REUNION IN MARRIAGE

LYNNE GRAHAM
MELANIE MILBURNE
KATE HEWITT

MILLS & BOON

First Published 2020
Second Australian Paperback Edition 2024
ISBN 978 1 038 91805 5

First Published 2020
Second Australian Paperback Edition 2024
ISBN 978 1 038 91805 5

First Published 2015
Fourth Australian Paperback Edition 2024
ISBN 978 1 038 91805 5

Published by
Mills & Boon
An imprint of Harlequin Enterprises (Australia) Pty Limited
(ABN 47 001 180 918), a subsidiary of HarperCollins
Publishers Australia Pty Limited (ABN 36 009 913 517)
Level 19, 201 Elizabeth Street
SYDNEY NSW 2000
AUSTRALIA

Printed and bound in Australia by McPherson's Printing Group

CONTENTS

The Innocent's Forgotten Wedding

Lynne Graham

Books by Lynne Graham

Harlequin Modern

The Greek's Blackmailed Mistress
The Italian's Inherited Mistress
Indian Prince's Hidden Son

Conveniently Wed!

The Greek's Surprise Christmas Bride

One Night With Consequences

His Cinderella's One-Night Heir

Billionaires at the Altar

The Greek Claims His Shock Heir
The Italian Demands His Heirs
The Sheikh Crowns His Virgin

Vows for Billionaires

The Secret Valtinos Baby
Castiglione's Pregnant Princess
Da Rocha's Convenient Heir

Visit the Author Profile page
at millsandboon.com.au for more titles.

Lynne Graham was born in Northern Ireland and has been a keen romance reader since her teens. She is very happily married to an understanding husband who has learned to cook since she started to write! Her five children keep her on her toes. She has a very large dog who knocks everything over, a very small terrier who barks a lot and two cats. When time allows, Lynne is a keen gardener.

CHAPTER ONE

MILLY'S HEARTBEAT SPEEDED up with excitement when she saw Brooke's name flash across the screen of her cheap mobile because it had been a while since she had heard from her famous and glamorous half-sister.

When Brooke phoned, however, it meant that Brooke *needed* her and that truth more than made up for Brooke's often cold and seemingly critical attitude towards her. Milly loved being needed and, in any case, deep down inside, Milly was convinced that her sister *cared* about her even though she might be too proud to admit it.

After all, why else would Brooke confide in her about so many private things if she did not, at heart, see Milly as a trustworthy friend and sister? Furthermore, aside of each other, neither one of them had a single living relative. Nor was it surprising that Brooke would need her services again when her life was in such turmoil, thanks to that dreadful possessive tyrant of a man she had mistakenly married. What sort of a man would try and come between Brooke and her career? What sort of man would divorce a wife as beautiful and talented as Brooke simply over ugly rumours that she had had an affair?

'He won't listen to a word I say!' Brooke had wept when she'd confided in Milly. 'He set me up because he wants rid of me.

I'm convinced he *paid* that creep to lure me into a hotel room and lie about having sex with me!'

'Brooke?' Milly exclaimed warmly as she answered her phone.

'I need you to pretend to be me for a few days.'

'A few...*days*?' Milly stressed in dismay, for that request went far beyond anything her sister had asked of her before. 'Are you sure I'll be able to manage that? I'm OK until people speak to me and expect me to be you!'

'You'll be holed up in a fancy hotel in the heart of London,' Brooke told her drily. 'You won't be required to talk to anyone but room service. You won't need to leave the room at all.'

Milly frowned. 'For how long?' she pressed anxiously.

'Five or six days. That's all,' Brooke informed her briskly.

'I *can't*, Brooke,' Milly protested apologetically. 'I've got a job and I don't want to lose it.'

'You're a waitress, Milly, not a brain surgeon,' her half-sister reminded her tartly. 'You can pick up casual work anywhere at this time of year. And if it's a matter of me paying your rent *again* for you, I'll do it!'

Milly flushed and subsided again because it was true, she could find another job relatively easily, and if Brooke made up her loss of wages to cover the rent on her bedsit as well, she had no grounds for complaint either. When it occurred to her that she had ended up sleeping on a friend's sofa the last time she'd needed help to cover her rent, she suppressed the memory. Brooke had forgotten to give her the money she had promised but Milly felt that that oversight was her own fault because she had been too embarrassed to remind Brooke. She couldn't help but shrink from highlighting the financial differences between her and her sister, and wasn't one bit surprised that Brooke had always refused to be seen in public with her or invite her into her more exciting world even briefly, except in Milly's guise as a lookalike. What else could she expect? Milly asked herself ruefully. In truth, she was lucky to have *any* kind of relationship with her sibling at all…

Brooke had first sought out Milly when she was eighteen and fresh out of a council home for foster kids. Milly had already known that she was illegitimate, but she had been shocked by what her newly discovered half-sister had to tell her—well, shocked and initially repulsed by Brooke's view of the circumstances of her birth. But then, slowly, she had come to understand Brooke's feelings of betrayal and had forgiven her sister for her offensive wording.

'Your mother was the slut who almost broke up my parents' happy marriage!' Brooke had told her sharply.

To be fair to Brooke, Milly's mother *had* been the other woman who slept with a married man, inflicting considerable suffering on that man's innocent wife and child. Brooke and Milly's father, William Jackson, a wealthy wine importer, had had a long-running affair with a model called Natalia Taylor and had threatened to leave his wife over her.

Sadly, a heart attack had taken William's life when Brooke was fifteen and Milly was nine. Natalia had died in a bus crash only a couple of years later and Milly had ended up in council care, where she had remained until she reached eighteen. At first meeting, both young women had been taken aback by the likeness between them, for they had both inherited their father's white-blonde curly hair and dark blue eyes. Milly, however, had had a large bump in her nose and somehow the features that made Brooke a stunning beauty had blurred in Milly's case, putting her into the pretty rather than beautiful category.

It had been Brooke's idea that she could use Milly as a stand-in either to avoid an event she considered boring or, more frequently, to mislead the paparazzi that dogged her footsteps and who occasionally followed her places where she didn't want to be seen or photographed her with individuals whom she didn't wish to be seen with. Brooke was obsessed with airbrushing and controlling the public image she wanted to show the world.

In the same way she had pointed out that Milly couldn't help her unless she was prepared to go that extra mile and have her nose 'done' so that it mirrored Brooke's far more elegant nose. At first, Milly had said a very firm no to that idea, not because she was fond of her less than perfect nose but just because it was hers and she was accustomed to her own flaws.

Brooke had had a huge row with her over her refusal and Milly had been devastated when her half-sister had cut off all contact with her. When Brooke had called her again six weeks later, Milly had been so grateful to hear from her that she had agreed to the surgical procedure and before she could change her mind she had been whisked into a private clinic and her nose had been skilfully enhanced to resemble Brooke's. Once that had been achieved, expert make-up had completed her transformation.

The first time Milly had pretended to be Brooke to enable her sister to evade a boring charity event, she had been terrified, even dressed in her sister's clothes and made up to look like her, but nobody had suspected a thing and, for the first time in her life, Milly had felt like an achiever. Brooke's gratitude had made her feel wonderfully warm inside and the second time, when Milly had had to simply step out of a limousine and walk into a shop while Brooke was many miles away, she had felt even better. She had discovered that it was fun to dress up in expensive clothes and pretend to be someone she was not and there had been very little fun in Milly's life before Brooke entered it.

And with Brooke in her current predicament, struggling to deal with her broken marriage, Milly knew that she should definitely go that extra mile for her sister. 'Where will you be while I sit in this hotel?' she asked curiously.

'Having a very discreet little holiday, so I'll need your passport,' Brooke advanced. 'I daren't travel on my own.'

And Milly frowned at that reference to her passport but could only smile at the mention of a holiday. A holiday was exactly what her poor sister needed at this stressful time in her life and if Milly room-sitting in some fancy hotel was all that was required, it would be utterly selfish of her to refuse to help. 'OK. I'll do it.'

'You can only bring one small bag with you. I've packed a case for you, and you can change into my clothes in the car,' Brooke informed her. 'I'll do your make-up in the car too. I'm better at it than you are.'

After Brooke had arranged to pick her up, Milly straightened her hair and threw her passport, fresh underwear, a couple of books and a range of craft items into a bag before heading out. It was a filthy wet day and she didn't step out onto the pavement until she had her umbrella up to protect her hair for Brooke's hair was always a perfect blonde fall without even a hint of curl.

First, however, Milly took ten minutes to walk down the street and quit her waitressing job in a local café, mentioning a family emergency. She hated letting people down, but Brooke had been right, she would probably find another job quite quickly, she reasoned, guilty at having let an employer she liked down at short notice. But, my goodness, Brooke *did* deserve a holiday after everything she had recently been through and if she could help her sibling achieve that, then she could be proud of herself because family needs came first, family should *always* come first, she thought ruefully, regretting that neither of her parents had lived by that truth.

Brooke looked amazing when Milly glimpsed her inside the limo, all groomed and flawless in a black jacket, a tomato-red sheath dress and very high-heeled stilettos. It was likely, though, to be a struggle for her sibling to get out of that dress in the back of the limo, no matter how spacious it was, Milly ruminated.

'Quick, get in!' Brooke snapped at her. 'We can't be seen together!'

'What about the driver?' Milly asked in bemusement as the passenger door closed to seal the two women into privacy.

'I pay him well to keep quiet!' Brooke fielded, snapping shut the privacy screen between the front and the rear seats. 'Now help me out of this dress… Oh, yes, don't forget that I need your passport too.'

'It has to be against the law for you to travel on my passport,' Milly muttered uncomfortably. 'Do you *have* to borrow it?'

Brooke settled furious dark blue eyes on her. 'I don't have a choice. I'll be traced if I travel under my own name. With your name, I'm nobody, and nobody is the slightest bit interested in me or where I go.'

Reluctantly accepting that reality, Milly handed over her passport and proceeded to help her sibling out of her tight dress.

'Good grief, I don't see you for a couple of months and you let yourself turn into the ugly sister. Your nails are awful!' Brooke complained, snatching at one of Milly's hands to frown down at the sight of nails that were an unpainted and modest length. 'I'm always perfectly groomed. When you're checking in, keep them hidden and get a manicurist to come to the room and fix them before you check out again!' she instructed impatiently.

'I'm sorry,' Milly muttered, choosing not to point out that she couldn't afford to have her nails done professionally. Brooke regarded expensive treatments in the beauty field as essential maintenance and never ever considered the cost of them. 'When do you think you'll be back?'

'Hell…you're putting on weight again too, aren't you?' Brooke said in frustration as she urged Milly to breathe in to enable her to get the zip up on the fitted dress.

Milly had been born curvier and almost an inch shorter than Brooke and she didn't respond. She knew she wasn't overweight but since meeting Brooke, who was thinner, she had deliberately dropped almost a stone so that she could fit better into her sister's clothes. Unfortunately, that had meant avoiding all her favourite comfort foods and reining in her love of chocolate. Beside her, Brooke kicked off her shoes and began to dress in jeans and a long concealing top, bundling her hair up under a peaked cap. Digging into her bag she produced moist wipes and began to wipe off her make-up.

'It's like being a spy,' Milly remarked with helpless amusement.

'Don't be so childish, Milly!' Brooke snapped impatiently. 'Have you any idea how much is riding on this holiday I'm having? This is too important to joke about. I'm meeting someone while I'm away who may put my name forward for a film part.'

'Well, it's exciting for me,' Milly confided with a little wrinkle of her nose and a look of guilty apology. 'Sorry. I expect it'll be pretty boring stuck in that hotel room though, so this is the fun part.'

'You'll need my rings...for goodness' sake, don't lose them! I may need to sell them somewhere down the road,' Brooke admitted stiffly, threading her wedding and engagement rings off her long manicured finger and passing them over. 'That *bastard*, Lorenzo! He could have slung me a few million for the sake of it, but he stuck to the letter of the pre-nup. I'm not getting a penny I'm not due. Still, he'll just be a bad memory a few years down the road. My next husband will be a fashion icon or an actor, *not* a banker!'

Disappointed by her sister's bad mood, Milly donned the rings and slid her feet into the shoes while Brooke passed her bag and jacket over. 'Do you think that when you come back we could spend an evening together?' she asked hesitantly.

'Why would I want to do that?' Brooke demanded.

'It's been ages since we spent any real time together,' Milly pointed out quietly. 'I would really enjoy that and maybe talking over things would make you feel better.'

'I'm feeling fine.' Brooke snapped open the privacy screens and lifted her make-up kit before pausing to communicate with the driver and telling him to speed up because she didn't want to check in late for her flight. 'When I first went looking for you, I was curious about you. But I'm not curious any more. I've been very good to you too, sprucing you up, fixing your face. What more can you expect from me? It's not as though we could ever be friends, not with your mother having slept with my father while he was still married to *my* mother. Do you realise that my poor mother tried to *kill* herself over their affair?'

Milly paled at that new revelation and dropped her head. 'I am so sorry, Brooke, but I've been hoping that in time…well, that we could get over that history because we're still sisters.'

Brooke pushed up Milly's chin to outline her mouth with lip liner. 'Smile…yes, that's the ticket. There is no getting over the fact that your mother shagged my father and I don't do friends. Friends let you down and talk behind your back.'

'I wouldn't *ever*!' Milly protested.

'Well, you haven't so far,' Brooke conceded grudgingly. 'And you've been very useful to me, I'll agree. But we have nothing in common, Milly. You're poor and uneducated and you wouldn't even be able to talk properly if I hadn't sent you to elocution classes. You knit and you go to libraries. What would we talk about? I'd be bored stiff with you in five minutes.'

Milly paled and stiffened and called herself all kinds of a fool for running blindly into such abuse. She had closed her eyes too long to Brooke's essential coldness towards her, hoping that Brooke would eventually accept her as her sister and leave the sins of their mutual parents behind her in the past where they belonged. But for the first time, she was recognising that Brooke was as angry and resentful now about their father's affair as she had been when she'd first met her. Brooke tucked away her make-up kit and told the driver yet again to speed up, the instruction sharp and irritable in tone.

The rain had got so heavy that it was streaming down the windows and visibility was poor. It was a horrible day weatherwise, Milly conceded wryly, suppressing her hurt at being labelled boring. It was true that she and her sister had little in common apart from their paternity and their physical likeness to one another. Evidently, however, Brooke didn't feel an atom of a deeper connection to her because of their blood bond. When

Brooke had confided in her about her problems, had it meant anything to her at all? Possibly, Brooke had grasped that Milly was trustworthy in that line and unlikely to reveal all to some murky tabloid newspaper. Or maybe Milly had just been there at the right moment when Brooke had needed to unburden herself.

'This will be the last time I stand in for you, Brooke,' Milly said quietly but firmly. 'If I'm honest, I kind of wish I'd never started it.'

'Oh, for heaven's sake, why do you have to start getting difficult right now?' Brooke demanded wrathfully.

'I'm not being difficult and I'm not about to let you down,' Milly responded tautly. 'But once this is over, I won't be acting as your stand-in again.'

Brooke flashed one of her charming smiles and stretched out her hand to squeeze Milly's. 'I'm sorry if I've been short with you but this has been such a frantic rush and I'm living on my nerves. We're almost at your hotel. Make sure you don't get into any conversations with staff. I never chat to menial people. Stay in your room and eat there too and don't eat any rubbish. I am known for my healthy eating regime and I have an exercise video in the pipeline. You can't be seen after you've checked in. People will understand. They know my marriage is over and I wouldn't look human if I wasn't seen to be grieving and in need of some private downtime...'

Milly was not fooled by that fake smile or the apology. She could see that she was only receiving it because Brooke was scared she would pull out on her at the last minute and it saddened her to see that lack of real feeling in the sister she had come to care deeply for.

Their driver was travelling fast when he suddenly jammed on the brakes to a jolting halt to make a turn. Milly peered out at the traffic. There was a large truck coming through red stop lights towards them and she gasped in fear.

Beside her Brooke was shouting at the driver and as Milly braced herself and offered up a silent prayer she tried to reach out for Brooke's hand, but her sister was screaming and she couldn't reach her. There was a terrible crunch on impact that jarred every bone in her body and then she blacked out in response to the wave of unimaginable pain that engulfed every part of her. Brooke... *Brooke*, she wanted to shriek in horror, because her sister had released her seat belt while she was changing...

Lorenzo Tassini, the most exceptional private banker of his generation and a renowned genius in the field of finance, was in an unusually good mood that morning because his soon-to-be ex-wife had finally signed the divorce papers earlier that day.

It was done. Within a few weeks, Lorenzo would be free, *finally* free, from a wife who'd lied, cheated, slept around and created endless embarrassing headlines in the newspapers. Brooke hoped to build an acting career on the back of her notoriety. Lorenzo might despise her, but he blamed himself more for his poor judgement in marrying her than he blamed her for letting him down. In retrospect, he could barely comprehend the madness that had taken hold of him when he had first met Brooke Jackson, a woman totally outside his wide and varied experience of the opposite sex. Lust had proved to be his downfall, he reflected grimly.

Brooke's white-blonde beauty had mesmerised him but the two years he had been with her had been filled with rage, regret and bitterness, for the honeymoon period in their marriage had been of very short duration. The ink had barely been dry on their marriage licence before he'd realised that his dream of having a wife who would give him a happy home life was unlikely to come true with a woman who had absolutely no interest in making a home or in having a child or indeed spending time with him any place other than a noisy nightclub.

But then what did *he* know about having a happy home life? Or even about having a family? Indeed, Lorenzo would've been the first to admit his ignorance in those fields. He, after all, had been raised in a regimented Italian palazzo by a father who cared more about his academic triumphs than his happiness or comfort. Strict nannies and home tutors had raised him to follow in the footsteps of his forebears and put profit first, and his dream of leading a more normal life in a comfortable home had died on the back of Brooke's first betrayal. All that foolish nonsense was behind him now though, he assured himself staunchly. From now on, he would simply revel in being very, very rich and free of all ties. He would not remarry and he would not have a child because ten to one, with his ancestry, he would be a lousy parent.

The police called Lorenzo when he was on the way out to lunch. He froze as the grim facts of the crash were recited. The driver was dead, one of *his* staff. The other passenger was dead. What *other* passenger? he wondered dimly, reeling in shock from what he was hearing. His wife was seriously injured, and he was being advised to get to the hospital as soon as possible. He would visit the driver's family too to offer his condolences, he registered numbly.

His wife? Seriously hurt? The designation shook him inside out because he had already stopped thinking of himself as a husband. But in an emergency, he was Brooke's only relative and if she was hurt, she was entirely *his* responsibility, and no decent human being would think otherwise, he told himself fiercely. Without hesitation, he headed straight to the hospital. He had stopped liking or respecting his wife a long time ago, but he would never have wished any kind of harm on her.

The police greeted him at the hospital, keen to ask what he might know about the other woman, who had died. According to the passport they had found, her name was Milly Taylor, but he had never heard of her before. The police seemed to think that, with it being a wet day, Brooke might have stopped the car to give some random woman a lift, but Lorenzo couldn't imagine Brooke doing anything of that nature and suggested that the unknown woman might be one of Brooke's social media gurus or possibly a make-up artist or stylist because she frequently hired such people.

He wondered if the accident had been his driver's fault. Consequently, was it *his* fault for continuing to allow Brooke the luxury of a limo with driver? Although the pre-nup Brooke had signed had proved ironclad in protecting his assets and his fortune, Lorenzo had been generous. He had already bought and given Brooke a penthouse apartment in which to live and had hesitated to withdraw the use of the car and driver as well until she had officially moved out of Madrigal Court, his country home. And Brooke had stalled about actually moving out because it suited her to have staff she didn't have to pay making her meals for her and doing the hundred and one things she didn't want to have to do for herself. *Madre di Dio*...what total nonsense was he thinking about at such a grave moment?

The police reassured him that the accident had not been his driver's fault. A foreign truck driver had taken a wrong turn, got into a panic in the heavy traffic and run a set of stop lights, making an accident unavoidable.

Brooke, he learned, had a serious head injury and he was warned by the consultant neurosurgeon about to operate on her that she might not survive. Lorenzo spent the night pacing a bland waiting room, brooding over everything that he had been told. Brooke had facial injuries. The tiny glimpse he'd had of her before she went into surgery, he had found her unrecognisable and he was appalled on her behalf because he had never known a woman whose looks meant more to her. He would engage the very best plastic surgeons to treat her, he promised himself, shame and discomfiture assailing him. As long as she was alive, he would look after her in every way possible, just as if she were *still* a much-loved and cherished wife. That was his bounden duty and he would not be tried and found wanting in a crisis.

When he learned that she had come through the surgery he breathed more freely again. She was in a coma. Only time would tell when she would come out of it or what she would be like when she came round, because such head traumas generally caused further complications and even if she recovered she might be different in some ways, the exhausted surgeon warned him. Furthermore, Brooke was facing a very long and slow recovery process.

He was given her personal effects by a nurse. He recognised her engagement ring, the big solitaire he had slipped on her finger with such love and hope, the matching wedding band he had given her with equal trust and optimism. He swallowed hard, recognising that he was at a crossroads and not at the crossroads of freedom he had expected to become his within weeks. Brooke was his wife and he would look after her and support her in whatever ways were necessary. In the short term, he reflected tautly, he would put the divorce on hold until she was on the road to recovery and capable of expressing her own wishes again.

CHAPTER TWO

THE WOMAN IN the bed was drifting weightless in a cocoon, her awareness coming to her in weird broken flashes.

She heard voices but she didn't recognise them. She heard sounds like bells, buzzes, and bleeps but she didn't recognise them either. And she couldn't move, no matter how hard she strained her will to shift a finger, wriggle a toe or even open her eyes. Her body felt as heavy as lead. And then she heard one voice and, although she didn't recognise it either, she clung to it in her disorientation as though it were a lifeline.

It was a man's voice, deep and dark and measured. It made her listen but at first she couldn't distinguish the words, and even when she began picking up stray words she couldn't string them together into a coherent sentence or think about what the words meant. Maybe it was a television, she thought, wondering why it was constantly tuned to a foreign channel because early on she identified a faint but very definite foreign accent that stroked along his vowel sounds like silk, sometimes softening them, sometimes harshening them. Time had no meaning for her while she listened to the voice.

And then there was the music that came and went in the background. It was the sort of music she had never listened to before, mainly classical. But occasionally she heard birdsong or the surge of waves on the shore or even noises she imagined might be heard in a jungle, as if someone had compiled a diverse sound collection just for her. She loved the birdsong because it made her feel that if she could only try a little harder to wake up, she would waken to a fresh new day.

Lorenzo studied his wife while he stood at the window of her room. Superficially, if one discounted all the machinery and the tubes, Brooke looked as though she were simply asleep, her cascade of white-blonde curls tumbling off the side of the bed in a glorious curtain. They called her, 'the sleeping beauty' in the high-tech care home he had moved her to when the hospital could do no more. She had moved from the coma into a vegetative state and there was no sign of recovery after fifteen months.

Fifteen months, Lorenzo conceded, driving a long-fingered hand through his luxuriant black hair, for fifteen crisis-ridden months, his life had revolved around her treatment. Fifteen months during which she had been in and out of Intensive Care, in and out of surgery, both major and minor, and now she was repaired, broken limbs mended, cuts and bruises healed, her face restored by the very best surgeons and daily physiotherapy keeping her muscles from wasting...but still, she wasn't *fixed.*

Fixing her every problem, banishing the physical damage caused by the accident and readying her for a return to the living had kept Lorenzo going, even when the hopes of the medical staff had begun to fade. He could not let her go, he could *not* allow those machines to be switched off, not while there was hope, and he was fortunate that he was wealthy enough to fly in specialists from round the world, only unfortunately all of them had different opinions on Brooke's prospects of recovery. He had never been humble but it was finally beginning to dawn on Lorenzo that he was not omnipotent and that she might *never* be fixed and might never open her eyes again.

He sat down by the bed and scored a forefinger over the back of her still hand. Her nails were polished, just as her hair was regularly washed and styled. They had wanted to cut her hair short but he had simply brought in a hairdresser to take care of it instead, just as he had brought in nail technicians. It was what Brooke would've wanted, although he had told the hairdresser to stop straightening her hair and leave the natural curls. He knew she would never have agreed to that change and if he accidentally brushed a hand through those glorious tumbling white-blonde ringlets he felt guilt pierce him.

'I *did* love you once,' Lorenzo said almost defiantly in the silent room.

And a finger twitched. Lorenzo froze and studied her hand, which remained in the same position, and he told himself he had imagined that movement. It wouldn't be the first time that he had imagined such a thing and he was being fanciful.

It bothered him that Brooke was so alone and that he was her sole visitor aside of the occasional specialists. He had never realised how isolated she was until after the accident when paparazzi had tried to sneak in and catch pictures of her but not one single friend had shown up. There had only been cursory phone calls from her agent and various other people engaged in building her career and those enquiries had soon fallen off once the news that she was in a coma spread. The fame she had gloried in had, sadly, proved fleeting. There had been a burst of headlines and speculation in the wake of the crash but now she seemed to be forgotten by everyone but him.

Early the following morning, alarm bells rang and lights flashed from the machinery by the bed. The woman came awake and went into panic, eyes focusing on an unfamiliar room and then on the arrival of two nurses, their faces both concerned and excited at the same time. She clawed at the breathing tube in her throat because she couldn't speak and the women tried to both restrain and soothe her, telling her over and over again that the doctor was coming, everything would be all right and that there was nothing to worry about. She thought they were crazy. Her body wouldn't move. She could only move one hand and her arm felt as if it didn't belong to her. How could she possibly have nothing to worry about? Why were they talking nonsense? Did they think she was stupid?

The panic kept on clawing at her, even after the doctor arrived and the breathing tube was removed. He kept on asking her questions, questions she couldn't answer until she couldn't hide from the truth any longer. She didn't *know* who she was. What was her name? She didn't *know* why she was lying in a hospital bed. She didn't have a last memory to offer because her mind was a blank, a complete blank. It was a ridiculous relief to receive an approving nod when she evidently got the name of the Prime Minister right and contrived to name colours correctly.

'What happened to me?' she whispered brokenly, her breath rasping. 'Have I been ill?'

'You were in an accident.' The doctor paused there, exchanging a glance with the staff surrounding the bed.

'What's my name?' she asked shakily.

'Your name is Brooke… Brooke Tassini.'

The name meant absolutely nothing to her, didn't even sound slightly familiar.

'Your husband will be here very soon.'

Brooke's eyes widened to their fullest extent in shock. *'I have a husband?'*

For some reason, the nurses smiled. 'Oh, yes, you have a husband.'

'A very handsome husband,' one of the women added.

Brooke stared down at her bare wedding finger. She was married. Oh, my goodness, she was married. Did she have children? she asked. No…no children as far as they knew, they said, and a tinge of relief threaded through the panic she was only just holding at bay. Then she felt guilty about that sense of relief. She liked children, *didn't she*? But it was scary enough to have a husband she didn't remember—it would be simply appalling if she had contrived to forget her children as well.

* * *

Lorenzo stood outside in the corridor studying the middle-aged doctor babbling at him. And it *was* babble because the care-home staff were not accustomed to their comatose patients waking up and excitement laced with frank worry had taken over.

'It's post-traumatic amnesia, perfectly understandable after a serious head injury. You need someone more qualified than me in the psychiatric field to advise you on her condition, but I would warn you not to tell her anything that might upset her more at the moment. I wouldn't mention yet that other people died in the accident or that you were…er…splitting up at the time of the crash,' the doctor muttered hurriedly, visibly uncomfortable with getting that personal. 'She's in a very high state of stress as it is. Try to calm her, try to keep it upbeat without divulging too much information.'

Lorenzo had been in an early board meeting when the phone call came. He had been so shocked by the news that Brooke had recovered consciousness that he had walked out without a word of explanation. Now that he was on the brink of speaking to her again, he was, for once, at a loss. Brooke didn't *remember* him? Could he believe that of a woman willing to use anything and everything to create a furore in the media? What better way to spring back into the public eye than with an interesting story to tell? When he had first met her, such suspicion would have been foreign to him and momentarily he was furious that he had to consider that she could be faking it. But he had learned the hard way that Brooke was a skilled deceiver.

The door opened and Brooke froze against the pillows, her chest tightening as she snatched in a breath. And there he was in the doorway and there was nothing familiar about him. Indeed, it immediately occurred to her that no normal woman could possibly have forgotten such a man.

He stood well over six feet tall, wide-shouldered, lean of hip and long of leg, and he wore a dark pinstriped suit with a blue tie and white shirt. And he was, undeniably, absolutely breathtaking in the looks department. His hair was black and cropped short and it was the sort of thick springy hair that a woman wanted to run her fingers through. His bronzed features were all high cheekbones and interesting hollows, dissected by a narrow blade of a nose, while his wide sensual mouth was accentuated by the faint dark shadow of stubble surrounding it. His eyes, deep set and very dark and framed with lashes lush as black fans, were even more arresting and resting on her now with a piercing gleam. She could feel her skin heating because that appraisal could have stripped paint.

No, he *couldn't* be her husband, she decided immediately. He had to be some sleek, highly qualified consultant come to suss her out. Instinct seemed to be telling her that her husband would be a much more ordinary sort, maybe a bit homely, a bit tousled, but when his wife woke up after being in a coma, he would, at least, be smiling with relief and happiness. This guy didn't look as if he smiled very often. He was downright intimidating even in the way he stood there, radiating raw masculinity and authority.

'Brooke…' he murmured without any expression at all, walking in and shutting the door behind him and then those amazing eyes were locking to her again and it was a challenge to breathe. 'How are you feeling?'

Her heart was hammering so hard with nerves she felt her throat close over, her already sore throat, still tender from the removal of the breathing tube. But when he spoke, she froze in wonderment because his voice was familiar. 'I know your voice… I *know* your voice!' she gasped with a sense of attainment. 'In fact it's the first thing I've recognised since I woke up…but I don't recognise you. Who are you?'

'Lorenzo Tassini.'

'I'm *married* to *you*?' Brooke yelped in open disbelief.

Lorenzo's brows drew together. He was trying very hard not to stare at her because she was a vision of natural beauty, this woman he had married who had only shown him the ugliness she kept hidden on the inside. With her dishevelled hair hanging across her shoulders, framing her entrancing heart-shaped face, and those huge incredible dark blue, verging-on-violet eyes, she looked utterly angelic. And different, startlingly different, because he didn't think he had ever seen Brooke without her cosmetic enhancements. Brooke would climb out of bed at dawn to put her make-up on, no matter how often he had told her she didn't need it to look good.

But, of course, there were differences in her appearance. She was thinner, for a start, painfully thin in spite of the nourishing diet she had been fed by tube. She looked frail and somehow younger. The surgeons had restored her to perfection, but his acute gaze had already spotted the changes. Her mouth seemed a little wider, a little lusher in its pout, her nose shorter, less defined, and her eyes, those beautiful violet eyes were as bright and inquisitive as a bird's. And he had never ever seen such an expression on Brooke's face before. Brooke rarely showed emotion of any kind but, right now, he was seeing uncertainty, shock and intense curiosity fleeing across her face and it was a novelty for him to be able to interpret her feelings.

'Yes, you're married to me,' he confirmed flatly, recalling the doctor's warning, striving to abide by it when his conscience wanted him to throw the truth out there and be damned for it because he wanted no more lies between them. But if he told her about the divorce, he would lose her trust, her ability to depend on him, and she *needed* him right now. She needed to trust that he would not harm her and that she could rely on him because he knew there was no one else to take his place.

Brooke swallowed painfully and closed her eyes. A headache was beginning to pulse behind her brow. She was ridiculously tired for someone who had only been awake for a couple of hours.

'Would you like a drink?' Lorenzo prompted, lifting the glass with the straw in it.

'Yes…thanks.' Her eyes flickered open again and she sucked eagerly on the straw, the cool water easing her throat. 'I've got so many questions.'

'We'll answer them one by one.'

'But why don't I remember *you* when I remember your voice?' she exclaimed in frustration. 'How long have I been here? Nobody would tell me.'

'You've been here over a year.' Lorenzo watched her eyes round in further disbelief and once again savoured the newness of being able to read her face. 'After the first few weeks, when you failed to come out of it, the prognosis wasn't optimistic, so it is a source of great satisfaction for me to see you awake.'

'It *is*?' Brooke repeated, brightening in receipt of that acknowledgement. 'Then why don't you show it?'

'*Show* it?' He frowned.

'Smile, look happy. You walked in here looking like the Grim Reaper,' she told him, reddening at her boldness in being that blunt. 'I feel so alone here.'

Ramming his ever-present doubts about Brooke's veracity to the back of his mind, Lorenzo closed a hand over her limp fingers. 'But you're not alone.'

'Sit down beside me…here, on the bed,' she heard herself urge.

He looked as startled as if she had suggested he get into the bed with her and she stiffened in mortification. Instead of doing as she asked, he backed away and sank into the chair by the window. He was very reserved, she decided, adding to her first impression of him, not a guy who relaxed or who was easy with informality. It was impossible to imagine that she had ever been in bed with him and, at the thought, her face burned.

'How long have we been married?' she pressed.

'Three years now.'

Then, she had *definitely* been in bed with him, Brooke realised, and she would have squirmed with embarrassment had she had the ability to move normally. But nothing was normal about her body or her brain throwing up random embarrassing thoughts, she conceded ruefully, and nothing was normal about their situation either, and it had to be causing Lorenzo equal discomfort that he had a wife who didn't remember him.

'I'm sorry about all this. I'm sorry I don't know you and that I've caused you all this trouble.'

'You haven't caused me any trouble whatsoever,' Lorenzo lied, wondering what was wrong with her because Brooke's view of the world was generally one-sided. She didn't consider other people or their needs. She valued those around her strictly in accordance with the benefits they could bring her. She could be charm personified to get what she wanted but would then dispense with a person's services the instant she achieved her objective. But, of course, he reminded himself darkly, he *was* valuable to Brooke at this precise moment when she had nobody else to fall back on.

'It's kind of you to say that but all these months I've been lying here like a rock and I must've been the most awful worry for you,' she mumbled, her words slurring.

'I think you need to rest now,' Lorenzo told her, rising from his seat. 'I need to make arrangements for you to be moved to a more suitable facility where you can convalesce.'

Her head heavy, she turned her eyes back to him. 'I just want to go home,' she whispered weakly.

'I'm afraid that's not an option. Right now, you need a rehabilitation programme to regain your strength and medical support to deal with your amnesia,' Lorenzo explained smoothly.

'How did we meet?' she muttered drowsily, her brain spinning on and on, in spite of her exhaustion, wanting answers to countless questions.

'At a party in Nice. I was there on business.'

'You're a businessman?' she slurred.

'A banker,' he advanced.

'I don't like banks,' she mumbled, and then thought in surprise, Where did that thought come from?

Brows pleating, Lorenzo paused at the door to look back at her searchingly. 'Why don't you like banks?'

With an enormous effort she opened her eyes again and there he was, standing directly below the lights, his hair blue-black, his eyes transformed into liquid-gold pools of enquiry. He looked devastatingly handsome and she smiled at him sleepily. 'I don't know. It was just a random thought that came out of nowhere,' she admitted.

'Go to sleep, Brooke,' he urged. 'I'll see you tomorrow.'

'No kiss goodbye?'

Lorenzo froze at what struck him as an almost childlike question, which was laughable, he told himself, for anyone acquainted with Brooke's past history. 'No kiss. You're too sleepy and I like my women awake.'

'That's mean,' she mumbled.

Lorenzo stood at the foot of the bed watching her sleep. He should've been on the phone looking into convalescent facilities. He should've been seeking out a top psychiatrist to treat her. He should've told her that he wouldn't see her tomorrow because he was flying to Milan for an international banking conference. But he did none of those sensible things. He stood and he watched her sleep, feeling guilty at leaving her but all the while thinking in rampant disbelief that he might have married Brooke, but suddenly he was feeling as though he didn't know *her* either. Everyone had layers, he told himself irritably. Maybe this was how Brooke was when she was unsure of herself and no longer knew who she was. Restored to her fantastic wardrobe and her make-up and her headlines, she would once again become the woman he remembered.

Brooke sank into a seat in front of Mr Selby, her psychiatrist, and stowed the stick she was using. After a physio session she was always very sore and the slight limp she still had made her clumsy as she tired towards the end of the day, but she didn't complain because just being able to walk again felt like a precious enough gift.

'How have you been over the last few days?' the psychiatrist enquired over the top of his eccentric half-moon glasses.

'Great, but no flashes, no memories yet,' she said uneasily. 'Everything still feels so strange. Lorenzo brought me this giant metal case of cosmetics to replace the one that was destroyed in the accident and I think he was expecting me to be ecstatic, but I couldn't identify half the stuff in the box. I used a bit of it for his next visit. I didn't want him to think his present was a disappointment.'

'You seem to care about Lorenzo a great deal,' her companion remarked.

'Surely that's healthy when I'm married to him?' Brooke replied.

'Of course, you've been forced to depend on him, but it will be even more healthy for you to embrace a little independence as you recover your physical strength.'

Brooke's nod of acknowledgement was stiff. Over the past two months, she had learned just to let advice she didn't relish pass over her head. Everyone she met in the rehabilitation centre seemed to want to give her advice. She had dealt with surprise after surprise since her arrival. She had discovered that she was married to an extremely wealthy man and piece by piece she had learned that, before the crash, she had been a minor celebrity, a known fashion icon and often a source of media interest.

Those revelations hadn't felt natural to her and hadn't seemed to fit in very well with the quieter, less confident image she had slowly been developing of herself. But when she asked Lorenzo when she could go on the Internet to research her own previous life, he had insisted that it would be the wrong thing to do and that her memories would have a much better chance of returning if they weren't forced.

'What will I do if the memories never come back?'

'You will rebuild yourself. You've been very lucky. Your injury was severe, but you have no other ongoing problems,' Mr Selby reminded her bracingly.

Except a husband she *still* couldn't remember, a reality that tormented Brooke every time he visited her. But he wasn't able to visit her as often as he had hoped because he was an exceptionally busy banker, who went abroad several times a month. And her initial impression of Lorenzo had been spot on in its accuracy. He *was* very reserved. He rarely touched her in even the most fleeting way. It was a little as though she had an invisible force field around her, she conceded with a regretful grimace. Obviously he was deeply uncomfortable with the fact that she didn't remember him but his hands-off approach wasn't helping her to feel any closer to him. It was a subject she needed to tackle…and soon, she told herself ruefully.

He hadn't walked away while she was in a coma, so why was he keeping his distance now? Did he love her? Did he still find her attractive? Or was their marriage in trouble?

She agonised over the options in the giant box of make-up because he was coming to see her that evening. She even leafed through the totally impractical garments he had had brought to her, which hung in the wardrobe, and selected a dress because greeting Lorenzo in the yoga pants that she wore for physio sessions hadn't got her anywhere. Lorenzo was used to a fashion queen, so she would strive to please and maybe that would warm him up.

Her skin heating at that enterprising thought, she did her face and put on the electric-blue dress that she thought was hideously bright, almost neon in shade, but presumably she had bought it and liked it once. She slid into it and then embarked on the matching shoes. She wasn't supposed to wear heels yet but she wouldn't be moving around much, which was just as well because the shoes pinched painfully at the toes.

Lorenzo stepped out of his chauffeur-driven limo and studied the modern building with disfavour as he braced himself for another visit to his wife. If she didn't recover her memories soon, he was likely to be forced to the point of telling her the truth about their marriage. And the psychiatrist had warned him that Brooke wasn't ready to deal with that reality, that he had become her 'safe place' and if that support was suddenly withdrawn, it might well disrupt her fragile mental state and send her hurtling back into panic mode, which would set back the recovery process.

He was already in major conflict with his lawyers' warnings. They didn't take a humane approach to the situation he was in, merely cautioning him that frequent visits to his estranged wife would only convince a judge that granting him a divorce would get in the way of what could be viewed as a potential reconciliation. And he didn't want to do that, no, he definitely did not *want* to stay married to Brooke. There had to be a hard limit to his compassion and care. But that wasn't what was really bothering him, was it?

He wanted her: that was the *real* problem. In fact, he lusted after her more, it seemed, than he had ever lusted after her. Why? Because she was different, *so* different he couldn't believe it sometimes and, quite ridiculously, he *liked* her now. How was that possible? Logic told him that he was seeing Brooke as she might have been before the lust for fame and the infatuation with her own beauty had taken hold of her. Even more shockingly, Brooke *au naturel* was a class act.

Only he didn't *think* it was an act any longer because he was convinced that the woman he remembered could never ever have carried off that outstanding mix of artless naivety and innocence she showed him. In short, Brooke was all sorts of things she had never been before with him...caring, unselfish, undemanding. She had made him like her again, but he was determined not to be sucked back into that swamp a second time, he reminded himself grimly. She was recovering well and soon he would be able to cut their ties again and slot her into that penthouse apartment.

Lorenzo strode in and Brooke leapt upright at speed, wanting him to see that she had made the effort, wanting him to see that she was truly getting back to normal…*and* ready to go home.

'You look…more like yourself this evening,' Lorenzo commented as she regarded him expectantly.

Her violet eyes, bright with what he recognised as excitement, unsettled him.

'I think I'm ready to leave here…to come home,' she told him urgently. 'I'm sure it would be better for me to be in a familiar place. They're very kind to me here but I'm going crazy cooped up like this and it's so boring and uneventful. Your visits are the only highlights in my week.'

With difficulty, Lorenzo mastered his consternation. 'I'll speak to your doctors tomorrow. We don't want to rush into anything. After all, you couldn't even walk two months ago.'

'I'm getting stronger every day!' Brooke argued. 'Why don't you see that?'

'I *do* see it,' Lorenzo countered levelly. 'But until you recover your memory, it's too risky.'

Brooke's hands coiled into tight fists, the sudden burst of temper that ignited inside her an explosion of the frustration she had been fighting off for days. 'Am I going to stay here for ever, then, as a patient?' she exclaimed angrily. 'Because I've already been told, and you must also know, that I might *never* get my memory back!'

Lorenzo gritted his teeth. He did know that, but he had confidently put the warning to the back of his mind because every time he saw her, he expected to see her change back into the woman he remembered. 'Sit down,' he urged. 'We'll discuss this calmly.'

Brooke dropped down on the side of the bed. Lorenzo studied her. She had been all built up to ask him to take her home and now she was upset, and he felt as if he was being cruel even though he knew that he had no other choice. Sitting there, she was a picture with her tangled ringlets half concealing her piquant face, the faint pout of her luscious pink mouth, the long length of her legs displayed to perfection in that dress and those shoes. A punch of lust tightened his groin and he tensed, willing back his desire, fighting for control. The yoga pants had driven him crazy, showing every curve, every indent, but Lorenzo wasn't easily tempted, not where Brooke was concerned, and he had fought that reaction every rigorous step of the way. He stood by the window gazing out at the tranquil courtyard garden in the centre of the building, striving to calm himself.

'Before the accident...' Brooke began hesitantly. 'Our marriage was in trouble, wasn't it?'

At that moment she didn't want the positive answer she suspected to be her new reality. Even so, she felt she still had to ask and had to be strong enough to confront such an unwelcome truth because, in that scenario, pretending wasn't fair to either of them.

Disconcerted, Lorenzo froze in position. 'What makes you think that?' he enquired in a deliberately mild tone.

'It doesn't take a rocket scientist,' she framed a little unevenly. 'You never touch me unless you can't avoid it. You never mention anything personal and if I ask questions in that line you stall. You don't want me home either. Just be honest, Lorenzo. I *can* take it. And then, just go home or back to the bank because you seem to work eighteen hours a day.'

Lorenzo almost ground his teeth in frustration. It would have been the perfect moment to speak had he not had to consider her condition. He glanced across at her and saw the tears shimmering like sunshine on water in her eyes.

Angrily aware of the tears prickling, Brooke dashed them away with an impatient hand. 'Stop treating me like a child, stop choosing your words. I'm twenty-eight years old, for goodness' sake, not a little girl! It's bad enough not remembering stuff, but it's a *torment* to be sitting here wondering all the time what sort of relationship we have...'

In disconcertion, Lorenzo strode forward just as she leapt up in haste, determined not to cry in front of him. 'Just go home!' she told him fiercely as she headed for the door and the sanctuary of the patients' lounge. 'I'll see you another day—'

But she tried to move too fast in the high heels and her weaker leg flailed and tipped her over. She was within inches of crashing down painfully on the hard floor when Lorenzo snatched her up, lifting her clean off her tottering feet and settling her down in front of him in the circle of his arms. The scent of him that close was like an aphrodisiac to her senses, an inner clenching down in her pelvis instantly responding. She closed her arms round his neck because she had decided that if he couldn't even kiss her, obviously he no longer felt attracted to her, and she would get her answer to how he felt about her one way or another.

Lorenzo collided with her wonderfully unusual eyes and, involuntarily, he bent down and kissed her, damning himself for even that momentary surrender. But he was too clever by half with women not to guess that she was giving him the green light to test him. One brief kiss and nobody was catching it on camera, he reminded himself, and then her soft, succulent mouth opened invitingly under his and suddenly all bets were off because the taste of her went to his head and his groin like a bushfire licking out of control.

She tasted like...she tasted like... His primal nature threatened to take over, almost made him forget that since she had lost her memory this was their *first* kiss as far as she was concerned. Quite deliberately he tried to rein himself back. But Brooke was still blown off her feet by the explosion of passion Lorenzo delivered with his mouth. His lips were hard and urgent and demanding, somehow everything she had been craving without realising it for endless weeks, and he crushed her to his tall, powerful frame.

It was off-the-charts exciting.

Her hands bit into his broad shoulders to keep her upright while the intoxicating chemistry of his mouth on hers left her breathless and dizzy and afflicted with all sorts of reactions that felt entirely new to her. Of course, they couldn't be new to her, but her heart was racing and her nipples became tight and almost sore in their sensitivity beneath her clothes. At the apex of her thighs, there was a burn, a sort of pulsing ache that inflamed her senses and, against her abdomen, she could feel the literal effect she was having on Lorenzo as well and somehow that shocked her when it shouldn't have done.

Indeed, for Brooke, Lorenzo's sizzling kiss was the first true gift she had had in all the weeks of her frustrating convalescence while she worried and wondered about who she truly was and wondered even harder how Lorenzo wanted her to behave. She was in constant conflict, struggling between what little she knew about her past self and the newer and equally unknown self that often prompted her to behave differently. But that kiss restored her equilibrium. It was *acceptance*, it was proof positive that her husband *still* wanted her and that she had been fretting herself into a state about nothing.

As he lowered Brooke down onto the bed and broke their connection with a slight shudder of recoil, Lorenzo was reminded very much of a saying a teacher of his had been fond of recounting to him: 'between a rock and a hard place'. 'Damned if you do, damned if you don't,' struck him as more apt. Still, what was one kiss? he reasoned wrathfully, instantly going into damage-limitation mode and stepping back from her. He was awesomely aware of the arousal he couldn't hide below the finely tailored trousers, the coolness he couldn't yet slide into place, and so furious with himself for succumbing to her again that his lean brown hands clenched into fists.

Lorenzo had once liked to pride himself on being an unemotional man like his late father but the unemotional man who had married Brooke had discovered otherwise. He had felt *tortured* by the endless dramas and he had shut that weak and disturbing part of himself away again, closed it down, re-embraced his calm, his control, his...sanity. He wasn't going back there, no, not even for the sake of honour or decency!

'That was wonderful.' Brooke gave him a huge smile, utterly impervious to his feelings at that moment. 'I feel so much better about us.'

'Good,' Lorenzo gritted between his perfect teeth, because it felt like another nail in his coffin that she had come alive in his arms as she never had before. He was in shock, he conceded, acknowledging the fact that Brooke had never kissed him back that way in their entire acquaintance, had never shown him an atom of the desire he had assumed she had for him when he married her. He shook his handsome dark head slightly as though to clear it. She was *so* different, but hadn't the doctors warned him of that possibility?

He trained his dark deep gaze on her. 'I'm not an emotional man, Brooke.'

'You don't really need to tell me that. It's kind of obvious,' Brooke pointed out. 'You've never shown me any emotion in your visits and it worried me about us but obviously we managed to get married anyway and right now I can see how tense you are.'

Lorenzo was starting to feel like the accused in the dock. 'I'm not tense,' he insisted.

But the tension was engraved in his lean, darkly handsome features, Brooke recognised with relief. Lorenzo might be locked up tight in his reserve, but he had shown her wonderfully strong emotion in that kiss...*hadn't he*? Or had that only been sexual hunger? And why didn't she know the difference? The way she seemed to just know other things? Like the names of the seasons, the days of the week? She swallowed hard, afraid to get carried away by her expectations of him, afraid to expect too much.

'Will you bring me home this week?' she just asked him baldly. 'I'm ready even if the doctors fuss about the idea. I can't stay here for ever...unless that's what you'd prefer?'

That anxious question shot through Lorenzo much like a whip because he could see the stress and the level of concern she was trying, very poorly, to hide from him, and he marvelled all over again at the complete absence of her once unrevealing shuttered expressions. 'Of course not,' he responded by rote. 'I'll speak to them.'

Content to have received that response, Brooke slid off the bed and walked over to him. 'I won't be any trouble to anyone. It's not like I'm depressed or mentally troubled in some way. I've only lost my memory. I just want my life…' *and* my husband, she added inwardly, 'back.'

Suddenly, Lorenzo found himself smiling at the almost enthralling prospect of reuniting Brooke with her wardrobe, her jewellery and her precious scrapbooks and files of headlines and articles. Nothing surely was more likely to revive her memory than her possessions and her media triumphs? What the hell had he hoped to achieve when he kept her in a sterile medical environment? Deprived of everything she valued and enjoyed in life? Nothing in the private clinic was familiar to her and nothing here would appeal to her tastes. In such a place there was no stimulation that could help her to recover her memory. *Sì*... He would take her to her supposed home and in all likelihood she would recover there and remember that she hated him. He could bear a few more weeks—*couldn't he*?

Even more enchanted by his rare smile, Brooke went pink. She had virtually thrown herself at him and, while it had taken a lot of initiative to act that way with him and had felt horribly pushy, the ploy had indisputably worked. As long as she didn't mention their marriage or love or anything of that nature, Lorenzo could handle it, but for the first time she was questioning what in their marriage or in his background had made him so uncomfortable about ordinary feelings.

CHAPTER THREE

IN THE LIMOUSINE that wafted her down the long driveway towards the giant building that sat at the bottom, Brooke sat wide-eyed with wonder but striving to conceal the fact. It seemed that she was married to a man who was very much wealthier than she had understood, and that was a shock too. But acting shocked got old quickly and she was slowly trying to learn how to school her face into less revealing reactions every time she got a surprise about herself. This was *her* life, after all, she reminded herself soothingly, *her* home.

And Madrigal Court was gorgeous, she thought helplessly, as the sunlight glinted off the rows of windows and the old brick with its intricate designs and so many chimneys—a country house that must've been hundreds of years old. Tudor? she wondered with a frown, disconcerted to find that term popping up in the back of her brain. Seemingly she knew more about old buildings than she had assumed, or could it have been a memory? She was desperate to recall something concrete: an event, an image, a face, a fact, anything really, she acknowledged ruefully, but so far there had been nothing and that had to be incredibly frustrating for Lorenzo.

Without even thinking about it, she reached for his hand because she had been so very flattered that he had taken a day off to share her homecoming with her. She was extremely conscious that he worked very hard and for very long hours and she thought that might have been why she had concentrated equally hard, it seemed, to make a separate role and career for herself. Clearly, Lorenzo had married a strong, independent and confident woman and Brooke was desperately trying to shore up those traits in herself.

There would be no clinging, no whinging, when he disappeared abroad for days at a time, no mention of the truth that she missed him terribly when he was gone. He wouldn't want to hear that kind of stuff and he would be disappointed in her. And hadn't he had enough disappointment already, sufficient to end many a marriage, she reminded herself, when his wife wakened and didn't know him from a stranger in the street?

Totally shocked by that gesture, Lorenzo flicked a covert black-lashed glance down at their linked hands and breathed in deep and slow to embrace calm. His enthralling vision of her walking into her wardrobe and shrieking in delight, 'I'm home!' still refused to retreat. But this new version of Brooke didn't shriek, and her voice was low-pitched, just one of the many, many changes in her that unsettled him. It was almost as though she had had a personality transplant, he mused. *Per Dio*, she had *cried* when he told her that her parents had passed away before he met her and that she had no other relatives, nobody, who could fill in the blanks of the memory loss she was enduring now. Of course, there might be photos of her family somewhere in Brooke's stuff, he reflected hopefully, because he knew that would please her.

At her request, he had retrieved her wedding ring from the home safe and she had threaded it on as though it were something special, not the plain band that she had originally dismissed as 'not very imaginative'. Nothing that didn't glitter with valuable jewels had once incited Brooke's admiration.

She listened to his advice now as well. She hadn't asked for a phone or even the Internet again, which impressed him as being even more weird, for Brooke had *lived* on her phone. How could she not be missing it? Of course, she didn't know *who* or what she had to miss, did she? Lorenzo's lean bronzed face hardened. Not least the very married film star who had recently had an aide contact Lorenzo to enquire after his wife's health, evidently having heard a rumour that Brooke was recovering from the accident. Lorenzo suspected there had been an affair between them, but he reminded himself that Brooke's sex life was, thankfully, no longer any of his business. They might remain legally married but there was nothing deeper involved.

Brooke walked up the worn stone steps into the house and smiled at the middle-aged man opening the door for their arrival. 'And you are?'

'Stevens, madam,' the older man supplied in surprise.

'Thank you,' she said quietly, moving indoors and stopping dead to take in the big imposing entrance hall made cosy by the low fire burning in the ancient fireplace to one side. 'Oh, this is beautiful!' she claimed, startling Lorenzo.

'You hated this house,' Lorenzo heard himself murmur in soft contradiction. 'You wanted a modern home, a McMansion. I refused to move because this was my mother's family home and, although I never knew her, I enjoyed the knowledge that she had once lived here.'

'*Hated* it?' Brooke exclaimed in disbelief, spinning round to look at him. 'I don't think that's possible.'

Watching her flounder with uncertainty as soon as she had spoken and accepted that such a former attitude was perfectly possible, Lorenzo registered his error in being that honest and at speed he strode over to a door to throw it wide. 'Lots of married couples have different tastes.' He dismissed that hint of contention smoothly. 'This room is more your style.'

What style? Brooke almost asked for every piece of furniture was gilded and the drapes, the upholstery and even the carpet were pristine white. Even the vase of flowers on the low table was filled with white blooms. In her opinion, it was stark and uninviting, but it certainly gave a striking effect.

'And this is you…' Lorenzo indicated the large professional photograph on the wall in which she posed on the same sofa for a *Dream House* magazine interview she had, according to him, given only weeks before the accident.

Brooke stared in fascination at the woman in the photograph and her fingers went up to pluck uneasily at her loose ringlets as she studied that smooth straight fall of hair in the image. 'I should be straightening my hair!' she gasped suddenly.

'I like it natural,' Lorenzo dared to impart.

'Honestly?' she queried tautly as she stared at that flawlessly groomed, almost inhumanly perfect image with a sinking heart. It was undeniably her, but it was *not* the version of her that she was currently providing him with.

'Honestly.'

In that moment, Brooke felt overwhelmed. Coming home was proving more of a challenge than she had expected. Was it possible that the head injury had altered her tastes? She supposed it was. When she had expressed her concern about such changes to Mr Selby, he had been very reassuring, never failing to remind her that she was lucky to be alive and relatively unscathed as if the loss of her every memory from childhood was something she simply had to accept. And perhaps it was, and there was nothing less attractive than self-pity, she told herself fiercely, moving back into the hall.

'Let's go upstairs,' Lorenzo urged. 'I'll show you your room.'

Your room, Brooke noted. 'Don't we share?'

Lorenzo cast her a lazy, careless smile because he was fully rehearsed on that answer. 'You like your own space and you often took your stylist up there to decide on outfits. Sharing wasn't practical.'

'You know more about my life than I know about yours,' Brooke couldn't help commenting.

'I don't think that there's anything in the world of finance that would interest you,' Lorenzo parried. 'Unless, of course, you've decided to set up a business or something of that nature.'

'Not just at the minute, no,' she quipped, breathing in deep.

So, separate bedrooms, little wonder Lorenzo was so physically detached from her and prone to treating her as though she were a friend rather than a wife. Even though they lived in an enormous house, they didn't seem to share much as a couple. Not a bed, not taste, not their lives. It was unhealthy but perhaps Lorenzo liked his marriage that way even if it didn't appeal to her, she ruminated worriedly. How had she let the man she loved move so far from her in every way?

Obviously she loved him. She couldn't believe that she would have married him for any other reason. His money, his giant house and his servants all made her feel intimidated. But *he* didn't intimidate her, he made her...happy. Mr. Selby had urged her to think about whether or not that was just her insecurity talking and had asked her how she could possibly still love a man she didn't remember. But she knew that she did in the same way she knew that the sun would rise in the morning. She had remembered Lorenzo's voice and it was the *only* thing she remembered, which to her signified and proved his overwhelming importance in her life.

Brooke walked into another blindingly white room, but this time it was a bedroom and she decided that the absence of colour did give a certain feel of tranquillity.

'And then there's your favourite place,' Lorenzo proclaimed, casting wide another door.

Brooke froze on the threshold of an amazing dressing room. But it was so big, so packed with stuff it didn't really qualify for that description. Racks and racks of shoes and bags lined the walls in glass cabinets. Rails and rails of zingy, colourful garments hung in readiness. It was a feast of conspicuous consumerism, a rebuttal of the 'less is more' mentality, and she thought, Oh, dear heaven, I'm greedy and extravagant and spoilt rotten! And then a calmer voice switched on inside her, reminding her that being a fashion icon had sort of been her job. She forced herself deeper into the room to browse through the clothes, hoping for something to jar her memory, glancing at labels and surprised that she only recognised the household names of famous designers that everyone knew. In the general knowledge sense, her fashion antenna seemed to be running on an empty tank.

'Of course, you'll have to throw it all out.'

Brooke whirled, violet eyes huge. *'Throw it out?'* she gasped incredulously.

'Because everything in here is old and out of fashion now.' Lorenzo tossed out that award-winning lure with deep satisfaction because he had already worked out how best to occupy his soon-to-be ex-wife. 'Your wardrobe is out of date. You'll need to start from scratch again and replace it all.'

'But that would be horribly wasteful,' Brooke framed in disbelief, fingering through a rack of jeans, searching for an ordinary pair but finding only slashed, sparkly or embroidered ones, marvelling that her former self had apparently never succumbed to a desire to simply wear something comfortable.

'It's the way that you live.' Lorenzo shrugged, brilliant, thickly lashed dark eyes cynical and assured. 'Every season you start again, so I imagine you'll be shopping until you drop for weeks.'

Brooke nodded jerkily since it seemed to be what he expected from her. 'It seems a very extravagant way to live,' she remarked uneasily.

'I can well afford extravagant,' Lorenzo intoned, wondering why she wasn't one bit excited at the prospect of shopping, wondering why she looked kind of lost standing there in the middle of the room, rather like a little girl contemplating a giant dress-up box that frightened her. This was Brooke's world, from the fashion magazines piled on the coffee table to the immaculate shoe collection. And she *didn't* recognise any of it, he acknowledged grimly.

At least now, she could explore her life, Brooke reminded

herself, for there had to be personal things tucked away somewhere within the two rooms, surely photos of her late parents and that kind of stuff, she reasoned as Lorenzo departed. As for the fashion end of things, she clearly wasn't able to become a fashion icon again in her current state of mind and she would just have to move on from that and find something else to keep her busy. Reinventing yourself was all the rage these days, she reminded herself dully. It was not as though she had a choice when she couldn't imagine wearing a see-through lace dress or jeans that exposed her bottom cheeks.

That reflection, however, threw yet another obstacle into her path. Almost certainly that more audacious woman was the woman Lorenzo knew and had chosen to marry. Brooke paled at that acknowledgement. A *sexier* woman. Was that the common denominator at the heart of her marriage? That together sexier Brooke and more reserved Lorenzo meshed like magnets? Was that why Lorenzo was now so distant with her? Because she wasn't putting out the right vibes any longer with her clothing and her manner? Well, she was just going to have to fake it, wasn't she?

What do you know about being sexy? she asked herself limply. But she had to *know* those things to make such daring clothing choices! She relived that kiss and a slow burn reignited low in her pelvis and she shifted restlessly. Maybe she was sexier in bed than she imagined and when it happened it would all just come seamlessly together for her...but what if it didn't? What if her apparent stock of general knowledge didn't include the bedroom stuff? What if she lay there like a graven image and freaked him out? And why was she even having these thoughts, she asked herself, when to date even getting a kiss out of Lorenzo had entailed practically falling on him? Maybe *she* was the partner who made all the sexy, inviting moves, she thought anxiously, and if that was true, the onus would be on *her*...

Perhaps Lorenzo had simply been waiting to bring her home, she reasoned, and tonight, when she was tucked up in bed, he would visit?

CHAPTER FOUR

'I'D LIKE SOME details about the accident,' Brooke declared over dinner two weeks later.

'I don't think that's a good idea,' Lorenzo informed her lazily.

For the first time ever, Brooke wanted to slap her husband for still treating her like a vulnerable child to be protected from every ill wind. 'I disagree. Since I wasn't driving—I mean, you told me that—who *was* driving?'

'An employee. I'm afraid that he died,' Lorenzo told her smoothly.

Brooke lost colour and stilled. 'Oh, how dreadful! I should go and see his family. Will you give me the address?' she pressed.

'He didn't have a family as such. He lived with an elderly mother. I've ensured that she is financially secure. You don't need to get involved,' Lorenzo assured her.

'I think the least I can do is visit his mother to offer my condolences,' Brooke responded firmly.

Lorenzo almost rolled his eyes at this new caring, sharing display of Brooke's. He compressed his hard mouth. Every time he saw her, she annoyed him by being so beautiful, so...*tempting*. There she sat, hair foaming in ringlets and cascading round her like some cartoon mermaid, triangular face bare of cosmetics, violet eyes bright and friendly and natural and, in truth, she remained drop-dead gorgeous. Yet she was wearing jeans, simple plain jeans, and flat shoes. She was another almost unrecognisable incarnation of Brooke and one he didn't intend to waste time on because the transformation wouldn't, *couldn't* possibly last. Inevitably, her indomitable will, her piranha-fish appetites for sex, media exposure and money would resurface and he, for one, would be a great deal happier.

He didn't want to be reminded of that treacherous kiss in the clinic when he had inexplicably contrived to overlook all the other men she had betrayed him with. Of that kiss, it was enough to recall that she had burned him alive and filled him with a hunger he refused to satisfy. He was even more astonished that she could *still* have that effect on him. Only days before the accident he had enjoyed the definitive proof that he was completely impervious to her looks and her seductive wiles. He could only suppose that being forced into a protective role for so long with his estranged wife had somehow softened his previous hard shell of cold disinterest. After all, he had never been the kind of foolish man who returned to explore his worst mistake and that was what Brooke genuinely was to him: *his worst mistake*.

'Do you want the full story of the accident? Even if it's distressing?' he prompted, reminding himself that keeping such secrets from her wasn't doing anything to help her adapt to her return to the land of the living.

Feeling a little threatened now and worried about what he might have held back from her, Brooke nodded urgently. 'Yes.'

'There was another woman in the limo with you and she died as well. We don't know what she was doing with you because, although I looked into her history before the funeral, I couldn't see anything relevant that would have brought you together that day.'

Brooke's smooth brow furrowed. 'That's a puzzle. Who was she?'

'She was a waitress in a London café, although she'd quit

her job that same day, quoting a family emergency, but when I investigated it turned out that she had no family and there was nothing of interest about her,' Lorenzo recounted with a fluid Italian shrug of dismissal. 'I suppose we'll never know what she was doing in the car with you that day unless you regain your memory.'

Brooke was troubled by the discovery that some mystery woman had been with her on the day of the crash. She had already discovered a severe absence of personal possessions in her bedroom. She had waded through a dozen files packed with press clippings and some rather suggestive headlines, depicting her with other men in nightclubs, but she hadn't found a single picture of her parents or indeed of anyone else. Her life, evidently, had been lived solely through the media and nothing else had much mattered to her, and that saddened her because her previous existence now seemed shallow to her and empty of real purpose.

As for her marriage, she ruminated regretfully, it didn't appear to be much healthier than her lifestyle had been because she barely saw Lorenzo except at the dinner table. When she had made the effort to rise at dawn to breakfast with him, he had not seemed remotely appreciative of her company and had buried his nose back in the *Financial Times*, the one and only media publication that came to the house.

It was ironic that she had actually been spending more personal time with her husband when he had been visiting her at the clinic. Now that she was back home, he was perfectly polite and pleasant, but it was almost as if she didn't really exist on his terms, which was weird, *wasn't it*?

But everything was weird in their relationship, she conceded wretchedly. Why didn't he sleep with her? Why didn't he want sex when popular parlance suggested that men always wanted sex? What was wrong with her? Or what was wrong with their marriage? She had tried to ignore the signs that something was not quite right but after a fortnight of being treated like a house guest rather than a wife, Brooke felt that she could no longer disregard suspicions that were a deep source of concern to her. After all, if Lorenzo didn't want her any more, what was she doing living in *his* house? Obviously she could only be uncomfortable with the fear that she wasn't truly welcome below the roof of the place she had mistakenly assumed was her true home.

'Why do you never take me out anywhere with you?' Brooke asked with a directness she had not dared to utilise with Lorenzo before.

Lorenzo glanced up from his plate, beautiful dark deep-set eyes shrewd and level, and she experienced that same maddening little prickling of awareness that his gaze always evoked and her heart started to thump faster inside her tight chest. 'We've always had separate social lives. And, unhappily, if we *are* seen in public together, you would be mobbed by the paparazzi because you are the former beauty maven who has now returned from the dead and many people are very curious about you. I don't like press attention in my private life...however, you do.'

'Oh...' Brooke breathed, crushed by those truths delivered so instantaneously. 'You think there might be headlines?'

'I *know* there would be. Brooke...' Lorenzo sighed and lounged back in his chair, devastatingly good-looking and infuriatingly calm. 'There have been cameras waiting at the foot of the drive to catch a photo of you since the day I brought you home. If you'd even once gone shopping, you would've seen them there. Maybe you don't feel like having that media attention right now?'

'I don't,' she confirmed.

'But it's still a very large part of who you used to be,' Lorenzo reminded her. 'And the paps aren't going to give up and go away any time soon.'

Having dealt that final blow, Lorenzo left for the Tassini Bank while Brooke retired to her white bedroom to read a book she had bought online about Italians, seeking in some small way to redress her ignorance of her husband. But there seemed little point reading about how Italians highly valued their families and seeking such a trait in Lorenzo. He was diligent in assuring that her medical needs were covered with regular online sessions with Mr Selby and physio sessions with a personal trainer, but his care never ever got more personal than that. She was fed, housed, clothed, medicated and that was that.

Along with jeans and casual tops, she had bought a dress, low-necked, short and scarlet in hue, and high heels. She viewed the more decorative fitted outfit as a move forward, a first step in becoming the woman whom Lorenzo obviously expected her to be. Now, sadly, she wasn't even sure she would have the nerve to wear it because he had shut her down again.

Two other people had died in that accident and *she* had survived. She was much luckier than she had ever appreciated, and she knew that her first outing would include a visit to the driver's mother and a respectful call at the cemetery to the grave of the woman who had been with her that day. Maybe she had been a friend, Brooke reflected sadly, for she could hardly have failed to note that she didn't seem to have friends in the way that other women had. Hadn't she liked other women? Hadn't other women liked her? The lack of a friend or relative to turn to sometimes made her feel very alone…

Blasted self-pity, she told herself off firmly, and returned to her book while wondering if she had the nerve to wear that dress for dinner and whether Lorenzo would even notice what she wore, because he didn't seem to look at her that much.

Just then, however, when she was least expecting it, the door literally burst open and she jerked bolt upright on top of the bed, her violet eyes wide with surprise.

The very image of innocence, Lorenzo thought in a rage as he strode across the room to slap the newspaper he had bought for that purpose down on the foot of the bed. The lurid headline ran: *She Doesn't Know Who She Is!*

He was furious with himself most of all for starting to trust her again even though he knew she was a liar and a manipulator. It wasn't like him to lose his temper, but when he had seen that newspaper headline, he had felt betrayed, and then he had wondered *why* he felt betrayed when Brooke was only doing what she had always done in seeking to shape her public image and stoke press interest. He should've been better prepared, should've expected such behaviour from her. It was his own fault that he felt as though she had deceived him. When, after all, had he begun to forget what kind of a woman she was?

'I should've guessed that you'd have your own more direct but *sly* way of dealing with the media!' Lorenzo fired down at her.

Brooke was frozen to the spot in disbelief by his behaviour because Lorenzo had never once raised his voice to her before. But at this moment, he was ferociously angry with her and it showed in every honed, hard lineament of his lean, darkly handsome features. 'Go on…look at the article and tell me you're not responsible for this outrage!' he challenged with contempt.

Trembling, Brooke lifted the tabloid newspaper, shaken to see the photo of her in the blue dress she had worn at the clinic now adorning the front page. She recalled the friendly nurse who had asked if she could take a picture on her phone. Brooke had said yes, had believed that it was the dress that the woman was interested in. She hadn't known enough about safeguarding herself from such exploitation to say, no, sorry, she conceded in dismay. So, it *was* absolutely her fault, just as Lorenzo believed, that that picture was in a newspaper.

'Obviously it was more than your vanity could bear to have the press speculating that you could be scarred or in a wheelchair!' Lorenzo bit out in raw condemnation. 'You tell me you don't want media attention and then you do…*this*? You give an interview to them? *Madre di Dio*, why the hell am I acting surprised?'

'An interview?' she whispered, turning the page with shaking fingers, intimidated more than she liked to admit by his sheer dark fury. There was more volatile emotion than she had ever thought he possessed emanating from him and lacing the atmosphere with brutal tension. Unfortunately, it wasn't how she would've wanted to discover that he was much more emotional in nature than he was prepared to show.

'*Sì*, an interview. While I'm busy hiring extra security to *protect* you, you're still feeding the fire to gain the attention you crave from your admirers!'

Brooke took a mental step back from the toweringly tall, dark man raging over her and concentrated on the article. She was quick to recognise that stray comments she had made and medical info that should've been kept confidential had been cobbled together and leaked in the form of an interview that had been faked. 'I didn't give anyone an interview, Lorenzo. I did let one of the nurses take a photo of me and I'm sorry she gave it to the press, but I didn't exactly know who I was supposed to be then or that I shouldn't allow that,' she confided uncomfortably. 'Read it properly and you'll see I'm telling the truth. It's a *fake* interview. I wouldn't want people to know that I'm suffering from amnesia because that's embarrassing—'

'Unfortunately for you,' Lorenzo countered glacially, 'I already know that I can't trust a word you say because you're a gifted liar. You lie about the most ridiculous things and then shrug indifferently when the truth comes out. I've never been able to trust you!'

While Brooke had contrived to remain calm and in control while Lorenzo vented his wrath over a naïve mistake she had made, those words fell on her like hand grenades that exploded on contact with her shrinking body. In shock, she drew up her knees and hugged them. All her natural colour had gone into retreat while her tummy stirred sickly. She had told her husband lies and he had found her out in them? *She* was a liar? It dawned on her then that for the very *first* time Lorenzo was giving her what he deemed to believe was the absolute truth about herself, yet only raw anger had drawn that honesty from him. For just a few minutes he had forgotten to treat her like someone too delicate to handle reality.

All of a sudden, she was being forced to face the fact that, regardless of how hard she had tried to explain away her husband's cool attitude towards her, their relationship *did* have problems. Indeed, Lorenzo saw her as a liar he couldn't trust. Shaken and appalled by that revelation, she rocked back and forth where she sat, struggling to deal with that new sobering knowledge.

Lorenzo stared down at her and then he blinked and the explosive rage that had powered him, most ironically a rage that had never once seized him with Brooke before, vanished as though it had never been. Stricken by what he had dumped on her in a temper, he came down on the side of the bed and hauled in a deep shuddering breath, cursing his lack of control and the damage he had inflicted. She looked so small, so lost, so unlike the woman he remembered, the woman he needed to *bury* and forget about because *that* version of Brooke might never return, he finally acknowledged.

'I'm sorry. I shouldn't have lost my temper,' Lorenzo conceded heavily and reached for her hand. 'When I saw that paper, a fuse just blew somewhere inside me *and—*'

'We're both living in a very stressful situation,' Brooke pointed out in a wobbly undertone. 'It's sure to be affecting you as well.'

Lorenzo didn't feel that he was in a stressful situation because naturally he was in possession of facts she had yet to learn. But he did feel guilty, horrendously guilty for shouting at her, condemning her and causing her distress. When her hand pulled away from his, rejecting that hold, he was disconcerted by that withdrawal.

'You don't need to pretend any longer, Lorenzo,' Brooke sighed in explanation. 'You've let the cat out of the bag. We don't have a good marriage, which actually explains *a lot*.'

Unprepared for that far-reaching conclusion being reached at such speed, Lorenzo hesitated only a moment before reaching across the bed and bundling her small resisting figure into his arms and settling her down across his long muscular thighs with an intimacy he had never dared to embrace before. 'No, it only explains that I have a terrible temper, which I usually manage to keep in check,' he breathed as he heard her swallow back the sobs making her tremble within his grasp. 'It doesn't mean anything.'

'But you said I was always telling lies and that you couldn't trust me!' Brooke sobbed outright.

Lorenzo was usually very fast at thinking on the back foot, as it were, but a quicksilver tongue somehow evaded him when he had Brooke struggling to hold back sobs in his arms. *He* had done that; *he* alone had distressed her to that extent. Yet she had borne every unsettling, scary development bravely from the outset of her recuperation. Even so, he had, and for the second time, reduced her to tears. He felt like a complete heel. When had he become so tough, bitter and selfish that he only went through the motions of giving her a roof over her head while at the same time utterly ignoring her presence in every other way? Of course, she had noticed that he wasn't behaving like a husband, of course she had become anxious about it.

'Did I lie about money?' Brooke whispered chokily. 'I mean, I can see by that wardrobe that I was kind of a bit...spendthrift.'

Lorenzo seized on that option with intense relief. He was rich enough to support a thousand spendthrift wives but rows over extravagance and lies concerning that extravagance were far less damaging to her self-image than the truth would be. 'Yes,' he confirmed, relieved to feel some of the jerking rigidity in her small frame drain away. 'Nothing I couldn't deal with, but you kept on doing it.'

'Well, I won't any more,' Brooke whispered shakily, the worst of her crushing anxiety draining away. 'I promise you, absolutely promise that I won't tell you any lies or spend too much money. There's no limit on those credit cards you gave me, is there?'

Lorenzo breathed in deep and slow. 'I don't think we need to worry about that now. You've only spent a couple of hundred pounds since you arrived,' he reminded her ruefully. 'Believe me, you can be a lot more spendthrift than that. I don't want you worrying about that either.'

'Maybe getting married to someone with money like you have sort of went to my head and I got carried away,' Brooke suggested thoughtfully.

Lorenzo registered the one salient fact that he should have shared with her sooner. 'No, you weren't penniless when I married you—your father left you a decent trust fund. He was an affluent wine importer and you were an only child.'

Brooke focused huge violet eyes on him as she flung her head back. 'I have money of my own?' she exclaimed incredulously.

'Yes, although we agreed when we married that I would take care of all the bills.'

But Brooke was still gripped by amazement that she had her own money. 'That really surprises me because I don't feel like I've ever had money. I suppose that sounds weird to you when I obviously have, but everything like the staff here and the limousines and the grandeur makes me feel…overwhelmed,' she finally confided. 'I assumed it was because I hadn't had time yet to become accustomed to your lifestyle.'

'Your parents weren't rich, only comfortably off,' Lorenzo suggested, the feel of her body heat, the brush of her breasts against his shirtfront and her proximity combining to increase the hard arousal thrumming at his groin and remind him of just how long it had been since he had had sex. As gently as he could, he scooped her up, rose upright and laid her back down on the bed. 'You should rest. I upset you.'

Brooke sat up again. 'I'm fine now. The nurse that took that photo was called Lizzie and if you read the supposed interview, you can see it's just put-together stuff aside of the amnesia.'

Lorenzo lifted the paper he had slapped down in front of her and spread his free hand, long brown fingers flexing. 'My temper went off like a rocket. I didn't read it and I'll inform the clinic about the nurse.'

'I don't want her to get in trouble!' Brooke protested.

'She sold a photo of you and revealed confidential medical facts. The clinic needs to protect their patients,' Lorenzo murmured smoothly, still incensed by the condemnation he had immediately laid at his wife's door and the distress the episode had caused her.

The distress *he* had created by jumping to conclusions without proof and venting freely. He swore to himself that it would be the very last time he awarded blame to her on the basis of her past sins. He really hadn't thought through the extent of the responsibility he was taking on in bringing her back to what had once been her home. And now he was stuck fast, neither married nor divorced, his own life in limbo alongside hers...

And for how long could he tolerate that injustice?

Lorenzo returned to the bank. Brooke went out to the garden, which she loved, strolling along gravel paths, enjoying the sunlight and the flowers and greenery all around her. A little dog bounded out from below the trees and began to bark at her. Brooke laughed because it was a tiny little thing, a mop of tousled multi-shaded brown hair on four spindly legs.

'Now who do you belong to?' she asked, settling down on a bench when natural curiosity brought the dog closer. He jumped up against her legs, more than willing to invite attention. She petted him, lifted him and discovered that *he* was a girl and laughed again, letting her curl up on her lap and settle there.

The gardener nearby, engaged in freshening up a bed with new plants, glanced across the sunken garden at them in apparent surprise. When she moved on, the little dog followed at her heels and she said to the gardener. 'Who does the dog belong to?'

'Topsy's yours, Mrs Tassini,' he said without hesitation and she realised that her amnesia was no longer a secret, if it ever had been, in the household.

Only a slight flush on her cheeks, Brooke walked on before stooping to pet the little animal. Her dog had found the way back to her and she smiled, delighted to discover that she had a pet and that she liked animals. It was uplifting to learn that there had been a positive side to the self she no longer remembered because so far she only appeared to be finding out negative stuff, she conceded ruefully, thinking about the extravagance and the lies that had clearly damaged her marriage. At the same time though, it was better to be forewarned that there could be further obstacles ahead, she reflected ruefully. What else had she done that she would be ashamed to find out?

At least, Lorenzo had resisted the very human urge to just dump all her mistakes on her at once, she thought fondly. That had been generous of him in the circumstances. He was doing everything by the book and shielding her from unpleasant truths. How could she not love a man like that?

Brooke dressed for dinner that evening with greater care than usual. Finally, she surveyed her reflection in one of the several mirrors in the dressing room and something strange happened. For a timeless instant as she gazed into the mirror, she became dizzy and she saw another woman. No, it wasn't *another* woman, she realised with a spooked shiver of reaction, it was herself clad in a black jacket with her hair straight and wearing a different red dress. She had been sitting in the back of a limousine. She blinked rapidly and realised that she had *finally* remembered something from the past and she couldn't wait to tell Mr Selby about that promising little glimmer.

It wouldn't be worth mentioning it to Lorenzo though, would it? Just as she hadn't thought to mention that none of the ravishing shoes in the cabinets even fitted her any longer because evidently her feet had grown a little fatter and those shoes pinched like the devil. A tiny little flashback that only involved seeing herself and that showed her nothing important wasn't worth telling Lorenzo about. Even so, it was a promising start to a complete recovery.

Lorenzo was still upstairs when she arrived in the dining room and she walked out onto the terrace that overlooked the garden, wondering if it would be acceptable to suggest that they ate outside during the summer months because the evenings were so beautiful and she did love the fresh air. Careful in the high heels that she was still a little wobbly in and with Topsy in tow, because the little dog hadn't left her side all day, she descended the steps that led down to the garden and roved along a path that led into a shrubbery backed by natural woodland. Topsy went scampering ahead and then started barking so ferociously that she almost levitated off the ground.

'Topsy,' she began to say and then, before she could gather her breath, a man leapt out of nowhere in front of her and gave her such a fright that she screamed.

And screamed again, backing away in absolute terror, every natural instinct on high alert, her heart thundering in her ears with fear. The man threw up his hands in apparent disbelief and then two men appeared from behind him and pulled him away.

An arm snaked round her quaking figure from behind. 'Are you all right?' Lorenzo's very welcome and familiar voice enquired, and relief made her sag like a ragdoll in his arms. 'I was in the dining room when I heard you scream. I've never moved so fast in my life!'

'Who was he?' she prompted shakily. 'What did he want?'

'A paparazzo chancing his arm,' Lorenzo imparted. 'Didn't you notice his camera?'

'No… I thought… I thought he was a rapist or something,' she contrived to explain unevenly, her breath still see-sawing in and out of her raw throat. 'That's what I assumed. I didn't think about this being a garden and how unlikely that would be, which was stupid.'

Lorenzo's dark eyes glittered with wildly inappropriate appreciation of that explanation for Brooke's reaction to a member of the press and he made no comment, seeing for himself that she was still pale and trembling with fright. He closed an arm round her to direct her back indoors. 'You can blame me for this frightening experience as well,' he told her instead in an exasperated undertone. 'I was about to double our security before I saw that newspaper headline this morning and then I *forgot*.'

'You're allowed to overlook stuff occasionally,' Brooke told him, still struggling to get her breathing under control. 'Anyway, how can it be *your* fault when it's obvious that my love of attracting publicity caused all this nonsense?'

'It wasn't wrong for you to like attracting publicity,' Lorenzo countered levelly. 'That was your world. I shouldn't have given you the impression that it was a bad choice, because it wasn't for you.'

But it was a bad choice for anyone married to you, Brooke completed inside her head, for everything about Lorenzo implied that he was a very private man and the last man imaginable to enjoy that kind of exposure. Clearly, her past self hadn't much cared about that, and she had continued to relentlessly pursue her own goals. She was twenty-eight years old and could scarcely blame that decision on immaturity. She had put her media career first, *not* her marriage.

'Topsy!' she called, and the dog raced over to her, long silly ears flopping madly, tongue hanging. Without hesitation she scooped the little animal up and started telling it that it was a great little watchdog while Lorenzo looked on in disbelief.

Brooke didn't *like* animals, but some nameless admirer had gifted her the puppy when handbag dogs were in vogue. She had brought the dog home and abandoned it in the kitchen and, as far as he knew, had never looked at it again. Lorenzo decided it was time for him to have another chat with her psychiatrist and ask how it was possible that his wife could be displaying entirely new personality traits as well as different tastes. Brooke wasn't even eating salads any longer, never mind fussing about her diet. She no longer used the gym and barely touched alcohol aside of a glass of wine at dinner. The changes were piling up to the extent that he no longer knew what to expect from the wife he would once have sworn that he knew inside out.

'Would you like a drink after that...er rather unnerving encounter?' he asked calmly.

'No, thanks. But thanks for being there this morning and this evening to ground me,' Brooke murmured in a rush, staring up at him with a great burst of warmth rushing and spreading through her veins, because she was grateful, *so* ridiculously grateful that Lorenzo existed and that she was married to him. He was her rock in every storm.

'I wasn't there for you this morning in the way I should've been,' Lorenzo corrected with a sardonic twist of his beautiful shapely mouth, tensing as that warm look in her eyes somehow contrived to arrow straight down to his groin. 'I attacked you, misjudged you.'

Determined violet eyes connected with his. 'But I forgive you.'

'Too easily,' Lorenzo chided, trying to keep some distance between them while he was as hard as rock and throbbing with arousal.

Brooke realised that she was literally backing him into the wall and she laughed in surprise, wondering if Lorenzo was always so slow on the uptake, so businesslike, so prone to saying and doing only the right thing that he couldn't even grasp when his wife was coming on to him! She lifted her hands and ran them up over his ribcage over the shirt below his tailored jacket, sensitive fingertips learning the lean mouth-watering musculature hidden beneath, and she stretched up and literally face-planted her mouth on his.

Two very masculine hands sank into her mane of ringlets and held her fast and she smiled against his parting lips, her mouth opening eagerly for the plunging urgency of his. It was everything she remembered from the clinic, a chemical explosion of sheer hunger and demand. Oh, yes, her husband *wanted* her all right, she savoured with pleasure, he only needed encouragement while she needed no encouragement whatsoever when keeping her hands off him was more of a challenge. Her body was coming alive with a host of sensations from the tightening of her nipples, to the swell of her breasts, to the aching hollowness that tugged at the heart of her.

There was a sound somewhere behind her and Lorenzo yanked her back from him as though he had been burned. Stevens was muttering an apology and Lorenzo assured him that dinner *right now* was fine.

Her face hot as hellfire, so hot she wanted to die for a split second, Brooke retreated to her designated dining chair and grasped her wine glass with new fervour. She couldn't look at Lorenzo, she absolutely couldn't look at him in that instant, she was so mortified by her own forward behaviour, but honestly, it was as if he were a magnet that pulled at her until she couldn't resist the charge any more. She was convinced that she had never felt desire so strongly before...and yet how could that be?

Lorenzo infuriated her then by acting as if nothing had happened. He asked her about her day and her enjoyment of the garden. Slowly, painfully, her equilibrium returned. It wasn't *his* fault that she wanted him to be the sort of guy who said to hell with dinner and carted her off to the nearest private spot to take advantage of her willingness...*was it*?

CHAPTER FIVE

IT WAS NOW OR NEVER, Brooke challenged herself, because on a deep inner level she was cringing about what she was about to do.

The many mirrors in her dressing room showed a slender figure garbed in a white satin and lace nightdress. Wearing it felt weird because Brooke was convinced that, at heart, she was a pyjama girl rather than the fashionable, sexier image she was sporting, but, going by the decorative lingerie collection in the dressing room, her past self had never given way to the weakness of putting comfort first. Pyjamas weren't sexy though and she *needed* sexy, needed it desperately, she acknowledged apprehensively, because in spite of reading the book she had found in the bedside cabinet on 'how to thrill your lover,' she *still* felt as if she didn't have a clue!

After all, suppose Lorenzo *rejected* her? How would she ever rise above that humiliation? She breathed in deep. Her need to have a normal marriage, added to the desire she definitely felt for him, was motivating her and what was wrong with making a major effort? Why would he reject her when he kissed her as though his life depended on it? she asked herself, striving to bolster her flagging courage as she ranged closer to the connecting door between their bedrooms and reached for the handle. The blasted door was locked! She couldn't believe it, and so afraid was she of losing her nerve altogether that she stalked straight out of her bedroom and walked down the corridor to let herself into his room with a fast-beating heart.

She couldn't believe her luck when she heard the shower running in the en suite. In one frantic leap she made it into the bed and hit the lights on the wall to plunge the room into darkness. Maybe that was a little too cowardly, she reasoned with a grimace, because that amount of self-consciousness wasn't sexy either. Stretching up, she put the lights back on and surveyed his bedroom décor, which was much warmer and comfier in ambience than her own stark white bower of rest.

Brooke was still all of a quiver, like a real scaredy-cat. She shrank at the prospect of being confronted by Lorenzo's shock, surprise and, ultimately, his rebuff. But if he said no, he would have to explain why not, wouldn't he? And then another little piece of the mystery of their marriage would fall into place, so, at the cost of her dignity, she would find out more even if he did dismiss her.

Lorenzo was in a dark brooding mood as he stepped out of the shower and snatched at a towel to dry off his hair. It was a challenge for him to believe that sharing a roof with Brooke could wind him up like a clockwork toy with sheer lust. How had that happened? *When* had that happened? It was damned near three years since he had experienced that hunger and then Brooke had woken up after the accident and somehow that primal urge had come back with a vengeance, engulfing him without reason or logic. It infuriated him.

When Lorenzo strode naked out of the bathroom and saw her lying in his bed, the last chain of restraint snapped inside him and set him free. Suddenly he had had it with self-discipline and had it with continually hearing his legal team's warnings in the back of his mind and all he could think about was that there were no cameras in his bedroom and he could do whatever the hell he liked with the woman he had married. Brooke was still his wife. He wanted her and *she* wanted *him*. If he kept it that simple, he didn't need to even think about anything else, and it *was* simple, basic sexual instinct and nothing more.

'I th-thought…' Brooke stammered, peering in awe at him over the top of the duvet, striving to grab up some bad-girl sass from somewhere down deep inside her, so deep she couldn't find it. She felt like a woman who had never been in a man's bed in her life and that was unsettling her more and increasing her nerves.

'Great minds think alike,' Lorenzo quoted, all smooth and dark in tone like the finest chocolate laced with that delicious accent of his.

And he smiled at her, he actually *smiled*, and the charisma of that smile set her heartbeat racing and released butterflies in her tummy. In an abrupt movement, Brooke pushed back the duvet with valiant hands and sat up against the pillows, the worst of her nerves conquered by the suspicion that she could have looked as though she was hiding in his bed like a little kid. A deep heat assailed her face when she registered that he was naked, absolutely naked, all bronzed and hair-roughened and aroused naked, and her mouth ran dry.

'So,' she breathed shakily. 'You're not going to throw me out?'

Lorenzo tilted his tousled and damp dark head to one side and sent her a smouldering appraisal from dark glittering eyes that speared her where she sat. 'You want me?'

Unnerved a bit by the change in his attitude, Brooke nodded jerkily like a marionette.

'Say it,' Lorenzo commanded, needing to hear the words because he knew she didn't remember being with him before and that for her this was her first time with him.

'I want you,' Brooke practically whispered, so hard was it to get sufficient oxygen into her struggling lungs.

'*Dannazione*... No, I'm not going to throw you out,' Lorenzo told her thickly.

'I want us to have a normal marriage,' she muttered tightly.

'It's been a long time since we had normal,' Lorenzo admitted.

'But why *is* that?' she pressed.

'That's not something we want to get into at this moment,' Lorenzo growled, tossing aside the towel still clutched in one lean brown hand and climbing into the bed.

Brooke felt almost as if she couldn't breathe with Lorenzo that close, the heat of his body warming hers even before he touched her, and then his wide sensual mouth crashed down on hers and breathing began to seem a much overrated pursuit as every sense she possessed flew off on a wild and wonderful trail of discovery. The very scent of him, soap, designer cologne and clean male, overwhelmed her and the minty taste of him against her tongue was delicious. As for the actual feel of that long, lean, hot, heavy body pressing against hers, it invoked a delirious wriggle closer from her hips while she pushed her breasts against the hard wall of his chest.

Great minds think alike.

She loved that phrase, which suggested that he had been waiting for her. Maybe this had always been their way—she came to him—and the idea no longer bothered her because he was pushing the welcome mat out with irrefutable enthusiasm.

Think about what you're doing.

The words sounded somewhere in Lorenzo's brain like an alarm bell but he suppressed them fast. He was way past caring *how* Brooke had contrived to make him want her again. He was fed up with being sensible when she drew him now on a very primitive level that kept him awake at night, wondering, fantasising about a woman who only eighteen months earlier he could not wait to kick out of his life. He stressed too much about making mistakes, he told himself impatiently. For once he would just go with the flow and do what seemed entirely natural.

Without ceremony he stripped off the nightdress and her breath caught in her throat again as she looked up at him. He had such beautiful eyes, lustrous gold in the lower lighting and framed by dense black lashes that curled up at the ends. Breathless, she lay there entranced until his warm, sensual mouth sealed to hers and a great swoosh of heat rushed up through her as a large masculine hand curved round a plump breast, the thumb rubbing at the sensitive tip until she gasped. Instantaneously she wanted more and when he utilised his mouth instead to suck at the swollen bud, she marvelled that even amnesia could make her forget such distinct sensations.

The tug on her nipple set alight the burn between her thighs, the pulsing liquidity that turned her to mush. She pushed against him in helpless need and he laughed softly, even that sound surging through her like an added aphrodisiac. She ran her hands down his sleek, satiny back with new confidence, smoothing over a lean flank, mentally recalling the book that had specified 'firm, assured' as the most desirable touch and wondering how on earth she could've forgotten something so basic as how to make love to her husband. However, when she touched him, he froze, and she jerked her fingers away again in swift retreat from that daring.

'No…no, don't back off,' Lorenzo positively purred in her ear, returning her small fingers to their former destination and revelling in her enthusiasm. 'I *like* being touched.'

Confidence renewed, Brooke stroked her hand along that smooth velvety skin, fascination powering her in her exploration of all that made them different. But a little of her attention seemed to go a long way and, before she got very far, Lorenzo was spreading her across the mattress like a starfish and she was a little nervous of that position until he began to work his path down her splayed body employing both his mouth and his hands to investigate her curves. The warm damp feeling at her core increased exponentially, leaving her craving his touch to an extent that was almost unbearable to her straining body.

'You've been driving me crazy with hunger for weeks,' Lorenzo growled, kissing a deeply intimate trail up her inner thigh, reducing her to uneasy little twists and jerks of a curious but self-conscious nature.

'Have I?' she pressed, half an octave higher, the words strangling in her throat as he ran his tongue over her most sensitive area, and her hands snapped into fists of restraint because she wanted to sink her fingers into that tousled dark hair of his.

'Every time I look at you, I want you,' Lorenzo grated, stringing a line of kisses across her quivering belly.

'Doesn't show!' she gasped, ridiculously grateful that she had gone leaping into his bed and weak with relief because Lorenzo didn't show things, didn't usually talk like this to her. Evidently, he needed a certain level of intimacy to get comfortable enough to share such truths.

He dallied between her thighs, making moves that drove her to the outer edge of hunger, and every nerve ending was screaming for release and then it happened, in a magical great whoosh that exploded through her being like a shooting star, a drowning absolute pleasure that drenched every limb and left her with a sense of shock that anything could feel that physically good.

That achieved, Lorenzo shifted over her with an intense look of hunger in his dark glittering eyes and it made her feel like a million dollars and as if every path in her life were paved with solid gold. Her heart clenched because the more she found out about him, the more she wanted him, and it was a heady moment that made her eyes prickle with tears, making her blink and turn her head away as his hands slid beneath her hips to tilt her up to him.

And in the next moment, he surged into her ready body, although her body didn't react as though it had been ready for that masculine invasion. It hurt, it hurt *a lot* and almost startled Brooke into crying out, but she mercifully managed to hold onto the cry that almost parted her lips because she was sure that that would have spoilt everything. He would have blamed himself for causing her pain when surely the only reason she had suffered pain lay in the reality that it had been well over a year since she had had sex. And that wasn't anybody's fault, she conceded ruefully.

It was a relief when the discomfort ebbed entirely, and she was able to lose herself again in the intimacy. Her heart began to pound with every lithe thrust of his body over and inside hers, excitement climbing, breathlessness ensured as she wrapped her legs round his lean hips and savoured the sweet throbbing pleasure engulfing her. The hunger came back, urging her body to shift up to his, and little sounds escaped her without her true awareness since it was a passion beyond anything she thought she could ever have felt. The excitement was overwhelming, all-consuming and she wanted more and more until she rose against him on a feverish wave of wild pleasure and another orgasm took her in a rush of high-wire energy.

'Wow,' she whispered in the aftermath, flaking out back against the pillows, limp and drained but secretly triumphant as well because she had achieved exactly what she had set out to do.

'Incredible,' Lorenzo commented, collapsing down beside her out of breath while he dimly wondered how sex could possibly be so different with her that even her behaviour had changed, and he felt as though he was with a different woman. Yes, he was definitely going to see Mr Selby for the question and answer session that he badly needed. Although he doubted if he would mention their new intimacy because that was private… wasn't it? Was *anything* between them private now? he asked himself in disbelief at the concept.

'I'm not on the pill,' Brooke murmured with a sudden stab of anxiety, for she suspected that the very last thing they dared risk in a marriage that appeared to need rebuilding would be a child. 'Did you—?'

'You have an IUD,' Lorenzo assured her while it dawned on him that, even so, he should have taken precautions because she had been with other men. On the other hand, while in medical care she had been saturated with every antibiotic known to man.

His contraceptive omission, however, was another concern that he was in no mood to deal with. It was, after all, a reminder of the true state of play between them and he suppressed the thought of it because if he thought about it too much, it would drive him crazy. The entire situation was *already* driving him crazy, he acknowledged as he questioned the secrecy he had been urged to embrace for her benefit.

But *was* it for her benefit?

Would she have slept with him were she herself?

And without warning, Lorenzo was snatched back into a black and white world with no forgiving shades of grey again. Brooke had hated him when he demanded a divorce and hadn't once spoken a civil word to him during their time apart when he had been forced out of his own house by her infidelity into a city apartment he had hated.

'We shouldn't have done this!' Lorenzo exclaimed with startling abruptness, feeling as though he had taken unfair advantage of her even though *she* was the one who had issued the invitation. 'You're not yourself…you don't know what you're doing.'

Brooke was galvanised out of her comfortable relaxation while thinking how weird it was that he had known she was on birth control when she did not. Even so, it was something she could live with until he said what he did, which filled her with a sensation very close to panic because she did not want him regretting what they had just shared. 'No, *no*, it's not like that!' she argued fervently.

'It is exactly like that,' Lorenzo contradicted gravely. 'I don't *like* that it feels like that but facts are facts.'

'No! You're not allowed to think like that now!' Brooke told him almost fiercely as she scrambled up and literally perched on top of him like a naked nymph, he reasoned in wonderment as arousal kicked in again for him with shocking immediacy.

'Why not?' Lorenzo breathed almost bitterly. 'I took advantage of you.'

'No, you didn't!' Brooke protested, leaning over him, her hands planted either side of his head on the pillows, the twin peaks of her luscious breasts brushing his chest. 'I got into *your* bed, for goodness' sake! I wanted you and we had a great time and that's all there is to it!'

Lorenzo blinked at that hail of keen protest and gazed up into vivid violet eyes and a flawless heart-shaped face surrounded by a tangle of platinum curls. His hands went up before he even knew it himself and he tasted her pouting pink lips like a man starving for that particular flavour. Need surged through him stronger than ever, a bone-deep driving need that threatened to unnerve him.

'I think I'm falling in love with you again, Lorenzo,' Brooke declared.

Lorenzo froze as though she had paralysed him. It was an interesting response from a husband in receipt of such a proclamation, she acknowledged unhappily.

'You can't love me...you don't know me,' he told her levelly.

'I beg to differ. It's almost three months since I came out of that coma and throughout that time you have been my biggest and best support team,' Brooke countered strongly. 'I have got to know you. I have got to see how you put me and my needs first *every time*. I have been here while you lived through a profoundly challenging situation with me and still took nothing for yourself. So please don't tell me that I *can't* love you because I don't know you. I do know what I've seen and how it makes me feel. I'm *definitely* falling for you.'

Lorenzo took a deep breath and parted his lips as if he was about to say something. But then he closed his mouth again and tugged her back down to him. 'Whatever,' he breathed, urgently conscious of her curvy body moving over his groin. 'I still want you.'

'Nothing wrong with that,' Brooke assured him, her colour rising headily as he gazed up at her full of blatant sexual intent.

'Dio...cara mia,' Lorenzo ground out, all self-discipline beaten down, even that affectionate label extracted from him by the encouraging feel of her in his arms. 'So, I'm free to live out my every fantasy, then?'

'Pretty much,' she whispered, barely recognising herself from the shy, uncertain woman she had been a mere hour earlier.

'I have quite an appetite built up,' he warned her thickly.

'It seems I have too,' Brooke whispered, recognising the hot tight sensation in her pelvis for the desire that it was this time around and ever so slightly proud of herself for no longer feeling either so ignorant or insecure about her own body. Lorenzo wanted her; indeed he had said that every time he looked at her, he wanted her. Why hadn't she had the perception to see that for herself in the man she had married? Why was her brain so dense where he was concerned? Why wasn't there even a glimmer of natural insight?

Stashing away her increasing frustration with her inability to remember what she needed to remember, Brooke fell into Lorenzo's blazingly sexual kiss, every concern about her ability to be sexy laid to rest. She was enough for *him* and really, at that moment, that was all that mattered to her or seemed the least bit important. He settled her down over him and raised her hips and, seconds later, she realised that it was all beginning again as he eased into her slow and sure, controlling her every movement in an innately dominant way while touching her in a way that sent her flying off the planet again within minutes. Exhausted then, she rested her head down on a smooth brown muscular shoulder and smiled dizzily.

Lorenzo surveyed his wife over breakfast with a faintly dazed light new to his shrewd dark gaze. There she was, curled up in a chair being all affectionate, playful and teasing while munching on toast and feeding Topsy pieces of crust. Brooke didn't eat carbohydrates; Brooke treated carbs like poison. He had never known her to be affectionate or playful either, even before he had married her. Within the hour, he was meeting with her psychiatrist in search of advice.

'Yes, I think it's perfectly possible that she could be a *very* different person without that celebrity frame of reference that was once so crucial to her self-image,' the older man declared with confidence. 'There are documented examples of cases of this nature but I'm afraid I can't tell you how to proceed. That is *your* decision, but I suspect it may soon be time to tell her that you were pursuing a divorce before the accident.'

Lorenzo mulled that challenging suggestion over on the way to the Tassini Bank for a board meeting and he grimaced. Last night they had had sex. Today he admits they're in the midst of a divorce? He breathed in slow and deep and groaned. That wouldn't work. He would sense the right moment to tell her when it arrived, he reasoned, recognising that he didn't want to rock the boat or cause her distress. It was still his role to be supportive, *not* destructive.

On the other hand, he was equally aware that he would never consider *staying* married to Brooke—he could not pardon either her lies or her infidelity. And that acknowledgement plunged him straight back into the same, 'damned if he did' and 'damned if he didn't' scenario…

Quite unaware of Lorenzo's thorny dilemma, Brooke was getting dressed to go out, which was something of a challenge given the glitzy nature of the contents of her dressing room. She knew that she didn't have to wear black to offer condolences, but it seemed a matter of respect for her to wear something other than a party outfit. She chose a navy pencil skirt and a silk striped top but she couldn't get the skirt to zip up and had to take it off again and accept with a wince that she had evidently put on weight. A pair of loose dark palazzo pants replaced the skirt. As she left the house for the first time since her arrival, she felt stronger and braver and relieved that she had finally got the gumption to do what she felt she had to do to lay her accident to rest in her own mind.

Lorenzo's PA at the bank had sounded surprised when Brooke phoned her but had been happy to pass on the address and the details she knew about the driver and the passenger who had died in the crash. Brooke bent her head out of view when she saw the cluster of paparazzi at the foot of the drive. Lorenzo's disdain for their interest in his wife had been palpable and she marvelled that she had married a man who cherished his privacy when her own interests had clearly pushed her in a very different direction.

The driver's mother was delighted with her gift of flowers and pleased to have the chance to talk about her late son. She referred several times to the substantial tips that Brooke had regularly given her son and Brooke smiled, relieved to hear that she had been generous. Visiting Milly Taylor's grave, however, put her in a more sombre mood. Although enquiries had been made, only the young woman's former employer had claimed to know her, and that café would be Brooke's final destination.

The gravestone was simple. Brooke set down her floral offering and sighed, wondering if the woman had been a friend. It would make sense that she had had *one* friend, wouldn't it? But would she have made friends with someone from such a very different background? What would they have had in common?

The café was within walking distance of the cemetery and she had asked her driver to pick her up in half an hour. On the way there she passed a newsstand on the pavement and something caught her eye on a front page. She paused to lift the magazine. It was her face and across it was splashed: *Divorce or Reconciliation?*

'You need to buy it to read it,' the vendor told her irritably and she dug into her purse for the cash, her face heating.

She stood in the street reading the article inside and shock went crashing through her in wave after wave. Her tummy succumbed to a queasy lurch and she felt dizzy. Suddenly everything she had believed she knew about Lorenzo was being turned on its head! And equally, everything she had believed she knew about herself was being torn to shreds. Rumours of affairs? Yes, she had seen those photos of her in nightclubs with other men, but she had assumed those men were work contacts or social connections, had never dreamt *that*...?

And Lorenzo had a business trip to Italy, for which he was leaving that very evening, and he would be away for a week. If she wanted the chance to speak to him, she couldn't afford to wait, no, she needed to see him immediately...

CHAPTER SIX

'YOUR WIFE'S HERE to see you,' Lorenzo was informed an hour later at the bank.

Taken aback by that unexpected announcement, because Brooke had never once in all the time he had known her come to see him at the bank, Lorenzo rose from behind his desk.

Brooke entered and the instant he saw her face he knew that something was badly wrong. Her eyes had a sort of glazed look and she was very pale, her stance as she paused uncertainly halfway towards him stiff and unnatural.

'What's wrong?' he asked quietly. 'Although possibly I should be asking you what's right. This *is* the first time you've emerged from the house since you left the clinic.'

'I shouldn't have come here…er…where you work,' Brooke muttered in belated appreciation of what she had done in her distraught frame of mind. 'I should've waited until you came home, so I'm going to just do that and we can talk before you leave for the airport.'

Lorenzo hauled out a chair from the wall before she could leave again. 'No, sit down. I can see that you're troubled about something. Tea? Coffee?'

'A coffee would be good,' she conceded flatly, hoping the caffeine would cut a path through the tangled turmoil of her emotions and miraculously settle her down at a moment when she felt as though the floor beneath her feet had fallen away.

She *was* too dependent on Lorenzo, she acknowledged with a sinking heart. Lorenzo was irreversibly stitched into everything she had thought and done and worried about since she had first wakened from the coma. Since awakening, she had built an entire life around him, and the idea that their marriage was simply a cruel mirage cut her off at the knees and left her drowning in a sea of insecurity and regrets.

The coffee arrived in record time and she was relieved to have something to occupy her hands as she cradled the bone-china cup and marvelled that it was a cup instead of a beaker. That random thought brought a wry smile to her lips. In truth, she recognised, she was eager to think about anything other than the giant chasm that had opened up beneath her feet.

'I went to see Paul Jennings's mother this morning,' she revealed as an opening.

Lorenzo leant back fluidly against the side of his desk, embracing informality for her benefit while both his exquisitely tailored dark suit and her surroundings screamed huge influential office and very powerful occupant. He was gorgeous, she conceded rather numbly, and it was hardly surprising that she had become attached to the idea that he was *hers*. Any woman in her circumstances would've done the same thing, she told herself bracingly. Not only was he gorgeous and sexy and terrific in bed, he had been a rock for her through every step of her recovery process. Whatever the truth of their marriage was, she still owed him gratitude for his generosity.

'Yes, my PA mentioned your plans. I thought it was great that you were finally emerging from the house,' Lorenzo commented. 'So, what went wrong?'

'Oh…nothing went wrong,' Brooke assured him tautly. 'I bought a magazine because I saw my face on the cover.'

'Dio...' Lorenzo bit out, tensing. 'I should've foreseen that you might do something like that.'

Quite deliberately, Brooke lifted her chin, her violet eyes clear and level, giving no hint of the turmoil inside her. 'You can't protect me from everything, Lorenzo…and you shouldn't be *trying* to protect me from the truth,' she told him tightly. 'If it's true that we were getting divorced before the accident, you should've told me weeks ago.'

Lorenzo shifted a lean brown hand in a sudden imperious movement that sought to silence her as he took a step forward.

'Of course, I know *why* you didn't tell me because someone like Mr Selby or some other clever doctor warned you that it might be too much for my battered little brain to handle,' Brooke framed steadily, ignoring his gesture. 'But I disagree with that kind of over-protective attitude because I'm back in the real world now and I *have* to adjust to it, no matter how tough or destabilising it is. I'm not a child.'

Lorenzo surveyed her, feeling strangely appreciative of her control and dignity in a very taxing situation, two responses that he had least expected from her. Brooke had always been more about hysterics and ranting and blaming everybody but herself when anything went wrong. He breathed in deep and accepted the inevitable. The truth was out and he couldn't deny it. 'We *were* pursuing a divorce at the time of the crash,' he admitted levelly.

'Why?' Brooke asked baldly.

Lorenzo studied her. She looked tiny in that chair and she was as white as a sheet. How was he supposed to tell the woman that she now was that she had played away with multiple men, indeed any man who suggested that he could advance her goal of breaking into the screen industry? Lorenzo had never had the slightest difficulty in delivering bad news. Indeed, it was integral to his role as a banker, but when it came to shattering the woman seated before him, he just couldn't drop the ugly truth on her at that moment. The divorce would've been a big enough blow to a woman who had told him that she thought she might love him only the night before. Never mind that that professed love was simply an assumption brought on by her amnesia. She was still being very brave and he admired that, and bad news was never *quite* as bad if it emerged piece by piece over a lengthier period of time, he told himself grimly.

'We were ill-suited, different goals, different outlook on life,' Lorenzo responded. 'I wanted children but you didn't. I wanted a home. You only wanted an impressive backdrop for your photos. Divorce was inevitable.'

Brooke nodded valiantly. 'And…er…the men, the affairs?'

'Rumours,' Lorenzo asserted valiantly. 'But I didn't enjoy the rumours.'

Brooke bent her head but breathed a little easier at that release from her biggest fear: that she was capable of that kind of betrayal and of cheating on him. 'Of course not,' she agreed flatly. 'Even without my memory, I can see that the woman I was and the man you are weren't a good match.'

Lorenzo had gone very quiet. He was thinking hard and fast, wondering whether to take her straight to that penthouse apartment he had bought her to cement their separation back into place. In rapid succession he pictured her there alone and potentially lost and he recoiled from that image while questioning his own sanity.

'And I really shouldn't be living in your home any more,' Brooke completed quietly, raising the point she knew she had to raise to set him free from feeling responsible for her.

Lorenzo's black lashes dropped down over his glittering eyes and every muscle in his lean, powerful frame jerked rigid. He *couldn't* let her go, at least, *not just yet*, he reasoned fiercely. She wasn't fit to be abandoned to sink or swim and that might not strictly be his business any more, but he still *felt* as though it were. Right now, a separation would be premature.

'I have a better solution,' he heard himself say before he had even quite thought through what he was about to say, a divergence from habit that shook him even as he spoke. 'I suggest you accompany me to Italy this evening.'

'To Italy?' Brooke gasped as if she had never heard of the country before, so disconcerted was she by that proposal at that particular moment.

'Yes, it would be good for you to escape the paparazzi and the publicity and enjoy some breathing space. You're a UK celebrity, pretty much unknown—' he selected that last word tactfully '—in Italy. We'll be left alone, free of this constant media speculation. A break is what we need.'

Brooke lifted her head, her heart, which had slowed to a dulled thud, suddenly picking up speed again. 'We?' she queried in a near croak.

'We,' Lorenzo stressed with vigour, some of his tension ebbing now that he could see a provisional way forward out of the current chaos.

'But we're getting a divorce,' Brooke reminded him shakily.

'The divorce has been on hold since the day of the crash. A few more weeks aren't going to make much difference at this point,' Lorenzo informed her with assurance. 'We can separate or divorce at any time. Let's not allow past decisions to control us in a different situation. Let's be patient a little while longer and see how things progress. Your memory may yet return.'

Brooke was plunged deep into shock all over again, the price of having been thrown from one extreme to yet another. She had come to his office to confront him with her heart being squeezed in a steel fist of pain. She had believed that their marriage was an empty charade already all but over and that it was her duty to finally set Lorenzo free, even though she loved him. She remained absolutely convinced that, even though she had made a mess of their marriage, she *still* loved him.

But to her astonishment, Lorenzo was reacting in an utterly unexpected way by offering her a second chance at their marriage. Wasn't that what he meant? For goodness' sake, what else *could* he mean? He didn't want to immediately reclaim his freedom as she had assumed. He was willing to wait...he was willing to continue living with her as her husband. A shaken, shuddering breath forced its passage up through her constrained lungs because relief was filling her almost to overflowing, liberating all the emotions that she had been fighting to suppress since she read about their divorce proceedings in that awful gossipy magazine. Her eyes stung horribly and flooded. She blinked rapidly, warding off the tears and hastily sipping at her cooling coffee.

Lorenzo reached down and rescued the shaking cup and saucer to set it aside, and scooped her up into his arms. It wasn't pity driving him, he told himself with ferocious certainty, it was a crazy, impossible mix of lust, responsibility, sympathy and fascination with the woman she now was. He was taking her to Italy with him. It was a done deal.

'I'm sorry,' she briefly sobbed against his shoulder before she got a grip on herself again and glanced up at him with a grimace of apology. 'It was the shock. I was *expecting*—'

'Keep it simple, like me,' Lorenzo urged. 'I'm practical and calculating and very typical of the male sex. I'm expecting you in my bed at night.'

An indelicate little snort of laughter escaped Brooke then, drying up the tears at source. 'Is that so?' she mumbled, a sudden shard of happiness piercing her.

'You haven't even asked me yet what *I* did wrong in our marriage,' he reproved. 'The mistakes weren't all on *your* side. I worked long hours, left you alone too much and only took you to boring dinner parties where everyone was talking about finance. You weren't happy with me either.'

'We'll see how Italy goes,' Brooke murmured softly. 'As you said, we can choose to part at any time, so neither of us need to feel trapped.'

'You're feeling trapped?' Lorenzo demanded without warning, an arctic light gleaming in his beautiful dark eyes.

'No...' Brooke toyed with a button on his jacket, striving not to flatter him with too much enthusiasm. 'I don't feel trapped at all. Maybe I've grown up a bit from the person I was before the crash. Obviously I've changed. I don't seem to want people with cameras chasing me. I seem to have lost what seems to have been an overriding interest in fashion and clothes...gosh, I'm going to be forced out shopping if you're taking me travelling. A lot of the clothes, and particularly the shoes, don't fit me now,' she confided ruefully.

'I'll organise someone to come to the house this afternoon and kit you out. I'll postpone the flight until early tomorrow morning,' Lorenzo informed her arrogantly. 'But that means I'll have to work late tonight... OK?'

'OK,' she agreed breathlessly.

Lorenzo stared down at her heart-shaped face while a *what-the-hell-am-I-doing?* question raced over and over through his brain. He concentrated instead on that luscious pink mouth and the ever-present throb at his groin and bent his head to taste those succulent lips.

Brooke fell into that kiss like honey melting on a grill. Her insides turned liquid and burned. It happened every time he kissed her, a shooting, thrilling internal heat that washed through her like a dangerous drug, lighting up every part of her body. She wanted to cling, but she wouldn't let herself, stepping back with a control that she was proud to maintain after her earlier emotionalism.

She reddened as she connected with his brilliant dark eyes, which packed such a passionate punch. Maybe this very hunger was what had first brought them together and kept them together even when their relationship didn't work in other ways. Sadly, it was a sobering thought to accept that sexual attraction might have been the most they had ever had as a couple and all she had left to build on.

Obviously, naturally, she wanted more, she reflected ruefully. She wanted him to *stop* feeling as responsible for her as a man might feel about a helpless child. She wanted him to see and accept that she no longer needed to be handled with kid gloves, that she was an adult and able to cope with her own life, even if it did mean losing him in the process. And possibly that was what it *would* mean, she conceded unhappily, bearing in mind that their marriage had apparently been rocky from the start.

Yet where had the ambition-driven woman she had been gone? Where had all the knowledge she must have accumulated from the fashion world gone? Why didn't she care now about what style was 'in' and what was 'out'? Why was she most comfortable in a pair of ordinary jeans? Where now was the brash confidence that had fairly blazed out of the magazine cuttings in her press scrapbooks? Those were questions that only time, or the recovery of her memories, would answer. But facing up to more challenging situations alone would probably strengthen her and do her good, she told herself fiercely. She resolved to make that visit to the café to ask about Milly Taylor on the drive home. Perhaps that would help her work out what the connection had been between two ostensibly very different women.

The café was also a bakery and Brooke waited patiently until the queue of customers had gone and the older woman behind the counter looked at her for the first time. The woman's eyes rounded, and she paled, stepping back as though she had had a fright.

'Milly?' she exclaimed shakily, her hand flying up to her mouth in a gesture of confusion as she stared at the younger woman. 'No, no… I can *see* you're not Milly, but just for a moment there, the resemblance gave me such a shock!'

Brooke's brow pleated as she asked the woman if they could have a chat. 'I'm Brooke Tassini. Milly died in the crash that I was injured in. You seem to think I resemble her… I've lost my memory,' she explained with a wince. 'I'm still trying to work out who Milly was to me.'

'Brooke? I'm Marge,' the middle-aged woman said comfortably as she moved out from behind the counter. 'When I get a better look at you, the resemblance isn't as striking as I first thought it was. But Milly had the same long curly hair and the same colour of eyes. Look, come and see the photo of her.'

Brooke crossed the café to scrutinise the small staff group photo on the wall, but it wasn't a very clear picture and she peered at the smiling image with a frown because she could see the extraordinary similarity of their features and colouring. 'When she was working here, did she ever mention me? I'm wondering now if she could be some distant relation, a cousin or something?'

'Milly didn't ever mention you,' Marge told her apologetically. 'She was a quiet girl. To be honest, I don't think she *had* much of a life outside work and she only worked here for a couple of months. I got the impression that she had moved around quite a bit, but I was still surprised that morning when she chucked her job in, because she had seemed content here. She said she had to quit because she had a family crisis.' Marge made a face. 'She seemed to forget that according to what she had once told me, she didn't *have* a family.'

'Oh…' Brooke breathed, acknowledging that she was no further on in her need to know who her companion had been and why they had been in the limousine together. The resemblance, though, that was a new fact, something that hadn't come out before, possibly because Marge wasn't in the right age group even to know who Brooke Tassini was or what she looked like, she reasoned while thanking the woman for her time.

As she walked to the door to leave, a startling image shot through her brain and for a split second it froze her in her tracks. In the flashback a man was standing over her where she sat in the café and shouting drunkenly at her while Marge flung the door wide to persuade him to leave. Brooke tried to hang onto that snapshot back in time, frantic to see more, know *more*. But nothing else came to her and embarrassment at the time she had already taken out of Marge's working day—Marge, who was already serving a new queue of customers at the counter—pushed her back out onto the street again in a daze.

Why did she never remember anything useful? she asked herself in frustration. Obviously she had visited the café at some point, presumably to see Milly, and Marge hadn't remembered her, which wasn't that surprising in a busy enterprise. What did still nag at Brooke, though, was the resemblance that Marge had remarked on and she had seen for herself. That was a rather strange coincidence, wasn't it? But how could it relate in any way to why that woman had been with her in the car?

CHAPTER SEVEN

BROOKE WAS RELAXED and calm on the drive from the airport in Florence.

Even the crack of dawn flight had failed to irritate her because the change of scene was a relief and an escape from her repetitive and anxious thoughts. Those exact same thoughts had threatened to send her out in search of more gossipy magazines that would enable her to find out additional stuff about her marriage. Aware of that temptation and the futility of such an exercise, when she already knew as much as she needed to know for the present, she had made herself concentrate instead on the selection of a capsule wardrobe with the stylist, who had arrived at Madrigal Court the previous afternoon. It had been a disappointment, though, that Lorenzo had come home so late that he had evidently chosen to sleep in his own room.

The crisp white and blue sundress she wore was comfortable in the heat of an Italian summer. It was neither edgy nor trendy but it was elegant and flattering, skimming nicely over those curvy parts of her that she was beginning to suspect were a little *too* curvy. Was a tendency to gain why she had once watched her diet with such zeal? But she had been too thin when she emerged from the coma and was now content to be a healthy weight, she reasoned. In any case, Lorenzo had been with her when she was flawless in figure and physically perfect and, clearly, it had done nothing to save their marriage. Now she had scars and more curves and neither seemed to bother him, although, to be fair, the scarring was minimal, thanks to the expert cosmetic surgery she had received, she acknowledged gratefully.

'Have I ever been to this house of yours before?' she asked Lorenzo.

'No. I tried to bring you here a couple of times, but it never fitted your schedule. There was always some event, some opening or fashion show that you couldn't miss.'

'Did you grow up in this house?' she prompted with curiosity.

Lorenzo surprised her by laughing, amusement gleaming in his lustrous dark golden eyes. 'No. I bought and renovated it. Sometimes, I forget how little you know about me now. I grew up in a splendid Venetian palazzo on the Grand Canal with my father.'

'No mother around?' she pressed in surprise.

'No, sadly she died bringing me into the world. She had a weak heart,' Lorenzo volunteered. 'And I don't think my father ever forgave me for being the cause of her death. He told me more than once that she was the only woman he had ever loved and that I had taken her from him.'

'But that's so unjust. I mean—'

'Do you think I don't know that?' Lorenzo sent her a wryly amused glance at her bias in his defence. 'He was a self-centred man. My mother wanted a baby and took the risk of getting pregnant against doctor's orders and I got the blame for it. I believe my father could have adjusted quite happily to *not* having a son and heir. Maybe a daughter would've brought out a softer side to him…who knows? He died last year, and we never had a close relationship.'

'That's so sad, such a waste.' Brooke sighed regretfully. 'I wish my parents had lived long enough for you to meet them and then you could have told me something about them.'

'Being without family never seemed to bother you. I think that it was natural for you to be a loner.'

'Is that why you think I didn't want children?' she asked abruptly.

Lorenzo expelled his breath in a measured hiss. 'No, you had multiple reasons for that. The effect on your body, the risk to your potential career, the responsibilities that would eat into your ability to come and go as you pleased.'

Brooke nodded, getting the message that in the past she had *definitely* not wanted a child. Evidently, her career had meant everything to her and that tough decision surprised her because she had found herself watching young children visiting their relatives in the clinic and had easily and quickly warmed to their presence. But Lorenzo had to know the woman he had married best, particularly now that he was no longer glossing over the more sensitive subjects simply to keep her in the dark and supposedly protect her from herself. But how on earth was anyone to tell her how to cope with a self that she, increasingly, didn't like very much?

'Did I tell you that I didn't want a family before we got married?' she pressed.

'No,' Lorenzo framed succinctly. 'Knowing *that* I wouldn't have married you but, to be fair, you didn't lie about it either. Later, I realised that you had merely avoided saying anything that would've committed you.'

Brooke still saw that as sly, just as he had once labelled her, but she said nothing because the picture of their marriage she was getting was still better than the blank she had had before, even if the more she learned, the more she suspected that saving such a troubled relationship could be a steeper challenge than even she had imagined.

'Why are we even talking about this?' Lorenzo demanded with wry amusement. 'The last complication we need now is a child.'

'Yes,' she agreed a little stiffly because it was true: they had quite enough on their plate with her amnesia. 'So, what happened to the Venetian palazzo you grew up in? Or didn't you inherit it?'

'I did inherit. I converted it into an exclusive boutique hotel. I had no personal attachment to the place. My childhood memories aren't warm or fluffy,' he admitted.

'I wonder if mine are,' she murmured ruefully.

'I should think so. The way you told it, you were an adored only child.' Lorenzo closed a hand over her restive hands where they were twisting together on her lap. 'Stop fretting about what you don't know and can't help.'

'I've had a couple of flashbacks!' she heard herself admit rather abruptly. 'Mr Selby thinks that's very hopeful.'

Lorenzo frowned in disconcertion, annoyed that she hadn't told him first. 'What did you remember?'

'Only an image of me seated in a limo and one of me in that café where Milly Taylor worked and where I must have gone to meet her. Not very helpful or interesting,' she remarked with a sigh.

'But promising,' Lorenzo commented, wondering why he didn't feel more excited over the prospect of her reclaiming her memory and, consequently, her life. Was it possible that after so many months he had reached some stage of compassion fatigue and disappointed hopes where he was simply guilty of secretly wishing that his life would return to normal?

Dannazione, why didn't he just admit the truth to himself? This current version of Brooke was his unparalleled favourite. He was in no hurry to reclaim the original version. As she was now, she was likeable, desirable and surprisingly appealing. Naturally he preferred her this way, he conceded with gritty inner honesty, no great mystery there. Only a masochist would have craved the old Brooke. What was wrong with being truthful about that? The woman he was with now was neither the woman he had married nor the woman he had been divorcing.

Brooke peered out of the windows as the limo drove up a

steep twisting lane hedged in by dense trees and her eyes widened with appreciation as the lane opened out to frame the rambling farmhouse that sat on top of a gentle hill, presiding, she suspected, over a spectacular view of the Tuscan countryside. 'It's a beautiful site,' she remarked.

'It's remote,' Lorenzo warned her as he climbed out of the car. 'You may find it quite isolated here while I'm away on business.'

'I think I'll be fine,' Brooke declared, waiting for the driver to open the car and bring Topsy's travelling carrier out. She bent down to release the little animal, accepting the frantic affection coming her way with a wide grin. 'I can go for walks with Topsy, sit out and read, maybe even do a little exploring.'

'I'm not planning to work *every* day,' Lorenzo told her with a sudden flashing smile. 'I don't want you going too far on your own, so save the exploration until I'm here and it will be much more comfortable for you.'

Topsy bouncing at her heels, Brooke walked into the house, violet eyes sparkling with pleasure at everything she saw. Her hand stretched out to brush the weathered pale sun-warmed stone of the house as if she couldn't resist its appeal. 'I love old things,' she told him cheerfully.

Lorenzo stoically resisted the urge to contradict her with his superior knowledge of her tastes. 'She's discovering herself again,' the psychiatrist had told him. 'Give her that freedom.'

'When did you buy this place?' she asked.

'Long before I met you. I wanted a home base in Italy, and I assumed I would use it for holidays but, to be frank, I've hardly been here since the renovation project was completed.'

Brooke gave his shoulder a playful mock punch. 'Because you work too hard,' she pointed out, gazing around the rustic hallway and caressing the smooth bannister of the old wooden staircase that led up to the next floor.

'You used a designer, didn't you?' she guessed, moving from doorway to doorway to study the pale drapes and the subtle palate of colours employed to provide a charming and tranquil backdrop to antique rustic furniture and comfortable contemporary sofas.

Lorenzo laughed, his lean dark features extraordinarily handsome in that moment as he stood in the sunshine flooding through the open front door. 'How did you guess?' he mocked.

'Whoever you used was really good,' Brooke was saying appreciatively when a sparely built older man appeared in the hallway and greeted them in a flood of Italian.

'This is Jacopo. He and his wife, Sofia, look after us here,' Lorenzo informed her, closing a hand round hers to urge her towards the stairs. 'When would you like lunch?'

'Midday? After our early start, I'm quite hungry.' She shot an uncertain glance up at his lean dark face, ensnared by vibrant and lustrous black-lashed golden eyes that left her breathless.

Lorenzo informed Jacopo and led her upstairs. 'Sofia likes a schedule to work to. She's a great cook.'

'Did I ever cook for you?' Brooke enquired.

'Never.'

Her brows lifted in surprise. 'I wonder why not. I like reading recipes, which makes me think that I must've enjoyed cooking at some stage of my life,' she told him, walking into a breathtaking bedroom as complete in charm and appeal as the ground-floor reception areas. Turning round, her head tilted back to appreciate the vaulted ceiling above, she sped through the door into the corner turret room to laugh in delight when her suspicions proved correct and she discovered a deftly arranged circular bathroom. 'It's a wonderful house, Lorenzo. Was it a wreck when you found it?'

'A complete ruin,' he confirmed. 'I loved the views and the old courtyard out the back, which was completely overgrown. I didn't really appreciate how much potential the house itself had or, indeed, how large it was. We certainly don't require the half-dozen bedrooms we have here.'

The doors had been secured back on a balcony on the opposite wall and she strolled out, relieved the ironwork was thick enough to prevent a nosy little dog from sliding between bars and falling, because there was no use pretending, she thought fondly, Topsy wasn't the brightest or most cautious spark on the planet. Seconds later she was so enthralled by the view of the Tuscan landscape, she simply stared.

A hint of early morning mist still hung over the picturesque walled stone village on a nearby hilltop and somehow it almost magically enhanced the lush green of the vines and fruit orchards in the valley below. Ancient spreading chestnut trees marked the boundary of the garden, the turning colour of their leaves hinting that autumn was on its way. 'It's really beautiful,' she sighed.

The only outstandingly beautiful object in his vision at that moment, Lorenzo acknowledged abstractedly, was her, a foam of curls falling naturally across her bare shoulders in a white-blonde mass, the pretty, surprisingly simple blue dress only adding to the fragile femininity that she exuded and the slender, shapely legs on view. Hunger stabbed through him as sharp and immediate in its penetration as a knife and he strode forward.

Brooke relaxed back into the warmth of his lean powerful frame as his hand came down on her shoulder, a roaring readiness within her taut body to do whatever it took to ensure that their relationship had a fighting chance of survival. His sensual mouth dropped a kiss down on her other shoulder and she trembled, her body coming alive as though he had pressed a magic switch, and by the time he shifted his lips to the considerably more sensitive flesh of the slope leading up to her neck, her hips were pushing back against his in helpless response.

The zip of her dress eased slowly down and he spread the parted edges to run his mouth down over her slender back and she wriggled and jerked, learning that she had tender spots she had not known she possessed. The snap of her bra being released unnerved her when she was standing out in the fresh air, *in public*, as she saw it, even though it was a very rural area. She spun in his arms.

'I don't want anyone to see me,' she mumbled nervously, suddenly wondering if that reaction was a passion killer as he looked down at her in seeming surprise at her inhibitions. 'I mean, there might be...er...workers in the vines or something.'

Lorenzo laughed soft and low and swept her up into his arms as if she were a lightweight, when she knew she was not, and carried her over to the bed. He skimmed off her bra with almost daunting expertise. Her violet eyes shot up to lock to his lean bronzed face. 'You must've been with an awful lot of women,' she heard herself say, and five seconds later cringed at that revealing observation, her face burning as hot as hellfire.

Taken aback, Lorenzo looked down at her in surprise. 'The usual number before we married,' he conceded.

'And not...er...*since*?' Brooke prompted, unable to stifle that question. 'I mean...we were separated...and then I was in a coma for well over a year...'

'I haven't been with anyone else since the day I married you,' Lorenzo spelt out with a level of precision that disconcerted her even more. 'I don't break my promises.'

A controversial topic, she recognised uneasily, but she was impressed nonetheless by that steadfast fidelity that many men would surely have forsaken during a legal separation. It was one more gift to appreciate, wasn't it? In one statement he had both surprised and delighted her, affirming her conviction that they might still have a marriage worth saving. He had not turned to another woman for either sex or consolation and that said so much about the sort of guy he was. She wanted to tell him that she loved him again, but she swallowed the words, which would strike him as empty when she didn't have the luxury of even recalling their past relationship.

'We're getting too serious,' Lorenzo told her with a sudden flashing smile that didn't quite reach his gorgeous eyes.

'Blame me,' she muttered ruefully. 'I was the one asking awkward questions.'

'You should feel free to say whatever you like to me,' Lorenzo told her, backing away from the bed to slam the door shut and shed his jacket, his tie and his shoes in rapid succession.

Brooke swallowed hard, wondering why she always felt so shy with him, wondering why she wanted to cover her bared breasts from view. She *had* to be accustomed to such intimacy. That she could be innately shy in the bedroom, after all, went against everything she had so far learned about herself. Women who were shy or modest about showing their bodies didn't wear teeny-tiny shorts and incredibly short skirts, she reminded herself impatiently.

There was nothing shy about Lorenzo either, she acknowledged as he strolled, buck naked, back to the bed like a very, *very* sexy bronzed predator, all lean, rippling muscle and hair-roughened thighs. Just looking at Lorenzo almost overwhelmed her because she still experienced a deep, abiding sense of wonder that such a rich, powerful and important man had married her. Yet where did that low self-esteem come from? She was supposed to be so confident, a woman in possession of a trust fund, both prosperous and successful in her own right. Had she always been scared on the inside and confident on the outside?

'*Dio*... I can't wait to get inside you,' Lorenzo growled.

That graphic assurance sent a flush running right up over her breasts into her face and that out-of-her-depth sensation that had grabbed her on the only night she had so far spent with him returned.

'What's wrong?' Lorenzo scanned the rapid changing expressions on her taut face. 'And why have you turned red?'

'I don't know,' Brooke gabbled, suddenly snaking free of the dress round her hips and kicking off her shoes to scramble below the sheets, desperate to be doing something rather than freezing guiltily beneath that far too shrewd and clever gaze of his. He picked up on her insecurities and it was not only embarrassing but also unnerving because it stripped away what little poise she retained.

'You're blushing!' Lorenzo laughed in apparent appreciation of that achievement.

'Did you have to mention it?' Brooke groaned. 'To me, being with you like this still feels very *new*. I know that's silly but that's how it is.'

'No, it's not silly. I'm being insensitive,' Lorenzo sliced in with lingering incomprehension at the concept of Brooke being embarrassed about anything on the planet. But he could see that, as far as she was concerned, she was telling him the truth and once again he marvelled at the transparency of her expressions.

'I'm the one out of step here with the norm, not you.' Brooke stretched up a hand to grasp his, trying to bridge the gap between them.

Lorenzo ceased trying to wrap his head around the inexplicable and came down on the bed to rub an appreciative hand over a succulent pink nipple and close his mouth there instead. When had she got so serious? When had *he* begun to behave as though what was only a temporary identity were the *real* Brooke? She was driving him insane again, only it was in a very different way from the first time around, he conceded fiercely. Here he was craving his almost ex-wife like an addictive drug. For the first time since the crash he wanted to walk away…and then her fingers tightened round his and she looked up at him and she smiled, and his thoughts evaporated as though they had never existed.

She stretched up, clumsily gripping his arm for support, and settled her ripe pink lips against his and the scent of her, the sweet delicious taste of her as her tongue darted against his, turned Lorenzo on so hard and fast, he flattened her down to the bed with two strong hands, his dominant nature taking over with all the passion he had once had to restrain in the marital bed. But there were no curbs now and he could not resist that lure of being himself for the first time with her or the temptation of not being with a woman who lay back like a goddess inviting worship and never touched him.

Brooke felt the change in him and welcomed his passion, realising that she had almost frightened him off with her insecurities. Her fingers delved into his luxuriant black hair and smoothed down his high cheekbones to the roughened blue shadow of stubble that highlighted his wide sensual mouth. She gasped as he dipped his head over her breasts and seized a swollen pink crest and grazed it with the edge of his teeth. She was *so* sensitive there that her back arched and then his skilled hands were travelling lower, tracing the damp cleft between her thighs, probing the tight entrance, making her hips rock up and a low-pitched cry part her lips.

'You're so ready for me,' Lorenzo husked in satisfaction, shifting position to roll her over and up onto her knees.

Her whole body clenched in sensual shock as he drove into her hard and fast. It was electrifying, every skin cell and nerve ending in her body powering the excitement that made her heart race and her breath catch in her throat. Every sleek, powerful thrust of his body sent sensation tumbling and cascading in seismic waves through her quivering body and heightened the tight clenching low in her pelvis. Her internal muscles contracted and sent her careening with a cry into a climax that detonated like a bomb of sheer pleasure inside her trembling body. It felt so good tears of reaction burned her eyes and she blinked rapidly. But he wasn't finished, no, far from it, and as the pressure began to build and tighten unbearably inside her again, it only took one expert touch at the most sensitive spot in her body for another orgasm to fly through her in a violent storm.

Shattered, she collapsed down on the bed, while he groaned in satisfaction and his arms tightened round her, flipping her round so that his wicked mouth could tease her parted lips and then slide between, sending a quivering tremor through her drained length.

'Not moving for anything ever again,' she swore limply.

'The helicopter's picking me up at two but I'll be back by nine this evening,' Lorenzo intoned, brilliant dark eyes connecting with hers. 'Sleep this afternoon because you won't be getting much sleep tonight, *cara mia*.'

'Promises, promises,' Brooke teased, feeling wonderfully relaxed. 'You could be absolutely exhausted.'

Lorenzo smoothed her tumbled curls off her pale brow and curled her slight length close. 'I won't be too tired for you,' he intoned huskily, purposely closing off every logical thought and living in the moment. *She* was doing that and if he wasn't prepared to let her go yet, so must he.

Four weeks later, after Lorenzo had repeatedly extended their stay, Brooke stood back to study the table she had laid on the terrace at the side of the house. She was humming under her breath as she walked back into the kitchen to check the bubbling pots. Tonight, she was cooking because Sofia was away visiting her daughter but she wasn't quite as adept a cook as she had hoped when she first came up with the idea of providing dinner. Sofia, however, had given her some useful tips and some even more useful shortcuts and, with a little preparation and help behind the scenes beforehand, Brooke had felt able to tackle a simple menu.

She glanced at the tiny half-knitted garment that Sofia had left lying on the dresser. The older woman was knitting a cardigan for her first grandchild. Brooke picked it up, unable to explain why it had attracted her attention in the first place as she found herself scanning the intricate pattern, and then registered that she could name every one of the stitches used and even identify a mistake. She blinked and something tugged almost painfully deep within her brain. She shook her head again in surprise. So, she knew how to knit, like lots of other people, she acknowledged dismissively, and rubbed her brow until the tightness there began to evaporate.

As she walked back out to the terrace, a bout of unnerving dizziness made her head swim and her legs falter and she swiftly took a seat, lowered her head and breathed in deep and slow.

She didn't know what was amiss with her and already planned to visit a doctor when they flew back to London the following day. She didn't think that the faintness or the headache were linked to her head injury, any more than the nausea that had assailed her at odd moments in recent days, but she thought it was time that she had herself checked out all the same. Perhaps she was coming down with some virus, she thought ruefully.

A slim figure in white cropped jeans and a vest top, she stood up again and studied the view of the tranquil patchwork of vines and orchards and fields that spread out beyond the garden boundaries. She had never dreamt that they would end up staying an entire month in Italy and the time had fairly raced past. Lorenzo had flown off to loads of business meetings but every other day he was at home, either working or taking her out somewhere, and their peaceful stay had done wonders for her state of mind.

Regrettably, she had experienced no further flashbacks, which was a considerable disappointment to her, but, on the balance side, she was sleeping well, eating well and generally felt much stronger. A lot of that related to her improved relationship with Lorenzo though, she conceded. He hadn't promised to make a special effort when he had said that they would see how their marriage went but he had definitely been trying.

Regardless of how busy he was, he had made time for her. She had drunk a glass of the local wine in the Piazza Grande in Montepulciano, strolled under the trees by the walls of Lucca, explored the labyrinth of underground caves in Pitigliano and wandered silent in appreciation through the gardens of Garzoni in Collodi. There had been dinners out as well in wonderful restaurants in Florence, but she had enjoyed the picnic in the orange orchard below the house even more because Lorenzo had surprised her with a sapphire pendant that took her breath away and had then made passionate love to her.

She had never felt so close to anyone as she felt to Lorenzo, and sometimes it scared her because she knew that she wasn't in a safe or settled marriage and that, at any time, Lorenzo could again decide that he wanted a divorce. When she allowed herself to think along those lines, her nervous tension went sky-high and so she tried to enjoy what they currently had without thinking too far ahead into the future. She didn't tell him she loved him now, no longer dared to be that confiding. Had she known the true state of their marriage, she would never have said it in the first place. She didn't want Lorenzo to feel trapped or that he couldn't tell her the truth, and her telling him that she loved him could only make him feel uncomfortable.

By the time the helicopter landed, Brooke had laid out the first course on the table and she stood back, smiling, as Lorenzo strode up the slope towards her, eye-catchingly gorgeous in his exquisitely tailored dove-grey suit, his luxuriant black hair ruffled, his spectacular dark golden eyes locked to her.

And, truth to tell, there was not a single cloud on Lorenzo's horizon at that moment and his lean, dark, serious face flashed into a smile at the sight of her waiting for him. It probably made him a four-letter word of a guy but he enjoyed the knowledge that his wife's world seemed to revolve entirely around him. She was a slender but curvy figure dressed entirely in white, her cloud of curls framing her piquant features, eyes purple as violets.

'I made dinner,' Brooke announced. 'But you have to sit down now.'

Lorenzo tensed. 'I was heading for a shower first—'

'You can't…if you do that the main course will be ready too soon and it will spoil,' Brooke told him earnestly. 'If you want to eat, it's now or never.'

Lorenzo grinned. 'I'll make a bargain with you. I sit down now to eat, and you join me in the shower afterwards…'

'That's a deal.' Brooke went pink and sank down at the other side of the table. 'Dig in. It's quite a simple meal but this timing thing is complicated.'

'I can't believe you've made a meal for us,' Lorenzo confided truthfully.

'It may not win any awards but I think I should be able to make a decent meal,' Brooke contended seriously. 'It's a basic skill.'

'How are you feeling about returning to London tomorrow?' he prompted.

'Kind of sad,' she confided, laying down her fork to finger the sapphire gleaming below her collarbone. 'I love it here and I've relaxed a lot more but we can't live cut off from the rest of the world for ever.'

'No, we can't,' Lorenzo agreed and, as he pushed his plate away to indicate that he was finished, he lounged back in his chair and spread his hands. 'Why did you go to all this trouble for a meal? We could've eaten out. That's what I usually do when Sofia takes a night off.'

'It's our last night here.' Brooke shrugged in an effort to be casual and pushed back her chair to return to the kitchen. There she drained pans, whisked the sauce again and put the main course together on delicate china plates to take them out to the table.

'It looks great,' Lorenzo said softly.

'Wait and see how it tastes,' she urged.

He ate in deliberate silence, cleared the plate and then sent her a wicked grin of appreciation. 'That's it. You're on kitchen duty every night that I can spare you.'

'And how often would you spare me?' she enquired as she pushed her own plate away and went to fetch dessert.

'Not very often,' Lorenzo confessed, following her into the kitchen to tug her back against his lean, hard frame, his hands smoothing down over her hip bones to lace across her flat stomach. 'You have a much more important role to fulfil, *cara mia*.'

Insanely aware that he was aroused, she instinctively pressed back into him, loving the sudden fracture in his breathing and the way his fingers instantly slid up to the waistband of her jeans to release the button and delve down over her quivering tummy to the heart of her. 'And what would that role entail?' she prompted shakily, suspecting that he wasn't likely to let her make it as far as dessert.

Interpreting the damp welcome below her silk knickers, not to mention the encouraging gasp parting her lips, Lorenzo laughed appreciatively. 'I think you already know, *gatita mia*.'

'Well, you *have* to make a choice. Me...' Brooke told him, battling her hunger for him to gently step away and fasten her jeans, 'or the last course.'

Lorenzo snatched her back to him. 'I'm Italian...the woman wins every time.'

'Maybe *if* you're really, really good,' Brooke teased, 'I'll bring you dessert in bed.'

In answer, Lorenzo spun her round and kissed her with voracious hunger, his mouth crushing hers, one hand anchored in her mass of curls. Beneath that onslaught, she gasped and he wasted no time in bending down to scoop her up and head for the stairs. 'Bossy...*much*?' she taunted.

'You know you like it,' Lorenzo breathed with inherent dark sensuality, dropping her down on the bed and following her there to pluck off her shoes and divest her of the rest of her clothes.

'No, you undress first,' Brooke instructed, feeling daring as she pushed his jacket off his broad shoulders and yanked at his tie, her fingers deft on his shirt buttons. Pushing the fabric back, she spread her hands over the warm hair-roughened musculature of his chest.

Lorenzo vaulted off the bed to remove the rest of his clothes. 'Off with the jeans and the top,' he commanded impatiently.

Brooke made a production of shimmying out of her tight jeans, sliding out one slender bare leg, then the next. Bending back, she released the hooks on her top and peeled it off over her head, her teeth tightening at the over-sensitivity of her engorged nipples as the air stung them. Her breasts had felt weird for several days, tender and swollen, and she had thought that had to be a sign of her menstrual cycle kicking in. Although she had had periods while she was still in the clinic, she had not had one since she left medical care and she knew that she would have to mention that to the doctor when she saw him as well. Possibly that IUD Lorenzo had mentioned was causing her problems, she reasoned wryly, and perhaps she would have to consider another method of birth control.

Lorenzo feasted his eyes on her with unashamed appreciation, his attention lingering on the luscious swell of her breasts. She must've put on weight and it really, really suited her, he acknowledged hungrily. 'I'm burning up for you—'

'Since when? You woke me up at six this morning,' Brooke reminded him helplessly, as always, almost astonished by his constant desire for her.

Lorenzo grinned and came down beside her. 'That was this morning and it was a lifetime ago, *bellezza mia.*'

'Will we still be like this when we go home?' Brooke heard herself ask in sudden fear that their new intimacy would somehow vanish when they left Italy.

'You're moving into my bedroom,' Lorenzo asserted.

'Am I?' Brooke smiled like a cat that had got the cream, reassured by that statement, that change in attitude that signified togetherness rather than separation.

'Are you thinking of arguing about that?' Lorenzo husked against her reddened mouth.

Her fingers speared into his black hair to draw him down to her, the same intense hunger firing through every atom of her being. 'No.'

A long while later, she lay in perfect peace in his arms and drifted off to sleep in a happy daze, which made the dream that followed all the more frightening because she wasn't prepared for it, couldn't *ever* have been prepared for the images that went flashing through her brain and made her scream so loud in the dark that she hurt her throat.

She saw the crash. She saw Brooke as she reached for her and failed to catch her hand, experienced the agony of knowing she had *failed* to save her sister, her only living relative. And in the shaken aftermath, when she must have regained consciousness for a split second, reliving that unimaginable pain and primal fear, she saw her knitting needles strewn in the smoking wreckage of the car…

'It's OK…it's OK…' Lorenzo soothed as she sat bolt upright in the bed, rocking back and forth, her head down on her raised knees as she sobbed. 'You had a nightmare. It's not real, none of it's real. *Dio*, you screamed so loudly I thought we were being attacked!'

But it was real, it was *very* real, Milly recognised, her frantic thoughts tangled and befogged by layer after layer of shock and growing disbelief. Somehow she had got her memory back, the memory she had once been so desperate to retrieve. Her true self had slipped back without fanfare into place during that nightmare, clarifying everything that had previously been a complete blank. But, disturbingly, reclaiming her memory and her knowledge of who she was had plunged her into an even more frightening world.

Brooke was dead and she was devastated by that knowledge, even though the last time she had been with her half-sister she had finally appreciated that Brooke was unlikely ever to accept her as a true sibling. But it was one thing to accept that, another entirely to accept that Brooke was now gone for ever and that their relationship could never be improved.

Her sister was dead and Milly had been mistaken for her. How had that happened? But the more she thought about it, the easier it became to understand. After all, she had been wearing Brooke's jewellery and Brooke's clothes and she had had facial injuries. The strong resemblance between the two women had gone completely unnoticed, presumably because Brooke had been seriously injured too. Her reddened eyes stung with fresh tears.

How on earth could she ever put right all that had gone wrong?

Lorenzo would be devastated.

Lorenzo didn't even know he was a widower. How could he? He had spent months looking after his injured wife's needs, caring for her because she had no one else and then, ultimately, living with and having sex with the woman he naturally believed to be his wife. But she *wasn't* his wife, she was a stranger, just as he had been a stranger to her when she first wakened out of the coma. Only, sadly, neither of them had recognised that reality.

Trembling, retreating fast from Lorenzo's attempts to soothe her, she hurried into the bathroom, for once taking no pleasure in her surroundings. She ran a bath as an excuse to stay there alone. Lorenzo appeared in the doorway, tall, dark and bronzed, and she chased him off again, telling him she just needed a warm bath and a little space to relax. Tears ran down her cheeks then as she sat in the warm water, all the mistakes she had made piling up on top of her, and she didn't know, she really didn't know *how* to go about telling Lorenzo the truth. He had said nothing was real in her nightmare, but he was wrong—it was all *too* real and the harsh facts could not be ignored. She had wakened from a nightmare to find herself entangled in a worse nightmare, because she was living her dead sister's life with a man she loved, who did not love her. Lorenzo was wrong: nothing was OK and it never would be again…

CHAPTER EIGHT

'DON'T TELL ME that you're fine again,' Lorenzo warned her in a raw-edged undertone, his lean, darkly handsome features set in stern lines as the limo wafted them through the London traffic from the airport. 'Obviously you're anything but fine. Something has upset you a great deal and it's time that you shared it with me.'

'We'll talk when we get back…er…home,' she told him shakily, in no hurry to get there and deal with his outrage, his disbelief and his belated grief.

Lorenzo had never been hers and her tummy lurched at the knowledge that everything that had happened between them had been based purely on his conviction that she was his wife. His *every* word, his *every* decision, his *every* caress had been bestowed on Brooke, not Milly, she reminded herself doggedly, shrinking guiltily from the knowledge that *she* had encouraged *him* into sharing a bed. Brooke had hated Lorenzo, she reminded herself, reluctantly thinking back to her sibling's conviction that Lorenzo was a possessive tyrant, who had unjustly accused her of infidelity in order to divorce her.

Obviously there had been a great deal of bitterness in their relationship by that stage. But Milly liked to think that, had Brooke seen how very supportive Lorenzo had been in the wake of the crash to the woman he believed to be his wife, she would have forgiven him for their differences. On that score, his behaviour had been above reproach. He could've walked away, let the divorce go ahead, leaving her to the tender mercies of the healthcare system and some legal executor. But Lorenzo hadn't done that. He had stood by the vows he had once taken...*in sickness and in health.*

Her head was aching again with all the stress of her feverish thoughts and she rubbed her brow, wishing foolishly that there were some miraculous way of avoiding what lay ahead of her. Obviously, she would have to leave Lorenzo's house and as soon as possible. Unfortunately for her, she had nowhere to go and not a penny to her name and no close friends either, because she had moved around too much to form lasting friendships.

It was a shame that she hadn't worked harder at the many different schools she had attended during her years in foster care, she reflected with regret. Sadly, the knowledge that she would inevitably be shifted to a new foster home and a new school with different exam boards and course content had removed any enthusiasm she had had when she was younger for studying. The continual changes had made her unsettled, undisciplined and distrustful of forging close relationships with anyone because, sooner or later, everyone seemed to leave her and move on.

Perhaps that was why she had repressed every qualm to stay friendly and involved with Brooke, generally accepting whatever treatment Brooke dealt out. She hadn't wanted to lose that all-important link with Brooke and had been eager to offer her half-sister all her love and support. Hadn't she clung to Lorenzo in much the same way? Pathetically eager to offer love even when he wasn't looking for it? Inside herself, she cringed for her weakness and susceptibility. But then had she *ever* been loved?

Her memories of her mother were very hazy because Natalia had died when Milly was only eleven years old, but Natalia *had* been affectionate and caring. Her father, however, had never paid her any attention when he visited them, hadn't seemed to have the slightest interest in her, she recalled sadly, although possibly his apparent indifference had come from his guilt at cheating on his wife. Had her mother not told her that William Jackson was her father, she would never have known because his name wasn't on her birth certificate. Although he had supported her mother financially, he had refused to officially acknowledge Milly as his daughter.

'We're home,' Lorenzo imparted flatly.

But Madrigal Court was *his* home, not hers, Milly ruminated, and immediately wanted to kick herself for that forlorn thought. Like many children raised by the state, she had always longed for a stable and permanent home. It was not a bit of wonder that when she had been deprived of her memory that deep-based need had surfaced and made her latch onto Brooke's home and husband like a homing pigeon eager to find a permanent roost.

'I'm afraid I can't understand how a bad dream can cause you this much stress,' Lorenzo breathed impatiently as he herded her into the pristine white drawing room and closed the door behind them. 'What on earth is the matter?'

Milly breathed in deep and slow to steady her nerves. 'I remembered the accident,' she admitted. 'And then my memory came back.'

Lorenzo paled and his lean, powerful frame went rigid. 'Just like that?'

'Just like that,' she confirmed sickly. 'But the real problem is that when I regained my memory I realised that I'm not the person everyone assumed I was…'

His brow pleated as if he was still trying to penetrate the meaning of that statement. 'What are you talking about?'

'I'm not Brooke Tassini, Lorenzo. I'm *not* your wife. I'm Milly Taylor.'

The fringe of his lush black lashes shot up over incredulous dark golden eyes and then he swung round and headed back to the door, pulling out his phone. 'That's not possible.'

'Where are you going?' she gasped.

Lorenzo compressed his lips. It was obvious to him that his wife was having some sort of nervous breakdown. He had not a clue how to deal with such an astonishing statement, but he was convinced that her psychiatrist would know. 'I'm contacting Mr Selby so that you can discuss this with him.'

'I don't want to see Mr Selby right now. I need to get things straight with you first,' Milly declared tautly. 'That's more important.'

'There *is* nothing more important than your mental health,' Lorenzo contradicted, sending her a censorious glance from his position by the door. 'Why did you keep quiet about this? Why didn't you immediately tell me what you were going through last night?'

'I had to get my head straight,' she protested. 'It was a big shock for me too and I feel terrible about everything that's happened. I don't know how the heck you'll ever sort out all the legal stuff.'

An imperious ebony brow elevated. 'What legal stuff?'

Milly dragged in another steadying breath. 'Brooke's... Brooke's dead, Lorenzo, and I've been declared dead but I'm still alive. That mistake will have to be rectified...*somehow*.'

Lorenzo was holding his phone so tightly between his fingers that he almost crushed it. Was she suffering from what he had heard referred to as a psychotic break? He studied her pale, rigid face, reading her distress. She really *believed* this stuff she was telling him, he registered in consternation: she had decided that she was not his wife, that she was the other woman in the car. Why would she do that?

'Brooke was my sister,' she murmured tautly.

'Brooke doesn't have a sister,' he overruled.

'Not officially. I'm illegitimate,' Milly admitted stiffly. 'William Jackson had an affair that went on for years with my mother and I was born during their affair. He never recognised me as his child and never treated me as if I was his and I didn't know back then that he was a married man with another family. Brooke traced me and came to see me out of curiosity when I was eighteen and just leaving foster care. She was my half-sister…'

Lorenzo released his breath in a slow, measured hiss. He hadn't had Milly Taylor's birth and background checked out, hadn't considered her past relevant in establishing who she had been to his wife. He could not yet accept the enormity of what he was being told but he also could not imagine how or why his wife could have come up with such a detailed and fanciful story overnight.

'Brooke would've mentioned a sister.'

'She didn't tell anyone about me and was careful never to be seen in public with me. My very existence was…' Milly hesitated before forging on with a frown '…pretty much a source of resentment and annoyance to her. She knew about the affair and the amount of unhappiness it had caused *her* mother. My mother was dead by the time Brooke sought me out, but I suspect that the bitter anger she felt towards my mother transferred to me to some extent.'

Lorenzo was frowning. 'A half-sister? But that doesn't explain anything! If Brooke didn't like you or find you useful in some way, what would you have been doing in that car with her on the day of the crash? Nothing about this story makes sense!'

Milly stood up slowly, her violet eyes deeply troubled. 'I can help it make sense but you have to try to keep your temper.'

Lorenzo flung his arrogant dark head back and dealt her a scorching appraisal. 'Of course, I can keep my temper, but I still don't think you're going to be able to explain this nonsense, and discussing it as if it's true fact isn't helping the situation or you.'

'Brooke used me as her stand-in on several occasions,' Milly admitted starkly. 'We looked very alike, even more alike after I had had cosmetic surgery done on my nose,' she continued doggedly as Lorenzo continued to stare at her as though she had sprouted horns and cloven hooves. 'Brooke paid for the procedure and I didn't want to get it done but when I said no, she dropped me, and I was so desperate to hang onto our relationship that eventually I agreed.'

Lorenzo was frowning in disbelief. 'You looked alike? What was wrong with your nose?'

'It was too big. Nobody would have mistaken me for her if I hadn't agreed to the surgery. After that, she used me a couple of times to stand in for her at charity events where I didn't have to do much pretending. I'm no actress,' she confided tightly. 'Sometimes, she didn't want to attend events or she wanted to mislead the press about where she was and then she would phone me up and ask me to go in her place. She would give me her clothes and her jewellery to wear.'

His frown had laced his bone structure with hard lines of tension. 'You are telling me that you engaged in deception with Brooke to trick other people, including me?'

Milly bridled. 'That isn't how I saw it and you were never involved. I was just helping my sister out. Smoothing out her life when she was too busy to meet all the demands on her time,' she protested.

'You were deceiving people,' Lorenzo contradicted with glacial disapproval. 'If this far-fetched story is true, tell me where you were going on the day of the crash.'

Milly winced. 'I was to go to a hotel and stay there for several days pretending to be Brooke while she was away somewhere on holiday, having travelled on my passport. But, of course, we never got as far as the hotel or the airport…'

'She was using *your* passport?' Lorenzo demanded incredulously. 'But that's illegal! Where was she going?'

'I don't know. She didn't tell me,' Milly replied numbly. 'Sometimes she told me stuff, sometimes, she told me nothing. It depended on her mood.'

And that *was* a startlingly accurate description of Brooke's unpredictable, temperamental nature, Lorenzo conceded grudgingly, because in spite of all logic he was beginning to listen, beginning to put facts together to finally see a picture forming that could make some kind of sense. He could certainly check out whether a Milly Taylor had failed to turn up for her flight that day and he could look deeper into her background to see if he could establish an official link that would bear out her story.

From Milly's point of view, Lorenzo's attitude seemed oddly detached. He was dealing with the facts, avoiding the harsher realities of their situation, she suspected ruefully.

'Well, anyway,' she mumbled. 'That's what I was doing in the limo on the day of the crash. Brooke gave me the clothes she was wearing and her jewellery and I put them on while she got changed. I expect that is how I came to be identified as her.'

'You were unrecognisable,' Lorenzo admitted starkly, shifting his attention away from her as if he could no longer bear to look at her, his big, powerful frame rigid. 'You are telling me that my wife is dead, that she actually died eighteen months ago in the accident…'

'I'm so sorry. I'm sorry about everything that's happened!' Milly muttered in a driven rush of regret. 'If I hadn't been suffering from amnesia, I could have identified myself and you would have known the truth months ago…'

Lorenzo expelled his breath and raked a long-fingered brown hand roughly through his cropped black hair, his emotional turmoil palpable. 'Brooke is gone…'

'Yes,' Milly whispered, tears lashing her eyes. 'Do you believe me now?'

'Only once I have had time to confirm the extraordinary facts you have given me,' Lorenzo told her flatly.

Milly suppressed a shudder, feeling dismissed, sidelined, set back at a new and disturbing distance from him while he worked out whether she was a fantasist or a woman having a breakdown. All of a sudden everything had changed between them. Lorenzo was changing before her very eyes. It was as though their personal relationship had never happened, she acknowledged painfully. But then it had all been a lie, based on the false premise that Brooke was still alive, and at this moment

Lorenzo was fathoms deep in shock and struggling to deal with the reality that his wife was dead. That was all he had the ability to consider right now and how could she expect anything more from him?

She studied his tall dark figure and the forbidding tension locking his facial muscles tight. It was selfish of her to feel rejected by his new reserve when she had no claim on him or his attention. She was nothing to him, never had been. Everything he had done for her had really been done for Brooke. On his terms she didn't really exist. And now that he knew that she *did* exist, he would never touch her again and would never look at her again as he once had.

And she had to deal with that reality and come back down to earth again, which would be challenging. After all, she had been living a kind of fantasy life with Lorenzo, a waitress from a very ordinary background, suddenly swept off into a billionaire's luxury lifestyle with private jets, servants and a level of wealth and comfort previously beyond her imagining. But it wasn't those expensive trappings she would miss, she conceded wretchedly, it would be Lorenzo.

Lorenzo, whom she loved to pieces, who didn't want her any more, who would never want her again. She felt as though her heart were breaking in two inside her and, tensing her slight shoulders, she compressed her lips, determined not to say or do anything emotional. Right now, Lorenzo didn't need that added stress and probably didn't even want to recall that he had had sex with her believing that she was his wife. No, the faster she got back out of his life again, the happier Lorenzo would be.

Lorenzo was looking back down through the months and marvelling that he had allowed the medics to silence his every misgiving about the woman who had come out of the coma. From her first wakening every atom of his ESP and intelligence had combined to send him continual warnings that Brooke's personality and character had apparently changed out of all recognition. He had listened to the doctors because it had naturally never occurred to him that the woman in the convalescent clinic could be anyone other than his wife.

Dio mio, she had been identified as his wife at the scene of the crash, presented to him as his wife when he was handed her jewellery for safekeeping before surgery. That an appalling mistake could've been made had not once crossed his mind or anyone else's. How could it have done when nobody had been aware of the striking resemblance between the two women? Of course, he hadn't had access either to her clarifying explanation about the nature of her relationship with Brooke. Brooke, indeed, had probably only latched onto her half-sister in the first place because of that resemblance, seeing how she could use that to her advantage. Milly had been acting as Brooke's stand-in, her *lookalike*. Distaste with her for having taken on such a deceptive role flared inside him, chilling his hard dark eyes to granite.

'I'll move out as soon as I can,' Milly muttered in a rush.

'Where are you planning to go?' Lorenzo lifted an ebony brow. 'Straight to the press to sell the story of the century for a fat price?'

Milly was aghast that he could even harbour such a suspicion and she turned white as milk, her violet eyes standing out stark against her porcelain skin. 'Of course not! I wouldn't do that to you or me.'

'Not even for the money?' Lorenzo prompted doubtingly.

Lorenzo's brain was awash with disconnected confused thoughts. He could not yet process what he had just learned. He struggled looking back through the long months with the woman he had believed to be his wife and accepting that she was an entirely different woman. And a stranger, his logic chipped in. A complete and total stranger. He grasped that he needed time and peace to come to terms with what he had just learned.

Milly went rigid, struggling to credit that only the night before Lorenzo had been making passionate love to her and holding her close in the aftermath as if she meant something to him. 'No, not even for the money,' she said sickly.

Lorenzo swung away from her as he could no longer stand to look at her. 'Pack,' he instructed grimly, recognising that he had to immediately get her out of the house if he was to avoid a sordid scandal. 'I have somewhere for you to live sitting ready for occupation and you might as well live there. Once I've checked out the information you've given me and consulted my lawyers, we'll sort this mess out.'

Pack?

Pure shock resonated through Milly and momentarily her head swam, and she felt dizzy. Evidently, he couldn't wait to get rid of her and the immediacy of his demand that she pack and move out disconcerted her. She might have told herself that he would want her to leave as soon as possible but her mind had yet to accept that idea. She hadn't been prepared for that change to take place so quickly and she blinked rapidly, her eyes dazed.

'I have nothing to pack. I don't own anything here,' she said flatly, because it was true when she didn't even own the clothes she wore because he had paid for everything.

'Don't be ridiculous!' Lorenzo growled. '*Anything* you have worn, *anything* that you have been using, is yours to take with you. Brooke is gone and she's not coming back.'

Milly nodded jerkily and quickly stood up, the dizziness she was still enduring dampening her face with perspiration. She felt ill, nauseous, but that was a weakness she had to hide. Lorenzo might be throwing her out but she was not about to play the poor little victim who couldn't cope. She had had enough of being weak and vulnerable while she was still in medical care.

As she opened the door to leave, Topsy hurled herself at her knees in greeting.

'You can take the dog with you too,' Lorenzo murmured. 'She's got used to you now. It would be cruel to separate you.'

But, seemingly, it wasn't cruel to kick out a bogus wife at such short notice, Milly reflected, heading upstairs with a straight spine, still battling to hold the dizziness at bay. Some sort of stupid virus she couldn't shake off, she thought wearily. As soon as she got settled, she would go and see a doctor, she promised herself. The clothes she had worn in Italy were still in the cases they had returned in and not yet unpacked, but even as she started to assemble the few items that she hadn't taken abroad with her, a maid arrived with empty cases for her to use. Lorenzo had already told the staff that she was leaving and her still-sensitive stomach rebelled to send her racing into the en suite to be sick.

Afterwards, she cleaned her teeth and with all the animation of a robot she went back to doggedly packing. She didn't have very much to show for her months in Lorenzo's life. She stripped off the rings, the diamond-studded watch and the sapphire pendant and laid them on the dressing table because they weren't hers, or at least had been gifts that weren't intended for her.

She might feel as though her life were over but, really, it was only beginning another phase, she tried to tell herself. Being hurt that Lorenzo wanted her out of his house was foolish. He had to mourn Brooke and adjust to the knowledge that the wife he had watched over for months while she was in a coma had not survived as he had believed. He had to draw a line under the past months and obviously he didn't want her around while he was trying to do that.

The cases were stowed in the limo and Milly climbed into the passenger seat, clutching Topsy to her like a tiny hairy comfort blanket. Lorenzo emerged last from the house, his lean, darkly handsome face wiped clean of emotion or any form of warmth, and barely a word was exchanged during the drive into London.

It was a fabulous apartment with its own private lift. Milly stood looking around her at the sea of crisp white furnishings and swallowed apprehensively.

'I had it decorated for Brooke,' Lorenzo breathed in a roughened undertone. 'She loved it.'

'It's spectacular,' she said woodenly, wanting him to leave

so that she could ditch her game face. But at the same time, she was dreading the moment when he would actually leave and already wondering how long it would be before she saw him again.

'It's yours now. You can make any changes you want...at my expense,' he added impatiently when she glanced at him in astonishment. 'Legally, this will ultimately be *your* apartment.'

Milly frowned in bewilderment. 'How on earth could it ever be mine?' she queried.

'I signed it over to Brooke before the accident and, according to my lawyers, everything that once belonged to Brooke is likely to go to you in the end because I refused to take it. I don't want anything that belonged to her,' he confessed quietly. 'Of course, it will take weeks, if not months, to disentangle the legal threads concerning the misidentification that has been made and free up her funds. In the meantime I will ensure that you are financially secure. The apartment is serviced. The fridge should be packed with food.'

'I don't want your money,' she whispered and flinched inside herself because standing in an apartment he had bought, wearing clothing he had purchased and making such a statement struck her as absurd. But the knowledge that he had evidently consulted his lawyers about their situation before she had even left his home chilled her to the marrow.

'Nonetheless, I will not leave you destitute. That would be unpardonable,' Lorenzo bit out in a fierce undertone. 'You have done nothing wrong. In your role as Brooke's lookalike you may have innocently contributed to the mistaken identification that was made but your life has been disrupted as much as mine by what happened. It's my responsibility to ensure that you don't suffer for that.'

Milly was already suffering, and she didn't want to hear that he still viewed her as his responsibility, not when he was in the act of casting her off like an old shoe. Her stomach lurched again and she crossed her arms defensively. She said nothing while she watched him from below her lashes, committing every beloved feature to memory. Those beautiful lustrous dark eyes of his were hard and dark without even a redeeming hint of gold. Yet he still looked amazing, sleek and dark and devastatingly handsome. And even the thought made her feel guilty because she was lusting after her sister's husband, wasn't she?

Instead she opted to wonder what his precious lawyers had told him to do. Handle her with kid gloves? Give her no cause for complaint or any excuse to run to the press and tell all? Even after all they had shared, did he still think so little of her that he could believe that she would betray him like that? And what did it matter what he thought of her now when everything was over?

Topsy on her lap, she sat still long after he had departed. She had a new life to plan now, she told herself urgently. She didn't want to return to being a waitress. Living Brooke's life had made her more ambitious, just as the long struggle to recover from the accident and handle living with amnesia had made her stronger. She would look into other jobs and work out if she could qualify for a training course and take it from there. She might feel as if losing her sister for ever and then losing Lorenzo as well had left her with a giant black hole inside her chest, but she couldn't afford to give way to such feelings or they would eat her alive.

Right now, she was at rock bottom but, from here on in, her life could only improve…

CHAPTER NINE

THE NEXT MONTH passed painfully slowly for Milly.

She had no contact whatsoever from Lorenzo, but she received more than one visit from his lawyers, seeking affidavits and signatures to documents while also persuading her to consent to a DNA test. They kept her informed of her legal position and of what would happen next. And it being the law, it moved at a leisurely pace but, finally, the day of Brooke's funeral arrived.

The media storm that had erupted at the news of Brooke's death, and the half-sister who had mistakenly been identified as her, had died surprisingly swiftly, firstly because Brooke had become old news, and secondly because they could neither find Milly to ask her to tell her story nor identify the woman who was Brooke's half-sister.

Milly had lived very quietly, walking miles through the streets with Topsy to keep herself busy while struggling to suppress her memories of the time she had spent with Lorenzo. There was no point looking back to a relationship that should never have happened in the first place, she told herself sternly. He wasn't hers, never had been hers, and never would be hers again.

All the same, even in the midst of her grief there came a day when she could no longer close her eyes to the complication that had developed: she was pregnant with Lorenzo's baby. And a joy that laced her with guilt filled her almost to overflowing at a development that only *she* was likely to welcome. For too long, she had ignored her symptoms, and by the time she went to a doctor to have her pregnancy confirmed, she had already done a home test and had fully come to terms with the reality of her condition.

And that she had fallen pregnant really wasn't that surprising, she reasoned ruefully. She had had sex with Lorenzo countless times and no precautions had been taken. Lorenzo had believed she had an IUD fitted because at the time he had believed that she was Brooke and she hadn't had the knowledge to contradict him.

He would be upset when she told him, and Milly knew that eventually she would *have* to tell him. How could she not? He had a right to know his child—even if the woman carrying his child wasn't the one he would have chosen for the role.

Even when he had believed she was Brooke he had said, *'The last complication we need now is a child.'*

But she wasn't the same person she had been on the day of the crash, she recognised wryly. Her recuperation and dealing with life as an amnesiac in a rocky marriage had taught her that she was far more mentally and physically robust than she had ever dreamt. Neither of them were to blame for her pregnancy. She was happy about her child, even excited about her future. Lorenzo could hurt her, she conceded ruefully, but he wouldn't *break* her.

Those were the thoughts on her mind as she dressed for her sister's funeral, bundling her hair below a hat, doing her utmost to ensure that nobody would notice her and catch on to the powerful resemblance between her and Brooke. The lawyers had assured her that nobody expected her to attend. For nobody, she had read Lorenzo, and she had grimaced and had said that of course she would attend her sister's reburial.

A car picked her up at ten. The church was almost empty, there being few mourners this long after Brooke's demise but the paparazzi were out in force outside the church, peering suspiciously at everyone, in search of the half-sister they had heard about but had not yet contrived to identify. Her head bent, her slender body shrouded in a deliberately unfashionable black coat, Milly dropped into a pew at the back of the church, listening to the service while striving not to stare at the back of Lorenzo's arrogant dark head.

How could she think of him as the father of her baby when it wasn't even acceptable to approach him at the funeral, lest someone snatch a photo of them together? At the graveside, tears burning at the backs of her eyes for the sister who was gone and for the sibling affection she had never managed to ignite, she stole a fleeting glance at Lorenzo. He dealt her a faint nod of acknowledgement. His lean, strong face had a tougher, harder edge. He had lost weight. But then Milly had lost weight as well. She felt nauseous much of the day and it was an effort to remember to eat as one day drifted into another. Usually she tried to eat when she was feeding Topsy.

Lorenzo studied Milly from the other side of the cemetery. He hadn't wanted her to attend. He had needed her to stay in the background and out of sight, had assured himself over and over again that that was the only sensible solution. But there she stood, lost in the folds of a voluminous coat, her incredible hair hidden below a trilby hat, her delicate face shadowed by the brim and barely recognisable. She looked thinner, younger, but naturally she looked younger because she *was* years younger than Brooke had been. Milly would only be twenty-three on her next birthday he reminded himself doggedly. It was all over, *finally* over, the whole distasteful business of his marriage to Brooke, done and dusted, he reflected, fighting to block memories of his time in Italy with Milly: long golden days lazily drifting past, the scent and the taste of her, the sound of her laughter and the readiness of her smile.

It would do him no good to dwell on the past. He had married Brooke and it had been a disaster from start to finish. And Milly was Brooke's half-sister and by acting as her unofficial stand-in had knowingly engaged with Brooke in an unsavoury deception to fool innocent people. Evidently, she had seen nothing wrong with that kind of behaviour. In other words, the same thread of dishonesty that had run through his late wife like poison had an echo in Milly as well. But she could learn to do better with his guidance, he reasoned squarely. After all, nobody was perfect. And after the ordeal of living with Brooke, he wasn't perfect either because he found it very hard to trust a woman again. He had needed time away from Milly to recover from the fallout of his failed marriage and the drama of discovering that he had been living with another woman.

He remembered Milly cooking for him, remembered her giving him pleasure as he had never known, and his teeth gritted. It was done: the connection had to remain broken for the moment, lest the paparazzi go into a feeding frenzy over Milly's very existence. Hopefully, their interest in identifying her wouldn't last much longer. But were they to discover her and place her within his life, they would tear her apart, implying this, implying that, *hurting* her as she did not deserve to be hurt.

When the vicar had finished, Milly watched Lorenzo swing on his heel and walk away, wide strong shoulders straight as girders beneath his black cashmere overcoat, his back even straighter, and suddenly she couldn't bear it. In fact, her temper soared. So much remained unsaid between them and she didn't even have his phone number! What had she done that was so bad that he was treating her as though she didn't exist? And she *had* to tell him about the baby. She had no choice on that score. There was no way she was prepared to ring his lawyers and tell *them*! He owed her a hearing, didn't he?

'Lorenzo!' she exclaimed, darting frantically in his wake,

her face heating with embarrassment at being forced to abandon her hard-won dignity.

Lorenzo wheeled to a sudden halt and turned back to face her.

'I need to see you to talk about something,' she told him in an angry rush. 'Do you think you could call round this evening?'

'Tomorrow evening. If I must,' Lorenzo gritted, his glorious dark golden eyes locked to her with an intensity that brought her out in goose bumps.

'You *must*,' Milly declared with bold emphasis. 'I wouldn't ask to see you if I didn't have a good reason for it.'

'Around eight, then,' Lorenzo confirmed coolly. 'Are you sure it isn't something my lawyers could handle?'

'No, it's too personal for that,' Milly retorted in a tight tone of annoyance, her colour higher than ever at being required to make that distinction.

'We'll talk over dinner. I'll pick you up at eight.'

Lorenzo strode towards his limousine, enraged at the shot of adrenalin now coursing through his veins and the undeniable sense of anticipation that powered it. He had been trying to stay away from her for weeks and she had just made that impossible, looking up at him with those haunting violet eyes. Of course, he could get through one dinner with her and behave! And go home *alone*? What was too personal? What the hell could she be referring to? Lorenzo did not like to meet anyone without knowing beforehand exactly what he would be dealing with. His strong jawline clenched hard.

He couldn't fault her behaviour, though, since she had moved out. She had asked for nothing from him and she hadn't gone to the press. She hadn't contacted him, hadn't clung, had, in short, done exactly as he had supposedly wanted. To all intents and purposes, they were finished. Only, it hadn't taken more than a day for Lorenzo to register that while he had acted in the shocked conviction that he didn't have a choice, absence wasn't what he wanted or needed from Milly.

He had told himself that he was free again, had wondered

why he was so angry and why the knowledge that he was free wasn't the relief that he had expected it to be. And now he knew. Milly was looking skinny and that tore him up. Her fine-boned face was downright thin now and her ankles seemed too delicate to support her. In terms of weight there hadn't been much of her to begin with, he reasoned...but *was* she looking after herself properly? The idea that she might not be now that he was no longer around to watch over her welfare nagged at him and made him decide that a dinner was a very good idea because he could check her out without making a production out of it. And to hell with the paparazzi!

CHAPTER TEN

THE NEXT DAY Milly rushed round the apartment, feeding Topsy and tidying up. She hadn't slept well the night before, haunted as she had been by memories of her sister and the guilty strain of finally laying those memories to rest. Perhaps had she had more time with Brooke or more in common with her, they would have become closer.

Late afternoon, she took Topsy out for a walk and then let her out onto the roof terrace where she liked to wander among the potted plants. That done, she hurried into the bathroom and had a shower.

Why was she fussing about her appearance simply because Lorenzo would be taking her out to dinner? For goodness' sake, it wasn't a date! She would put on jeans and a sweater, she told herself, so that he could see that she had no silly expectations.

After the shower, she put on her smartest jeans and a simple top, but it was a heck of a struggle to get the zip done up on her jeans. Inexorably her shape was changing and, although she had got thinner, her breasts were still larger, her waist was expanding and her stomach was developing a definite outward curve. There was nothing she could do about any of that, she scolded herself as she examined her reflection and winced at the biting tightness of her jeans. She could tell that the need for maternity wear was only just round the corner.

Five minutes later, she tore off the jeans and the top and pulled out a dress instead, the pretty red dress she had bought when she was living with Lorenzo, only, unhappily for her, the dress was now much too tight over her boobs. In a feverish surge of activity she dragged out her entire wardrobe, trying on outfit after outfit until she found a sundress with a looser cut that was reasonably presentable even if it was a little odd to be wearing a sundress when winter was on the horizon. Lorenzo probably wouldn't even notice what she was wearing. He had hardly looked at her at the cemetery, after all, and once she told him about the baby, he would have much more important things to focus on.

At that point her nervous tension and worries threatened to overwhelm her. The discovery that she was pregnant had made a nonsense of her tentative plans for a better future in which she had planned to work while studying. There were so many things she wouldn't be able to do with a child dependent on her. She had hoped to move out of the apartment and sever her last ties to Lorenzo but how could she do that when she needed somewhere to live while she was pregnant?

The lawyers had assured her that, as William Jackson's younger daughter and Brooke's sibling, she was entitled to inherit Brooke's estate because Lorenzo had refused to accept it. But in her heart, Milly suspected that her half-sister would not have wanted *her* to benefit and that made her squirm. Brooke hadn't been fond enough of her and that made it even more difficult for Milly to contemplate being enriched by her sister's demise. She didn't feel entitled to Brooke's trust fund yet how could she refuse it when she had a baby on the way and desperately needed that security? As for taking any more money from Lorenzo, that was out of the question. Baby or not, she wasn't planning to hang on his sleeve for ever!

* * *

Lorenzo worked late at the bank and then headed straight to the apartment. That enervating word, 'personal', had played on his mind throughout the day. Did she still believe that she loved him? She had never mentioned love again after that first time when he had failed to reciprocate. Back then he had been relieved by that silence because he had still been planning to divorce her. After all, leopards didn't change their spots. He had never doubted that they would end up divorced and discovering that Brooke was, in fact, *Milly* had simply set him free sooner and more quickly than he had expected.

The dream scenario, his most senior lawyer had commented cheerfully, and Lorenzo had felt like punching him because the past month had been anything but a dream for him.

Milly opened the door with a fast-beating heart. Knowing that he was coming up in the lift had simply increased her nerves about what she was going to say. Lorenzo would be completely unprepared for her announcement and yet shouldn't he have become aware of the risk he had run with her the minute he had realised that she wasn't Brooke? Had that contraceptive oversight completely escaped his attention? She supposed it had, just as it had initially escaped her attention in the emotional turmoil of their break-up.

Lorenzo strolled through the door in a charcoal-grey pinstriped suit, blue-black stubble accentuating his wide mobile mouth and hard masculine jawline, imbuing his dark good looks with an even tougher edge. 'I can't work out what you could have to say that falls into the category of personal,' he admitted coolly.

'Believe me, it's very personal to both of us,' Milly retorted, annoyed by his continuing determination to keep her at a distance. 'I wouldn't have asked you here otherwise.'

Lorenzo gazed at her, dark eyes narrowed and shrewd, his attention lingering on the blue and white dress, which he remembered all too well. He remembered it best in a heap on the bedroom floor. He remembered taking it off to reveal her curvy little body. He remembered persuading her out of its concealing folds at a picnic and convincing her that they would not be seen in the shelter of the trees. Indeed, seeing her *wearing* it rather than seeing himself stripping it off her was a novelty, a novelty and a reminder that his libido didn't need. He clenched his teeth as a pulsing wave of arousal assailed his groin.

'Let's go to dinner and talk,' he urged thickly before he let himself down and just grabbed her and carried her back to his cave like a Neanderthal who hadn't seen a woman in years.

The soft blue cashmere stole she had put round her shoulders kept the chill of the evening air off her skin.

Lorenzo remembered buying that for her in Florence when he saw her shiver one evening. Indeed, he seemed to have an extraordinarily photographic memory for everything she had ever worn and everything he had taken off. The limo didn't have to travel very far before they arrived at a small bistro where they were immediately escorted to a dimly lit corner booth.

Lorenzo sank gracefully down. 'There's something I need to say first…'

'Go ahead,' she encouraged as she opened her menu.

'When you regained your memory, we needed a complete break from each other for a while,' he breathed tautly. 'You needed peace to come to terms with everything that had happened. I had to accept that Brooke was gone and deal with that appropriately. I couldn't have done that with you still living with me and I was keen to keep the press out of our relationship.'

'Yes,' Milly conceded uneasily. 'But, perhaps now you can accept that I have no desire to talk to the press *or* embarrass you in any way?'

'If you didn't crave publicity exposure, why did you agree to act as Brooke's stand-in and deceive people?' Lorenzo asked with unnerving suddenness, his disapproval of her behaviour obvious to her for the first time.

Milly flushed because she hadn't yet confronted the embarrassing fact that he viewed her actions as Brooke's stand-in as a form of deception. 'I didn't crave the publicity but it *was* exciting for me to wear her expensive outfits and to be greeted by people as if I was *somebody* for the first time in my life,' she admitted, mortified at having to make that lowering admission. 'But mainly I agreed to do it because I wanted to please her and help her out. It made me feel needed and I truly believed that it would make her fonder of me.'

Disconcerted by that honesty, Lorenzo frowned. 'Then you were very naïve. Brooke didn't like other women. She saw them as rivals and she didn't trust them. Did she pay you for your services?'

Milly reddened even more uneasily. 'She promised that she would but she never actually did. I was missing work and I couldn't afford to and still pay my rent. I once lost a job over it and had to move,' she confessed awkwardly. 'I didn't like to ask her for money and bring our relationship down to that level. I didn't want to be someone she paid like hired help. I wanted to be a sister coming to her aid and I hoped she would eventually appreciate that...'

As Milly fell silent to take note of the waiter hovering, Lorenzo frowned and voiced their selections while also ordering wine.

'How many times did you stand in for her?' he asked bluntly when they were alone again.

'The day of the accident would have been the fifth time but a couple of the times she used me it was simply a matter of me being seen entering or leaving a shop she was publicising,' Milly revealed, worrying anxiously at her lower lip with her teeth. 'But the last time? That was a big deal for me because I was to stay hidden in the hotel room she had booked for six days, which meant that I had to quit my job.'

'I've since learned where she was planning to go,' Lorenzo volunteered as the first course was delivered to the table. 'Brooke was flying to Argentina.'

'Argentina?' Milly gaped. 'Why Argentina?'

'Presumably to meet up with Scott Lansdale, because he was filming on location there,' Lorenzo supplied very drily.

'Scott Lansdale the *movie star*?' Milly whispered in a feverish hiss, both incredulous and ironically impressed by that famous name. 'But he's a married man!'

'She was having an affair with him, probably in the belief that he would put her name forward for a part in his next film,' Lorenzo explained flatly. 'Brooke didn't sleep with men out of love or lust. She picked men she expected to advance her career. If they didn't deliver, she moved on.'

'You say that as if it happened more than once during your marriage,' Milly muttered with a frown, pushing away her glass when the wine arrived and opting instead for water.

'It did. Sex was only another weapon in her arsenal. After the first time I caught her out and she lied about it, I never slept with her again. We were living entirely separate lives by the time I started the divorce,' he completed.

'So, the rumours about other men weren't just gossipy stories like you first said they were?' she pressed in dismay.

'No, they weren't,' he confirmed steadily. 'At the time I didn't want to upset you by telling you the truth about our marriage… well, about my marriage with Brooke.'

Milly dropped her head, suddenly understanding so much more about Lorenzo. He had gone for a divorce as soon as he saw that his marriage was beyond saving. She could easily understand why he had initially steered clear of any further intimacy with her. 'Why on earth did Brooke marry you in the first place?' she pressed.

'Her trust fund didn't run to the designer clothes she adored and my wealth gave her unlimited spending power. Our marriage also propelled her up the social ladder, which gave her more opportunities to meet influential people in the film and television world.'

Milly swallowed hard. 'You think that she never loved you, that she just used you for what you could provide?'

Lorenzo shrugged and thrust his big shoulders back into a more relaxed position. As he shifted lithely his jacket fell back from his chest and the edges parted to display lean muscles rippling below the fine shirt and Milly's mouth ran dry as dust. 'She betrayed me so early in our marriage that she couldn't possibly have loved me. I never saw anything in her that made me think otherwise. I have to be truthful with you on that score. I didn't hate her, I certainly didn't wish her dead, but by the end of the first year when the marriage had died, I had few illusions about her character.'

As the main course was delivered, Milly breathed in slow and deep and thought of the way Lorenzo had looked after her after the accident, refusing to allow his own feelings to influence his attitude. That had taken an immense force of will and self-discipline that in retrospect shook her. But his strength and protectiveness had been powered purely by the mistaken conviction that she was his wife and deserving of his care.

'I'm glad that you felt that you could finally tell me the truth,' she confessed, wondering how the heck they had strayed so far from her intent to tell him that she was carrying his child. However, she didn't believe a public setting was suitable for such a revelation and resolved to tell him only when he had taken her home again.

'Hopefully that's cleared the air. Now, perhaps you'll tell me what was too *personal* to discuss with my lawyers,' Lorenzo murmured smoothly.

Her heart started beating very fast inside her chest, depriving her of breath, but she shook her head vehemently. 'I'll tell you as soon as I get home.'

His ebony brows pleated. 'Why the secrecy?'

'I don't want you to feel constrained by our surroundings,' she admitted stiffly.

When they stepped out of the restaurant, immediately flashbulbs burst all around them, blinding and startling her. As shouted questions were aimed at them like bullets by the paparazzi, Lorenzo curved a protective hand to her spine and urged her unhurriedly in the direction of the car.

'For goodness' sake, we shouldn't have come out together in public!' Milly gasped, stricken, in the back of the limousine. 'Why did you risk it? Before you know it, I'll have been identified.'

'And so what if you are?' Lorenzo incised impatiently between clenched teeth. 'Neither of us has done anything wrong and nobody knows what happened between us. It's nobody else's business either. But I do believe that it's past time for this relationship to come out of the closet and be seen.'

Taken aback by that far-reaching statement that suggested that they still *had* a relationship, Milly climbed breathlessly out of the limo and accompanied him into the lift. He leant back against the wall, all lean, sinuous male, his beautiful dark golden eyes intent on her, and desire clenched low in her pelvis, dismaying her because she had believed that she had better control than that.

'I'm not used to you keeping secrets from me,' he confessed. 'You were always very open.'

Milly recalled how she had told him that she loved him and barely restrained a wince at the recollection of how trustingly naïve she had been in those early days. 'I haven't changed but maybe I've learned a little more discretion,' she parried.

They emerged from the lift into the shadowy foyer of the apartment. Lorenzo strode ahead of her to hit the lights. Milly forged on into the lounge, leaving him to follow.

'So now...' Lorenzo drawled with wry amusement. 'I gather it's finally time for *the big reveal*.'

Milly breathed in so deep that she felt dizzy as she exhaled again and she braced her hands on the back of a sofa, reckoning that hint of amusement would be short-lived. 'I'm pregnant,' she informed him apprehensively.

Lorenzo did a complete double take, his dark head jerking up and back, his dark eyes gleaming sharp as rapier blades. *'Pregnant?'* he emphasised in astonishment.

Milly sighed as she sank wearily down on the sofa. 'I'm almost three months along because *I* wasn't using any birth control while we were together and *you* didn't take any precautions,' she reminded him.

Lorenzo hovered with an incredulous look stamped on his lean, strong face, his dark eyes glittering like polar stars. *'Pregnant?'* he repeated a second time as if he could not comprehend such a development. 'By…*me*?'

'Oh…are you infertile? You never mentioned it,' Milly shot back at him to punish him for that inexcusable second question, her colour warmer than ever.

Unexpectedly, Lorenzo dropped down fluidly into the seat opposite her, lustrous vibrant eyes fringed by black lashes pinned to her. Hurriedly she looked away, wishing he weren't quite so spectacularly handsome that he distracted her every time she looked at him. On some level her eyes were in love with those hard, chiselled features of his. But she needed to be cool, calm and collected, not tied in emotional and physical knots by her memories of her time with him, she reminded herself doggedly.

'I *could* be infertile,' Lorenzo mused almost conversationally. 'I don't know. Unprotected sex is a risk I've never taken with a woman…you're the single exception.' The instant he was forced to concede that point, he was plunged back into shock and the colour slowly leached from below his bronzed skin as her first words finally sank in. He stared at her, his dense black lashes framing his bemused gaze. *Pregnant?* How was that possible? But he now accepted that it was perfectly possible, even if he had not foreseen that possibility and that knowledge silenced him.

'But as you said, it's a risk you took many times with me,' Milly reminded him shakily, her courage beginning to flag because he still looked absolutely stunned. 'I'm not Brooke. I didn't have the IUD you assumed I still had, and you didn't protect me.'

'No, I didn't,' Lorenzo acknowledged in a low, driven undertone. 'I just assumed it would be safe.'

'And I took your word for it.' Milly sighed.

'Madre di Dio,' Lorenzo groaned. 'I've always wanted a child but not like this.'

'I feel the same,' Milly admitted heavily. 'I've always wanted to be a mother, but this is hardly an ideal situation. Even so, I still plan to make the best of it. I won't be considering termination or adoption or any other way out of this situation. I *want* my baby.'

'I wouldn't have suggested those options,' Lorenzo asserted in stark reproof.

'Yet only minutes ago you were quite happy to suggest that this baby might not be yours,' Milly reminded him curtly. 'That was very offensive.'

'How am I to know who you might have been with in recent weeks?' Lorenzo countered in a driven undertone. 'The idea that you could be out there seeing other men has driven me crazy over the past month!'

Milly stared back at him in wonderment. 'I haven't *ever* been with anyone but you!' she told him with a decided edge of bitterness. 'I was a virgin but *you* didn't notice...and although it hurt like hell I just thought it was a question of it having been too long since I'd last had sex, so I didn't say anything about it at the time.'

Lorenzo vaulted upright. 'You were a virgin?' he breathed rawly.

'Yes. And I was planning to stay that way until I was in a serious relationship,' she admitted with spirit.

Lorenzo raked long brown fingers through his ruffled blue-black hair. *'Dio mio...* I'm sorry. You should've told me that I'd hurt you.'

'I didn't want to spoil the moment...engaged as I foolishly was in trying to save my rocky marriage...the marriage that didn't actually exist,' she completed tightly.

'This...*us*...it is an unholy mess!' Lorenzo growled in sudden frustration.

'Well, I've told you now. Perhaps you would have preferred me to approach your lawyers with this little problem.'

'No. Not with anything that relates to our baby and, by the way, our baby is *not* and will never be a problem,' Lorenzo declared, moving restively about the room, obviously too shaken up by her news to settle again.

Our baby was a label that warmed Milly's heart and she hastily looked away from him, telling herself that she was simply relieved that he wasn't angry or resentful. He *wanted* their child. That was a more positive response than she had even dared to hope for. 'I'll make tea. I'm afraid I don't have any alcohol.'

Lorenzo flashed her a sudden unexpected smile that radiated charisma. 'May I have coffee instead?'

'Of course, you can,' Milly told him cheerfully as she jumped up, a sense of reprieve making her body feel shaky as she walked into the sleek kitchen.

'I want you to come home with me tonight,' Lorenzo announced with staggering abruptness from the doorway.

Wide-eyed with astonishment, Milly whirled round to face him where he lounged gracefully against the frame. 'Why the heck would I do that?'

'You're expecting my child,' Lorenzo countered evenly, as if her question was a surprising one. 'And you've lost a lot of weight. I don't want you living here alone.'

Her facial muscles locking tight with self-discipline, Milly turned away again to put the kettle on, grateful to have something to do with her hands. 'You threw me out, Lorenzo. I'm not coming back.'

'I didn't *throw* you out,' he argued vehemently.

'It's not worth fighting about,' Milly parried quickly. 'You were right when you said our relationship was an unholy mess. So, let's not dig ourselves into a deeper hole. Leave things as they are.'

'But I don't *like* how things are,' Lorenzo framed without apology. 'This child will be my child as well and I want him or her to have my full attention from the start. I can't achieve that if we're living apart.'

Milly's slight shoulders sagged wearily. 'I'm not sure I'd have told you if I'd known you were going to make this much fuss. I'm pregnant...deal with it,' she advised. 'And once you've thought us over, you'll appreciate that we were an accident that should never have happened. But that doesn't mean that we can't still respect each other and maintain a civil relationship for the sake of our child.'

Lorenzo's sculpted features had shadowed and set hard. 'I strongly disagree with everything you just said,' he responded in unambiguous challenge. 'I don't think we were an accident and nor is our baby. I want more than a *civil* relationship with the mother of my child. I'm a traditional man. I want my child's mother to be my wife.'

The mug in Milly's hand dropped from her nerveless fingers and smashed into a million pieces on the tiled floor. She jerked back a step to avoid being splashed by the hot liquid and then gasped as a tiny flying piece of china stung her leg, before stooping down in an automatic movement to pick up the broken china.

Lorenzo's hands closed over hers and yanked her upright again. 'Are you burned?'

'No,' she said limply.

'But your leg's bleeding,' Lorenzo pointed out, bending down to lift her unresisting body up and settle her down on the kitchen counter out of harm's way.

'It's only a little cut!' she protested.

Lorenzo yanked the first-aid box off the wall and broke it open while frowning down at the blood trickling down her leg. Milly sucked in oxygen to steady herself, but she couldn't get her whirling thoughts under her control. All she could hear was Lorenzo saying, 'I want my child's mother to be my wife.' Had that been a marriage proposal? Surely not? That would be crazy. She blinked rapidly, wincing as he tugged the tiny sliver of china from her calf with tweezers and cleaned her up, covering the cut with a plaster as though she were a kid.

'Thanks,' she said as she watched him gathering up the broken china and cleaning up the mess she had made. Slowly, carefully, she slid back down to the floor and poured him a cup of coffee, extending it silently when he had finished.

'Yes, I *meant* what I said,' Lorenzo breathed in a raw undertone before she could speak again. 'I want us to get married as soon as possible.'

'You're not in a fit state to marry anyone, least of all me,' Milly told him roundly. 'A year and a half ago you were getting a divorce. Then your principles forced you into staying married and pretending. You got tangled up with me but that was only a sexual thing and clearly very casual when it all went wrong. Now you're single again. You need to start again with someone fresh. You've already walked away from me.'

'And look how that turned out for me!' Lorenzo urged impatiently. 'I'm back and I'm not leaving you again. And what we had *wasn't* casual and it *wasn't* just sex.'

'Maybe not on my side, *then*,' she specified with precision. 'But I was working blind in a marriage that was already dead, only I didn't know that. I assumed that I had married you because I loved you. Now I know that I was never married to you at all...and, Lorenzo, no offence intended, but I don't *want* to be married to a man who's only marrying me because I'm pregnant.'

'Well, at least I know you don't want me for my money,' Lorenzo replied with a wry smile. 'But you *know* that I want you and I want our child as well.'

'You can't buy me like a package deal. I won't come cheap

or easy,' Milly responded, tilting her chin at him before walking back towards the lounge with her tea. 'Amazing sex isn't enough to base a marriage on.'

'Was I amazing?' Lorenzo probed huskily behind her and she almost dropped a second mug at the same time as an involuntary smile tilted her lips.

'You know you were…but then I don't have anyone to compare you to yet, so—' she protested jerkily.

'Yet?' he queried, removing the mug from her hand to press her down into a seat, setting the tea down on the coffee table in front of her. Glittering dark eyes pierced her. 'If I can't have you, no other man can.'

'I'm afraid it doesn't work like that.' Milly sighed. 'We are both free agents now.'

'You're not free while you've got my baby inside you,' Lorenzo shot at her, his lean bronzed face fierce and forbidding.

'When you've finished your coffee, you should leave. I'm sorry but I'm very tired. Between the exhaustion and the morning sickness, I tend to go to bed early most nights,' she confided. 'I'm not in the mood to argue with you—'

'I'm not trying to argue. I'm trying to make you see sense.'

'You're not getting any further with me than I got with you. You said you wanted to marry me, but I don't think you've thought it through,' Milly said anxiously. 'There's a lot more to marriage than sex and having a child together.'

'I know. I love you,' Lorenzo confessed without the smallest warning. 'I was going to wait another month before approaching you again. I suppose I was trying to be a better man than I am. I didn't want the newspapers writing stuff about you and upsetting you. I thought that if I waited long enough, they would lose interest in us both. But I can't *live* another month without you, so here I am being bloody selfish and weak!'

Milly heard only the first half of that speech and his claim that he loved her knocked her for six. 'You *can't* love me,' she told him weakly.

'I began to fall in love with you the day you awakened from the coma. I fell deeper in love with every visit. At first, I told myself it was just sexual attraction even though it had been years since I'd been physically attracted to Brooke. I assumed that once you recovered your memory you would switch back into being the Brooke I remembered, and I knew I would continue the divorce eventually.'

'But before we went to Italy, you said we'd see how things went for us.'

'By that stage, I was secretly hoping that you would *never* recover your memory and, to be frank, I really didn't have a proper game plan,' Lorenzo confided grimly. 'I only knew that I couldn't face letting you go. I had fallen head over heels in love with a woman who was kind and compassionate and loving and I was revelling in every moment of the experience.' A smile slashed his lean dark features. 'I was extremely happy with you and I want that back. But I want to do everything the right way round this time. I want you to be my wife.'

'Oh...' was all Milly could bleat at that moment.

'You're not saying a flat no any more?' Lorenzo was quick to recognise that she was weakening.

'I'm thinking it over,' Milly muttered, her cheeks colouring. 'Why didn't you at least phone me while we were apart?'

'I was trying to be strong for both of us and I thought we were safer from press intrusion if nobody, including you, knew how I felt about you,' he admitted grimly. 'But I found it very hard to cope without you. I buried myself in work. It didn't help. I came home at night and I couldn't sleep and the house didn't feel like home any longer without you in it.'

Milly began slowly to smile, and her hand crept up to frame one high cheekbone in a tender caress. 'I love you, Lorenzo. I've missed you so much.'

Lorenzo tugged her gently into his arms and held her close. 'How can you still love me after the mess I made of things?'

Milly jerked her head back playfully, a foam of silvery blonde ringlets falling against one cheekbone. 'If you were perfect, you'd be boring. But you must stop hiding stuff from me in the belief that I have to be protected from every adverse event. I'm more resilient than I look,' she told him firmly. 'Yes, there would've been unpleasant stuff in the tabloids if it got out that we were together but we could have got through it. We are stronger together than we are apart.'

His ebony brows pleated. 'I didn't think of that angle.'

'I know. Your glass is always half empty while mine is always half full,' she teased, her violet eyes sparkling as she gazed up at him. 'Let's not care what anyone says or thinks about us. I learned how to do that at school. You must've been more protected than I was. I was always the kid in the unfashionable shoes, who got free lunches because she was the poor foster kid...'

Lean brown hands framed her animated face. 'And now you're going to be the wife of a billionaire.'

Her nose wrinkled. 'It just goes to show...you *can* sleep your way to the top!' she joked.

'*Madre di Dio...* I love you so much, *cara mia*,' Lorenzo husked, his mouth crashing down on hers with all the hunger he had fought to suppress for weeks giving her the strongest message yet that he needed her.

They stood there kissing, urgently entwined, too long separated to bear the idea of being apart even for a moment, both of them studiously ignoring Topsy, who was barking at their feet. She backed him up against the window, wrenching at his tie while he claimed urgent little biting kisses from her luscious mouth.

'I gather I'm staying,' Lorenzo pronounced with a wicked grin.

'Wait until you're invited,' Milly told him, waited a heartbeat. 'You're invited.'

He carried her into the all-white bedroom and dropped down on the side of the bed, holding her between his spread masculine thighs. He made a production out of sliding down one strap on her shoulder and then the other, pushing them gently down her arms to her wrists so that the dress slid down baring the full swell of her breasts cupped in a strapless bra. He undid the bra, let it drop away, studying her ripe curves with reverent intensity. 'You are perfect,' he breathed.

'You are not in the mood to be critical,' Milly laughed, taking in his arousal clearly outlined by the fine fabric of his trousers.

'Perfect,' Lorenzo repeated aggressively as he splayed the gentle fingers of one large hand across her stomach. 'You've got my baby in there...and that means the world to me.'

'And me,' she agreed as the dress fluttered to her feet and he gathered her into his arms and settled her down on the bed.

For a long time afterwards, there was nothing but the sheer urgency of the passion they had feared they might never experience again together, and then, in the tranquil aftermath, the real world intruded again.

Lorenzo fanned her tumbled hair back from her face and stared down at her with an adoring glow in his intense scrutiny. 'We start again fresh from this moment with no ghosts from the past between us,' he murmured sibilantly. 'The house has already been cleared. I had mementoes put aside for you, photos and scrapbooks and such, but I donated the contents of the dressing room and the jewellery I bought her to a charity auction. It's all gone.'

Milly nodded uncertainly, surprised and relieved and sad all at the same time. 'We wouldn't have met but for Brooke,' she reminded him gently.

'I can't stand to think of a world in which I might not have met you,' Lorenzo confessed. 'So that is something to be grateful to her for.'

'If her trust fund does come to me, I'd like to donate it to a good cause because I would never feel it was mine,' Milly admitted ruefully. 'I mean, our father never acknowledged me and neither did she really. She never once made me feel that she accepted me as an actual sister. It wouldn't be right for me to keep it.'

'As you wish. Just don't let the past poison anything that we share,' Lorenzo urged her anxiously.

Tender fingers stroked his roughened jawline. 'I love you too much, Lorenzo Tassini, to ever let that happen,' she whispered.

'I hope that means that you love me enough to get married soon,' he murmured softly, dropping a kiss down onto her reddened mouth.

Her eyes widened. 'How soon?'

'A couple of weeks?'

'No, that's far too soon,' she told him firmly.

'Well, if I had my choice it would be tomorrow,' Lorenzo admitted unrepentantly.

'Could we get married in Italy?' she asked wistfully. 'I'd love that.'

Lorenzo smiled. 'I think that could be arranged and still give you time to find a beautiful white dress.'

'I can't wear white. I'm pregnant!' Milly gasped with a wince.

'That's an old-fashioned concept,' Lorenzo overruled. 'You deserve to wear white and if I have anything to do with the decision, you will.'

Milly lifted her nose, knowing how bossy he was, resolved not to let him have anything to do with that decision. 'We'll see.'

'Is that you placating me?' Lorenzo asked suspiciously.

'Possibly.' Milly looked up at him, her whole face wreathed with happiness. 'I love you. I can't think of anything else right now.'

His dark eyes shimmered pure gold. 'Why should you think of anything else? I love you too, more than I ever thought I could love anyone, *bellezza mia*.'

Milly slipped into a dreamy sleep. Lorenzo lay awake planning the wedding and Topsy, suspecting that she wouldn't be welcomed into her usual spot in the bed, went for a nap underneath it.

* * *

Two months later, Milly adjusted her short veil and looked in the cheval mirror with a wide contented smile.

Her dress was a dream. Sheer lace encased her arms while a Bardot neckline exposed her shoulders and the fitted lace bodice drew attention away from the swell of her pregnant stomach, the tulle and organza layered skirt tumbling softly to the floor. Milly hadn't needed to hide her bump to feel presentable. She was proud to be carrying her little girl. It was only a few weeks since they had learned that they were to have a daughter and they both liked the name Liona. While Lorenzo was hopeful that Liona would inherit her mother's colouring, Milly was hopeful that she would inherit her father's.

Clutching her beautiful bouquet of wildflowers, she stepped into the car that would whisk her up the hill to the village church where they would take their vows. Lorenzo's senior lawyer had offered to lead her into the church and down the aisle. As they had become well acquainted during the proceedings that had established her sister's death and her own survival, she had laughed and agreed, especially after he had unbent sufficiently to admit that they had been taking bets in the office about how long it would take Lorenzo to admit that he had fallen madly in love.

Her eyes were intent only on Lorenzo when she entered the crowded church. A large number of Lorenzo's friends had chosen to accept their invitations and fly out for an autumn weekend in Tuscany. Many of them had already met her because once she had moved back in with Lorenzo he had begun entertaining again for the first time in several years. Initially her resemblance to Brooke had unsettled people, but once they had got talking to her and realised how friendly and unassuming she was that unease had melted away. In fact, for the first time ever, now settled and secure and confident in the happiness she had found, Milly was making friends.

Sunlight slanted through the stained-glass windows of the

chapel, illuminating the man at the altar, who was very tall beside the small, rounded priest. His hair gleamed blue black in strong light, his eyes gilded to gold in his lean dark face and he was smiling at his bride and she grinned back, barely able now to dredge up the recollection of the forbidding, reserved and very serious man he had once appeared to be. He covered her hand with his. 'You look radiant,' he told her proudly.

And the ceremony began, short and sweet and with no flourishes, because neither of them needed anything fancier than the love they had for each other and the child that was on the way to make them into a family. A slender platinum ring was slid onto her finger and then one to his. Lorenzo kissed his bride without a second's hesitation, and they walked out into the sunlight smiling and united.

The reception was held in the village hall where the earlier civil ceremony had taken place. It was merry and fun-filled and utterly informal, very much in the bride's style. Lorenzo had bought a yacht, an uncharacteristic act of conspicuous consumption that had attracted a lot of flak from his colleagues, and in a day or two they planned to cruise the Caribbean for their honeymoon. That first night of their marriage, though, they returned to the peaceful farmhouse in the hills and ate by candlelight on the terrace with the stars twinkling above them before retiring for the night.

'Happy now?' she teased him as he helped unhook her from her dress.

Lorenzo spread the parted edges of the dress back and kissed a trail across her smooth pale shoulders. 'Yes, now you're officially mine. I feel safer being happy.'

'Nobody's going to take our happiness away from us,' she soothed, spinning round as the gown dipped dangerously low over her full breasts to fall to her waist as she slowly extracted her arms from the tight lace sleeves. 'We worked hard for it, and you earned it every week that you watched over me when I was in a coma.'

'I still don't deserve you,' Lorenzo breathed gruffly, trying without success to drag his attention from her truly magnificent cleavage.

Milly let the dress fall to her feet and stepped out of it. 'Yes, you do. You deserve your happy ending just like everyone else. And I'm going to be it.'

'No complaints here.' Lorenzo laughed, lifting her gently to set her down on the bed, stroking the firm mound of her stomach with a possessive hand. 'Are you tired?'

'More elated now that we've finally got here, where we wanted to be,' she confided quietly. 'It was a glorious day, exactly what I dreamt of.'

'I wanted it to be really special for you, *bellezza mia*,' Lorenzo confided.

'Believe me, it was,' Milly assured him, running her fingertips lazily through his luxuriant black hair, a shiver of sensual awareness quivering through her as his stubbled jaw rubbed across her nape. 'Oh, do *that* again,' she urged helplessly.

Her unashamed enthusiasm made Lorenzo laugh. 'I love you to pieces, Milly.'

'I love you too…'

'And that little girl you're giving us will be as special as you are,' he told her.

And Liona *was*, coming into the world with all her mother's zest for life.

Two years later, she was followed by Pietro, as dark in colouring as his sister was fair, and rather more serious in nature.

Four years beyond that, when their parents naively thought their family was complete, fate surprised them with Cara, blonde with dark eyes, a little elf of a child with a mischievous smile. And together they were the family that both Lorenzo and Milly had always dreamt of having.

* * * * *

The Return Of Her Billionaire Husband

Melanie Milburne

Books by Melanie Milburne

Harlequin Modern

The Tycoon's Marriage Deal
A Virgin for a Vow
Blackmailed into the Marriage Bed
Tycoon's Forbidden Cinderella

Conveniently Wed!

Bound by a One-Night Vow
Penniless Virgin to Sicilian's Bride
Billionaire's Wife on Paper

One Night With Consequences

A Ring for the Greek's Baby

Secret Heirs of Billionaires

Cinderella's Scandalous Secret

The Scandal Before the Wedding

Claimed for the Billionaire's Convenience
The Venetian One-Night Baby

Visit the Author Profile page
at millsandboon.com.au for more titles.

Melanie Milburne read her first Harlequin novel at the age of seventeen, in between studying for her final exams. After completing a master's degree in education, she decided to write a novel, and thus her career as a romance author was born. Melanie is an ambassador for the Australian Childhood Foundation and a keen dog lover and trainer. She enjoys long walks in the Tasmanian bush. In 2015 Melanie won the HOLT Medallion, a prestigious award honoring outstanding literary talent.

To all the parents who have lost a baby at birth.
Your journey through grief is unimaginably painful
and long lasting. My thoughts are with you. xx

CHAPTER ONE

THERE WAS A weird kind of irony in arriving as maid of honour for your best friend's destination wedding with divorce papers in your hand luggage. But the one thing Juliette was determined *not* to do was spoil Lucy and Damon's wedding day. Well, not just a wedding day but a wedding weekend. On Corfu.

And her estranged husband was the best man.

Juliette sucked in a prickly breath and tried not to think of the last time she'd stood at an altar next to Joe Allegranza. Tried not to think of the blink-and-you'd-miss-it ceremony in the English village church in front of a handful of witnesses with her pregnancy not quite hidden by her mother's vintage wedding dress. The dress that scratched and itched the whole time she was wearing it. She tried not to think of the expression of disappointment on her parents' faces that their only daughter was marrying a virtual stranger after she got pregnant on a one-night stand.

Tried not to think of her baby—the baby girl who didn't even get to take a single breath…

Juliette stepped down out of the shuttle bus and walked into the foyer of the luxury private villa at Barbati Beach. The scarily efficient wedding planner, Celeste Petrakis, had organised for the wedding party to stay at the villa so the rehearsal and other activities planned would run as smoothly and seamlessly as possible. Juliette had thought about asking to stay at another hotel close by, as she didn't fancy running into Joe more than was strictly necessary. Socialising politely with her soon-to-be ex-husband over breakfast, lunch and dinner wasn't exactly in her skill set. But the thought of upsetting the drill sergeant wedding planner's meticulous arrangements was as intimidating as a cadet saying they weren't going to march in line on parade. Juliette had even at one point thought of declining the honour of being Lucy's maid of honour, but that would have made everyone think she wasn't over Joe.

She most definitely was over him—hence the divorce papers.

'Welcome.' The smartly dressed female attendant greeted her with a smile bright enough for an orthodontist's website homepage. 'May I have your name, please?'

'Bancroft…erm… I mean Allegranza.' Juliette wished now she had got around to officially changing back to her maiden name. Why hadn't she? She still didn't understand why she'd taken Joe's name in the first place. Their marriage hadn't come about the normal way. No dating, no courtship, no professions of love. No romantic proposal. Just one night of bed-wrecking sex and then goodbye and thanks for the memories. They hadn't even exchanged phone numbers. By the time she'd worked up the courage to track Joe down and tell him she was pregnant, he had insisted—not proposed, *insisted*—on marrying her soon after. They'd only lived together as man and wife for a total of three months. Three months of marriage and then it was over—just like her pregnancy.

But once Joe signed the papers and the divorce was finalised she would be free of his name. Free to move on with her life, because being stuck in limbo sucked. How would she ever be able to get through the grieving process without drawing a thick black line through her time with Joe?

She. Had. To. Move. On.

The receptionist click-clacked on the computer keyboard. 'Here it is. J Allegranza. And the J is for...?'

'Juliette.' She wondered if it would be pedantic to insist on being addressed by her maiden name while she was here but decided against saying anything. But why hadn't Lucy told the wedding planner she and Joe were separated? Or were Lucy and Damon still hoping she and Joe would somehow miraculously get back together?

Not flipping likely. They shouldn't have been together in the first place.

If her childhood sweetheart, Harvey, hadn't taken it upon himself to dump her instead of proposing to her, like she'd been expecting, none of this would have happened. Rebound sex with a handsome stranger. Who would have thought she had it in her? She wasn't the type of girl to talk to staggeringly gorgeous men in swanky London bars. She wasn't a one-night stand girl. But that night she had turned into someone else. Joe's touch had turned her into someone else.

Note to self. Do not think about Joe's touch. Do. Not. Go. There.

There was not going to be a fairy tale ending to their short-lived relationship. How could there be when the only reason for their marriage was now gone?

Dead. Buried. Lying, sleeping for ever, in a tiny white coffin in a graveyard in England.

'Your suite is ready for you now,' the receptionist said. 'Spiros will bring your luggage in from the shuttle.'

'Thank you.'

The receptionist handed her a swipe key and directed her to the lifts across the hectare of marble floor. 'Your suite is on the third floor. Celeste, the wedding planner, will meet with the bridal party for drinks on the terrace, to go through the rehearsal and wedding timetable, promptly at six this evening.'

'Got it.' Juliette gave a polite movement of her lips, which was about as close to a smile as she got to these days. She took the key, hitched her tote bag over her shoulder and made her way over to the lifts. The divorce papers were poking out of the top of her bag, a reminder of her two-birds-one-stone mission. In seven days, this chapter of her life would finally be over.

And she would never have to think about Joe Allegranza again.

There was only one thing Joe Allegranza hated more than weddings and that was funerals. Oh, and birthdays—his, in particular. But he could hardly turn down being his mate's best man, even if it meant coming face to face with his estranged wife, Juliette.

His wife…

Hard to believe how those two words still had the power to gouge a hole in his chest—a raw gaping hole that nothing could fill. He couldn't think of her without feeling he had failed in every way possible. How had he let his life spin out of control so badly? He, who had written the handbook on control.

Mostly, he could block her from his mind. Mostly. He binged on work like some people did on alcohol or food. He had built his global engineering career on his ability to fix structural failures. To forensically analyse broken bridges and buildings, and yet he was unable to do anything to repair his broken marriage. Fifteen months of separation and he hadn't moved forward with his life. *Couldn't* move on with his life. It was as if an invisible wall had sprung up in front of him, keeping him cordoned off, blocked, imprisoned.

He glanced at the wedding ring still on his finger. He could easily have taken it off and locked it in the safe, along with Juliette's rings that she had left behind.

But he hadn't.

He wasn't entirely sure why. Divorce was something he rigorously avoided thinking about. Reconciliation was equally as daunting. He was stuck in no man's land.

Joe walked into the reception area of the luxury villa where the wedding party were staying and was greeted by a smiling attendant. 'Welcome. May I have your name, please?'

'Joe Allegranza.' He removed his sunglasses and slipped them into his breast pocket. 'The wedding planner made the booking.'

The reception attendant peered a little closer at the screen, scrolling through the bookings with her computer mouse. 'Ah, yes, I see it now. I missed it because I thought the booking was only for one person.' She flashed him a smile so bright he wished he hadn't taken his sunglasses off. 'Your wife has already checked in. She arrived an hour ago.'

His wife. A weight pressed down on Joe's chest and his next breath was razor-edged. *His failure* could just as easily be substituted for those words. Hadn't the wedding planner got the memo about his and Juliette's separation?

The thought slipped through a crack in his mind like a fissure in bedrock, threatening to destabilise his determination to keep his distance.

A weekend sharing a suite with his estranged wife.

For a second or two he considered pointing out the booking error but he let his mind wander first... He could see Juliette again. In private. In person. He would be able to talk to her face to face instead of having her refuse to answer his calls or delete or block his texts or emails. She hadn't responded to a single missive. Not one. The last time he'd called her to tell her about the fundraising he'd organised for a stillbirth foundation on their behalf, the service provider informed him the number was no longer connected. Meaning Juliette was no longer connected *to him.*

His conscience woke up and prodded him with a jabbing finger.

What the hell are you thinking? Haven't you done enough damage?

It was crazy enough coming here for the wedding, much less spend time with Juliette—especially alone. He had ruined her life, just like he had done to his mother. Was there a curse on him when it came to his relationships? A curse that had been placed on him the day he was born. The same day his mother had died. His birthday: his mother's death day.

If that wasn't a curse, then what the freaking hell was?

Joe cleared his throat. 'There must be some mistake. My…er…wife and I are no longer together. We're…separated.' He hated saying the ugly word. Hated admitting his failure. Hated knowing it was largely his fault his wife had walked out on their marriage.

The receptionist's eyebrows drew together in a frown. 'Oh, no—I mean, that's terrible about your separation. Also, about the booking, because we don't have any other rooms and—'

'It's fine,' Joe said, pulling out his phone. 'I'll book in somewhere else.' He began to scroll through the options on his server. There had to be plenty of hotels available. He would sleep on a park bench or on the beach if he had to. No way was he sharing a room with his estranged wife. Too dangerous. Too tempting. Too everything.

'I don't think you'll find too much available,' the receptionist said. 'There's several weddings on this part of Corfu this weekend and, besides, Celeste really wanted everyone to stay close by to give the wedding a family feel. She'll be gutted to find out she's made a mistake with your booking. She's worked so hard to make her cousin's wedding truly special.'

Joe's memory snagged on something Damon had told him about his young cousin, Celeste. How this wedding planning gig for her older cousin was her first foray into the workforce after a long battle with some type of blood cancer. Leukaemia? Non-Hodgkin's? He couldn't remember which, but he didn't want to be the one to rain on Celeste's first parade.

'Okay, so don't tell Celeste until I make sure I can't find accommodation. I'll do a ring around and see what I find.'

He fixed problems, right? That was his speciality—fixing things that no one else could fix.

And he would fix this or die trying.

Joe stepped back out into the sunshine and spent close to an hour getting more and more frustrated when there was no vacancy anywhere. Beads of sweat poured down the back of his neck and between his shoulder blades. He even for a moment considered making an offer to *buy* a property rather than face the alternative of sharing a room with his estranged wife. He certainly had enough money to buy whatever he wanted.

Except happiness.

Except peace of mind.

Except life for his baby girl...

His phone was almost out of charge when he finally conceded defeat. There was nothing available close by or within a reasonable radius. Fate or destiny or a seriously manipulative deity had decided Joe was sharing a room with Juliette.

But maybe it was time to do something about his marriage. Keeping his distance hadn't solved anything. Maybe this was a chance to see if there was anything he could say or do to bring a resolution to their situation. Closure.

Joe walked back into Reception and the young receptionist gave him an I-told-you-so smile. 'No luck?' she said.

'Nope.' Luck and Joe were not close friends. Never had been. Enemies, more like.

'Here's your key.' The receptionist handed it over the counter. 'I hope you enjoy your stay.'

'Thank you.' Joe took the key and made his way to the lift. *Enjoy his stay?* Like that was going to happen. He'd been dreading seeing Juliette again, knowing he was largely responsible for her pain, her sorrow, her devastation. But at least this way, in the privacy of 'their' suite, he would be able to speak to her without an audience. He would say what needed to be said, work out the way forward—if there was a way forward—and then they could both move on with their lives.

CHAPTER TWO

JULIETTE HAD A refreshing shower and was dressed in a luxurious bathrobe with her hair in a towel turban. The bespoke bathrobe—apparently all the wedding party had them—had her initials embroidered over her right breast—JA. Which was a pity because the bathrobe was absolutely divine and she hated the thought of tossing it in a charity bin. But maybe, once she got home, she could unpick the embroidery and embroider JB instead.

The wedding planner had certainly pulled all the stops out. There were handmade chocolates with the bride and groom's names on them by the bedside, plus spring water bottles labelled with a photo of the happy couple. It was hard to look at her friend's blissfully happy smile in that photo and not feel insanely jealous.

Why couldn't she have found a man to love her like Damon loved Lucy?

Juliette had thought her ex, Harvey, had loved her. How could she have been so blind for so long? Harvey had said the three little words so often and yet they had meant nothing.

She had meant nothing.

And Joe hadn't loved her either, but at least he hadn't lied to her about it. Their relationship hadn't been a love match but a convenient solution to the problem of her accidental pregnancy. A duty marriage. A loveless arrangement to provide a secure home and future for their child. She had known it from the start and still married him because she couldn't bear to face the disappointment on her parents' faces. The disappointment she had seen throughout her life—every school report, every exam result, every time she failed to gain their approval. Every time she failed to live up to the standards set by her exceptionally talented, high achieving older brothers. And her parents, with their multiple university degrees. Even her very existence had been a mistake. She was a mid-life baby born to older parents who thought their childrearing days were over. And they *were* over, so they'd outsourced the rearing of Juliette to a variety of nannies.

Juliette placed her hand on the flat plane of her abdomen, her heart squeezing as she thought of the precious life she had nurtured there for seven months. Her baby might have been an accident but no way would she ever think of Emilia as a mistake. Oh, God, she shouldn't say her name, even in her head. It brought her so much pain, so much anguish to think of Emilia's tiny little crinkled face, her tiny wrinkled legs and arms. Little arms that would never reach up to her to hold…

Juliette turned to the task at hand, determined to keep control of her emotions. She was moving on, processing the grief the best way she could. Part of that process was getting through this weekend and handing over the divorce papers to Joe.

She was still deciding which dress to wear to the drinks and rehearsal and had her choices laid out on the bed. The very *big* bed with cloud-soft pillows and gazillion thread-count Egyptian cotton sheets. It was similar to the bed she and Joe had spent that one-night stand in, having off-the-Richter-scale sex.

A night she couldn't erase from her brain or her body.

She swung away from the bed and snatched up her make-up bag from her open suitcase. She needed armour and not just the cosmetic sort. She needed anger armour. Anger was her friend now. Her constant companion. It simmered and smouldered deep in her chest like lava inside a grumbling volcano. Anger was her way of punching through the blanket of despair that had almost smothered her after losing the baby seven months into the pregnancy. A despair so deep and thick it had taken every particle of light out of her life. Happiness was something other people experienced. Not her. Not now. Not ever. A part of her was missing.

Broken. Shattered.

And all the King's horses and all the King's men were not going to be able to put her back together again.

Juliette was on her way to the bathroom off the bedroom to do her make-up when she heard a brisk knock on the door of the suite. Thinking it was a waiter bringing the pot of tea she had ordered a short time ago, she called out, 'Come in. Just leave it on the table, thanks.' And went into the bathroom and closed the door.

She heard the suite door open and the rattle of a tea cup and saucer as presumably the tea trolley was wheeled in. Then the door closed again with a firm click.

Should she have given the waiter a tip? Probably not while she was dressed in a bathrobe, even if it was the most deliciously soft fabric she had ever worn against her skin. Not that she had too much spare cash lying around for tips. She refused on principle to touch the obscenely excessive amount of money Joe put in her bank account every month. Guilt money? No. Those were relief funds. *His* relief. He hadn't got there in time for the birth, but when he came in half an hour later she hadn't seen a father grieving for his stillborn baby girl. She had seen relief washing over his features. She had seen a man who was relieved his sham of a marriage now had an excuse to end.

Their baby had died and so had any hope of them remaining together.

They were a mismatch from the start. Hadn't she always known that on some level? He was suave and sophisticated and super intelligent. A self-made man who answered to no one but himself. His cool aloofness had drawn her like a moth to a dangerously hot flame.

And it had burned her in the end. Even after three months living together as man and wife, he had always kept an emotional distance, which had reinforced every fear she harboured about herself. It mirrored the emotional distance she'd experienced from her parents while she was growing up. The sense she wasn't enough for them—not clever enough, not pretty enough. She always felt they were holding back, keeping her to one side, *compartmentalising* her.

Juliette picked up her foundation bottle, took off the lid and released a sigh. Joe had done the same. He had travelled abroad for most of the time they were married, leaving her stranded at his villa in Positano. As far as she could see, he hadn't made any adjustments to his life by marrying her. He had expected her to do all the adjusting. She had moved countries, left friends and family behind and lived in a large villa with no one for company other than a rotating agency-recruited team of household staff. None of whom stayed long enough for her to learn their names, much less their language.

Juliette picked up her foundation brush and ran her fingers over the soft bristles. Of course, she was always there waiting for Joe when he returned, and she couldn't fault their physical relationship. It was as exciting and pleasurable as ever but it niggled at her that he seemed to spend more time away than he did at home. What did that say about her? Hadn't her parents done the same? So many trips abroad, lecture tours, sabbaticals, leaving her languishing and lonely in boarding school.

Juliette applied some foundation to cover the dark shadows that seemed to be permanently under her eyes. There was nothing she could do about the shadows in her eyes—they were also permanent. She put on some eye shadow and then a coat of mascara but she left the lip-gloss for after she had her cup of tea. She unwound the towel from around her head and shook her shoulder-length hair loose. Looking at herself in the mirror, there was no sign she had ever carried a baby to seven months' gestation. Her weight was back to normal…well, the new normal, because her appetite was hardly what anyone could call enthusiastic these days. Her hair had grown and thickened up again after a lot of it falling out due to hormones and deep emotional stress.

She looked like the same person…but she was not.

Juliette came out of the bathroom and walked into the lounge area and immediately saw the tea trolley next to the table by the window. She heaved a sigh of relief. A proper pot of tea with a silver tea strainer. No musty little tea bags and lukewarm water for this wedding party guest.

Big tick for you, Celeste.

Juliette could smell the bergamot notes of the high-quality Earl Grey in the air…and something else. Something that struck a chord in her memory and made a faint prickling sensation tiptoe across her scalp.

She swung around from the tea tray to see her estranged husband, Joe Allegranza, seated on the sofa behind her. A gasp rose but died in her blocked throat, her hand coming up to her chest to hold her leaping heart in place.

'What the hell are you doing in my room?' Her voice was a fishwife screech, her pulse a thud-stop-thud-stop hammering in her temples.

Joe rose from the sofa, his expression as unreadable as one of her father's astrophysicist research papers. 'It's apparently our room.' His deep baritone with its rich Italian accent made something in her stomach swoop.

Juliette frowned so hard a year's supply of Botox would have given up in defeat. Two years' supply. '*Our* room? What do you mean "our" room?'

'There's been a mistake with the booking.'

She narrowed her eyes to hairpin slits. 'A mistake?' She knew all about mistakes. Wasn't he her biggest one? She wrapped her arms around her middle, wishing she wasn't naked under the bathrobe. Wishing she had more armour against the tall, unknowable man in front of her. She needed heels the size of stilts to get anywhere near his six-foot-four height. She needed her head read for even noticing how gorgeous he looked, dressed in dark denim and a sky-blue open-necked shirt that highlighted his olive complexion.

She drank in his features, hating herself for being so weak. The determined jaw, the slash of aristocratic cheekbones, the ink-black eyebrows over hooded eyes the colour of centuries-old coal. The sensual mouth that had wreaked such havoc on her senses from the first time he had smiled at her, let alone kissed her.

But she was not going to think about his kisses. No. No. No.

Nor his earth-shattering, planet-dislodging love-making. No. No. No.

What she had to concentrate on was her anger. *Yes. Yes. Yes.*

'Juliette…' His voice had a note of authority that made her spine stiffen. 'The way I see it, we have two options here. We either go downstairs and make a fuss and thereby draw a lot of attention to ourselves, or we suck it up and leave things as they are.'

Juliette unwound her arms from around her middle and widened her eyes to the size of the saucer under her bone china teacup. 'Are you out of your mind? Why can't we go downstairs and tell Reception they've made a monumental error? But wait—isn't this the wedding planner's mistake? Celeste Petrakis was the one who organised the accommodation. She's being paid a ridiculous amount of money to make sure everything runs smoothly. This—' she pointed her finger between him and herself '—is not what I'd call running smoothly.'

A frown drew his eyebrows closer together and he looked down at one of his rolled-up sleeves and flicked off an imaginary piece of lint. The gold glint of his wedding ring on his finger stopped her heart for a moment. *He was still wearing his wedding ring?* Why? She had left hers at his villa in Positano, but hardly a day went past when her thumb didn't go in search of them on her finger like a child's tongue checking the vacant space left by a missing tooth.

His gaze came back to hers—dark, deep, mysterious. 'Celeste is Damon's cousin. This is her first job after being sick with blood cancer. It would upset God knows how many relatives of his if we make a big deal about this. Greeks are all about family. Besides, this is Lucy and Damon's wedding and I don't want to draw unnecessary attention to our situation.'

Juliette chewed at her lip, knowing there was a lot of truth in what he said. Wedding party guests were meant to be the supportive team, not the main event. And it made sense not to make a fuss, given Celeste's health issues. She admired the girl for getting back out there, and with such focus and dedication. Juliette hadn't been able to illustrate another children's book since she'd lost the baby. Her publisher and editors, and Lucy who co-wrote the books with her, had been incredibly patient but how long would that continue?

'But what if one of us stayed in another room? Another hotel? There are plenty of hotels further down the—'

'No.' There was an intractable tone in his voice. 'I've already spent the best part of an hour trying to find somewhere and drawn a blank. Lucy and Damon wanted the wedding party staying in one place. And there are no other rooms vacant here. So we will have to share.'

Juliette swung away and began pacing the floor, her arms wrapping around her body again. 'This is ridiculous. I can't believe this is happening. A weekend of sharing a suite with you? It's…it's unthinkable.'

'You've shared much more than a suite with me in the past. Our first night together was spent in a room very much like this one, was it not?' His coolly delivered statement triggered a firestorm in her body, sending waves of heat coursing through her flesh.

She didn't want to think about that night and how her body so wantonly, greedily responded to him. How her senses had reeled under the ministrations of his touch. How many women since their breakup had enjoyed the pressure of his mouth, the smooth, hard thrust of his body, the sensual glide of his hands? A hot spear of jealousy drove through her belly, sending pain so deep into her body she only just managed to suppress a gasp.

Juliette sent him a glare hot enough to blister the paint off the walls. 'How many women have you shared a hotel room with since we separated?'

Something moved across his features like a zephyr across a deep dark body of water. 'None. We are still technically married, *cara*.' His voice had a low and husky quality, his eyes holding hers in a lock that felt faintly disturbing. Disturbing because she found it almost impossible to look away.

She frowned, opening and closing her mouth in an effort to find something to say. *None?* No lovers since her? What did that mean?

She swallowed and finally found her voice. 'You've been celibate the whole time? For *fifteen* months?'

His crooked smile made something kick against her heart like a tiny invisible hoof. 'You find that surprising?'

'Well, yes, because you're…' Her words trailed off and her cheeks grew warm and she shifted her gaze.

'I'm what?'

Juliette rolled her lips together and glanced at him again. 'You're very good at sex and I thought you'd miss it and want to find someone else, many someone elses, after we broke up.'

'Have you found someone else?' A line of tension ran from the hinge of his jaw to his mouth.

Juliette gave a choked-off laugh. Her, sleep with someone else? The thought hadn't even crossed her mind. Which was kind of weird, come to think of it. Why hadn't it? She was supposed to be over him. Wouldn't being over him mean she would be interested in replacing him? But somehow the thought of it sickened her. 'No, of course not.'

Joe's eyes were unwavering on hers. 'But why not? You're very good at sex too. Don't you miss it?' His deep and husky tone was like dark rich treacle poured over gravel.

It wasn't just her cheeks that were hot—her whole body was on fire. Flickering flames of reawakened lust smouldering in each of her erogenous zones. Erogenous zones that reacted to his presence as if finely tuned to his body's radar. Her body recognised him in a thousand and one ways. Even his voice had the power to melt her bones. Her flesh remembered his touch as if it were imprinted in every pore of her skin. Hunger for his touch was a background beat in her blood but every time his gaze met hers it sent her pulse rate soaring.

And she had a feeling he damn well knew it.

Juliette smoothed her suddenly damp palms down the front of her bathrobe, turning away so her back was to him. 'This is exactly why I don't want to share a room with you this weekend.'

'Because you still want me.' He didn't say it as a question but as a statement written in stone.

Juliette turned and faced him, anger rising in her like a pressure cooker about to explode. Her body trembled, her blood threatening to burst out of her veins. Should she mention the divorce papers burning a hole in her tote bag? The thought crossed her mind but then she dismissed it. She planned to hand them to him once Lucy and Damon left on Sunday morning for their yachting honeymoon. It would spoil the happy couple's celebrations if the hideous D word was mentioned.

But Joe had mentioned the other dangerous D word. Desire.

'You think I can't resist you?' Her voice shook with the effort of containing her temper.

His eyes went to her mouth as if he were recalling how she had shamelessly, brazenly pleasured him in the past. His gaze came back to hers and something deep and low in her belly rolled over. 'I don't want to fight with you, *cara*.'

'What *do* you want to do then?' Juliette should never have asked such a loaded question, for she saw the answer in the dark gleam of his chocolate-brown eyes.

Joe closed the distance between them in a number of slowly measured strides but she didn't move away. She couldn't seem to get her legs to work, couldn't get her willpower back on duty, couldn't think of a single reason why she shouldn't just stand there and enjoy the exquisite anticipation of him being close enough for her to touch.

He lifted his hand to her face and skated his index finger down the curve of her cheek from just below her ear to the bottom of her chin. It was the lightest touch, barely there, but every cell in her body jolted awake like a dead heart under defibrillator paddles. Every drop of blood in her veins put on their running shoes. Every atom of her willpower dissolved like an aspirin in water. She could smell the lime notes of his aftershave cologne. She could see the sexy shadow of his regrowth peppered along his chiselled jaw and she had to curl her hands into fists to stop from touching it. She could see the lines and contours of his sculptured mouth, could remember how it felt crushed to her own.

Oh, dear God, his mouth was her kryptonite.

'Take a wild guess what I want to do.' His voice was rough, his eyes hooded, the air suddenly charged with erotic possibilities.

Juliette could feel her body swaying towards him as if someone was gently but inexorably pushing her from behind. Her hands were no longer balled into fists by her sides but planted on the hard wall of his chest, her lower body pulsing with lust-heated blood.

His hands settled on her hips, the warmth of his broad fingers seeping into her flesh with the potency of a powerful drug. His black-as-night gaze went to her mouth and she couldn't stop from moistening her lips with the darting tip of her tongue.

He drew in a sharp breath as if her action had triggered something in him, something feral, something primal. He brought her even closer, flush against his pelvis, and her traitorously needy body met the hard jut of his.

His mouth came down to within millimetres of hers, his eyes sexily hooded. 'This was never the problem between us, was it, *cara*?' His warm hint of mint breath caressed her lips and her willpower threw its hands up in defeat and walked off the job.

Juliette's heart was beating so fast she thought she was having some sort of medical event. 'Don't do this, Joe…' Her voice didn't come out with anywhere near the stridency she'd intended.

He nudged her nose with his—a gentle bump of flesh meeting flesh that sent a wave of longing through her body. 'What am I doing, hmm?' His lips touched the side of her mouth, not a kiss but so close to it her lips tingled all over. He brushed her cheek with his mouth and the graze of his stubble made something hot and liquid spill deep and low in her core.

Juliette's lips parted, her lashes lowered, her mouth moved closer to his but then a stop sign came up in her head. What was she doing? Practically begging him to kiss her as if she was some love-struck teenager experiencing her first crush? She drew in a sharp breath and stepped back, glaring at him.

'What the hell do you think you're doing?' Nothing like a bit of projection to take the focus off her own weakness.

His cool composure was an added insult to the tumultuous emotions coursing through her body. 'I would only have kissed you if you'd wanted it. And you did, didn't you, *tesoro*?'

Juliette wanted to slap his face. She wanted to claw her fingernails down his cheeks. She wanted to kick him in the shins until his bones shattered. But instead her eyes filled with stinging tears, her chest feeling as if it were being squeezed in a studded vice. 'I h-hate you.' Her voice cracked over a lump clogging her throat. 'Do you have any idea how much?'

'Maybe that's a good thing.' His expression went back to his signature masklike state. Unreadable. Unreachable. Invincible.

Why wasn't she shrugging off his hold? Why wasn't she putting distance between their bodies? Why was she feeling as if this was where she belonged—in the warm protective shelter of his arms? Juliette slowly eased back to look up at his face, her emotions so ambushed she couldn't find her anger. Where was her anger? She *needed* her anger. She couldn't survive without it pounding through her blood. She blinked back the tears, determined not to cry in front of him.

'I don't know how to handle this…situation…' She swallowed and aimed her gaze at his shirt collar. 'I don't want to ruin Lucy and Damon's wedding but sharing this suite with you is…' She bit her lip, unable to put her fears into words. Unwilling to voice them out loud, even to herself.

Joe inched up her chin with his finger, meshing his gaze with hers. 'What if I promise not to kiss you. That will reassure you, *sì*?'

No! I want you to kiss me.

Juliette was shocked at herself. Shocked and shamed by her unruly desires. She stepped out of his hold and wrapped her arms around her body before she was tempted to betray herself any further.

'Okay. That's sounds like a sensible plan. Let's decide on some ground rules.' She was proud of the evenness of her tone. Proud she had got her willpower back into line. 'No kissing. No touching.'

Joe gave a slow nod. 'I'm fine with that.' He walked over to the sofa and sat down, hooking one ankle over his muscular thigh.

He was fine with that?

Everything that was female in Juliette was perversely offended by his easy acceptance of her rules. Surely he could have put up a little bit of resistance? But maybe he had someone else he wanted to kiss and touch and make love to now. Maybe he was tired of being celibate and was ready to move on with his life. It had been fifteen months after all. It was a long time for a man in his sexual prime to be without a lover. A tight pain gripped her in her chest and travelled down to tie tight knots in her stomach. Cruel twisting knots that made it hard for her to breathe. If she didn't pull herself into line, her grey-blue eyes would turn green. She had no right to be jealous. She had left their marriage. She had divorce papers in her bag, for pity's sake.

'Good.' Juliette's tone was so clipped it could have snipped through tin. 'But of course, that leaves the tricky problem of what to say to Lucy and Damon when they realise we're sharing a suite.' She walked over to the bar fridge and took out a bottle of water, unscrewing the cap and pouring it into a glass. She picked up the glass and turned to face him. 'Any brilliant suggestions?'

Joe's expression was still inscrutable but she could sense an inner guardedness. His posture was almost too casual, too relaxed, too calm and collected. 'We could say we're trying for a reconciliation.'

Juliette took a sip of water before she gave in to the temptation to throw it in his face. She put the glass down on the counter with a clunk. 'A reconciliation? For a marriage that shouldn't have come about in the first place?'

A knot of tension appeared beside his mouth, his eyes locked on hers in an unblinking hold. 'I wasn't the one who left our marriage.'

Juliette stalked over to the windows overlooking the white crescent of the sand and the turquoise water of the beach below. She took a shuddering breath. 'No, because you weren't fully in it in the first place.'

The silence was so long it was as if time had come to a standstill.

She heard the rustle of his clothes as he rose from the sofa. Counted his footsteps as he approached her but she didn't turn around. He came to stand beside her, his gaze focused like hers on the beach below.

After a long moment, he turned his head to look at her, the line of his mouth bitter. 'If you were to be truthful, Juliette, you weren't fully in it either. You were still getting over your ex. That's why we hooked up in the first place, because you couldn't bear to spend the night he got married to one of your so-called friends, on your own.'

Juliette wished she could deny it but every word he said was true. She had been shattered by Harvey's betrayal. They had been dating since their teens. His affair with Clara had been going on for months and Juliette hadn't had a clue. The night she'd thought Harvey was going to propose to her, he'd told her he was leaving her. Harvey Atkinson-Lloyd, her parents' choice of the perfect son-in-law for their only daughter. The daughter who, unlike their high-achieving sons Mark and Jonathon, had failed to do anything much else to win their approval.

Juliette ground down on her molars, torn between anger at Joe for pointing out her stupidity and anger at herself for making a bad situation worse by falling into bed with him that night.

She turned to face him, chin high, eyes blazing. 'So, what's your excuse for hooking up with me that night? Or do you regularly sleep with perfect strangers when you're working in London?'

An emotion flickered across his face like an interruption in a transmission. A pause. A regroup. A reset. 'It was the anniversary of my mother's death.' His tone was flat, almost toneless, but there was a stray note of sadness under the surface.

Juliette looked at him blankly. 'But I don't understand… I thought you told me your mother had emigrated to Australia. Wasn't that the reason she wasn't able to come to our wedding?'

'She's my stepmother. Both of my parents are dead.'

Had she misheard him back when they were together? She tried to think back to the conversation but couldn't recall it in any detail. She knew his father had died a few years back but he had barely mentioned his mother. She'd got the sense it was a no-go area for him, so she hadn't delved any further.

They hadn't done much talking about each other's family backgrounds, mostly because he was away such a lot. Their brief passionate reunions when he came home between trips were physical catch-ups, not emotional ones. She had wanted more than physical intimacy but hadn't known how to reach him. Every attempt to get closer to him had failed, with him leaving for yet another work commitment. It was as if he sensed her need for emotional connection and found it deeply threatening. But, to be fair, she too had been pretty sketchy with her own issues to do with her background, not wanting him to know how out of place she felt in her academically brilliant family.

'I'm sorry…' she said, frowning. 'I mustn't have heard you correctly when you told me that when we were living together.'

His lips moved in a grimace-like smile that didn't involve his eyes. 'My father remarried when I was a child. But when he died ten years ago, my stepmother and two half-siblings emigrated to Melbourne, where she has relatives.'

'Do you have much contact with them? Phone? Email? Birthdays—that sort of thing?'

'I do what is required.'

Juliette was starting to realise she didn't know very much about the man she had married in such haste. Why hadn't she tried a little harder to get him to open up? Her shock pregnancy had thrown her into a tailspin. And when she'd finally worked up the courage to call him and tell him, he had flown straight to her flat in London with a wedding proposal. A proposal she had felt compelled to accept in order to mitigate some of the shame she had caused her parents in getting herself 'knocked up' after a one-night stand.

She looked at him again, wondering how she could have been so physically close to someone without knowing anything about him. 'How old were you when your mother died?'

Joe glanced at his watch and muttered a soft curse. 'Isn't there a drinks thing soon?'

'Shoot.' Juliette gave a much milder version of his curse. 'I'm not dressed and I haven't done my hair.'

He picked up a tendril of her mid-brown hair, trailing it gently through his fingers. 'It looks beautiful the way it is.' The pitch of his voice lowered and his eyes were a bottomless black.

Juliette swallowed and tried hard not to look at his mouth. 'Ahem. You're touching me. Remember the rules?'

He released her hair and stepped back from her with a mercurial smile. 'How could I forget?'

CHAPTER THREE

JOE DROVE A hand through his own hair once Juliette had retreated to the bathroom. No touching. No kissing. Sure, he could abide by the rules. But he hadn't realised it would be as difficult as this. It had been hard enough trying to erase the memory of her touch when he was living thousands of kilometres away. But sharing a suite with her this weekend was going to test his resolve in ways he wasn't prepared for.

He hadn't expected the chemistry to still be there. He hadn't expected the hot, tight ache of desire to grip him so brutally. He hadn't expected to feel anything other than guilt about how things had panned out between them. The guilt was still there, spreading cruel tentacles around his intestines like a poisonous strangling vine. Tentacles that crawled up into his chest and wrapped around his heart and squeezed, squeezed, squeezed like a savage fist.

Truth was, he'd been almost relieved when she hadn't answered his texts and emails. It meant he didn't have to face the train wreck he'd caused. The further along her pregnancy went, the longer he'd stayed away on business. Business others under his employ could have easily seen to. But no, he had wanted—*needed*—to throw himself into the distraction of work, because watching Juliette growing with his child had secretly terrified him. What if she died during childbirth? What if, like his mother, she had a complication and no one could save her?

Had he caused the loss of their baby by not being there? Had his absence caused Juliette unnecessary stress? Hindsight was all very well, but he had thought he was doing the right thing at the time. They weren't in a love relationship. They had married for the sake of the baby and Juliette had seemed okay with that arrangement. Providing stability and security had been his focus.

His focus since their separation had been channelling his efforts into fundraising for a stillbirth research foundation. It had been his way of dealing with his own grief. He considered it far more productive than falling into a heap like his father had done. Joe wanted the money raised to help others, to prevent others from experiencing the devastation of losing a child at birth. Research was expensive and counselling services were always seriously underfunded. But that was changing as a result of his efforts. His own regular large donations along with the fundraising programme he had orchestrated would hopefully reduce the number of stillbirths across the globe.

Joe changed into his fresh clothes and unpacked the rest from his small travel bag and hung them in the wardrobe next to hers. He touched the silk sleeve of one of her tops, lifting it to his nose to smell the lingering scent of her signature perfume. For months after she'd left, he couldn't go into the bedroom they had shared. He'd got his housekeeper to move his things into another room. A room without memories and triggers.

He slid the door closed on the wardrobe, wishing he could lock away his desire as easily. He'd wanted to kiss her. No doubt about that. His lips still burned with the need to feel the soft press of hers. Joe knew he was wrong for Juliette. He was relationship poison. He couldn't seem to help destroying those he cared about. But seeing her again made him realise there was unfinished business between them. Was that why he hadn't made more of a fuss about the booking mix-up? Yes, he'd been concerned about upsetting Damon's young cousin, Celeste, but he might have found some way to resolve the situation even if he had to stay on the other side of the island. And, truth be told, he could have refused the invitation to be Damon's best man in the first place and no one would have blamed him.

But he hadn't because on some level, be it conscious or subconscious, he wanted to be here for the weekend on Corfu with Juliette. On neutral ground. Somewhere where there were no triggers and tripwires to the heartbreak of their past. It suited him to be in close proximity to her, to reassure himself he hadn't totally destroyed her as well as their relationship.

A relationship that might have had a better chance if their baby had lived.

A tight ache spread through his chest when he thought of that lifeless little body. His baby girl with her little wizened pixie face, her tiny feet and hands, her permanently closed eyes.

Was there some sort of curse surrounding him and birth? His own birth had brought about his mother's death. His birthday—the day in the year he dreaded more than any other—was the anniversary of his mother's death. The very same day he had met Juliette in that London bar that had changed both their lives for ever.

The bathroom door opened and Juliette came out with her hair fashioned in a stylish knot on top of her head. 'Bathroom's all yours,' she said, avoiding his gaze.

Joe swept his gaze over her candy-pink calf-length dress with its waist cinched in with a patent leather belt and her matching high heels that showcased her slender ankles. He had never met anyone who could look so effortlessly elegant. Whether she was wearing track pants and a sweatshirt or designer wear, she always took his breath away. And when she was naked he forgot to breathe at all. 'You look stunning.'

Her creamy cheeks pooled with colour. 'Thank you.' Her gaze flicked away from his and she moved past him to get to the wardrobe. 'I'll just get my evening purse.'

Joe had to clench his hands into fists to stop himself touching her. The suite wasn't large enough to keep a safe distance. It needed to be the size of a small nation for that. The suite was mostly open-plan with a king-sized bed dominating the bedroom area, with no door between that and the lounge area. No more than a metre or two from the bed was a sofa and single armchair and coffee table and there were minibar facilities near the windows to maximise the view over Barbati Beach. The en suite bathroom was luxuriously appointed but was hardly what anyone would call spacious. For a honeymoon, it would be ideal.

But they weren't on a honeymoon.

Juliette opened the wardrobe and took her purse from one of the shelf compartments. He watched as her eyes went to his clothes hanging next to hers. Saw her teeth sink into her bottom lip and a small frown pull at her forehead.

'Is that against the rules?' Joe asked, leaning against the wall near her. 'To have our clothes touching?'

She stiffened and then shut the wardrobe with a little more force than was necessary. Her cheeks were a fiery red, her grey-blue eyes reminding him of a storm-tossed sea. 'We wouldn't need rules if you would stop looking at me like that.'

'How am I looking at you?'

She pursed her lips and put her chin up at a haughty height. 'Like you want to touch me.'

'I do want to touch you but the rules are the rules.' Joe wanted to touch her so badly it was all he could do to keep his hands under control.

She swallowed and her blush deepened. She dropped her evening purse on the bed and adjusted the belt around her dress. 'I should never have slept with you in the first place. It was totally out of character for me to do something like that.'

'I know it was,' Joe said, pushing himself away from the wall to approach her. 'That's why that night was so memorable.'

She frowned. 'Are you saying...*you* found it special?'

He gave a crooked smile and, before he could stop himself,

he stroked a lazy finger down the curve of her cheek. 'I'd never met someone like you before.'

'Because I wasn't madly in love with you like most women are?' Her eyes glittered with sparks of cynicism.

He traced the outline of her lush mouth, knowing he was breaking the rules but unable to resist the temptation. 'You weren't interested in my money or my status. You just wanted to be distracted from a bad day, just like I wanted to be.'

Her tongue swept over her lips and she gave another audible swallow. 'Joe, we're going to be late for the drinks thing.'

Right now, Joe didn't care if they never made it to their friends' wedding. Being with Juliette—breathing in her scent, feeling the softness of her lips under his fingertip—made his blood pound with longing. A slow drag began pulling at his groin—a primal need he had shut down, ignored, blocked out with work, pulsed to vibrant and undeniable life. He slid his hand to the nape of her neck, meshing his gaze with hers. 'Why aren't you telling me to stop touching you?'

She gave a shuddery breath and her gaze dipped to his mouth. 'I—I don't know...' Her voice was whisper-soft.

He brought up her chin with his finger and locked her gaze with his. 'I'll tell you why, *cara*. Because deep down you want to be touched by me. You think a bunch of silly rules is going to damp down the explosive chemistry we still share?' It certainly wasn't damping down his. Not one little bit. He could feel the electric energy passing between them like a hot fizzing current. He could see it reflected in her eyes—the flicker of her eyelashes, the dart of her gaze to his mouth, the quick sweep of her tongue over her lips.

But then her gaze hardened and she placed her hand around his wrist and pulled it away from her face, shooting him a laser-like glare. 'There is no chemistry. I don't feel a thing where you're concerned. Not a damn thing.'

He captured her hand and tugged her close against his body. 'Want to put that to the test? One kiss. Let's see what happens.'

'Don't be ridiculous.' Her expression was scathing but her tone contained a trace of something else. Something that sounded very much like a dare.

Oh, he dared all right.

Joe breathed in the achingly familiar scent of her, brought his mouth as close to hers as he could without actually touching her lips. 'Just one little kiss.'

'You think I won't be able to help myself, like the night we met? But I can and I will.'

'Prove it.'

Her eyes went to his mouth. 'I don't need to prove anything to you.'

'Prove it to yourself then.'

She wavered for a moment, her eyes going to his mouth and back to his eyes. Then her eyes glazed over with chilly determination. 'Okay. I'll show you how immune I am to you.' She rose on tiptoe and planted a brief chaste kiss on his lips. She lowered her heels back to the floor and gave him an arch look. 'See? No fireworks.'

Joe gave a soft chuckle and released her. 'Probably just as well. I don't think anyone, least of all Damon and Lucy, are going to believe we've reconciled.'

A frown pulled at her brow. 'You're not going to…?' She clamped her mouth shut and turned away to reach for her purse on the bed. 'So, what are we going to tell them?' Her back was turned towards him, her hands fiddling with the clasp on her purse but he could see the tension in her slim back and shoulders as if she was bracing herself for his answer.

'We'll tell them the truth.'

She swung back round to face him, her expression wary. 'The truth?'

'That we're mature adults who are in the process of an amicable separation. Sharing a room for a couple of nights will not be a problem for us.'

Her brows rose. 'Amicable? Not a problem? Funny, but I don't see it quite that way.'

'Think about it, Juliette,' Joe said. 'We could go out there and pretend to be back together and then you'd have to allow me to touch you. Otherwise no one is going to buy it. I'd have to hold your hand, slip my arm around your waist, kiss you. You'd have to lie to your best friend. Is that what you want?'

Her small neat chin came up and her grey-blue eyes pulsated with anger. 'I want this weekend to be over. That's what I want.'

'Yeah, well, I want that too.'

Then maybe he could move on with his life.

CHAPTER FOUR

THE WELCOME DRINKS party was on the terrace in front of the infinity pool that overlooked the beach. The area was decorated with lanterns with golden flickering candles inside and honeysuckle and orange blossom scented the evening air. A champagne tower was on a table festooned with ribbons and posies of flowers on each corner. Two waiters dressed in white shirts, black trousers and black bowties were on standby to hand around a delicious-looking array of finger food. A string quartet was playing at one end of the terrace with a backdrop of cascading scarlet bougainvillea. There was a large sandwich board framed by pink and white flowers with a large love heart in the centre with Lucy and Damon's names written in beautiful calligraphy. Juliette had never seen such a romantic setting and tried not to compare it to her own wedding reception.

There certainly hadn't been any sandwich boards with love hearts on them.

Celeste Petrakis, the wedding planner, a slim young woman in her early twenties with short spiky black hair, was carrying a tablet in her hand and came dashing over to Juliette and Joe as soon as they came out to the terrace.

'Oh, my God, I'm so sorry but I think I've messed up your booking,' Celeste said. 'I only put down one J Allegranza on my list. I don't know how I got that wrong. I know Damon told me you guys were separated but I must have forgotten. Blame it on my chemo brain or something. I'm so embarrassed I want to die.' She clamped a hand over her mouth, her big brown eyes going wide as if she was worried she was going to get struck by lightning by a vengeful God. 'Oops. Didn't mean that. I've spent the last two years trying *not* to do that. But, seriously, I'm awfully embarrassed all the same.'

Joe stood close to Juliette but didn't touch her. 'It's fine, Celeste. We have no problem sharing a room.'

Juliette forced her lips into the semblance of a smile. 'Yes, indeed. So please don't worry, Celeste. You've done a brilliant job of organising everything. I've never seen such a lovely setting for a wedding. It looks like it's going to be an amazing weekend for Lucy and Damon.'

Celeste clasped a hand to her heart, her eyes dewy with emotion. 'Does that mean…? Oh, how romantic! I'm so happy for you both. We'll have a special toast for you guys later toni—'

'No.' Joe's tone was as blunt as a sledgehammer on a slice of sponge cake. 'We're not back together.'

Celeste's face fell and she bit down on her lip. 'Oh…sorry, I misunderstood. Do you want me to organise a fold-out bed for you? I mean, you might not want to share—'

'That would be wonderful, if there's one available,' Juliette said, trying to ignore the magnetic heat of Joe's body within touching distance of hers. If she moved even a fraction of a millimetre her arm would brush against him. It was almost impossible to control the urge to do so.

Touch him. Touch him. Touch him.

The chant was trying to keep up with her racing pulse.

'I'll see what I can do,' Celeste said, glancing between Joe and Juliette as if she couldn't quite work them out. 'I can only apologise again for this stuff-up. I would hate for you to be inconvenienced by my mishandling of—'

'Don't stress,' Joe said, moving slightly, his arm brushing

against the bare skin of Juliette's, sending a shivery sensation through her flesh. 'It's not a problem.'

Juliette moved half a step away and gave the wedding planner a rictus smile. 'We don't want to draw attention away from Lucy and Damon. It's their special weekend, not ours.'

'Thank you for being so amazingly good about it.' Celeste gave them a finger wave and dashed away to greet some other guests coming out to the terrace.

Juliette glanced up at Joe. 'I need to speak to Lucy. She'll stress if she thinks I'm not okay about this. It'll ruin her wedding day for her if she's worrying about me—'

'Then pretend to be okay. It's not that hard.'

She glowered at him. 'Easy for you to say, Mr Show No Emotion.'

Joe shrugged and turned to look at the guests coming out to the terrace. 'It doesn't mean I don't have them.' The bottom register of his voice throbbed with something she had never heard in it before.

Juliette frowned and chewed on the inside of her lip. He was always so aloof and distant. He was like a steep and rocky island she continually circled, looking for a place to anchor.

His eyes met hers in a lock that made the backs of her knees shiver. 'This weekend could be a blessing in disguise. It could be a chance to sort out some of our issues. Not in the presence of other people, but while we're alone.'

While we're alone.

Juliette had to do everything in her power *not* to be alone with him. The only time she wanted to be alone with him was to hand him those hot-off-the-press divorce papers. 'I don't think our issues are the type that can get sorted out over a weekend, Joe. Not even over a lifetime.'

'Maybe, but at least we should try. I have some regret over how I handled our relationship.'

He had regret? She didn't want to hear about his supposed regret. She had regrets in their multitudes. She had known he had only married her out of duty and she had married him anyway. He had been there for her on his terms, not hers. It had been a fly-in, fly-out marriage that was doomed from the start. Being with him now reminded her of how stupid she had been.

She'd foolishly believed their baby would bond them—would help him fall in love with her as well as their child. She had *wanted* him to love her. Wasn't that every girl's dream? If he had loved her then it would have made her feel better about how they had come together in the first place. It would absolve some of her nagging guilt about her own feelings. She had fallen in lust with him. Simple and bald and blatant as that. Lust was what she still felt for him and it had to stop.

She had to stop fuelling the fire that blazed inside her.

Juliette sent him an icy look. 'There isn't anything you could say to me that would make me want to resume our relationship. Nothing. So don't get any funny ideas that this weekend is going to magically fix what wasn't right in the first place.'

A waiter approached with a tray of drinks and Juliette took a glass of champagne. She was acutely conscious of Joe standing beside her, his arm brushing hers as he reached for a drink sending another hot shiver coursing through her body. Nerves and other emotions she didn't want to think about had her halfway through her drink before Joe had even taken a sip.

'Did you hear me say I want us to get back together?' There was a bite in his tone that nipped at her feminine pride. His eyes were espresso coffee dark and glittering with barely suppressed anger. 'That's the last thing I want.'

Juliette took another sip of champagne and then looked down at the remaining bubbles in her glass. 'Good to know.' It was good, wasn't it? He wanted out. She wanted out. Why then was her chest feeling as if something heavy was pressing all the air out of her lungs? She rapid blinked to clear her suddenly blurry vision, her throat so tight it felt as if a champagne cork was stuck halfway down.

Joe released a long slow breath and moved closer again, resting his hand on the top of her shoulder. The anger had gone from his gaze, to be replaced by a brooding frown. 'I apologise for being blunt but what's done is done and can't be undone.'

Juliette summoned her pride back on duty and brushed off his hand as if it was soiling her dress. 'I thought we agreed not to touch?' Her tone was sharp, her glare cutting.

'Please welcome the bride and groom.' Celeste's cheery voice rang out and the string quartet accompanied Lucy and Damon as they came out onto the terrace to cheers and applause from the assembled guests.

The press of the other guests gathering for a better view brought Joe to stand shoulder to shoulder with Juliette to make more room. Juliette painted a smile on her lips while her elbow landed a surreptitious jab in his ribs. He gave a low grunt that sounded far sexier than she had bargained for and a wave of heat rose over her skin. The steel band of his arm came around her and his hand glided down to her hip in a hold that was blatantly possessive. She glanced at his left hand resting on her hip and saw the gold glint of his wedding ring. The ring that claimed her as his. She was conscious of every point of contact as if her body had been finely programmed to recognise his touch.

She could have been blindfolded and still known it was him.

Lucy and Damon approached arm in arm and with wide smiles. An aura of happiness surrounded them and Juliette wished some of it could brush off on her. Why couldn't she have found happy-ever-after love?

'Oh my gosh, I can't believe my eyes,' Lucy said, grabbing Juliette in a bone-crushing hug that almost spilt the rest of her champagne. 'What's going on? Don't tell me you two are—?'

'No.' Joe's strident tone served to underline the word and land another free kick to Juliette's self-esteem. His arm dropped from around her waist and he added, 'There was a mix-up with the accommodation and we're trying to make it easy on Celeste, who double booked the room.'

'Oh, well, then…' Lucy's eyes began to twinkle as brightly

as the princess diamond ring on her finger. 'I hope it won't be *too* much of a problem for you sharing?' There was a wink-wink-say-no-more quality to her tone.

'No problem at all.' Juliette kept her features under tight control but she couldn't control the creep of warm colour she could feel pooling in her cheeks. Or the lingering hot tingle on her hip where Joe's hand had rested just moments before.

Damon grinned and grasped Joe's hand. 'Who knows what a weekend on Corfu will do, eh? Great to have you both here to share our special day with us.'

'I wouldn't have missed it for the world,' Joe said with an enigmatic smile.

After a moment or two, Lucy and Damon moved on to greet other guests, and Juliette lifted her glass to her lips and drained it. 'No problem sharing a room. Who knew what a consummate liar I could be? Go me.'

Joe's expression was shadowed by a contemplative frown. 'As I said, we could use this weekend to help both of us move forward.'

She raised her brows, sending him a scathing look. 'And how do you propose we do that? Hmm? Kiss and make up? Thanks, but no thanks.'

He took her empty glass off her and placed it on the stone balustrade nearby. 'It would be a start, don't you think?' His darkened gaze dipped to her mouth as if he were recalling every kiss they had ever exchanged.

Juliette's lips tingled and she fought not to lick her lips to draw any more of his attention to them. She sent him an arch look. 'That's how we got into this mess, if you remember. You kissed me.'

One side of his mouth came up in a sardonic half-smile. 'I seem to recall you made the first move.'

She ground her teeth so hard she was worried they would turn to powder on the spot. Did he have to remind her how forward and brazen she had been that night? So reckless and out of character. She shot him a pointed glare. 'You didn't have to take me up on it.'

'You seriously overestimate my willpower, *cara*.'

Juliette's chin came up. 'You'd better make sure it's in better shape this time around.'

One of his ink-black brows lifted. 'For when you beg me to take you to bed, you mean?'

Her hands clenched into tight balls by her sides in case she was tempted to slap him. 'Not going to happen.' She injected as much confidence in her tone as she could.

His lazy smile made the base of her spine fizz and tingle. He picked up one of her fists and gently prised open her fingers, his thumb stroking the middle of her palm in a way that was unmistakably sexual. His gaze held hers in a mesmerising lock no amount of willpower to resist could ever have matched. 'You shouldn't be ashamed of our chemistry.' The pitch of his voice lowered to a knee-weakening burr.

Juliette pulled her hand out of his, rubbing at it as if he had burned her. 'I'm not ashamed. I'm disgusted. And for God's sake, stop touching me.'

His smile didn't fade but a line of tension appeared next to his mouth and his eyes hardened. 'Careful, *cara*. We're in public, remember? Sheath those pretty claws until we're alone. Then you can rake them down my back to your heart's desire.'

Juliette had to blink away the scorching-hot images his words evoked. Her body was on fire, swamped with memories of his masterful lovemaking. It had taken her almost two years to be able to reach an orgasm with her ex and even then it was hit and miss thereafter. She had practically orgasmed on the spot the moment Joe kissed her the first time. He never took his pleasure before he satisfied her. He knew her body better than she knew it herself. She had explored every inch of his and, by doing so, had found a passionate and adventurous streak in her personality she hadn't known existed. Standing within touching distance now made her body miss him all the more. She could feel a magnetic pull towards him as if an invisible current of energy was calling her back to base.

To distract herself, she took another glass of champagne off a passing waiter. She figured it was better to keep her hands and mouth otherwise occupied.

'Do you know any of the other wedding party guests?' Joe asked after a long moment.

Juliette crossed her arms and cupped one hand under her elbow, holding her champagne glass in the other hand. 'Only Lucy. And Damon, of course. I haven't met any of the four other bridesmaids before because they're friends Lucy made since moving to Greece. What about you?'

'I'd heard about his cousin Celeste but not met her before today. But I've met two of the bridesmaids once or twice before.' He took a measured sip of his drink, lowering his glass from his mouth to glance at the view over the terrace.

A dagger of jealousy jabbed her in the gut. 'Oh, really?' Juliette made sure her tone was just mildly interested when in fact she wanted to know dates, times, places and whether he had been to bed with either of them. How could any woman resist him? She certainly hadn't been able to.

Joe turned to look at her with an unreadable expression. 'It's kind of ironic how Damon and Lucy met through us, isn't it?'

'Ironic in what way?'

He gave a one-shoulder shrug and looked down at the contents of his glass, twirling it to set the bubbles spinning. 'They seem pretty happy together. Whether or not it lasts is another thing.'

'Do you have to be so cynical? They're in love. Anyone can see that. That's what we were lacking. We married for all the wrong reasons.'

He didn't respond and instead tipped his glass back and drained it. She couldn't take her eyes off the strong tanned column of his throat and the peppery regrowth on his jaw that, in spite of a recent shave, was already vigorously reappearing.

How many times had she felt his stubble against her soft skin? On her face, on her belly, between her thighs…

Juliette suppressed a shudder and turned to look at the other guests milling about for the next part of the entertainment the wedding planner had organised. Which bridesmaids had Joe met before? The blonde one? The sleek raven-haired one? The one with the big boobs and legs that went on for ever?

Joe held out his hand for her empty glass. 'Would you like something soft this time? Orange juice? Mineral water?'

Juliette handed the glass to him, being extra careful not to touch his fingers. 'Are you hinting I might drink to excess and make a fool of myself?'

He drew in a breath and pressed his lips into a flat line before releasing it. 'Look, I know the situation this weekend is hard on you. It's the first time we've seen each other face to face since you left.' His hands were thrust in his trouser pockets, his broad shoulders rolled forward. 'I would have preferred meeting with you in London but you didn't respond to any of my attempts to contact you.'

Juliette had ignored his texts and emails for months. She had even blocked his number on her phone. It had been her way of punishing him for not being there when she'd needed him the most. But in a way she had punished herself because she had made herself completely isolated. Her friends and family had tried to support her but, a few months in, they were all suffering compassion fatigue. Even Lucy, with the distraction of her wedding preparations, hadn't been as available to her, especially since Juliette hadn't felt up to illustrating the books they wrote together since the loss of Emilia. She'd desperately needed to be with someone who knew and understood what she was going through—the grief, the pain, the loss. She looked down at the flagstones at her feet rather than meet his gaze. 'I wasn't ready. I found it too…triggering.'

He moved closer to her and lightly touched the back of her hand with one of his fingers. 'That's completely understandable.' His voice was gentle as a caress and her hand tingled as if it had been zapped by a live current.

Juliette brought her gaze up to meet his. 'Do you think about her?'

His eyes flickered as if he was suffering a deep internal pain and only just managing to control it. 'All the time. That's why I've regularly donated to and been fundraising for a stillbirth research foundation for the last few months. I wanted to do something positive to help others in our situation. If you'd happened to read any emails from me, you would have known about it. I donated money on behalf of both of us.'

A stillbirth research foundation? Juliette's heart contracted. *He had been fundraising for a stillbirth foundation?*

The anger she wore like armour dropped away like a sloughed skin, leaving her feeling stripped of her defences. Defences she needed to keep her from getting hurt all over again. She hadn't read any of his emails for the last fifteen months. She had marked them as spam and felt immensely satisfied doing it.

Knowing now he was doing something for others was all very well, but what about helping her through the worst time of her life? She had stood by their baby's grave alone. Time and time again, she had grieved in isolation. 'But I don't get it. You tell me you've donated money and, knowing you, it would be a significant amount, but you haven't once visited her grave since the funeral.'

His mouth went into a tight line. 'Graveyards aren't my thing. I prefer to pay my respects in other ways.'

Every week when Juliette visited her baby's grave, she hoped to see flowers or a card or toy left by Joe. But there was nothing. She couldn't understand it and nor could she forgive it, in spite of his generosity to others. He came to London for work regularly—how hard would it have been to drop by the cemetery and hand-deliver flowers or a soft toy? Or didn't he want to be reminded of their baby and their broken marriage?

'Were you keeping away in case you ran into me?' She couldn't tone down the accusing note in her voice.

He looked down at her with an unreadable expression. His features could have been carved in stone. 'How often do you go?'

'Every week.'

'Does it help your grieving process?'

Juliette blew out a frustrated breath. 'Nothing helps with that. But at least I feel I'm not ignoring her.'

'Is that what you think I'm doing?'

She raised her chin to a combative height. 'Aren't you?'

He drew in another sharp breath and turned again to look at the view. His posture was stiff and tight as if invisible steel cables were holding him upright. 'There's no right way to grieve, Juliette. What works for one might not work for someone else.' He spoke through gritted teeth, his hands thrust back in his trouser pockets.

'And is your grieving process working?'

He turned his head to look at her with a grim expression. 'What do you think?'

Juliette shifted her mouth from side to side and looked away. Trouble was, she didn't know what to think. He had never behaved the way she had expected him to behave. He hadn't expressed the words she had wanted to hear or done the things she had hoped he would do. Their relationship had been based on his sense of duty towards her and the baby, so when the baby was lost there was no reason to stay together. He hadn't given her a good enough reason to continue their relationship. He hadn't expressed any feelings for her. But then, neither had she for him. She had been incapable of expressing anything but profound grief, which had in time morphed into anger.

She schooled her features into coolly impersonal lines and turned to face him again. 'I think you're secretly relieved we no longer have a reason to stay together.'

His jaw worked for a moment and his mouth tightened into

a flat line. 'Let's leave that discussion until later. We're at our friends' wedding, remember?' And, without another word, he turned and left her with nothing but the company of the ocean-scented breeze.

CHAPTER FIVE

AFTER THE BRIEF wedding rehearsal Joe made idle conversation with some of the other guests but his mind was stuck on Juliette. He kept searching for her in the knot of people, a tight fluttering sensation going through his chest every time he caught sight of her honey-brown head in the crowd.

He had thought often of going to the cemetery where their baby was buried in England but each time he baulked. His father had dragged him to his mother's graveside to pay his respects on each and every birthday until he was a teenager. It had been a form of torture to stand by that headstone knowing he was the reason his mother was beneath it. No amount of wishing and praying and hoping could bring his mother or his baby daughter back. No number of visits, flowers or cards could undo what was done. He had always found his father's way of grieving a destructive process. Joe had chosen a different outlet—a constructive way of processing his grief by raising money for the research that would hopefully save lives and, no doubt, relationships.

But now, touching Juliette, standing next to her, breathing in the scent of her stirred his blood and upped his pulse and made him wonder if there was a chance something positive could come out of their situation. The chemistry was still there, as hot and electric as ever. The explosive chemistry that had kick-started their relationship was the one thing he could rely on to get it going again. He felt the pull of it like an invisible force drawing him to her. He'd had to stuff his hands in his pockets to stop reaching for her. He couldn't be in the same room as her without wanting her. Damn it—he couldn't be in the same country without aching with the need to take her in his arms.

Juliette turned and looked at him across the now moonlit terrace and a small creature scuttled through the ventricles of his heart. Girl-next-door-pretty rather than classically beautiful, she still had the power to snatch his breath. Her grey-blue eyes reminded him of a deep stormy sea with shifting shadows. Her slim frame was ballerina-like with a natural elegance of movement. And her skin was pale but she had a dusting of freckles over the bridge of her upturned nose that reminded him of sprinkled nutmeg. Her mouth was a Cupid's bow of pink lushness that drew his gaze like a magnet and he realised with a sharp pang how much he missed her sunshine-bright smile. Not those fake ones she flashed when required but a genuine one that lit up her face and eyes.

Juliette's gaze shifted back to the older couple next to her who were the bride's parents, but Joe could see she wasn't really engaged in the conversation. She kept chewing at her lower lip and fiddling with the clasp of her evening purse as if she couldn't wait for the evening to be over.

And soon it would be over and they would be alone in their suite.

The string quartet was playing dance numbers and several couples were dancing further along the terrace. He remembered the first time he'd danced with Juliette, how she had moved with him with such natural rhythm as if they had been dancing together for years.

Making love had been the same.

After their one-night stand and they had gone their separate ways, he hadn't been able to get her out of his mind. He'd had commitments back in Italy and then another project in Germany but he hadn't stopped thinking about her. And then, out of the blue, she'd called him and told him she was carrying his child. The news had stunned him. They had used protection but fate had decided to step in and create a new life. A life that hadn't lasted long enough to take a single independent breath.

Joe let out a long sigh as the familiar pain seized his chest whenever he thought of his tiny baby daughter. He blamed himself for not being there when Juliette went into early labour. Perhaps if he had been there to take her to hospital earlier things might have panned out differently. There were so many things he wished he had done differently.

Joe wove through the small crowd to join her, taking one of her hands in his. 'Would you like to dance?' He figured it was one way he could legitimately hold her in his arms. And, more importantly, stop her from dancing with anyone else.

She looked as if she were about to refuse, but then she shrugged, not quite meeting his gaze. 'Sure. Why not?'

Joe led her to the part of the terrace set up for dancing, overlooking the ocean below. The string quartet was now playing a romantic ballad and he gathered her close, moving with her to the slow rhythm of the music. 'You didn't look like you were enjoying the conversation you were having back there,' he said, breathing in the flowery scent of her hair.

Juliette glanced up at him with a frown. 'Was it so obvious?'

'Only to me.' He led her further away from the other guests who had joined them on the dance floor. 'Do you know Lucy's parents well?'

'Pretty well. I spent a fair bit of time at their house when Lucy and I were teenagers.' She gave a little sigh and added, 'I was really envious of her. Her parents were so different from mine.'

'In what way?'

She didn't respond for so long, he wondered if she hadn't heard him. But then she aimed her gaze at his shirt front and spoke in a low tone. 'They were so…so uncritical. I don't think

I've ever heard them say anything negative about her or the choices she made.'

Joe eased back to look down at her. 'And your parents were critical and negative?'

She gave a little eye-roll and lowered her gaze back to his shirt front. 'Not so much when there's an audience. They're way too polite and subtle for that. But I know how much I've disappointed them by not being as academically gifted as them and my two older brothers.'

Joe couldn't say he was all that surprised by her confession. But it niggled him that he hadn't drawn her out a little more on her family while they were living together. What did that say about him? What sort of husband didn't show an interest in his wife's background?

A husband with a troubled background of his own who wanted no questions asked, that was who.

Joe had only met her parents and brothers twice—at the wedding and then Emilia's funeral. The funeral was a bit of a blur to him and they hadn't been particularly warm towards him at the wedding—but he hadn't been expecting them to welcome him with open arms. They'd been polite in a stiff upper lip kind of way, but then his courtship of their only daughter hadn't exactly been ideal. A one-night stand pregnancy was hardly the way to impress and win over in-laws but he hadn't wanted his child to grow up without knowing him. Marriage had been the best option in his opinion.

Their child had to come first—the baby had been his top priority.

Her parents hadn't come to the hospital when they'd lost the baby as they were on a long-haul international flight. Juliette had flown to England to visit her parents before they'd left for a three-month tour abroad. She had been booked on a flight back to Italy the next day when she'd gone into labour. He'd flown back as soon as he heard but he got there too late.

'But you're so talented, Juliette. Your illustrations are amazing. Aren't they proud of your work?'

Her gaze was downcast, her mouth downturned. 'I'm the only person in my family without a PhD. I barely scraped through my GCSEs. A children's book illustrator isn't what they consider a worthwhile career, especially as I don't even have an art degree. They're proud I've had stuff published, sure, but they still see it as a kind of hobby.' She gave another sigh that made her slim shoulders go down. 'I haven't done a sketch in months so maybe they're right. It's time to find something else. I don't know how Lucy has put up with me this long. It's not just my career on hold, but hers too.'

Joe placed one of his hands along the curve of her creamy cheek, meshing his gaze with her troubled one. 'You don't need to think about a career until you're ready, *cara.* I've been depositing funds in your bank account to more than cover any loss of income.'

A tinge of pink spread across her cheeks but a determined light came into her eyes. 'I don't want or need your money. I haven't touched a penny of it.'

Joe brushed his thumb pad across the small round circle of her chin. 'You hate me that much?'

Something flickered in her gaze until her lashes came down over her eyes to lock him out. 'I never wanted your money. That wasn't why I married you.' She stepped out of his hold and crossed her arms over her body as if she were cold but the night air was balmy and warm.

'Yes, well, we both know why you married me.' Joe couldn't remove the cynicism from his tone in time. 'You wanted to show your cheating ex you'd moved on.'

She pressed her lips into a flat line, the colour in her cheeks darkening. 'That's not true. It had nothing to do with him. I can barely remember what he looks like now. I thought I was doing the best thing by the baby by marrying you. Anyway, you were the one who insisted on marriage. I would've been just as happy with a co-parenting arrangement.'

'Have you heard from your ex? Do you ever see him?' Joe wasn't sure why he was asking because he didn't want to know. He could do without the punishment, the torture, the despair of imagining her with someone else. He had never considered himself the jealous type. But the thought of her being intimate with someone else made his gut churn. The thought of her having another child with someone else sent a tight band of pain across his chest until he could hardly draw a breath.

Juliette flashed him an irritated look. 'I hardly see how it's any of your business who I see or don't see.'

Joe led her by the elbow away from the other dancers to a quieter part further along the terrace. 'It's my business because we're still legally married.'

He lowered his hand from her elbow but he had to summon up every bit of willpower he possessed to stop from pulling her back into his arms and crashing his mouth down on hers. To remind her of the passion that sparked between them. The passion that was charging the atmosphere even now.

Which brought him to a perplexing question—what the hell was he going to do about it? He had already made mistakes with Juliette. Big mistakes. Mistakes that couldn't be undone. Would it be asking for trouble to revisit their relationship? To see if it was worth salvaging?

Her gaze glittered with defiance. 'I find it highly amusing how you're suddenly so interested in my private life after all these months.' She glanced at his mouth as if she was expecting him to do what he was tempted to do. 'And why do you keep wearing your wedding ring? It seems rather pointless.'

Joe reached for her left hand, running his thumb over her empty ring finger. He was expecting her to pull away but, surprisingly, she didn't. Instead her gaze meshed with his and her tongue darted out to sweep across her lower lip, her throat rising and falling over a swallow.

'It's not entirely pointless. It keeps me free of unwanted female attention.' He waited a beat before continuing. 'I still have your wedding and engagement rings.' Joe wasn't sure why he was telling her that snippet of useless information. Did it make him sound like a sentimental fool who hadn't got over the walk-out of his wife? Should he tell her he hadn't removed one article of her clothing from his wardrobe? That he couldn't even use the same bedroom they had shared as it caused him too much gut-wrenching pain? And don't get him started on the nursery. He hadn't opened that door once. Not once. Opening that door would be tearing open a deep and devastating wound.

Juliette glanced down at their joined hands before returning her gaze to his. 'I'm surprised you haven't pawned them by now or found someone else to give them to.'

Joe stroked the soft flesh of her palm, watching as her pupils flared and her breath quickened. 'They belong to you.'

Her chin came up, an intransigent light sparking in her eyes. 'I don't want them.'

'Maybe, but still you want me.' Joe brought her hip to hip to his body, his gaze lowering to her mouth. 'Don't you, *mio piccolo*?'

Juliette licked her lips again, her eyes flicking to his mouth. 'No.' Her tone was firm but her body swayed towards him as if propelled by a force bigger than her will to resist.

He tipped up her chin, stroking her lower lip with his thumb. 'Pride is a funny thing, is it not? I would like to say I don't want you either but I would be lying to myself as well as you.'

She drew in a breath and released it in a shuddery rush. 'Joe...please...'

'Please, what?' Joe cupped one side of her face with his hand, the other hand going to the small of her back to bring her even closer to the throb and ache of his lower body. 'Are you going to deny what you're feeling right now? What you've felt from the moment I walked into the suite this afternoon? What you felt the first time we met? It's why you blocked my phone and emails, isn't it? You don't want to be reminded of what you feel for me.'

Juliette swallowed again, her hands creeping up to rest against his chest, her gaze homing in on his mouth. 'We're separated now and—'

'We're not separated this weekend. We're sharing a room. Sharing a bed.'

'No, we're not.' Her hands fell away from his chest, her gaze defiant. 'Celeste said she was going to get a fold-out for—'

'I spoke to her a few minutes ago,' Joe said. 'She wasn't able to get one in time for tonight but she'll try again tomorrow.'

Her gaze flicked back to his, the line of her mouth pulling tight. She stepped back, her posture stiff, guarded. 'We both need to move on with our lives. It would only complicate things to go backwards instead of forwards.'

She placed her left hand against her temple and closed her eyes as if in silent prayer. 'Please, Joe. Don't make this harder than it needs to be.' She lowered her hand from her face and looked up at him again with an expression that shone anew with determination. 'I'm going back to the room. To sleep. *Alone.*'

Juliette managed to slip away without any of the wedding party noticing and went back to the suite and closed the door with a heavy sigh. She'd been so tempted to dance with Joe all night, to find any excuse to be in his arms again. But that was the pathway to heartbreak because they didn't belong together. Not then. Not now.

If only her body didn't keep betraying her. It was so hard to keep her distance when he only had to look at her and her resistance melted. She had lowered her guard enough to tell him about her frustrating relationship with her parents and her doubts over her career going forward. It was a moment of weakness and yet she had drawn comfort from sharing so openly with him. He had been supportive and understanding in a way she hadn't expected.

And then there was the stillbirth foundation…

She couldn't get it out of her mind—how he had raised money for much-needed research. That all this time she had been judging him for not grieving the way she expected, but he'd been doing what he thought would help others. It made it harder for her to access her anger, to keep her emotional distance.

But it didn't mean they had a future together.

How could they when they weren't in love, had never been in love and would only be together for the sake of physical chemistry? That wasn't enough to build a marriage on, especially a marriage that had suffered such a tragedy as theirs. A marriage that would never have come about if it hadn't been for her accidental pregnancy. She wasn't the type of woman he normally dated. She wasn't sophisticated or super-smart and no one could ever call her supermodel beautiful. She would never have been his first choice of bride if she hadn't fallen pregnant.

Juliette pulled the clips out of her hair and tossed them on the dressing table on her way to the bathroom. Joe's shaving things were on the bathroom counter and his bottle of cologne right next to her cosmetics. A soft fluttering sensation passed over the floor of her belly. Sharing a bathroom was such an intimate thing to do. Would she be strong enough to resist the temptation he offered? She picked the cologne bottle up, took off the lid and held the neck of the bottle to her nose, closing her eyes to breathe in the citrus notes. She put the bottle back down and put the lid back on.

She had to be strong enough.

She *had* to.

Juliette came back out to the bedroom and glanced at her tote bag, where the divorce papers were stashed. On Sunday, after Lucy and Damon sailed off, she would whip them out and wave them under Joe's nose, not before. It gave her a sense of power to know she had them there, waiting for the right moment. He thought he could snap his fingers and she would come running back to him as if nothing had changed. Everything had changed.

She had changed.

And she wasn't changing back.

Joe came back to the suite later that night to find Juliette asleep in the bedroom with a bank of pillows dividing the king-sized bed in two sections. The bedside lamp was still on and the muted light cast her features into a golden glow. She had taken her hair down and it was spread out over the pillow. Her make-up was removed, leaving her skin as fresh and glowing as a child's. Her mouth was relaxed in sleep, her lips softly parted, her breathing slow and even. He reached up and loosened his tie, slipping it from around his collar and tossing it to the chair in the corner of the bedroom.

Juliette's eyes sprang open and she sat upright, blinking at him owlishly. 'Oh, it's you…'

'Thanks for the hearty welcome.' Joe began to unbutton his shirt.

Her gaze narrowed and she pulled the bedcovers further up her body. 'What are you doing?'

'What do you think I'm doing?' He shrugged off his shirt and tossed it in the same direction as his tie. 'I'm getting undressed.'

'Can you do it in the bathroom?' Her cheeks were a bright shade of pink and her eyes kept avoiding his. 'And please wear boxers or something. And stay on that side of the bed.'

'It's a bit late to be shy, *tesoro*. I'm familiar with every inch of your body, as indeed you are with mine.'

She threw back the covers and dived for the bathrobe that was hanging over the back of another chair. He caught a tantalising glimpse of café-latte-coloured satin shortie pyjamas, one of the shoestring straps on the camisole top slipping off her shoulder to reveal the upper curve of her breast. She thrust her arms in the bathrobe's sleeves and knotted the waist ties around her middle with unnecessary force, sending him a scalding glare. 'Fine. Have it your way. You have the bed and I'll sleep on the sofa.' She began to stalk past him but he caught her wrist on the way and stalled her passage.

'Don't be so dramatic.' He let her arm go, opening and closing his fingers to ease the tingling sensation touching her had produced. 'I'm not going to force myself on you. You have the bed. I'll take the sofa.'

She bit down on her lip and glanced towards the other section of the suite where the smallish sofa was situated. 'You're too tall for it. You won't sleep a wink.'

He wasn't going to sleep a wink anyway, not with her so temptingly close. Seeing her all sleep tousled with so much of her creamy skin on show was already stretching the limit of his self-control. 'I'm sure we can manage to share a bed for two nights without crossing any boundaries.'

She fiddled with the waist ties of her bathrobe, her teeth still worrying her lip. 'Okay. But you have to promise not to touch me.'

He placed his hand on his heart. 'You have my solemn word.'

Juliette pursed her lips, her gaze searching his for a moment. 'Why do I get the feeling you're laughing at me?'

He lowered his hand from his chest and dropped it back down by his side. 'Believe me, *cara*. It's been a long time since I laughed.'

Her eyes fell away from his and a shadow crossed her features. She turned back to the bed and climbed back under the covers, pulling them up to her chin and turning her back to him. 'Goodnight.'

Joe's gaze went to the box of sleep medication on her bedside table. He came over to her side of the bed and perched on the edge. 'How long have you been taking those?' He pointed to the medication sitting next to a glass of water.

Juliette turned over onto her back, her expression defensive. 'I only use them when I can't sleep.'

'And how often is that?'

Her eyes shifted out of reach of his and her fingers began plucking at the hem of the sheet. 'More often than not…' Her voice was hardly more than a whisper.

Joe stroked back a strand of hair from her forehead, his chest so tight he could barely inflate his lungs to breathe. Guilt rained down on him over how he had handled the last few months. She had suffered alone when he should have been by her side. He'd thought keeping his distance was what she wanted but it clearly hadn't helped her through the grieving process. It certainly hadn't helped him either. So many platitudes sprang to his lips—like the irritating comments other people had made to him.

Time is a great healer.

It will get easier.

You'll be stronger for it.

Instead, he stayed silent.

Her shimmering gaze met his and his chest tightened another painful notch. 'I can't help blaming myself. Maybe I shouldn't have flown home to England to visit my parents before they went on their trip. I didn't need to go. I could have asked them to visit me instead.'

And why had she flown home to England? Because he'd been away on yet another work commitment, leaving her to fend for herself. If anyone was to blame, it was him. Joe took one of her hands and anchored it to his aching chest. 'No. You mustn't blame yourself.' His voice was so rough it could have filed through metal. 'You had a dream pregnancy up until then.'

Her mouth twisted. 'You weren't there for the first three months. It wasn't such a dream pregnancy then. I was sick just about every day.'

Joe wished he had been there but she hadn't told him until she was twelve weeks along. He laid her hand on his thigh, moving his thumb over the back of her hand in slow soothing strokes. 'I was going to contact you so many times after we slept together that night.'

A frown creased her smooth brow. 'Were you? You never told me that before.'

Joe gave a wry half-smile. 'We hadn't exchanged numbers but I managed to find your details online because of your publishing career. I thought of emailing you numerous times, suggesting we meet up for a drink or something.'

'Why didn't you?'

'You were still getting over your ex. I didn't think you were ready to move on.'

She lowered her gaze and slipped her hand out of his hold and grasped the edge of the bedcovers. 'I think I was over Harvey as soon as he told me he was in love with Clara. But you would've only been offering a fling back then, not something lasting.' She issued it as a statement rather than a question.

Joe stood from the bed and looked down at her, unwilling to confirm or deny it. He had never felt the need to settle down with anyone long-term. He'd preferred to live in a world outside permanent attachment. A safe world. A world where he couldn't hurt or be hurt in return. 'Try and get some sleep, *cara*. Goodnight.'

Juliette listened while Joe had a shower in the bathroom. She tried to stop her mind filling with images of him under the hot spray of water, tried to stop thinking of the times she had shared a shower with him in the past. The blistering passion, the drumming need, the explosive orgasms.

She groaned under her breath and turned so her back was facing the bathroom, tucking her legs up close to her torso and squeezing her eyes shut. She waited for him to join her in the bed, waited for the familiar press of his weight down on the mattress, her senses so alert she knew it would be impossible to settle into sleep. She opened her eyes and saw the medication next to her glass of water. She sat up, pressed one out of the blister packet and swallowed it down with a gulp of water.

She lay back down and waited for the slow but inexorable drag down into mindless slumber…

CHAPTER SIX

JULIETTE DIDN'T KNOW how long she had been asleep when she woke. It was still dark except for a beam of silvery moonlight peeping through a gap in the curtains, illuminating the bed… *the half empty bed.* She sat up and pushed her hair away from her face and frowned at the vacant space beside her. The pillows were undented, the sheets smooth, showing no sign Joe had even momentarily lain down beside her.

A perverse sense of pique washed over her. Why hadn't he slept beside her? Did he find her repulsive? Was he worried she might cross to his side of the bed? She pushed off the bedcovers and, ignoring the bathrobe laid over the chair, padded through to the sitting room area.

Joe was sitting in a slumped position on the sofa, his long legs stretched out in front of him, his head on one side, his eyes closed in a deep sleep. He was naked except for a bath towel anchored around his lean hips.

Juliette knew she should tiptoe back to bed. Knew she shouldn't feel a smidgeon of compassion for him for having spent an uncomfortable night sleeping upright. Knew she had no right to stare at his tanned athletic body bathed in moonlight, making him look like a Greek god rather than human. But her feet seemed to be anchored to the floor, her eyes drawn to him with the force of an industrial-sized magnet.

She wasn't aware of making a sound but suddenly his eyes opened and he blinked and sat upright, scraping a hand through his already tousled hair.

'Was I snoring?' he asked with a grimace.

'No. Is that a new habit you've acquired since we…?' She left the sentence hanging but couldn't explain why. He'd told her there'd been no one else since she'd left but one day there would be. That was something she didn't want to think about too closely. Someone else in his life. In his bed. In his arms. Experiencing the mind-blowing passion she missed to this day.

Joe drew his legs to a right-angled position, leaned forward and rested his forearms on his thighs. 'Not that I know of.'

There was a moment of silence. A silence so loaded the air seemed to be weighted, making it hard for Juliette to breathe.

'Why didn't you sleep in the bed?'

Joe lifted his head to look at her, his eyes so dark they could have been black holes in space. 'I didn't want to disturb you. You looked like you needed your sleep.' His voice had a rough edge that made something in her belly lose its footing.

Juliette rolled her lips together and came a little closer, drawn to him as if her body had a will of its own. 'Joe…it's okay if you want to share the bed. Really, we're both mature adults and—'

'It's fine. I got a couple of hours. It's all I need.' He rose from the sofa, securing the towel around his hips, and walked over to the windows, pushing the curtains further aside to look at the moonlit view.

She couldn't take her eyes off the sculpted perfection of his back and shoulder muscles, taut buttocks and his long strong thighs and calves below the hip-height towel. Just knowing he was naked under that towel was enough to send her female hormones into a cheerleading routine. Sensations stirred low in her body—sensual, erotic memories of his thick, hard presence moving within her.

Joe turned from the window and brushed his hair back from his forehead. 'Go back to bed, Juliette.' His tone was part stern authority and part growing impatience.

Juliette took a step towards him. 'Joe…'

He closed the distance between them and placed his hands on the tops of her shoulders. The warmth of his fingers seeped into her flesh, awakening needs and desires she wasn't sure she could control. His hooded eyes drifted to her mouth, his breath hitching, his body so close her breasts brushed against his chest. The smooth satin of her shortie pyjamas couldn't hide her body's reaction to him. She could feel the tensing of her nipples, the spreading tingles in her breasts, the smouldering heat in her core.

His hand cupped one side of her face, his thumb moving across her cheek like the arm of a slow-beating metronome. 'Kissing you would be the easy part. Stopping at one kiss, however, would be something else.' His voice was so rough it sounded as if he'd been gargling with gravel.

Juliette's gaze lowered to his sensually shaped lips and something in her stomach fell off a high shelf. 'Who said I wanted you to kiss me?' Her voice was too breathy to relay the cool indifference she'd aimed for.

One side of his mouth tipped up in a crooked smile that did serious damage to her resolve to resist him. His thumb stroked across her lower lip, back and forth in a mesmerising, spine-tingling rhythm. 'When I arrived here this weekend I was so determined I wasn't going to do this.'

Juliette hadn't realised she'd moved until she found herself flush against him, the hard jut of his hips, the proud rise of his male flesh setting her body on fire. 'Do what?' Her voice was so soft it could barely be called a whisper.

'You know exactly what.' And his mouth came down and covered hers.

Juliette knew she should have pulled away right then. She should have stopped it from going any further. She shouldn't have allowed herself to be tempted, much less give into it. But as soon as his lips met hers, something hard and tight and bitter inside her collapsed like a house of cards. His lips moved against hers in an exploratory fashion, as if he was reminding himself of her contours, her taste, her texture. She groaned and opened to him and his tongue met hers in an erotic dance that made the hairs on the back of her neck tingle and the base of her spine fizz.

Her hands moved from his chest to link around his neck, her fingers playing with the thick black strands of his hair. He made a low growling sound deep in his throat and changed position, deepening the kiss until the bones in her legs threatened to melt like candlewax in a cauldron.

Joe's hands framed her face, his breathing almost as hectic as hers. After long breathless moments he lifted his mouth off hers, gazing down at her for an infinitesimal pause before sealing her lips once more with a softly muttered curse, as if he too hated himself for his weakness where she was concerned.

One of his hands left her face and went to the small of her back, pressing her closer to the tantalising ridge of his male flesh. His other hand went to the nape of her neck, his long fingers splayed into the tingling roots of her hair. Shivers coursed up and down her back, her inner core hosting a welcome party, darts of pleasure shooting between her legs.

Joe lifted his mouth off hers and placed his hands on her hips, stepping back from her a fraction. 'I think it might be time to stop.' Something in his tone belied his words—the gruffness, the rueful note, the chord of longing so low she might have missed it if she hadn't been feeling it herself.

Stop? Now?

When her body was screaming for the release it craved? And why the hell hadn't *she* been the one to stop this madness? She felt hot shame flushing into her face and she shoved his hands off her hips and stepped further back, chest heaving as if she were an affronted heroine in a period drama. 'What the hell do you think you're playing at, kissing me like that?'

One of his ink-black eyebrows rose in a sardonic arc. 'I could ask you the same question.'

Juliette couldn't hold his gaze and swung away. 'I'm going to have a shower. It'll soon be time to get up and get ready for the wedding anyway.' She strode into the bathroom and locked the door, leaning back against it with a ragged sigh. Why had she allowed him to prove how weak she was? How vulnerable to his touch? How lacking in immunity?

How dangerously ambiguous her feelings...

The wedding was to be held in the morning on the beach. Somehow Juliette had managed to shower and dress without running into Joe. He had left the suite while she was in the shower, and because she was heading to Lucy's room for a hair and make-up session with the other bridesmaids she didn't expect to see him again until the ceremony.

Lucy handed Juliette a glass of champagne on arrival. 'Get that into you. Now, tell me how last night went. Did you guys kiss and make up?'

Juliette took the champagne but decided against taking anything but a token sip. 'Let's talk about you, not me. Are you nervous?'

Lucy beamed. 'Me? Nervous? I can't wait to marry Damon.' Her smile dimmed a little. 'I just wish things were better between you and Joe. Are you sure there's no hope of a reconciliation?'

'It's not what either of us wants.'

'Are you sure about that? I saw the way he was watching you last night. He could barely take his eyes off you. And when you two were dancing, well, anyone would have thought you were—'

'We're not.' Juliette's tone was emphatic. She opened the

long narrow box that contained Lucy's hand-embroidered veil. 'He slept on the sofa.'

'Oh…'

Juliette turned to look at her friend. 'I don't want your wedding to be spoilt by my dramas with Joe.' She painted a bright smile on her face. 'Now, let's get you ready to marry the man of your dreams. Your dress looks amazing, by the way.'

Lucy twirled this way and that in her voluminous tulle and satin dress. It made her mixed-race complexion look all the more stunning. 'You don't think I look too much like a meringue?' There was a dancing light in her eyes. 'It was a toss-up between this one and the figure-hugging one we looked at together in Mayfair but I've always wanted to be a princess for a day.'

'You look exactly like a princess,' Juliette said, trying to ignore a tiny jab of envy. 'A princess in love.'

Joe stood next to Damon under the canopy of tropical flowers that had been set up on the beach. He was trying not to think of his own wedding, how different it was from this one. If he and Juliette had married in a more relaxed and informal setting, would it have helped? His goal had been to get married to her as soon as possible for the sake of the baby. The cold and austere village church where generations of her family had been christened, wed or buried would not have been his first choice. But he had wanted Juliette to feel supported by her family, given he had none to speak of.

Damon nudged him. 'Here they come.'

Joe turned and saw Juliette leading the way up the flower-strewn red carpet that had been laid down on the sand. She was dressed in a deep blue satin dress the colour of the ocean that pulsed nearby. The dress clung to her body like a slinky glove, outlining the gentle swell of her hips, the narrow waist, the slight globes of her breasts. There was a garland of flowers in her hair, giving her an *A Midsummer Night's Dream*, almost ethereal look. His chest tightened, his breath stalled, his guilt throbbed. He had failed her in so many ways. He had made promises to love and protect her but he had failed on both counts. Romantic love was something he had never committed to. He doubted it even existed except perhaps in rare cases.

It had certainly never existed for him.

But seeing Juliette walking towards him now, something shifted in his chest. A slippage. A softening. A tightly locked space slowly opening…

He snapped it shut. *Bang.* Bolted the door.

He was comforted by the all too familiar jolt of his emotions shutting down. It was safer not to feel too deeply. To leave stray feelings unexplored. To deny them access through the firewall of his control tower.

Juliette met his gaze and a tremulous smile formed on her lips. The soft lips he had kissed early that morning and only just managed to stop kissing before he lost control. Kissing her made him realise how dangerous it was to be around her. It made him want her. Need her. Crave her. But how could he hope for a rerun of their relationship? What right did he have to insist on a second chance? It would only cause more pain, more heartache. It was practically his brand—projecting pain, heartache and loss onto the people he cared about. It was better he didn't care. It was better he didn't want. It was better not to hope.

Her gaze moved away and a sense of disappointment sank in his stomach like a stone.

Her smile was for the crowd, for appearances' sake.

It wasn't for him.

Juliette couldn't look at Joe without blushing over their kiss that morning. She couldn't look at him and not think about their own wedding. Their cold and duty-bound wedding where the promises he made had meant nothing.

But had hers meant something? Anything? Juliette gave an inward frown, wondering why her conscience was bringing this up now. She hadn't been the one to insist on marriage. She had done the right thing in telling him he was to be a father, to give him the option of being involved or not. She could have refused his offer… *Why hadn't she?*

Juliette stood to one side of Lucy and Damon as they exchanged their vows. Both had tears shining in their eyes, their love for each other plain to see. She glanced at Joe to find his gaze trained on her, his expression grave. She bit her lip and looked away again, her heart feeling as if squeezed by an invisible hand.

Maybe she had judged Joe too quickly. Hadn't her parents always complained about her impulsive nature? Her tendency to act first, ask questions later had often caused her to regret her actions in hindsight. She had not only not asked Joe the questions, she hadn't even allowed him to contact her. She had blocked him at every turn.

It was excruciatingly painful to confront her role in the breakup of their relationship. Would she be making a huge mistake in pursuing a divorce? But how could their marriage continue if Joe didn't love her?

The newly married couple kissed and the guests clapped and cheered and again Juliette was reminded of the brief kiss Joe had given her at their wedding, and the less than enthusiastic applause from the handful of guests, her parents in particular.

After Lucy and Damon's official photos were taken further along on the beach, the mostly informal and relaxed reception was held in the villa's ballroom overlooking the beach.

Juliette got up to dance with three of the other groomsmen to avoid dancing with Joe. She was worried she would betray herself in his arms, reveal things about herself she knew she shouldn't be feeling while she had divorce papers to hand to him. Dance after dance, drink after drink, she worked the room as if she had graduated as star pupil at Social Butterfly school. But inside she was shrivelling up, struggling to cope with pretending to be happy. One of the guests—another cousin of

Damon's—was heavily pregnant and every time Juliette looked at her she felt a hammer-blow of sadness crash over her.

Juliette took yet another glass of champagne off a passing waiter and turned to find Joe standing beside her.

'Is that a good idea?' He nodded towards her glass, his expression brooding.

She arched her brows. 'Since when did you join the Temperance Society?'

He took the glass out of her hand and placed it on a nearby table. 'I think you've had enough.'

'I think you need to back off,' Juliette said, glowering at him. 'Just because you're not having a good time doesn't mean I can't.'

'*Are* you having a good time?' His gaze was as pointed as his tone. But then he released a heavy breath and added with a frown, 'You're pretending, just like I am. But doing a much better job of it than me.'

Some of Juliette's anger faded. She couldn't explain why—it just slumped inside her like a windless sail. 'It's a form of torture, isn't it? Watching other people being happy.'

'Sì.'

Juliette tried to read his expression but it was like trying to read a cryptic code. Or maybe it was because her head was starting to pound from all the champagne she'd consumed. Or maybe it was because she knew she was getting closer to the moment when she would hand Joe the divorce papers. She couldn't allow her defences to let her down now. She had come on a mission to get those papers signed. One kiss did not a reconciliation make. She pinched the bridge of her nose and winced. 'I think I need to go to bed. Do you think Lucy and Damon would be offended if I slipped away now before they leave?'

Joe glanced to where the happy couple were dancing cheek to cheek. 'No. I don't think they'll mind. Come on—' he held out his hand '—I'll walk you back to our room.'

* * *

Joe led Juliette back to their room. *Their room.* One last night suffering the torture of having her close enough to touch. Close enough to remember the potent magic that brought them together in the first place. Close enough to regret how he had handled every step, every stage of their relationship. Close enough to wonder if there was a chance—a slim chance—she would consider trying again.

The idea crept into his head and looked around for a place to get comfortable, pushing his conscience, his fears, his doubts out of the way. He wasn't imagining the chemistry still between them, was he? It was as strong and pulsing as ever. Their kiss had proven how strong their connection still was.

How could he forgive himself for not at least exploring the possibility of reconciling?

Joe closed the door of their room but he realised immediately his timing was way off. Not only was there a fold-out bed set up in the sitting room area but Juliette looked tense and on edge. Her teeth chewed at her lip, her eyes not quite meeting his.

'Are you okay?'

She nodded and sat on the sofa and held a scatter cushion against her body like a shield. 'I will be. I just need a glass of water.'

Joe fetched her one and brought it back to where she was sitting. She took the glass from him, guzzled down the water and then handed the glass back. 'Thanks.'

'Another one?'

'Not right now...' She tossed the cushion aside and reached for her phone in her purse and switched it off silent. 'I forgot I promised I'd send my mother a picture of Lucy and Damon.' She clicked the necessary keys and the sound of the message pinging through cyberspace filled the silence. She continued to look at her phone, her forehead wrinkling in a frown. 'Joe?'

'Mmm?'

She lifted her head to look at him with a puzzled expression.

'This email here that just popped into my inbox. Is it spam? It says you and I have been nominated for some sort of fundraising award. It says we're Fundraising Couple of the Year.' She held the screen up for him to inspect.

Joe leaned down to read the email, and then straightened to take out his phone and clicked on his own emails. He was copied into the same email she had received. What sort of twisted irony was that? *Couple of the Year?* They were no longer a couple. He slipped his phone back in his pocket. 'No, it's not spam. Remember I told you I'd donated on your behalf? And raised funds through various other means. I sent you emails about it but you chose not to read them. There's a fundraising dinner in Paris next month. We've been invited to go and—'

Juliette sprang off the sofa as if one of the springs had poked her. 'Are you out of your mind? I'm not going to Paris with you. It's completely out of the question. Everyone will think we're still together.'

'So, what if they do?'

'We're not together, Joe.' A stubborn edge came into her voice, her grey-blue eyes steely. 'Just because we've shared a room this weekend doesn't mean anything.'

Joe took a deep breath. No way was he going to that fundraiser without her. It was the perfect opportunity to spend more time with her. This weekend wasn't enough. How could it ever be enough when he wanted her this badly? 'Juliette. This is not about us. It's about helping others who experience what we went through. If we don't show up as a united couple, then how will it look?'

Her expression tightened. 'It will look exactly as it is. We. Are. Separated.' The emphasis on each word was like three punches to his gut. She went over to her tote bag in the corner of the room and pulled out some papers and came back to thrust them at him. 'Here. I've been saving these for now.'

Joe's gaze narrowed as he saw what it was. Legal papers. *Di-*

vorce papers. A pain spread like fire through his chest, searing through flesh, pulverising bone, taking away his breath.

So, his time in limbo was over.

Juliette had already made up her mind. She had come to their friends' wedding with divorce papers for him to sign. It was over. No sequel. No reruns.

The End.

A streak of stubbornness steeled his spine and his gaze. Their marriage would end on his say-so, not hers. No way was he signing divorce papers at his best mate's wedding weekend. He took the papers off her and tossed them onto the seat of the sofa as if they were nothing more than yesterday's newspaper. 'I'll sign those when I'm good and ready. Come to Paris with me and then I'll give you a divorce.'

Her chin came up and her eyes flashed. 'You're blackmailing me?'

He gave a grating laugh. 'Damn right I am. What were you thinking, bringing those to your best friend's wedding? I thought you had more class.'

She picked up the legal papers and carefully fed them back inside the envelope. Her movements were calm and controlled but he could see the effort it cost her. Her jaw was tight, her mouth pressed flat, her anger a palpable presence in the room. She put the envelope back in her tote bag and faced him with fire and ice in her gaze. 'We'll discuss this again in the morning. I have a headache and don't want to argue with you right now.'

Joe locked his gaze on hers, his own anger stiffening his spine. Anger so thick and throbbing he could feel it pulsing in his veins like a thousand pummelling fists. 'You'll hear the same thing from me in the morning. I will not sign those papers until I'm good and ready. End of.' He turned and walked out of the suite and closed the door behind him as firmly as a punctuation mark.

* * *

Juliette winced as the door shut behind him. She let out a ragged breath. *That went well.* She tugged at the pins holding her hair up and shook her head to loosen the strands. It didn't help her headache, nor did the thought of confronting Joe again with the divorce papers. Why was he being so stubborn and obstructive? Hadn't he said being together again was the last thing he wanted? Or was he interested in a little affair with her until after Paris? She couldn't allow herself to be used in such a way. She wouldn't allow herself to be exposed to more hurt when he failed to support her in the way she wanted. *Needed.* He was all for helping others in their situation, but what about helping her? Supporting her?

When Juliette woke the next morning, after a fitful sleep, she found a note propped up on the bedside table, written in Joe's distinctive handwriting.

See you in Paris,
Joe.

She glanced around the room. His luggage was gone. There was no trace of him in the suite. It was as if he had never been there with her.

Isn't that the truth?

She gritted her teeth and scrunched the note up in a ball and threw it at the nearest wall. 'I'll see you in hell first.'

CHAPTER SEVEN

One month later...

JULIETTE WEIGHED UP the options of informing Joe she would be calling on him at his villa in Positano or showing up unannounced, to hand deliver the divorce papers. She would get those papers signed if it was the last thing she did. She'd had zero contact from him since Lucy and Damon's wedding—not that she had contacted him either. Still seething with anger at the way he had issued her with an ultimatum, and the way he'd left without saying goodbye, it had taken her this past month to feel ready to face him again.

She was *not* going to be controlled by his outrageous demands.

In the end, Juliette decided to just show up at his villa, suspecting if she gave him the heads-up he might find a convenient excuse for not being there. She had heard via Damon that Joe was currently at his luxury villa high in the hills overlooking the Mediterranean ocean, so she was confident it wouldn't be a wasted journey. Besides, she still had a key and, unless he had changed the locks, she would stay there until he returned even if it took a week or two. Those papers needed to be processed and they could only be processed if he signed them.

That was her goal.

Her mission.

Get a divorce. Get on with her life.

But, due to travel delays and her taxi taking several costly—and she thought deliberate—wrong turns, Juliette didn't arrive until late in the evening. Which was deeply annoying, as she hadn't planned on staying longer than the five or ten minutes it would take to get the papers signed. She dismissed the taxi, figuring she would call another one as soon as she was done and then go to the hotel she'd booked online before flying back to London tomorrow.

She was reassured that some lights were on in the villa and pressed the doorbell. No answer. She pressed it again. And again. Still no answer. There was a security camera at the front entrance, so she knew if Joe was inside he could see it was her. Why wasn't he answering the door? And if he wasn't home and one of the household staff was there, why weren't they responding?

It was way too early for Joe to be in bed…although if he had someone with him… Juliette tried to ignore the sharp jab of pain that suddenly assailed her. He had to move on some time. He would definitely do so once their divorce was finalised.

Why was she getting upset about it? It was petty and immature of her. She was over him. She *had* to be.

There was no going back.

Juliette reached in her bag for her key and placed it in the lock, praying he hadn't changed the alarm code, otherwise the security system would screech loud enough to hear in Naples. She opened the door and, wheeling in her overnight bag, stepped inside and closed the door softly behind her.

'Hello?' Her voice echoed through the marble foyer and somewhere further inside the villa she heard something fall over and then Joe's deep voice letting out a filthy curse.

Juliette left her overnight bag at the front door and walked further into the villa. 'Joe?' She went to the smaller of the two sitting rooms, where she could see a pool of soft light shining from the door that was ajar. She pushed the door further open and saw Joe standing near the drink's cabinet with a shot glass of spirits in his hand. The room was in disarray. The sofa scatter cushions were askew, one of them on the floor some distance away as if it had been thrown there. The air was stale as if the windows hadn't been opened in days. Newspapers littered the floor and there was an empty pizza box with traces of topping—olives, capers, mushroom—stuck to the cardboard.

If Joe looked shocked to see her suddenly appear announced at his villa, he didn't show it on his face. He simply raised the glass to his lips, tipped back his head and drained the contents, before wiping the back of his hand across his lips.

'To what do I owe this honour?' His tone was bitter, his eyes bloodshot, his hair tousled, his lean jaw shadowed with at least two days' stubble. His shirt was creased and untucked from his trousers, giving him an unkempt look that was at odds with the man she knew. It was one of the things she secretly admired about him. He took care with his appearance. He wasn't a junk food eater. He didn't drink to excess. He was careful about over-indulging. Unlike her ex, whose idea of a gourmet meal was a deluxe burger at a fast food chain. And who had embarrassed her on more than one occasion by drinking too much and acting inappropriately.

Like *she* could talk after all the champagne she'd drunk at Lucy and Damon's wedding, but still…

Juliette frowned, shocked to find Joe in such a state. 'Are you…drunk?'

He gave a twisted smile that didn't reach his eyes. 'No, but it sounds like fun. Want to join me?' He placed his glass down on the drinks cabinet and reached for the bottle of spirits.

She dropped her tote bag on a nearby chair and came further into the room, stepping over the pizza box and a collection of newspapers. 'I'm not here to party, Joe.' She injected her tone with as much gravity as she could even though it made her sound like the fun police.

He poured a measure of spirits into the glass and she was relieved to see it was only a few millimetres, not centimetres. 'Want one?' He held the glass out to her with a daredevil light in his dark eyes.

'No, thank you.'

'I can open some champagne for you.' His smile had a hint of cruelty about it. 'We could get drunk together and see what happens.'

Juliette pressed her lips together as if she were channelling a starchy schoolmistress. 'That won't be necessary. I don't have anything to celebrate.'

The glint in his gaze hardened to flint. 'Not even my birthday?'

Juliette stared at him for a stunned moment. How could she not have realised? She had never actually celebrated his birthday with him as they hadn't been married long enough. She'd seen it on his passport, though—April the fifth.

But wait... That date rang another bell...

What twist of fate had her coming to visit him on the *exact* date they'd first met? 'I didn't realise until now—we met for the first time on this day. But I thought you said it was the anniversary of your mother's death?'

'Sì.' His expression was masked. Stony, cold, emotionless—all except for a shadow lurking at the back of his gaze.

She frowned as she tried to join the dots. 'Your mother died on your *birthday?*'

He put the shot glass down with an audible thud. *'Sì.'*

Her throat was so clogged it felt as if she'd swallowed one of the scatter cushions. 'How old were you?' Her voice quavered with emotion, imagining him as a young child dealing with the loss of his mother. Why hadn't he told her when they were together? Why had he kept such important information about himself a secret? And why hadn't she delved a little more deeply—tried to get to know him better? They hadn't been married long and they hadn't married for the usual reasons, but that didn't absolve her. She hadn't taken the time to understand him, to uncover the enigmatic layers of his personality.

'Thirty-three minutes.' His tone was flat but his eyes were haunted. Black, brooding, bleak.

Juliette's mouth fell open and her heart slipped from its moorings. 'Thirty…? Oh, Joe, you mean she died *having* you?'

He turned away to put the lid back on the bottle of spirits, a frown pulling at his forehead. 'It's why I try to ignore my birthday. There's nothing to celebrate in knowing your birth was responsible for someone's death.'

Juliette came over to him and touched him on the arm to get him to face her. 'I can understand how you, or anyone, would feel like that. But you mustn't blame yourself. It could have been a medical error or—' Even as she said the words, she realised how unfairly she had blamed him for their baby's stillbirth. Guilt was a heavy stone in her belly—crushing, punishing guilt.

He removed her hand from his arm. 'Look, I know you mean well but I'd rather not talk about it right now.' He rubbed a hand down his face, the rasping sound against his stubble loud in the silence. He let out a long breath and added, 'Why are you here? Have you changed your mind about Paris? It's next weekend. Don't forget—no divorce without it.'

The divorce papers could wait. Handing them to him on his birthday seemed a bit crass, considering the circumstances. Besides, her feelings of remorse were so overwhelming she didn't want to do anything she would regret later. She had enough regrets. As for Paris… Would it hurt her to go with him? Maybe it would help both of them find some measure of peace going forward.

'I'm not just here about the divorce. I wanted to come anyway…for another reason.'

Joe took a bottle of water out of the bar fridge and unscrewed the cap, his gaze watchful. 'Which is?'

'Erm…research for my next book.' It was a lie but she could make it true by doing a few sketches while she was here. That was if he hadn't thrown out her art materials. She had taken virtually nothing with her when she'd left. And he hadn't sent any of her things on to her. She couldn't possibly leave him tonight, not on his birthday. At first, she'd thought he was properly drunk, but she realised now he was in a brooding mood and tired. As if he hadn't slept in weeks. And he looked like he'd lost weight—his cheeks were hollow and fine lines ran down either side of his mouth.

He moved past her and sat on one of the sofas, his long legs stretched out in front of him and crossed at the ankles. He took a couple of mouthfuls of water, his gaze tracking back to her as if he couldn't help himself. 'How long do you plan to stay in Italy?'

Juliette sat on the opposite sofa and placed her hands on her thighs. 'I haven't decided. I thought I'd see how I go… It's been a while since I've drawn anything—I might not be able to do it any more…'

Joe took another mouthful of water and then his gaze locked back on hers. 'Where are you staying?' There was a guarded note in his tone.

'I booked a small hotel down near Fornillo Beach.'

His jaw worked for a moment. 'Are you with anyone?'

'No.'

Silence ticked past.

Juliette tucked a strand of hair back behind her ear for something to do with her hands. She felt restless and on edge, uncertain of how to behave around him. Way too tempted to behave in ways that would make a mockery of the legal document in her overnight bag, still on the floor in the foyer. She wished she had the courage to walk behind the sofa where he was seated and massage his tense neck and shoulders like she used to do.

Joe leaned his head back against the sofa cushions and closed his eyes. 'I'll let you see yourself out.'

She was being dismissed.

A wall had come up and she was on the wrong side of it. But something kept her seated on the sofa, something kept her gaze focused on the lines and planes of his face, something breathed life into a dead place deep inside her heart. Juliette felt the stirring in her chest, the slow unfurling of closed wings, the gentle flap of hope coming to life. Hope that their relationship might not be in its last throes but had the potential to rise again.

But better this time.

She hadn't taken the time to get to know him in the past. Her shock pregnancy had propelled them too fast into marriage without the appropriate getting-to-know-you lead-up. And the devastation of losing their baby had blinded her to the things that had worked well in their relationship. Could they possibly build on those things?

'Joe?'

He cracked open one eye. 'What?' His one word, somewhat sharp reply wasn't encouraging but Juliette was starting to realise he was probably feeling uncomfortable with her seeing him in less than ideal circumstances. He felt vulnerable and unguarded and for such a control captain that was anathema.

Juliette glanced in the direction of the kitchen. 'Do you mind if I make myself a cup of tea?'

'Go for it.'

'Do you want one?'

One side of his mouth tilted in a bad boy smile. 'I'm not ready to be a teetotaller.'

'I know you're not drunk. You're only pretending to be.'

He leaned forward to rest his elbows on his thighs and lowered his head into his hands. 'I didn't ask you to come here. I'd rather not have an audience right now.' The *keep away* quality in his tone didn't daunt her. Not now she knew how vulnerable and exposed he felt.

Juliette came over and perched on the arm of the sofa next to him. She raised her hand and began stroking her fingers through the thick strands of his black wavy hair. He gave a low deep groan but didn't push her hand away. Every now and again her fingers would catch on a knot in his hair and she gently untangled it.

After a while, he raised his head from his hands and looked at her with his pitch-black eyes and something slipped sideways in her stomach. 'You should have left five minutes ago.' His voice was so rough it made the hairs on the back of her neck tingle.

Juliette idly ran her finger down the slope of his nose. 'Why should I?'

He grasped her wrist with the steel bracelet of his fingers and her heart gave an excited leap. His fingers were warm, the tensile strength an erotic reminder of other parts of his body that were hot and strong and potent. 'Because I might not let you go.'

Was it the whisky talking? Or was he expressing feelings he had hidden from her in the past?

Juliette used her free hand to stroke his richly stubbled jaw. 'Joe…why didn't you tell me about your mother when we got married? You barely told me anything about yourself. And when I fished for information, you would shut me down or distract me with something else. Or disappear for days on end with work commitments.'

His gaze shifted from hers to stare at her wrist in his grasp on his lap. His other hand came over the top of her captured hand and his index finger traced each of the tendons on the back of her hand. 'There wasn't much to tell. My birth caused my mother's death and my father did his best to raise me but her death was a dark cloud over our relationship.'

'Do you mean he blamed you?'

He gave a lopsided twist of his mouth that wasn't anywhere near a smile. 'Not in so many words. But every year on my birthday since I was old enough to remember, he would take me to the cemetery and make me tidy her grave and put flowers there. I hated going. I found it creepy, to be honest. I put my foot down when I was fifteen and said I wasn't going again. And I haven't. Not once.'

Juliette's heart contracted. She could picture him as a small toddler, not quite understanding why he had to perform such a morbid duty. And then in the years while he was growing up, still being forced to confront the reality of his mother's death and his innocent part in it. So many pennies were dropping in her head she was surprised Joe couldn't hear the loud tinkling. Was that why he had been so distant and aloof at their baby's funeral? He had been almost robotic, hardly saying anything to anyone, not showing any emotion and not comforting Juliette in the way she had needed. Was that why he had never visited their baby's grave? And during Juliette's pregnancy, the further along it went, he had retreated into himself, closed off, distanced himself. Had he been terrified all along that the same thing could happen to her that happened to his mother?

'Oh, Joe…' Tears stung her eyes and she turned her hand over in his and gripped him tightly. 'I wish I'd known. How terrible that must have been for you as a small child.'

Joe released her hand and rose from the sofa, moving to the other side of the room with his back towards her. 'Why are you really here, Juliette?' His tone had a cold razor-sharp edge. Accusing, cutting, callous.

Juliette swept her tongue over her carpet-dry lips. 'I told you—I'm doing some research for—'

He swung around to face her with a brooding expression. 'You're a terrible liar.' He moved across the room and rummaged amongst some things on the small table near a pile of books. He picked up a pen. 'Got the divorce papers with you?' He clicked the pen open and smiled a savage smile. 'Where do I sign?'

Juliette rose from the sofa and hugged her arms around her middle. 'It's a really dumb idea to sign legal documents when you've been drinking even a small amount of alcohol. I think we should talk about this some other time.'

He clicked the pen on and off several times and she got the feeling it was his way of counting to ten to control his simmering anger. After a moment, he tossed the pen aside and walked past her out of the room, throwing over his shoulder, 'I'll let you see yourself out. I'm sure you haven't forgotten the way.'

Juliette closed her eyes against the sting of his parting words. But there was one thing she was certain of—no way was she leaving tonight. Not until they had chance to talk about things they should have talked about months ago.

Joe had enough trouble resisting Juliette when he was stone cold sober and even though he had only had a couple of shot glasses of whisky he knew it was wise to keep his distance. He was disgusted with himself for indulging in a pity party on his birthday. He mostly tried to ignore the date but this year had brought it all back. The anniversary of the day he'd met Juliette. The amazing night of hot sex he hadn't been able to forget. The amazing night that for once had made him forget what day it was. The amazing night that had cumulated in a pregnancy. A doomed pregnancy, because that was the sort of stuff that happened to him, right? He had a poisonous touch and it was no good thinking it was going to change any time soon. If ever.

He knew why Juliette was here. Those wretched divorce papers. He couldn't put off signing them for ever. English law stated a couple married in England could be granted a no-fault divorce after two years of separation. They had now been separated for sixteen months.

In another eight months they would both be free.

No-fault? Of course there was someone to blame.

Him.

CHAPTER EIGHT

JULIETTE WAITED DOWNSTAIRS until she was sure Joe had taken himself to bed. She went back out to the foyer and carried her overnight bag rather than wheel it, so as not to disturb him. There were several spare bedrooms on the second floor to choose from. The master bedroom door was closed and in darkness, so she assumed Joe had settled down for the night. She toyed with the idea of checking on him but decided it was best to leave him to sleep off his devil-may-care mood. She didn't trust herself around him, especially when he was in such a reckless state of mind. Besides, re-entering the room they had shared during their short marriage would test her in ways she wasn't sure she could handle. Too many images came to mind of her being in that bed with him, her legs entangled with his, her body responding to his surging thrusts with wanton abandon.

She suppressed a delicate shudder and continued on her way to one of the rooms further along the wide carpeted corridor until she came to the closed door of the nursery. She stopped outside, unable to take another step. It was as if a thick glass wall had sprung up in front of her and she could go no further until she glimpsed her baby's room—to see if it was as she had left it.

She had decorated the nursery herself, spending hours in there painting a frieze for the walls, making a mobile for the cot, placing soft toys on the floating shelves she had designed and got made specially. She'd chosen the pink fabric for the curtains with fairies and unicorns on it and made them herself. Every stitch, every brushstroke, every item had been placed there with love. Love for her baby.

They had found out at the twenty weeks scan they were having a little girl. At first, Juliette had wanted to leave it as a surprise but Joe had wanted to know. She understood so much more about him in hindsight—his uneasiness at that and the other appointments she'd managed to drag him to. She'd put his lack of enthusiasm down to the fact the pregnancy wasn't planned, that they weren't in love with each other, that they were only together because of the baby. But now she could see how difficult those appointments must have been for him. How he would be thinking of his mother and how his mother's pregnancy with him had ended in his birth and her death. If only she had known, if only he had told her, maybe their relationship wouldn't have floundered so badly after losing their baby.

Juliette still couldn't say her name out loud. Emilia. Once she'd been out in London and a young mother had called out to a small child with the same name. Juliette had to leave the store—she didn't even stay long enough to buy the things she had come for. She couldn't hear that precious name without going to bits.

How would it feel to walk into her nursery?

Or had Joe redecorated the room since she'd left? Had he stripped his villa of any record of her and the baby? The need to know was unbearable, even though she knew by opening the door she would be tearing open an already raw and seeping wound.

She took a deep breath and turned the handle and pushed the door open, reaching for the light switch on the wall. It was like a time capsule. Nothing had changed. The toys with their soft little bodies and sightless eyes were keeping watch over the empty cot. The hand-embroidered quilt was smoothly tucked in, the sheets neatly folded. The cross-stitched sampler she had made was framed above. *Emilia.*

Juliette's throat closed, her heart gave a spasm, her eyes filled. Joe hadn't changed a thing. Everything was the same. Everything. She walked further into the room and touched the mobile over the cot, sending it on a gentle rotation. She didn't have the courage to turn on the nursery rhyme music. There was only so much heartache she could stand.

She brushed at her eyes with the back of her hand, stepping away from the cot to pick up one of the soft toys off the shelf. It was a floppy-eared white rabbit with a pink satin bow. She held it to her face, breathing in the still newish smell, wondering if there would ever be a time when she would be able to think of her baby and not have this aching weight pressing down on her chest.

Juliette put the rabbit back on the shelf and went to the chest of drawers next to the change table. She pulled the first one open and looked at the tiny vests and booties and onesies lying there. She picked up a pair of booties—booties she had knitted herself. She swallowed and put them back and closed the drawer, her eyes burning, chest aching, emotions smashing through her like brutal, punishing waves.

She walked back to the door and turned for one last look at the room. Could there be anything more heartbreaking than an empty nursery, never used?

And then, with a sigh, she switched off the light and softly closed the nursery door behind her.

Juliette went further along the wide corridor to the spare room furthest away from the master bedroom. She opened the door and switched on the light but stopped short when she saw Joe lying face down on the bed. Naked. *Gulp.* He was soundly asleep, his strongly muscled legs splayed across the mattress, his arms resting either side of his head.

She ran her hungry gaze over his toned back and shoulders, feasted on the taut shape of his buttocks, his hair-roughened legs. She came closer, reaching for the throw rug on the foot of the bed, gently easing it out from under his feet and laying it over him to keep him from being cold, even though it wasn't a particularly cool night.

Why was he sleeping in one of the spare rooms? Why not in the master bedroom?

Juliette began to step backwards away from the bed to leave the room when he opened his eyes. He turned over onto his back, the throw rug slipping to barely cover his pelvis. Dark masculine hair arrowed down from his muscle-ridged abdomen, disappearing under the throw rug, but her memory filled in the rest of the picture for her. Hot colour rushed to her cheeks and her pulse flew off the starting blocks and raced and raced and raced.

'I—I'm sorry…' She backed further away from the bed. 'I didn't know you were sleeping in here.'

He sat up and pushed his hand through his sleep-tousled hair. 'I sleep better in this room.' He yawned and threw off the throw rug, stood and stretched, and her female hormones jumped for joy.

Juliette turned her back so quickly she became lightheaded. Or maybe that was because the sight of him naked was enough to make her faint. With desire. 'Could you please cover yourself?' She sounded like a prim spinster from another century but she couldn't look at him without wanting him.

Joe came over to her and placed his hands on the tops of her shoulders. Juliette sucked in a ragged breath, her senses reeling at his closeness. She could feel his body heat—*his naked body heat*—behind her, tempting her to lean back to feel the deliciously hard ridge she was almost certain would be there.

He leaned down to place a kiss just below her left ear and she tilted her head sideways to allow him access, her will to resist evaporating. 'Haven't you heard that saying—*let sleeping dogs lie*?' The soft movement of his lips against her skin, the waft of his warm breath, the deep rough burr of his voice was enough to make her legs fold beneath her like severed marionette strings.

'I told you—I didn't know you were in here. I was looking for somewhere to sleep and—'

He turned her to face him, his eyes sexily hooded and focused on her mouth. His thumb came up and brushed her lower lip, and something deep and low in her belly rolled over. 'Sleep with me.'

It was a command rather than a request and for some reason she was fine with that. More than fine. She didn't want to overthink why she was standing in the circle of his arms with her body burning with lust. But somehow, being back in this house with all the memories it contained shifted something in her—especially now she understood more about him. Things about his personality that made her see him in a totally different light. A light that drew her closer and closer like a storm-tossed dinghy towards the strong, steady glow of a lighthouse. Right now, all she wanted was to be in his arms, to feel the potent power of his body within hers, to feel nothing but passion, lust, longing and have those primal needs satisfied. By him.

Juliette placed her hands around his neck, pressing closer to the hard heat of his body, her body responding with humid heat of its own. She could feel the slick preparation of her inner core, the dew of arousal signalling her readiness, her eagerness, her wantonness. 'Are you telling me or asking me?' Her voice was just shy of a whisper but still managed to contain a spirited note.

He gave a crooked smile and drew her flush against him. 'Right now, I'd get on my hands and knees and beg if that's what you wanted me to do.'

She stepped up on tiptoe and brought her mouth to just a breath away from his. 'This is what I want you to do.' And then she closed the distance between their lips.

He made a desperate sound at the back of his throat and his arms tightened around her. His lips moved against hers in a series of hot presses, massages, nudges, teases. She opened to the commanding thrust of his tongue, the blatantly erotic movement sending lightning strikes of electricity straight to her core. Flickers and flames of want leapt through her body and she wondered how she had managed to survive so long without this conflagration of the senses. Her body was alive and wanting, aching with the need to have him deep within her.

Joe lifted his mouth off hers and started working on her clothes. 'Let's get rid of these. I want to look at you. All of you.'

Juliette tried to help him but her hands weren't cooperating. Besides, they were already occupied exploring his muscled chest and toned abdomen on her journey down to his erection. She took him in her hand and stroked him the way she knew made him wild for her.

Joe groaned and pulled her hand away. 'Let's get you naked first.' He continued to remove her clothes and each time a slip of fabric fell away from her body she shivered as his glittering gaze ran over her. 'You're so beautiful. So hot. I'm going crazy here.' His fingers struggled with the fastening on her top. 'Damn it. Why do you wear such complicated clothes?'

Juliette laughed and helped him with the fastening, leaving her in nothing but her bra and knickers. His hands cupped her breasts and even through the delicate barrier of lace her flesh leapt at his touch. Her nipples tight, her breasts tingling and sensitive, her inner core aching with need.

Joe placed his hands on her hips, his expression now gravely serious. 'Are you sure about this, *cara*? We can't undo this once it's done.'

Juliette brushed her lips against his. 'Totally sure. I want you. Don't make me wait any longer.'

He brought his mouth down on hers in a firm kiss that spoke of his own escalating need. Their tongues met and tangled, heat flaring between their bodies like an out of control fire. Joe deftly unclipped her bra and it fell to the floor at her feet. His mouth lifted off hers as he slid her knickers down her thighs. She stepped out of them, kicking them aside with one foot, and then moving close to his body again.

He cradled one of her breasts in his hand, his thumb stroking her budded nipple, sending shivers shooting to the core of her being. He brought his mouth down to her breast, his tongue circling her nipple, his teeth gently grazing the sensitive nub and his lips caressing the dark circle of her areola. Tingles coursed through her body, hot tingles and fizzes that sent her senses into a frenzy. Need throbbed and ached between her legs in a pounding rhythm in time with her racing blood.

'You have no idea how long I've ached to do this…' His voice had a ragged quality as one of his hands cupped her mound.

Juliette gasped with delight when he inserted one thick finger into her wet heat. 'Oh, God, I've missed this. I've missed you.' She shuddered from head to foot as his finger caressed her, his expert strokes sending hot streaks of longing down through her pelvis.

He brought his mouth back to hers in a long drugging kiss that made her forget about everything but the sensations coursing through her body. He tasted of salt and a hint of whisky and danger but she was addicted to all of it. Addicted to all of him. The flickering caress of his fingers sent her catapulting into a dizzying flight, spinning her into an abyss where she was conscious of nothing but the exquisite sensations rippling through her.

Juliette gripped his shoulders with her hands. 'Don't let me go. I might not be able to stand upright.'

'I'm not letting you go. I haven't finished with you yet.' His rough tone and strong hands made her insides quiver like an unset jelly.

He walked her to the bed, laying her down and coming down beside her, his dark eyes unashamedly feasting on her body. He trailed a lazy finger from the upper curves of each breast, down her sternum to the tiny shallow cave of her belly button. He spread her thighs and brought his mouth down to the secret heart of her body. She sucked in a breath, heady anticipation for his touch sending another hot shiver down her spine. His tongue tasted her, teased her, tantalised her into another earth-shattering orgasm. It went on and on, sending shudders throughout her flesh until she was breathless and gasping.

Joe placed his hand on her abdomen, his gaze doing a slow appraisal of her body. 'I want you.'

Take me. Take me. Take me.

Juliette panted it under her breath, her heart still hammering in the aftermath of ecstasy. But her body still craved him, it craved his presence deep inside and she reached for him, cupping him in her hand. 'What are you waiting for?' she said.

He eased her hand off his erection. 'I need to get a condom. Don't go anywhere.'

'I won't.' Juliette lay back and watched him hunt for a condom but it was taking too long. Her need for him was throbbing like a tribal drum between her legs—deep, pulsing, insistent.

He opened his wallet and swore, tossing it back down again.

Juliette propped herself up on her elbows. 'What? Don't you have one? What about in the bathroom?'

Joe came back over and leaned down to press a hot hard kiss on her mouth. 'I'll be right back.'

Joe hoped he still had condoms that weren't past their use-by date. Using protection was an issue, irrespective of whether they were officially back together or not. The thought of exposing Juliette to another pregnancy, another terrible loss was out of the question. But what was this...this interlude for Juliette? What was it for him? Just a quick scratch-the-itch-and-regret-it-in-the-morning?

Either way, it was a risk he was prepared to take. He wanted her. He wanted her with an ache so hot and hard and tight it was making him crazy. Making him think beyond tonight. Making him hope they might salvage something from the train wreck of their relationship.

Joe rummaged in the bathroom cupboard off the spare bedroom and found a couple of condoms in his toiletries bag he used when travelling. They had been there for months without him even noticing. But why would he have noticed them? He hadn't been interested in sleeping with anyone since Juliette had left. Not just because he considered he was technically still married, but because he couldn't stomach touching another woman. Being with any woman other than Juliette was repugnant to him. In the past, he'd had his share of casual flings—more than his share. His wealth and status made it easy to pick up casual dates. He had not even thought about it before he'd met Juliette. It was like following a script: drink and/or dinner, dive into bed with an equally enthusiastic and willing partner.

It had worked until it hadn't worked.

He'd met Juliette, they had a one-night stand and whoomph. He hadn't been the same since. He hadn't slept with anyone else since the night he'd met her. Not even when he had no contact with her for three months until she tracked him down to tell him she was carrying his baby. He'd blamed it on his work schedule—he was too busy, travelled too much, was too tired for the chase. All those things might well have been true but he knew deep down it was because sleeping with Juliette had shifted something inside him and he couldn't shift it back. But he would have to find a way, because there were no guarantees she would stay if he offered her a reconciliation.

He had to remember: she'd come here to get the divorce papers signed. Her willingness to sleep with him was probably nothing more than a parting gift. A farewell… Insert coarse swear word. That was all it could be, right? Why was he thinking it could be anything else?

Joe went back to the bedroom to find Juliette lying on her stomach with her chin propped up on her hands. He drank in the smooth curves of her spine and bottom, his lower body twitching with impatience to glide between her legs and thrust home.

'Did you find any?'

He held them up in his fingers. 'Only two, so if you have any ideas of a marathon you'd better hold that thought.'

Something passed over her features and her eyes momentarily slipped out of reach of his. 'What are your plans for the rest of the weekend?' Her tone was casual. Too casual.

Joe came and sat beside her on the bed, placed his hand on her hip and turned her so she was lying on her back. He leaned closer, placing his hands either side of her head, caging her in, his gaze feasting on the sweet globes of her breasts. His groin pounding with feverishly hot blood. 'Shouldn't I be asking *you* that question?'

Her eyes flicked to his mouth. 'I don't know what this is…' She touched her hand to his jaw, grazing her fingers along his stubble. 'I mean…what we're doing…'

'Seems pretty obvious to me, *cara*.' Joe leaned on one elbow and traced his finger around one of her nipples in a lazy circle. 'We're getting it on.'

She pulled her lower lip partway into her mouth, releasing it again, her eyes still troubled. 'Break-up sex? Or…something else?'

It was the million-dollar question Joe didn't have an answer for. He kept his expression casually indifferent when inside he was mentally holding his breath. 'What else could it be? You came here wanting a divorce.'

A small frown pulled at her forehead and her finger brushed over his lower lip. 'I came here determined to get you to sign those papers. It was my goal. My mission…but now…' She gave a tiny sigh and her hand moved to the back of his neck, bringing his head closer. 'I want you to make love to me. I know it's probably wrong or inconsistent of me when I've been waving divorce papers in your face, but it's what I want for now. Just while I'm in Italy.'

A break-up fling with his soon-to-be ex-wife.

But Joe wanted her any way he could have her. 'I want you to stay until after the Paris fundraiser.' He knew he was taking a risk using such a commanding tone but did it anyway.

Her eyes flicked to his mouth and her tongue darted out to lick her lower lip, tightening the ache in his groin another unbearable notch. 'Okay. I'll go with you to Paris.'

'Good. But as long as we're both clear on what this actually is.'

Was *he* clear? The only clarity he had was that this felt right. Having her here in his arms. The trouble was...how was he going to let her go when it was time for her to leave? Or could he dare to hope she would stay? But that would mean resuming their marriage and look at what a rubbish job he'd done of it the first time around.

'I want you, Joe.' Her voice was as soft as her touch.

'I want you so badly.' Joe covered her mouth and lost himself in the hot, sweet temptation of her lips. His tongue met hers and a lightning bolt of lust shot through his groin. He gathered her in his arms, their legs tangling in a way that was achingly familiar and yet no less thrilling. It was like discovering her body for the first time—the dips and slopes and contours, the honeyed secret of her centre, the taste of her mouth and the feel of her breath mingling intimately with his.

He left her mouth to kiss his way down the scented hollows of her neck, over the delicate scaffold of her collarbone, all the way to her breasts. He took each nipple in his mouth, rolling his tongue over the tightly budded flesh, his blood thrumming with excitement. Her soft breathless groans, the arching of her spine, the folding out of her knees to welcome him made his heartrate spike. No one could turn him on like her. No one got him so worked up and ready to explode. No one.

He slipped on a condom and, putting a hand under her left hip to tilt her towards him, entered her with a deep thrust that made the hairs on his scalp stand up and a shudder ripple through him. She welcomed him with a gasp and began moving with him, her smooth slim legs in a sexy tangle with his. It was too hard for him to slow down as he'd planned. Too hard to resist the magnetic pull of her silken body. He thrust and thrust, his blood racing like rocket fuel through his veins, his skin tingling from head to foot. He placed his hand between their rocking bodies to caress her.

She threw her head back, writhing and whimpering as her orgasm took her away and carried him with her. The tight rolling spasms of her body sent him flying into the stratosphere. He buried his face into the side of her neck and groaned and shuddered and shook as his release powered through him in pulses and waves and ripples, taking him to a place beyond thought. Beyond the ugly divorce word, beyond the lonely emptiness of a future without her in it.

Beyond anything but mindless, magical bliss.

CHAPTER NINE

JULIETTE WOKE TO find herself spooned in Joe's arms. One of his legs was flung over hers, his head buried against the back of her neck, where she could feel his deep and even breaths stirring her hair. One of his hands was resting on her ribcage and he murmured something unintelligible and glided it up to cup her breast. She shivered with longing, her inner core contracting with the muscle memory of their passionate lovemaking during the night.

He groaned and sighed like a satisfied lion and propped himself up, turning her so she was on her back, his dark gaze smouldering. He brushed her hair back from her forehead with a touch so gentle it made something in her chest spring open. 'So here we are. The morning after the night before.' His tone was playful but she sensed an undercurrent of gravity.

She pushed back his hair from his forehead with her splayed fingers. 'You probably need to find a better way of getting through your birthday without drinking on your own or having one-night stands with strangers.'

He circled her mouth with a lazy finger, his gaze suddenly inscrutable. 'Is that what last night was? A one-night stand with a stranger?'

Juliette lowered her hand to his jaw, stroking his lean cheek with a feather-light touch. 'You don't feel like a stranger to me now. Not after we talked about…stuff.'

A frown flickered on his forehead and his gaze became wary. 'Is that why you slept with me? Out of pity?'

She pulled her hand from his face and jerked her chin back in shock. 'How could you think that? I wanted to make love with you. I practically begged you to.'

He placed a firm hand on the flank of her thigh to keep her moving further away, the heat of his touch sending a fizzing current to her core. 'There's probably a lot of stuff I should have told you before. But I try to forget about how I came into the world. I don't like thinking about it, much less talking about it.'

Juliette slid her hand back to rest against his cheek, her thumb stroking back and forth over his prickly skin. 'It must be awful to not look forward to your birthday. It must have been so painful growing up without a mother, especially feeling so guilty about how you lost her. But it wasn't your fault. Your father should've made that absolutely clear.'

His gaze flickered with shadows, as if he was leafing through his childhood memories like fanning through the pages of a thick book. 'He was grieving for a long time. I didn't understand that until I was much older. He was like a zombie walking through life. He was only a young man. My mother was the love of his life—they met in primary school. They married at twenty-one.' His mouth twisted and his eyes briefly squeezed shut as if he was experiencing the most excruciating pain. 'And she was dead at twenty-two. She didn't get to live the life she'd planned. She didn't get to reach her potential, to do the things most people dream of doing.' He swallowed and continued in a strained tone, 'I hated going to visit her grave. I felt sick to my stomach, because I knew I was the one who put her there. Who robbed her of everything: the man she loved, the future she'd dreamed of, the family life she longed for. I took it all away from her.'

Juliette blinked back tears. 'Oh, Joe, I wish I'd known all that before. I feel so annoyed at myself for not pressing you to tell me more about yourself. Is that why you found my pregnancy so unsettling? I sensed you were staying away longer and longer, the further along the pregnancy went.'

He took one of her hands and brought it up to his chest, holding it against the steady thump of his heart. 'I wanted to support you—that's why I married you, to provide for you and the baby. But when I saw your belly growing bigger each week, a vague panic set in and I could only quell it by distracting myself with work. I don't think I was entirely conscious of it at the time—why I was feeling like that. I just felt compelled to work as hard as I could. But I see how you would've read that as something else.'

Juliette swallowed a knot of emotion in her throat. 'When you got to the delivery suite… I thought you looked relieved… I hated you at that moment. I couldn't believe you were being so brutally insensitive.'

A flash of pain went through his eyes and his fingers on her hand tightened. 'I was relieved. Relieved you hadn't died.' His voice sounded rough around the edges, raw and uneven. 'I didn't think about the baby at that point. All I could think on my way into that room was, *Has it happened again? Have I killed my mother and now my wife?*'

Juliette bit down on her lower lip until she was sure it would draw blood. She couldn't believe how blind she had been. How blinkered she'd been to think he hadn't cared about her and their child. She pulled her hand out of his so she could hug him around the neck. She rested her cheek on his chest, her throat so tight it was aching. 'I've made so many mistakes. I'm sorry for misjudging you.'

Joe rested his chin on the top of her head and stroked her hair with his hand. 'We've both made mistakes.' His voice was a low, deep rumble against her ear. 'I guess the thing to do now is not make any more.'

Was *this* a mistake? Lying in his arms, wanting him with a

need so strong it throbbed deep in her core. A need that made a mockery of the divorce papers she had brought with her. Joe hadn't said anything about loving her. And nor had she to him. She still wasn't sure how to describe her feelings for him. They had been under layers of bitterness and anger and grief and were only now rising to the surface. One thing she did know for sure—they didn't feel anything like the 'love' she'd thought she'd felt for her ex. They felt strong and lasting, healing and hopeful.

How long Juliette wanted to stay with Joe was not so easy for her to acknowledge—even to herself. She'd only booked her hotel for one night, as she'd planned to fly back to England once the divorce papers were signed. But spending the night with Joe and finding out so much more about his background made her reluctant to rush off home without spending a bit more time with him. To answer some important questions that were niggling at her conscience.

She felt foolish and immature for being so intransigent in Corfu about going to Paris with him, but was it too soon to jump back into their relationship? Was it too soon to hope he would grow to love her as she was growing to love him? Or maybe she had always loved him. From the moment they'd met she had felt something shift inside her. The connection they'd formed had rocked her to the core and not just because of the pregnancy and its tragic outcome. Her misplaced anger towards him had covered up her true feelings. Feelings that had sprouted at that first meeting but had been poisoned and almost destroyed by the tragedy of losing their little baby.

'I know you're busy with work but I can hang out here and sketch and relax by the pool until we go to Paris. I'll try not to get in your way.'

One side of his mouth lifted, his gaze gleaming with unmistakable desire. 'You can get in my way all you like.' He traced her mouth with a lazy finger. 'The more the better.'

Juliette shivered at his tingling touch. 'You don't mind me being here?'

'Not at all.' And his mouth came down and confirmed it.

Juliette woke later that morning to find the bed empty beside her. She glanced at the clock beside the bed and was a little surprised she had slept in for so long. How could it be nine in the morning? She couldn't remember the last time she had slept so soundly. Her nights were usually disturbed by restlessness and sleeplessness, rumination and regret.

She threw off the bedcovers and slipped on a bathrobe. *Joe's bathrobe.* She breathed in the scent of him, her senses whirling, her belly fluttering, her heart swelling as she recalled his exquisite lovemaking during the night.

How could she regret last night? It was impossible. She felt close to Joe in a way she had never expected to feel. Knowing more about his heartbreaking background had softened her anger towards him and directed it more at herself. Her own grief had blinded her to the reality of his. Didn't the untouched nursery demonstrate that? He hadn't changed a thing in that beautiful room. Last night, he had shown her with his lips and hands and body how much he'd missed her.

Juliette walked out of the bedroom to head downstairs, where she could hear Joe moving about in the kitchen. But as she was passing the door to the master bedroom she had previously shared with him, she stopped and reached for the door knob. Why did he no longer sleep there? What had motivated him to occupy one of the spare bedrooms instead? She opened the door and, leaving the door open behind her, walked further into the room.

Memories floated towards her, stirring her emotions into a way she hadn't expected. She walked past the king-sized bed where she had spent so many nights wrapped in his arms, when he'd come home from his work trips. She opened the door of the walk-in wardrobe and found her clothes still hanging there as if she had never left. She could even pick up a faint trace of her signature perfume. She came out of the wardrobe and entered the en suite bathroom. Some of the cosmetics and toiletries she hadn't bothered to take with her were on the marble counter and in the cupboards under the twin basins.

Surely he could have got one of his housekeepers to remove her belongings? Why hadn't he? Or had Joe been *expecting* her to return?

Juliette frowned and came out of the bathroom to find Joe standing in the open doorway of the bedroom, carrying a tray with tea and toast and preserves. His expression was hard to read. On the surface he looked relaxed and open but she could sense an inner tension.

'I was just bringing you breakfast in bed.'

'Why didn't you get rid of my things?'

He came further into the room and placed the tray on the bedside table. He straightened to face her. 'I figured if you wanted them you would've taken them with you when you left or asked me to send them to you.'

Juliette searched his unreadable gaze. 'Were you always expecting me to come back?'

Something flickered at the back of his eyes and his mouth took on a rueful twist. 'No. I had given up on that score.' His tone contained a flat note of bleakness.

She sat on the edge of the bed and looked up at him. 'Joe… why don't you use this room any more?'

He ran a hand around his shirt collar as if the fabric was prickling him. 'I told you last night—I sleep better in the other room.'

'But why?'

Joe released a harsh-sounding breath. 'For God's sake, do I need to spell it out?'

Juliette kept her gaze trained on his. 'Yes, I'm afraid you do.'

He drew in another breath but this time released it less forcefully. He sat down beside her and took one of her hands in his.

His fingers wrapping around hers in a protective cloak. 'Every time I came in here was another reminder of how I'd let you down. I couldn't be in here without thinking about you. It was easier not to come in here at all.'

Juliette lifted her hand to his cleanly shaven jaw. 'Is that why you left the nursery as I left it?'

A flash of pain went through his gaze. 'I can't even bear to say her name, much less go in there and be reminded of her.' His voice was raw with suppressed emotion, his jaw tightening against the cup of her palm.

Tears sprouted in her eyes. 'Oh, Joe, I can't say her name either. Some days, I can't even think it without falling to bits.'

Joe brought his hand to her face, blotting her tears with the pad of his thumb. His eyes were dry but pained. 'My whole career has been based on fixing things that are broken. Finding why things that shouldn't have failed, failed. But I couldn't fix any of this for us.'

Juliette put her arms around him and laid her head on his chest. 'I'm glad we're able to be so honest with each other now. It helps me to know I'm not the only one who feels so undone by what's happened.'

His hand stroked the back of her head in gently soothing strokes that made the last of the armour around her heart melt away. 'I wish I'd been there to support you better. There's so much I would like to have done differently.' His deep voice rumbled against her cheek—full of low, deep chords of regret and self-recrimination.

'It might have been different if we had known each other better at the time,' Juliette said, glancing up at him. 'I mean, if we'd had a normal period of dating before we married. I feel like I'm only getting to know you now.' When it was too late. Or was it?

He glanced at the tea tray with a wry expression. 'I'm trying to decide whether to feed you breakfast or give you a kiss first.'

Juliette linked her arms around his neck and smiled. 'Just one kiss?'

His eyes smouldered and he gathered her closer. 'Why stop at one?'

And he didn't.

A couple of days before the Paris trip, Joe came in to the morning room where Juliette was sketching. He had been on a lengthy Skype call in his study. 'Sorry that took so long,' he said, leaning down to press a kiss to the top of her head. 'Hey, it's great to see you sketching again.' He picked up one of her earlier sketches—one of him sleeping—and frowned. 'I look so relaxed.' He put the sketch back down.

Juliette swivelled on her chair to look up at him. Something in his expression sent off a distracted vibe. A subtle distance in his gaze. A slight disturbance in his tone.

'Is everything okay? Has something come up with work?'

'I've been thinking about this Paris thing.'

Juliette straightened in her seat, unsure what to make of his expression. 'You still want me to go…don't you?'

'I shouldn't have pressured you into going. I can go alone if you don't feel up to being social.'

Juliette rose from her chair and wrapped her arms around her middle, uncertain of what to make of his seeming reluctance to have her accompany him. Was he wary of being out in public with her in case people read more into their relationship than was true? After all, they weren't officially reconciled. They were having a break-up fling. Did he want to keep their involvement with each other out of the press? Or was there some other reason?

She turned her back to him and stared at the view of the ocean below the steep slopes, with their collection of old and luxury villas and the vivid splashes of colour and greenery. 'Are you worried I might say or do something I shouldn't? That I might disgrace you in some way?'

Joe came over to her and placed his hands on the top of her tense shoulders. He turned her around to face him, his expression etched in lines of concern. 'No. I'm worried people will make you feel uncomfortable. You know how it works at these gatherings. You get stuck next to someone who wants to know every detail about your life or tell you every detail of theirs.' He made a husky, clearing his throat sound and added, 'I know it's a fundraiser for stillbirth research and counselling services but people can still ask intrusive questions. I don't want you to be hurt by someone asking you about things you'd rather not talk about.'

Juliette's heart gave a funny little flutter-spasm.

He was concerned about her. He wanted to protect her.

She had done her usual jumping to conclusions by thinking he was somehow ashamed of her, worried she might drink too much and humiliate him. But it was nothing to do with any of that.

He genuinely cared about her.

She put her hands on his chest, her lower body flush against his. 'I've avoided a lot of social events for exactly that reason. What if someone asks me if I have any children? Or plan to try again? What am I supposed to say? Am I even allowed to call myself a mother when I didn't give birth to a live baby?'

Joe framed her face in his hands, his gaze tender as it meshed with hers. 'You will always be Emilia's mother. No one can take that away from you. No one.'

Tears stung her eyes and a lump formed in her throat. 'Y-you said her name…'

Joe stroked his thumbs across each of her cheeks in a slow soothing motion. 'Maybe some time in the future it won't hurt so much to say it. To think of her.'

'Maybe…' Juliette sighed and leaned her cheek against his chest. 'They say time is a great healer, but how *much* time?'

'As long as it takes, I guess.'

There was a small silence, broken only by the sound of his hand stroking the back of her head and their quiet breathing.

It was an enormous comfort to her that he felt the same sense of loss. She had unfairly assumed he was less affected because he hadn't been the one to carry the baby, to physically give birth, and that he hadn't been there to witness the birth. But she realised now his expression of grief was different from hers.

Not wrong, but different.

Juliette lifted her head off his chest and looked up at him. 'I can't avoid social events for ever. I want to go with you. It's important to support such valuable fundraising.'

A small smile flicked up the corners of his mouth and illuminated his gaze. 'We could make a long weekend of it. How does that sound?'

She linked her arms around his neck and smiled. 'It sounds wonderful. I haven't been to Paris for years.'

He pressed a kiss to her upturned mouth. 'How remiss of me not to have taken you before now.'

Juliette played with the ends of his hair that brushed his collar. But she was conscious of a small grey cloud of unease creeping closer. Paris. The city of love. Had he taken anyone else in the past? She wasn't aware she was frowning until Joe inched up her chin and smoothed the crease away from her forehead with a gentle finger.

'What's wrong, *mio piccolo?*'

Juliette forced a smile but it fell a little short of the mark. 'I guess you've been to Paris heaps and heaps of times with lots of other…people…' She couldn't bring herself to say the word *lovers*—the pang of jealousy was too intense.

His eyes softened and he drew her closer with one hand resting in the dip of her spine, the other gliding to the sensitive nape of her neck. 'You have no need to feel jealous, *cara*.'

Juliette slipped out of his hold and pretended an interest in straightening her sketches on the table. 'I'm not jealous. I know you've been to lots of places with lots of different people.'

'But none of them have been my wife.'

My wife. The words sounded so…so permanent. But they hadn't decided anything permanent about their relationship.

They had discussed a lot of issues, yes. And grown closer in so many new ways. But Juliette knew there would be other issues to discuss. Difficult, painful issues—whether or not to have another child, for instance. That was one of the questions she most dreaded. For months and months since the loss of her baby, she couldn't bear the thought of trying again. Going through another pregnancy with fear and dread on board as well as a baby. A baby there was no guarantee she would deliver alive.

Juliette held onto the back of one of the chairs and glanced down at her ring finger. The vacant space seemed to mock her. He referred to her as his wife but there had been no renewed promises. No official reconciliation. No renewed commitment. No declaration of love.

She brought her gaze back to his. 'Have you told anyone we're…?' She left the sentence hanging, not sure how to describe their relationship. A fling sounded so tawdry. An affair even worse.

'No. Have you?'

She pressed her lips together and released her grip on the chair, using one hand to sweep her hair back over one shoulder. 'I didn't think it was necessary…under the circumstances.'

'Precisely.' Something about the delivery of the word was jarring. Discordant. Like the wrong note played during a musical performance.

Juliette ran the tip of her tongue over her lower lip. 'It would be silly to get people's hopes up. Lucy and Damon, for instance.' *Not to mention her own hopes.*

'But what if the fundraiser draws a lot of press attention? Aren't people going to assume we're back together permanently?'

The ensuing silence was too long. Why wasn't he asking her to come back to him for ever? Why wasn't he dismissing her concerns with a declaration of love?

'There isn't a law about divorcing couples attending a social function together.' Joe's voice sounded tight. Constricted. 'If anything, it will demonstrate how civilised we're being about the whole damn thing.'

She studied his tense features for a moment, wondering if he was having second thoughts about their divorce. But, if so, why hadn't he said anything? 'Joe…?'

He scraped a hand through his hair and released a rough sigh. 'The press will probably make a big thing of it, but that's to be expected. I'll try and shield you as much as possible.'

Juliette approached him, touching him on the forearm. 'I want to be with you.' She couldn't think of anything she wanted more. Not just the Paris trip but with him all the time. For ever. Was she a fool for hoping he would agree to a reconciliation? Maybe the Paris trip would cement their relationship—take it to a new level that would make him realise they had a chance to make it.

The tension in his face relaxed slightly and he cupped her face in his hands. His eyes searched hers as if he was looking for something he'd lost and hoped desperately to find again. 'The dinner is only for a couple of hours. We can spend the rest of the time doing our own thing.'

She linked her arms around his neck and pressed closer. 'I can't wait.'

CHAPTER TEN

THEY ARRIVED IN Paris on Friday afternoon and once they had settled into their luxury hotel Joe suggested they go shopping.

'Shopping?' Juliette looked at him in wary surprise. 'But I don't need anything.'

'How about a new outfit for tomorrow night?' He wanted to spoil her. To make this weekend as special for her as he could. To make this weekend last for as long as he could.

'I brought one with me. You don't have to waste money buying me expensive—'

'I insist, *cara*.'

Something flickered across her features. A tightening. A guardedness. 'Are you concerned I won't dress appropriately?'

Joe mentally kicked himself. He should know by now how proud and sensitive she was. He took her by the hands and brought her close to his body. 'You always look amazing in whatever you wear. Indulge me, *tesoro*. Let me spoil you this weekend.'

Her gaze slipped to the open collar of his shirt, her teeth sinking into her lower lip. 'I feel guilty about all the money you're spending. This hotel, first class airfares, designer clothes.'

He tipped up her face to meet her gaze. 'Don't you think you're worth it?'

Her eyes swam with doubt. 'It's not about that…'

'Then what is it about?'

Her teeth did another nibble of her lip and she slipped out of his hold. 'We're not exactly acting like a soon-to-be-divorced couple, are we?'

'I wasn't aware there was a strict protocol we had to follow.' Joe couldn't remove the note of bitterness from his tone. The divorce word was becoming worse to him than the birthday and funeral words. Every time he heard it, his heart stopped and his gut clenched like a fist.

Juliette turned to pick up her silk scarf from where she had left it on the bed. She looped it around her neck and turned back to face him. 'It feels wrong, taking gifts off you when we're not—'

'Does it feel wrong sleeping with me?'

Her expression faltered for a moment. 'No.' Her cheeks pooled with a tinge of pink and her gaze drifted to his mouth. 'It doesn't feel wrong at all.' Her voice was a few decibels shy of a whisper. 'But I can't help feeling it should.' A frown pulled at her forehead as if she was trying to solve a deeply puzzling mystery.

Joe placed his hands on her hips, his body responding to her closeness with a hot rush of blood to his groin. 'It would only be wrong if one of us didn't want to. Or if one of us was involved with someone else. But, for now, we're involved with each other.'

Her mouth flickered with a vestige of a smile. 'Right.' She took a serrated breath and released it. 'For now.' She said the two words as if she was underlining them.

'If you're not okay with that, then you need to tell me.'

Her grey-blue eyes were clear and still as a lake but he sensed a disturbance just below the surface. 'I'm okay with it.' Her tone was confident, assured. Her smile a little too bright to be believed.

Joe reached for one of her hands and brought it up to his mouth. He pressed his lips to her bent knuckles, holding her gaze with his. 'Then let's make the most of it.'

* * *

A couple of hours later, Juliette felt as if she had stepped into Cinderella's shoes. Joe took her to various designer stores, where he proceeded to buy her not one, but several gorgeous outfits. She tried not to think about the money he was spending or why he was spending it on her. It was wonderful to be spoilt like a princess and wonderful to be in his company, walking hand in hand along the streets as if they were just like any other couple.

'Time for a coffee?' Joe said when they came across a street café.

'Lovely.' Juliette sat opposite him and took in the surroundings while they waited for the waiter to arrive. The leafy trees along the footpath created a canopy of dappled shade. The afternoon was mild with a light breeze that every now and again set the leaves above them into a shivery dance that sounded like thousands of pieces of tinsel. In the distance she could see the ancient cathedral of Notre Dame in various stages of repair after the devastating fire that had threatened the entire structure. It reminded her of her relationship with Joe—the savage fire of loss had ripped through their lives and left them both scarred shells of themselves. But maybe this time together would rebuild the framework of their marriage, making it stronger and more resistant to damage.

The waiter took their order and within a short time an espresso was placed in front of Joe and tea and a buttery croissant set in front of Juliette. She was conscious of Joe's gaze resting on her as she broke off pieces of the croissant. She glanced at him and held up a portion. 'Want some?'

He shook his head, his smile indulgent, and he patted his rock-hard abdomen. 'No, thanks. I have to think of my figure.'

Juliette laughed and put the piece of croissant back on her plate. 'Now you're making me feel guilty.'

There was a small silence.

'I've missed hearing your laugh.' He brought his cup up to his mouth, taking a sip without his gaze leaving her face.

Juliette could feel a light blush heating her cheeks. 'I can't remember the last time I laughed.' She sighed and added, 'It seems like a lifetime ago.'

He put his cup back on its saucer and reached for her hand across the table. His fingers gently squeezed hers, his expression sombre as he looked down at their joined hands. 'I think I was probably five or six years old when I first heard my father laugh. A proper laugh, I mean.' His thumb stroked the empty space on her ring finger. 'I asked him about it once. He said he felt guilty about being happy.' His eyes met hers. 'Like he was betraying my mother's memory.'

Juliette placed her other hand on top of his. 'It must have been so hard growing up without your mother. Mine drives me crazy at times but I can't imagine not having her in my life.'

His mouth flickered with a smile touched by sadness. 'I could mostly put it out of my mind but now and again something would remind me I wasn't like the other kids at school. Lots of them were in single parent families but mostly it was from divorce or separation, not the death of a parent. Parent-teacher interviews were difficult, and on Mother's Day, when the teacher got us to make cards, I made one for my *nonna* instead.'

'Were you close to your *nonna*?'

'I adored her. She was a widow herself so she understood what my father was going through but she died when I was nine.' His mouth twisted. 'I never met my mother's parents. They refused to have anything to do with my father. They weren't keen on him as a son-in-law in the first place, so you can imagine how they felt once she died. They blamed him for her death. I'm sure it didn't help his grieving process.'

Juliette's heart ached for what he had been through. So much sadness. So much loss. So much grief. Somehow it made what she had been through a little easier to bear. Just a little. 'I don't know how you coped with all that sadness. Did things improve at all once your dad remarried?'

'Yes and no.' Joe released her hand and picked up his coffee cup, cradling it baseball mitt style in one hand. 'My father was certainly happier. And my stepmother was nice enough but it was hard for her bringing up someone else's kid. A kid she had no history with, who she suddenly had to mother when she married my father. When they had two kids together, I felt even more of an outsider.' He lifted his cup to his lips and drained the contents, placing it back down on the saucer. 'And when my father died my stepmother no longer had to pretend to play happy blended families any more.'

If only he had told her this in the past. If only she had understood the trauma and sadness that had shaped his personality—the grief that had robbed him of a normal childhood and made him so cautious about relationships.

Juliette pushed her plate to one side and touched his hand where it was resting on the table. 'I wish I'd known more about your background when we first met.'

His eyes met hers, his fingers wrapping around hers in a gentle hold. 'I can't remember the last time I told anyone about any of this. It's not something I like talking about. Plenty of people have it much worse than I did.'

'Yes, but we were married and I should've understood you better.' She frowned and looked down at their joined hands. His wedding ring was a reminder that she was the one to leave their marriage, not him. Would he remove it once their divorce was finalised? Her stomach pitched at the thought of him being with someone else. She swallowed a tight lump and continued, 'I should've made more of an effort.'

Joe leaned forward and stroked a lazy finger down the curve of her cheek. 'None of this is your fault. You had your own stuff going on with your ex.'

Juliette sat back in her chair with a little thump and folded her arms and frowned. 'I wish you'd stop mentioning my ex. I don't even think I was truly in love with Harvey. I think I only continued with the relationship as long as I did as it seemed to please my parents.'

He studied her for a long moment. 'Were they pleased when we broke up?'

Juliette unfolded her arms and slumped her shoulders on a sigh. 'No. If anything, they thought I was being impulsive and letting my emotions overshadow everything. But I shut them down pretty quickly and they've said nothing since.'

'One could hardly blame you for being emotional, given the circumstances.' His tone was a disarming blend of gruffness and tenderness.

Juliette lowered her gaze, leaned forward and pushed a piece of croissant around her plate with her finger. 'I don't see much of them these days. They're always so busy with work. I know their careers are important to them but it always makes me feel I'm way down on their list of priorities.' She sighed and added, 'I wonder if it will change when they retire. *If* they retire, that is.'

There was a long silence.

Juliette chanced a glance at him but he was looking into the distance as if his thoughts had been pulled elsewhere. It gave her a moment to study his features—the frown of concentration, the sharply intelligent gaze, the chiselled jaw with its peppered regrowth, the sculptured contours of his mouth. Her belly flip-flopped when she thought about his mouth on hers, the silken thrust of his tongue, the heat and fire of his kiss.

He stirred his coffee even though she knew he didn't take sugar, his gaze focused on the tiny whirlpool he created in his cup. 'Some people live to work—others work to live.'

Juliette shifted uncomfortably in her chair. 'I suppose you think that makes me sound like a spoilt brat, insisting on being the centre of my parents' world.'

His gaze met hers. 'I don't think that at all. It can be difficult when our caregivers don't meet our expectations. Sometimes it's down to circumstances, other times to personality.'

Another silence ticked past.

Juliette shifted her gaze to the left of his. 'I was a change of life baby. An accident. A mistake.'

His expression clouded. 'Surely they didn't say they didn't want you?'

Juliette chewed the side of her lip. 'No. Never—it's just a feeling I've had over the years. Having a child at their stage of life must have been an inconvenience. My brothers were eighteen and twenty. I spent a lot of time with nannies and babysitters and, of course, boarding school, which I hated. I think that's why I never did that well at school. I disengaged out of emotional distress.'

He touched her hand where it was resting on the table. 'Don't be fooled into thinking a bunch of letters after your name makes you smart. You are an intelligent and hugely talented artist.'

Juliette hoped her creative drive would come back stronger than before but it had taken such a blow with the death of her baby. Her motivation had been totally crushed and was only now flickering into life. 'Thanks.'

He smiled and waved a hand at her teacup. 'Would you like a refill?'

'No. I'm done.' She pushed back her chair while he gathered the array of shopping bags around his chair.

He paid the bill and within a short time they were on their way back to the hotel. Once they arrived, Joe handed the porter the bags and accompanied Juliette to the private lift to the penthouse.

'Why don't you have a bit of a rest before dinner?' he said as the lift arrived at their suite. 'I have a couple of things to see to.'

Juliette tried to ignore the little stab of disappointment that jabbed her. 'Will you be long?'

He leaned down to press a light kiss to her lips. 'Not long at all.'

* * *

Joe walked the streets of Paris, ruminating on how he had approached life's challenges. Juliette's comment about her parents always working had struck a chord with him. Ever since he was a young child, he had thrown himself into tasks, study, work, to escape the shadows of his childhood. The loss that had defined him since he'd taken his first breath. Being successful, wealthy and hard-working had given him a framework for his life that had never let him down until he'd met Juliette.

But now he could feel the foundations of his personality undergoing a change, like a fine crack running through concrete. A gradual destabilisation of his identity as a man who needed no one.

Who kept himself emotionally separate, distant. Safe.

But the more time he spent with Juliette, the wider the cracks grew, allowing him to envisage the sort of man he could be if he was able to let go of the past. A man who could love and be loved in return. A man who would no longer need to keep his emotions locked down. A man who could embrace his vulnerabilities and face whatever life threw at him with emotional courage instead of cowardice.

His feelings for Juliette were something he had tried so hard to ignore. And he'd been damn good at it so far. So good he'd convinced himself not to beg her to come back to him when she'd left. So good he'd not revealed things to her he should have revealed while they were together. Things that might well have made a difference if he hadn't been so determined to hold himself apart, as he had done with every other relationship, both intimate and otherwise.

But now his feelings were tiptoeing out of their hiding place, their tentative footsteps leaving soft little impressions on his heart that felt almost painful.

He looked down at the wedding ring on his finger, the symbol of his commitment. A commitment he wasn't entirely sure Juliette wanted from him any more. She had made no commitment other than to spend the next few days with him before she went back to London.

Could he dare to hope to change her mind?

Juliette had showered and dressed and was putting the finishing touches to her make-up in preparation for the dinner when Joe returned to their hotel. She met his eyes in the mirror of the dressing table. 'You're cutting it fine. Isn't the dinner at seven-thirty?'

He gave a crooked smile. 'It won't take me long to get ready.' He came up behind her and, slipping one hand inside his jacket pocket, retrieved a rectangular jewellery box. 'I found something for you when I was out walking.'

Juliette turned on the stool and raised her brows. 'Found? Like on the footpath?' She gave him a mock frown and waggled a reproving finger at him. 'You've been spending money on me again.'

He handed her the box. 'And why shouldn't I spoil you?' He leaned down to press a light kiss to the top of her head. 'Mmm… You smell beautiful.'

Juliette lifted her face to meet his gaze. 'It's the same perfume I've always worn.'

His fingers brushed beneath her chin in an idle movement, his eyes dark and lustrous. 'I know. I smelt it everywhere in the house after you left.' His mouth turned down at the corners as if the mention of that time caused him pain. He glanced at the jewellery box in her hands. 'Go on. Open it.'

Juliette looked down at the box and ran her fingertip over the gold embossed designer label on the black velvet lid. She prised open the lid and gasped when she saw a glittering diamond on a gold chain as fine as a thread and two matching diamond droplet earrings.

'Oh, Joe, they're gorgeous.' She could only imagine how much they'd cost. It was the sort of jewellery designer where one didn't shop if one needed to see a price tag before considering purchasing anything.

'Here. Let me put the necklace on you.' His voice had a gruff edge, his expression hard to read.

She handed him the box and turned so she was facing the mirror again, watching him carefully remove the diamond from its plush white velvet bed. She shivered when his hands brushed the sensitive skin of her neck as he fastened the diamond in place. He handed her the earrings one at a time for her to insert into her earlobes. Then he rested his hands on her shoulders and met her eyes in the mirror.

'You look stunning.'

Juliette touched the diamond with her fingers, the earrings glinting like stars when she turned her head from side to side. 'I hope I don't lose one of them.'

He gave a grim smile that wasn't really a smile. 'There are worse things to lose, *cara*.' His deep tone echoed with a sadness that was almost palpable.

She placed one of her hands over one of his, pressing down on it in an I-know-what-you-mean gesture. Her throat thickened, her chest tightened, her eyes glistened. 'You'd better get dressed. It's almost time to leave.'

He looked as if he was about to say something—his brows moved closer together and his mouth opened as if in preparation to speak—but then seemed to change his mind. He gave her shoulders one last squeeze and turned away to get ready for the dinner.

The fundraising dinner was held in the ballroom of a private mansion within walking distance of their hotel. By the time Juliette and Joe arrived, the guests were making their way to their allotted tables after having drinks and finger food in the foyer. The room was decorated with simple and elegant arrangements of flowers and pastel-coloured paper rosettes and ribbons rather than less environment-friendly balloons.

Joe seemed to know many of the guests and introduced her to several people on the way to their place at the huge table but she found it hard to remember all their names. She smiled and shook hands with everyone, quietly wondering if any of them knew the circumstances about her and Joe's marriage.

Juliette was seated next to Joe, with a woman on her left in her mid to late forties called Marisa, who was on the board of directors for the charity.

'I'm so pleased to finally meet you,' Marisa said with a warm smile. She glanced covertly towards Joe but he was talking to the man next to him and added in a lower tone, 'We so appreciate what you and Joe have done for our charity. It's really lovely too that you could make it here with him.'

'Oh, well, it was really Joe who did all the fundraising. I'm afraid I had little to do with that at all.'

Marisa placed a gentle hand on Juliette's arm, her expression full of compassion. 'You don't have to explain. What you two went through is enough to tear apart any young couple. I should know. I had a stillbirth in between my first and third child. It was horrendous. I think of him every single day. We called him Alexandre.'

Juliette looked into the other woman's now shimmering hazel gaze and for the first time in months felt less alone and isolated. 'I'm so sorry.'

Marisa's mouth twisted. 'He would have been ten years old last month. You never really get over it. You carry it with you. I was lucky I already had a child. I'm not sure I would have been game enough to try again if I hadn't. But I'm so glad I did. My two girls are my biggest joy.'

Juliette swallowed a tight lump in her throat. 'How soon did you…try again?' Her voice was as tentative as her thoughts on the subject of having another baby. It was something she had been thinking about ever since she'd walked into the nursery. The thoughts were mostly at the back of her mind, but lately they were creeping closer and closer. Close enough for her to imagine cradling a beautiful baby in her arms.

A live baby.

Joe's baby.

'Months and months,' Marisa said. 'I could barely look at my husband without bursting into floods of tears. But I'd always wanted a family and Henri did too. We decided it would probably help us heal if we tried again. And it worked. It doesn't mean I don't still grieve. I do, and badly at times, and so does Henri. But the thing that helped Henri and me was setting up this foundation a couple of years after we lost Alexandre. Joe's contribution has been invaluable. It's meant we can do further important research as well as adding to our counselling services. It was so very kind and generous of him, when he was going through such a difficult time himself.'

Guilt rained down on Juliette anew. Joe might not have visited their daughter's grave but he had done what he could to stop such a tragedy from happening to others. Instead of trying to understand things from his point of view, she had pushed him away, rejected him, marched out of his life instead of sharing the burden of grief with him—without allowing him time to process his feelings, which were just as valid as hers.

'He's…a very kind and generous person,' she said, her heart so full of love for Joe she found it hard to take her next breath. Love that had grown from the moment she'd met him. The first kiss, the first night together—the night where she had given herself to him so wholeheartedly. The night that had bound them together with a subsequent tragedy. Could they move past it?

Marisa gently squeezed Juliette's hand where it was resting on her lap. 'You'll know when it's the right time to try again. You'll probably always feel worried during any subsequent pregnancy—that's entirely natural and unfortunately unavoidable. But the sheer joy of holding your baby at the end is worth it. There's really nothing like it.'

Juliette squeezed the other woman's hand in return. 'Thank you for sharing your experience with me. I've found it so hard to talk to anyone about it. Some people in my life think I should have moved on by now.'

'Not Joe, though?' Marisa frowned.

'No, not Joe.' Juliette sighed and continued. 'I've been so hard on him. I was so caught up in how I was feeling that I didn't realise he was feeling the same, only expressing it a different way.'

Marisa nodded in empathy. 'Tell me about it. I often was so angry at Henri for the most ridiculous things until I realised it was misplaced grief masquerading as anger. I could handle feeling angry. What I couldn't handle was feeling profound gut-wrenching, inescapable grief. But eventually we worked through it and are stronger and closer for it.'

Stronger and closer for it.

Juliette mulled over that phrase as the more formal part of the dinner commenced. The award was finally announced and Joe led Juliette up to the podium. Press cameras went off and later a journalist requested an interview. Joe spoke briefly about the foundation and skilfully steered the journalist away from their personal situation. It made Juliette all the more uncertain of what he ultimately wanted from her. A fling before they divorced—or did he want her to stay with him for ever?

Stronger and closer.

Would those words one day define her and Joe? The desire to heal was so strong in her now. Stronger than her anger, which seemed to have dissipated like fog under the hopeful beam of sunshine. And she realised now a part of that healing included fulfilling her dream of having a family. Of being part of a loving partnership with her husband, raising children in a house where love and acceptance and nurture were at the forefront at all times.

Time was reputed to be a great healer, but wasn't love the best healer of all?

CHAPTER ELEVEN

THEY WALKED BACK to their hotel in silence. Juliette had so many questions to ask, so many doubts to address, so many hopes to allow the freedom to grow. When they were back in their room she turned to look at him.

'Joe? I wish I'd known about your work with the foundation. It means so much to me that you've tried to help so many others like us. I'm sorry I blocked contact with you.'

He slipped off his jacket and hung it loosely over the back of a chair. His mouth was pressed flat for a moment and his eyes looked pained. 'I was almost glad you blocked me. I was worried about upsetting you. Every time we talk about the baby…' his throat rose and fell and his voice grew raspy '… I see what it does to you. It hurts you.'

Tears sprouted in her eyes and she went to him, wrapping her arms around his waist. 'But it hurts me more *not* to talk about her. Losing Emilia will always upset me. It's normal and unavoidable. We suffered a terrible loss. But I want to move on as best I can and that includes talking about how we're feeling and when we're feeling it.'

Joe cupped one side of her face, his other hand going to rest on her hip. His gaze held hers in a tender lock that made her heart contract. 'I felt so powerless and frustrated our baby died.

Giving to the foundation was the only thing I could think to do to remove some of that powerlessness. I figured by donating and raising large sums of money for research it would stop it happening to someone else. It helped me process my grief by actually doing something positive. I didn't want to be like my father, who was so prostrated by grief it took years for him to come out of it.'

Juliette stroked his jaw, leaning into his strong frame, her body responding to his closeness with its usual leap of excitement. 'I think you're amazing to have done that. It shows the wonderful man you are. Generous and kind and compassionate.'

He brought his head down so his mouth was just above hers. 'Don't make me out to be too much of a hero, *tesoro.* I have many failings.'

Juliette linked her arms around his neck. 'Kiss me, Joe. Make love to me.'

He drew her closer, his arms a strong band around her body, his mouth coming down on hers in a kiss that was soft and yet deeply passionate. Sensations swept through her body—hot, urgent sensations that made her weak at the knees. He lifted her in his arms, carrying her as if she weighed little more than a child, and took her through to the bedroom. He lowered her feet to the floor in front of him, his hands already setting to work on her clothes. Juliette got to work on his and within moments they were both naked and lying, limbs entwined, on the bed.

Joe's mouth came down on hers, firmer this time, his tongue entering her mouth to tease hers into erotic play. Molten heat pooled in her core, need pulsating deep in her feminine flesh. His mouth moved from her lips to explore the soft skin below her ear, his tongue flickering against her sensitive flesh until she writhed with pleasure. He went lower to her décolletage, tracing the fine structure of her collarbone and down to the gentle swell of her breasts. The action of his mouth and tongue evoked tingles and prickles and needles of pleasure through her breasts. Her nipples tightened, her spine melted, her need escalated.

His hand went to her hip, gliding to her bottom to tilt her towards him. '*Dio mio*, I want you so much.' His voice was a low, deep, agonised groan. He kissed her again, his tongue tangoing with hers until she was mindless with desire. He lifted his mouth off hers and rolled away to get a condom.

Juliette thought of telling him not to bother, that perhaps they should try for another baby instead of using protection. But she decided to keep that conversation for another time. A time when she had a better understanding of how he felt about her. He had never said he loved her. But she knew deep in her bones he cared about her. Cared more than he was probably willing to admit. And wasn't she a bit the same? She hadn't declared her love for him. Not yet.

Joe applied a condom and came back to gather her close. His eyes were so dark with desire they looked densely black. 'I'm glad you came with me to Paris.'

Juliette pressed a soft kiss to his mouth. 'I'm glad I came too. And, speaking of coming…' She hooked one leg over his and gave him a come-hither look.

'Leave it with me.' He smiled a sexy smile and brought his mouth back down to hers. 'I'll see what I can do.'

During the night Joe reached again for Juliette, his arms gathering her close to his body. She made a soft murmuring sound and nestled closer, her head resting on his chest right where his heart beat a steady rhythm—but not for much longer. He could feel the quick uptake of his pulse as his body responded to her silky skin, her smooth limbs, the soft waft of her warm breath. The scent of her filled his nostrils, the glide of one of her hands against his thigh making his breath catch. His groin swelled, heated, burned at the thought of her touching him. Desire rolling through him in ever-increasing waves.

The moonlight coming in through the window cast her body in silvery light, making her look like an angel that had flown from heaven and lain down beside him. *Heaven* just about summed up what it felt like to hold her. To make love to her. To feel her body enclose his, to feel her respond to him hadn't lessened his desire but rather fed it, nurtured it, expanded it.

Her hand crept ever closer until she was encircling him with her fingers. 'Are you awake?' Her voice was a whisper that made his flesh tingle all over.

He smothered a groan as his body throbbed under her touch. 'I am now.'

She glanced up at him with shining eyes, a cheeky smile curving her lips. 'Do you want me to stop touching you?'

Joe felt like he would *die* if she stopped touching him. He rolled her over to her back and leaned over her with his weight propped on his elbows. 'How about I touch you to even this up a bit?'

He cupped one of her breasts, rolling his thumb over her nipple, watching her response play out on her features, in the catch of her breath, the parting of her lips, her gaze flicking to his mouth. His hand went down from her breast to the tiny cave of her belly button and then beyond.

'Oh…' Juliette gave a breathless gasp, her legs folding outwards to welcome his touch. *'Oh...'*

Joe moved down her body, using his lips and tongue to bring forth her earth-shattering response—a response that never failed to thrill him. Making love with her was on another scale from anything he had experienced before. A scale he had never reached with anyone else. Her response to him touched him at the centre of his being. Making him *feel* every movement of her body, every stroke and glide of her fingers, every soft press of her mouth, as if his body's nerves had been tuned to another setting. A higher, richer, more pleasurable setting.

Juliette flopped back down against the pillows, her face flushed, her eyes bright as gemstones. 'I'm not letting you get away with that without a payback.'

'Is that a promise?'

She smiled and scrambled to a sitting position, pushing him

down so he was on his back. 'What do you think?' She straddled him and slid down his body until her mouth was close to his erection.

He sucked in a rasping breath. 'I can't think right now.'

'Then don't. Just feel.' And when she closed her mouth over him that was all he could do. He was reduced to sensations so powerful, so all-consuming, he thought he would lose consciousness. The teasing suction of her mouth, the sexy glide and the kittenish licks of her tongue made him fly into a vortex of mind-blowing, senses-spinning ecstasy.

He came back to earth with a deep sigh of contentment and brought her down so she was lying on top of him, her legs entangled with his. He stroked the length of her spine in slow movements, enjoying the press of her breasts against his chest, the beat of her heart against his, her hair tickling him where it cascaded over him like a mermaid's.

He listened to the gradual slowing of her breathing, felt her body gradually melt into full relaxation as she drifted off to sleep.

A long time later he too closed his eyes but it was a long time before he went to sleep...

On Monday morning Joe woke a little later than was normal for him. He turned to reach for Juliette but the space beside him in the bed was vacant. For a brief moment panic gripped him in the chest like a claw—a sudden, savage claw that reminded him of all the mornings he had woken without her beside him. But then the sound of her moving about in the bathroom relaxed his tense muscles like the injection of a prophylactic drug. Relief swept through him in deep calming waves.

After spending the weekend wandering around the city of Paris hand in hand, they were flying back to Italy this afternoon. He could not remember a time when he had felt such a deep sense of hope. Hope that their relationship had a chance to be restored, regenerated, renewed. But while Juliette had initially agreed to stay a couple of weeks, she hadn't said anything about staying longer. He *wanted* her to stay longer. He wanted to resume their marriage. To start afresh. To build on the new understanding they had now after spending time together.

Juliette came out of the bathroom already showered and dressed. 'Good morning, sleepyhead.' Her smile was as bright as the sunshine pouring through the window and his breath caught in the middle of his chest.

'Yes, well, you did wear me out a little last night.' Joe smiled and tossed off the bedcovers and slipped on a bathrobe in case he was tempted to take her back to bed and cause them to miss their flight.

She gave an answering smile but something about a look in her eyes gave him pause. 'Joe?'

He came over to her and ran his hands down from her upper arms to her wrists, gently encircling them with his fingers. 'What's on your mind, *cara*?'

She drew most of her lower lip into her mouth, holding it there for a beat before releasing it. 'You know how I said we should be honest about our feelings? Well, I don't want to go ahead with the divorce.'

Joe pulled her to him in a tight hug, his relief so immense it flooded his being. 'I don't want that either. I want you to stay with me.' His voice was hoarse with suppressed emotion, his heart thudding with joy. 'We'll start afresh. Go on a proper honeymoon this time. We can even renew our vows if that's what you'd like.'

She leaned back to look up at him, her grey-blue eyes clear. 'Why, though? Why do you want our marriage to continue?'

Joe could feel a ripple of unease slithering down his spinal column. 'You know why. We're good together. We understand each other better now.'

Her eyes drifted to his mouth. 'Joe, a marriage is not just about good sex.' Her gaze came back up to his. Direct. Determined. 'I love you.'

Joe knew he should fill the silence with the answer of those overused words but his mouth dried, his chest tightened. He had never said those words to anyone. Not even his father or Nonna. He had showed it in other ways, but saying those words out loud would trigger something primal in him. Born out of some kind of primitive desire to keep himself free of deep emotional entanglements.

'*Cara*, you know I care about you.' Somehow he spoke past the stricture in his throat.

Her expression faltered, hurt flickering through her gaze, her mouth sagging at the corners. 'I don't want you just to care. I want you to love me. And I want us to try for another baby. I'm ready now. Please say you're ready too?'

Something in his chest gave way as if his heart had suddenly been dislodged, like an industrial crane losing its heavy load. He couldn't take a new breath. He became lightheaded, disoriented. Panic beat in his chest as if fists were punching inside his heart to escape.

Another baby... Another pregnancy... Another nine months of worry. Of dread. Of anguish.

Joe let his hands drop from around her wrists and stepped back, fighting for air. For composure. For safety. 'Whoa there. That's not something I can even think about. Not right now.'

She frowned, her mouth opening and closing as if she couldn't think of what to say. Then she took a steadying breath. 'Joe.' Her tone was level, calm, rational. 'I know you're worried about what might happen to me or the baby or both. I suspect most husbands would feel that way if they were asked, especially after going through what we went through. But we'll have the best of medical care and we can only hope this time the baby will be okay.'

Joe shoved a hand through his hair, his brain reeling so much it felt as if his skull would fracture. 'I'm not ready to discuss this.'

'But, if we're to stay together, we have to discuss difficult things as they come up. Isn't that what we did wrong in the past? We pushed it under the carpet instead of airing it up front.'

He moved to the other side of the room, unable to get his thoughts out of their frenetic maelstrom. It was like a tornado of terror inside his head. 'I'm not willing to discuss it. No way.'

Her eyes widened, her cheeks losing colour. 'No way...*ever?*'

He scrubbed a hand down his face, his chest still so tight he could barely inflate his lungs. His gut prickled with anxiety, his head pounded, his brain log-jammed. He wanted a reconciliation. It was all he wanted—to have Juliette back in his life. But to go through the stress of another pregnancy, knowing it could end like the last one, would be a step too far. A dangerous, frightening step that made everything in him freeze in panic.

'Look, I'm happy to resume our marriage—really happy—but having another baby is out of the question. I just can't face it. I'm sorry.'

Her brow was furrowed with confusion. 'But I thought you cared about me? I even thought maybe you...loved me, even though you seem unwilling to say the words.'

Love was something Joe had never expected to feel with any intensity. Whenever he felt the stirring of emotions he couldn't handle he blocked them. Deadened them. Denied them. He let out a long breath. 'I told you—I care about you.'

She moved further away, crossing her arms over her body. 'But you're not in love with me.' Her tone was flat, resigned, dull.

Joe swallowed against another tight knot in his throat. 'I've never felt like this with anyone else, but as to whether it's the love you want, well, I can't guarantee it is.'

She met his gaze with a steady focus that was unnerving. Unnerving because he felt a horrible sense of history about to repeat itself. 'I spent so much of my childhood wondering if I was loved like my brothers were loved. Never quite feeling I made the grade. I didn't seem to tick the boxes my parents wanted ticked. I always seemed to disappoint them. It made me feel like an outsider in my own family. I don't want to live like that in our marriage. I want to be on an equal footing with you. A true partnership where we share everything openly and honestly.'

What could he say that he hadn't already said? He *was* being honest with her. Brutally so.

'I'm sorry you feel that way about your family. It's tough feeling like you don't belong. I get that. But a marriage like ours could be successful without the idealised, overly romanticised version of love you're talking about.'

Juliette ran her tongue over her lips and continued, her voice becoming husky. 'I could probably cope with you not being in love with me. I knew when you married me you didn't love me that way. But I want another baby at some point. It doesn't have to be right now. But how can we have a future together if you won't even discuss it?'

'Of course we have a future together,' Joe said, struggling to contain his poise. 'Hasn't the last week proved that? We're in a much better place than we ever were before. We know each other so much better and—'

'I know all that but it's not enough.' Her slim shoulders went back as if she was drawing on some inner strength to get her point across. 'I want a family, Joe. I want to be a mother so badly. I can't guarantee it will happen, especially given what happened last time, but I still want to try.'

The punching panic in his chest was at a manic stage, like a boxer going for the knockout blow. Desperate to get out of the ring no matter what.

'Look, children obviously are an important part of many people's lives. But we've been down this road and it nearly destroyed us. Why not quit while we're ahead? We can have a great life. Travel to anywhere at any time and never want for anything.'

Her eyes dulled, her expression faded, her throat tightened over a swallow. 'You never wanted her, did you? You never wanted a baby in the first place. That's why you don't want another one now. It's not part of your life plan. It never has been.'

'That's not true. I wanted our child as much as you did—'

'Tell me honestly. Do you *ever* want another child?'

The silence clawed at his guts, tore at his heart like talons.

'I'm not sure I can answer that.' He finally found his voice.

Her grey-blue eyes became glacial ponds, her expression hardening like a hoar frost. 'I think I get it now. Sorry for being so slow on the uptake.' Her tone chilled the temperature in the room to an arctic level. 'The problem as I see it is you don't want to have a baby with *me*. I'm the problem.' She batted her hand against her chest for emphasis. 'It's *me*.'

'That's not true,' Joe said, scrambling for a way out of this wretched conversation. He was in quicksand and sinking. He could feel it dragging him down, down, down. He had seen whole buildings crumple and disappear into sinkholes. Could there be a bigger, blacker pit of despair for him to fall in? To lose her again? Not once, but twice?

But…another baby?

No. No. No. He couldn't go through it again.

Her spine straightened, her gaze determined. 'If you don't want to be the father of my child, then it's time for us to say goodbye.'

No! The word was a silent scream inside his head. A siren of blind panic. A high-pitched screech of fear that made his blood run cold. But, rather than voice it out loud, Joe curled his lip instead, determined not to show how undone he really was. He would climb out of that damn sinkhole and take control. He *had* to. He'd done it before. He would do it again.

'Blackmail doesn't suit you, Juliette. And you should know by now, I'm not the sort of man to respond to it.'

Her small neat chin came up and her eyes glittered with defiance. 'Then we are at an impasse.'

'Don't be ridiculous,' he began.

'I'm not being ridiculous—I'm being realistic,' Juliette said.

'What would be the point in continuing our marriage if one of us isn't getting what we want? Who never gets what they want? I'd end up resenting you. Hating you for denying me the family I want so much.'

Joe strode over to her but refrained from touching her. If he touched her, he would agree to anything. He couldn't risk it. He needed time to process what she was demanding. It was too much for him to handle when they had only been back together a matter of days.

'There's always compromise in relationships,' he said, shocked at how calm and collected he sounded when on the inside he was collapsing like a badly constructed office tower. The very foundation of his being was under threat. He was teetering over an abyss of uncertainty, dread, uncontrollable danger.

Juliette met his gaze with a level stare. 'I know all about compromise. I'm the one who made all the adjustments, fitting into your life when we first got married. But I'm not prepared to compromise on this. It's not fair to ask me to. If you loved me, you would understand how important this is for me.'

'Then maybe I don't love you.'

One side of Joe's brain was shouting, *What are you saying?* The other was saying, *You're safe, for now.*

She flinched as if he had slapped her and, right at that moment, he had never hated himself more. But wasn't it better this way? He had always known on a cellular level he would not be enough for her. He wasn't good for her. He had all but destroyed her life by getting involved with her in the first place.

The blame for so much suffering was at his door.

'Then I think that's all that needs to be said.' Her voice was almost as calm and indifferent as his but he could see how much he had disappointed her. It was in every nuance of her face—the tight lips, the creased brow, the dullness of her grey-blue gaze as if a light had been turned off inside her. 'I won't be returning to Italy with you this afternoon. I'll fly straight home to London.'

Home to London.

The words were vicious hammer blows to his heart. But he had no way of defending himself without bringing more pain and uncertainty into both of their lives.

Juliette turned away and began packing her things into her weekend bag.

Stop her. Stop her. Stop her. Tell her the truth. Tell her how you feel about her. Don't let her leave like this.

But Joe did the opposite. He walked calmly, silently into the bathroom, and when he returned a few minutes later she was gone.

Later, Juliette could barely recall how she got to the airport and on a plane to London without displaying the devastation she felt. It was as if she had split herself into two people—one was calm and logical and rational, able to call a taxi, pay the driver and board a plane without a qualm. The other was a broken, shattered shell, limping through the steps to get her to somewhere safe where she could address her terrible wounds.

Joe didn't want another child.

Joe didn't love her.

He had never loved her.

She had fooled herself into believing otherwise. She had constructed a dream landscape where the pain of the past would fade into the background, not quite going away but no longer causing the distress it once had. A landscape where the birth of another baby would bind her and Joe in the joys of parenthood, their marriage thriving instead of dying. How could she have been so naïve? How could she have allowed herself to think they had a future when he was unable—*unwilling*—to love her?

Was there something wrong with her that she was destined to crave a love she couldn't have?

Juliette had always doubted her parents' love for her, seeing it as conditional rather than unconditional. She had thought Harvey, her ex, had loved her and had foolishly believed it when he'd said the words so often and so volubly. But that had also been a lie.

She huddled into her seat on the plane and looked listlessly out of the window at the clouds drifting by. Her heart ached as if an invisible corkscrew were driving through it on the way to her backbone.

So, it was finally over.

Her marriage to Joe Allegranza was dead.

Unsalvageable.

Could there be anything crueller than to dangle hope in front of her and then snatch it away? Every kiss, every touch, every time they made love, she felt that he loved her. How could she have been so misguided? So fanciful? So deluded?

It was time now to move on and forge a new path for herself. A new future.

Juliette's heart gave another painful spasm.

Without Joe...

Joe spent the first week after Juliette left throwing himself into work, largely helped by a bridge collapse in northern Spain. Fixing other people's problems was the only way to distract himself from his own unfixable ones. But, as much as he found his work rewarding and challenging in equal measure, he began to realise it no longer filled the gaping chasm Juliette had left behind. His work was like temporary scaffolding holding up a compromised building.

He was the compromised building, constructed from materials that were now seriously out of date.

Stoicism, self-reliance, a fierce desire for control, emotional lockdown, an isolationist mind-set were no longer materials in a man's life that worked, if indeed they ever had. They were destroying him like termites in the foundations, quietly, secretly, stealthily destabilising and destroying the man he had the potential to be.

But where to start to fix such deep-seated faults?

He knew exactly where—at the beginning.

Joe's mother's grave was sadly neglected and a deep sense of shame washed over him as he knelt down beside it and pulled out the weeds from around her plot. He placed the flowers he'd brought with him in the stone vase and sat back on his heels to read the words engraved on the marble headstone.

Giovanna Giulia Allegranza
A loving wife and mother
Missed for ever

He had no knowledge, no physical memory of his mother, and yet he sensed how much she must have loved him. He was touched that his father had insisted the word 'mother' was included on her headstone even though she hadn't regained consciousness to hold Joe in her arms. Why hadn't he noticed that before now? All those times his father had dragged him to the graveyard, Joe had stood sullenly to one side as his father tended the grave with tears pouring down his face. It had repulsed Joe, made him feel his father was weak and unable to control his emotions, that he had loved his wife *too* much.

Why had he adopted such toxic notions about manhood? Why had he denied himself for all these years the full breadth and depth of his humanity? The ability to feel and express deep emotion, the ability to willingly relinquish control over things that couldn't be controlled in any case, to acknowledge his grief over the loss of his baby daughter.

And the deep and abiding love he felt for Juliette.

Why else was he struggling to make sense of his future without her? The emptiness she'd left behind could not be filled with work. No amount of work could ever do that. He loved her with a love so strong it seeped into every cell of his body like the pouring of concrete on a building site. His love was the solid, dependable, unshakable platform on which they could plan a future.

Joe stood from his mother's grave and glanced at some of the other headstones nearby. There were numerous stories of love inscribed there. Old love, young love and everything in between. Life had no guarantees. You could be lucky to live to ninety. Some, like tiny Emilia, didn't survive the nine months of pregnancy. Some didn't survive childhood or middle age, and yet others lived long lives and still they were grieved. Grief had no age limit. It was a human response to loving someone. It didn't matter how old they were—they were missed when they were gone.

Like he missed his baby daughter...

Pain gripped him in the chest and he blinked against the moisture at the back of his eyes. Could he do it? Could he visit that tiny grave and confront the raw grief that threatened to overwhelm him?

CHAPTER TWELVE

JULIETTE WAS IDLY sketching at her flat in London, her mind preoccupied with missing Joe. She hadn't heard anything from him since she'd left him in Paris. Not that she'd expected to—they had both said all that needed to be said. But when the doorbell rang her heart leapt and her deadened hopes took a gasp of air.

She opened the door and her shoulders slumped on a sigh. 'Oh…hi, Mum…' Her tone was jaded and unwelcoming even though she was craving company. Any company to distract herself from her misery.

'Have I come at a bad time?' her mother, Claudia, asked.

Juliette forced a weak smile. 'Of course not. I was just doing some drawing…' She led the way into the kitchen, where she had set up her art materials.

Claudia glanced at the sketches. 'So, you're working again?'

'Sort of.' Juliette shuffled the papers into a neat pile. 'I'm thinking about doing a children's book on loss. I thought it might help when kids lose a parent or someone close to them. Or even a pet.'

'That's a wonderful idea,' Claudia said, pulling out a chair to sit. She waited a beat before adding, 'Did you get the divorce papers signed?'

Juliette hadn't told her mother about the few days in Italy

with Joe or the weekend in Paris, and realised now how awkward it was going to be to fill in the gaps.

She slid into the seat opposite. 'Mum…for a time I was considering going back to him. We caught up at Lucy and Damon's wedding and then I went to see him in Positano. I stayed for over a week and I really thought we had a chance to make things work. I found out his mother died having him. How tragic is that? I realised while I was there that I love him. I know this might sound a bit fanciful to someone as rational and logical as you, but I think I fell in love with him the moment I met him. And I want to have another baby but he's adamantly against even discussing it. I can't compromise on that. I know there's no guarantee I won't have another stillbirth but I want to try for another child.'

Claudia reached for Juliette's hand and gave it a motherly squeeze. 'Sweetie, falling in love like that doesn't sound fanciful at all.' She sighed and continued. 'I might appear rational and logical to you, but I'm not always like that on the inside. I fell in love with your father in much the same way. It was so sudden and I always felt as if I had to prove myself to his parents—your grandparents—to justify him marrying me.'

'Really? But I thought Nanna and Pop adored you.'

Claudia's smile was rueful. 'They did, eventually, but mostly because I did everything I could to please and impress them. My Masters and PhD? That was my way of showing them I was as intelligent and capable as their son. Worthy of him.' Her expression faltered. 'When I got pregnant with you, I had just enrolled in my PhD. I couldn't bear the thought of dropping out and yet I was so torn about you. There were times when I hated leaving you with the nanny and other times when I couldn't wait to get away so I could concentrate on my work. I couldn't seem to win, no matter what I did. And, being an older mother, well, I just didn't have the energy and drive I had with your brothers.'

'Oh, Mum…' Juliette stood and came around to give her

mother a hug around the shoulders. 'I think most mothers feel like they can't win.'

Claudia turned in her chair and grasped Juliette's hands. 'I wish I could make you happy, sweetie. The last few months have been so tough on you. But, given what you told me just now about Joe, it's been terribly tough on him too. He must have been beside himself the whole pregnancy. No wonder he doesn't want to go through that again. He wouldn't want to risk losing you.'

Juliette slipped her hands out of her mother's hold. 'He doesn't love me, Mum. He told me he cares about me. That's not enough. I want him to love me.'

Claudia frowned. 'Sweetie, are you sure he doesn't love you? One thing my long career in science has taught me is to look closely at the evidence. Examine every bit of data, check and double check and keep a rational perspective. Men aren't always good at expressing their emotions. Sometimes they don't even recognise what they're feeling. Years of being taught to suppress how they feel makes it hard for them to open up when they need to.'

Could her mother be right? But why had Joe let her leave both times without asking her to stay? Why hadn't he called or texted?

He'd left her stranded in a vacuum.

'I don't know…' Juliette sighed. 'I sometimes thought he loved me. He's so generous and kind. But he hasn't contacted me since I left him in Paris. Not even a text or phone call. If he cared about me, wouldn't he want to contact me?'

'We always expect people to respond to a situation the way *we* would respond, but each of us has their own way of doing things, their own framework or lens to view things through,' Claudia said. 'Joe strikes me as someone who takes his time to think about things before he acts. He's just taking longer than you would like.'

'But what if you're wrong?'

Claudia gave a soft smile. 'Look at the evidence, sweetie. It's all you can go on for now.'

After her mother left, Juliette bought flowers from her local florist and drove to the graveyard where Emilia was interned in a small village outside London. It never got any easier and it was particularly difficult on cold wet days when the miserable sky above felt as if it was pressing down on Juliette with the sole intent to crush her. But the sun was out today and birds were twittering in the shrubs and gardens that fringed the cemetery. The roses were in full bloom and the rich clove and slightly peppery scent wafted on the gentle breeze.

Juliette walked towards her daughter's grave but, as she got closer, something caught her eye. There was a new teddy bear with a pink tulle tutu sitting propped up next to the marble headstone. She bent down and read the card that was attached to the teddy bear.

To my darling Emilia
Love you for ever, mio piccolo
Rest in peace
Papà

It was Joe's distinctive handwriting. The combination of English and Italian a touching tribute to their baby girl's heritage. He'd been here. Recently. He had visited Emilia's grave for the first time since her funeral.

He was here in England.

Juliette turned and scanned the graveyard for any sign of him but, apart from an older couple standing next to a grave several metres away, there was no one else here. Her shoulders slumped and she turned back to Emilia's grave and set about placing the flowers in the vase. Just because he was in England didn't mean he would seek her out.

What else could he say other than what he'd already said?

Then maybe I don't love you.

How those words had tortured her, bruised her, destroyed her hopes like noxious poison sprayed on a delicate bloom.

Juliette drove back to her flat in London with a heavy heart. It was all very well for her scientifically trained mother to insist she look at the evidence, but how could she survive another rejection?

She turned the corner into her street and saw a tall figure standing at her front door. Her heart gave a leap, her pulse thudded, her hopes rose. She tried to play it cool by parking her car with casual ease, even though she felt like banging and crashing into the cars before and aft in her haste to get to Joe.

She walked towards him with her expression as blank as she could muster but she could do nothing about the way her heart was thumping. 'Hello.' How stiff and formal she sounded. As if she was addressing a cold caller or doorstep salesperson.

'Can we talk inside?' Joe's tone was gruff, his expression guarded.

'Okay.' She unlocked her door and went in, conscious of his tall frame coming in behind her. The scent of his aftershave teasing her senses, her body reacting automatically. Wanting to touch him. Be held by him. Loved by him.

The door closed behind him and silence descended. A weighted silence.

'I saw the teddy bear,' Juliette said.

'Yes, I went there this morning.' He swallowed and continued in a fractured tone. '*Cara*, can you ever forgive me for how I've handled everything? I'm ashamed of how blind I've been to how I feel about you.'

Juliette took a steadying breath, not quite ready to let her hopes run free. 'How do you feel about me?'

He smiled and took her hands in his. 'My darling, I love you. I think I've loved you since the first night we met but I've been denying it, suppressing it or disguising it as something else. It was cruel of me to say I didn't love you back in Paris.

I can never forgive myself for that. But I was so threatened by your desire to have another child. It made me shut down in a blind sort of panic.'

Could she believe him? Could she risk further heartbreak if she was wrong about his motives for being here?

'How do I know you mean it? You might be just saying it to get me to come back to you.'

His grip on her hands tightened as if he was worried she was going to pull away. 'I deserve your scepticism. The way I blocked any discussion about having another child was a knee-jerk reaction, sure, but it was unspeakably cruel to send you away as if I cared nothing. I love you with every beat of my heart. I can't imagine life without you by my side. It is no life without you. I'm a robot, a zombie like my father was when he lost my mother.'

'You're not just saying this because you want me back?'

'I'm saying it because it's true. I can't be who I'm meant to be without you. I never thought there was such a thing as a soulmate but I've realised you don't find a soulmate, you *become* one.' He squeezed her hands. 'I've become the man I want to be because of you. I didn't know I was capable of such depth of feeling.'

'Oh, Joe…' She blinked back tears. 'I'm so frightened I'm going to get hurt again. It was so hard losing both you and the baby.'

He brought one of her hands up to his mouth, his eyes holding hers in a tender lock. 'You're not going to lose me, *cara.* I will always be here for you, no matter what. I can't guarantee we won't lose another baby. No one can guarantee that, but what you can count on is this—I will be with you every step of whatever journey our lives take us on.'

Hope blossomed in her chest. 'So, are you saying you'd consider having another baby?'

He brought her closer, his eyes dark and tender, so full of love it made her heart turn over. 'I'll probably be a nervous wreck throughout your pregnancy, but it will be worth it if we are so lucky as to be blessed with a child. The thought of losing you like my father lost my mother haunts me. It haunted me from the start but when I visited my mother's grave the other day—'

'You visited her grave as well?'

Joe gave a rueful smile. 'It was long overdue but, yes, I did. It was strange. I didn't see it in the same way as I had as a teenager. I saw all those other graves—lives well lived, others cut tragically short—and I realised no one can guarantee you won't experience grief at some stage. Having another child will test me in ways I don't want to be tested. But it's part of being human to experience grief sooner or later. And being human, fully human, means being able to give and receive and openly express love.'

He stroked her face and looked deeply into her eyes.

'I love you so much. I can't bear the thought of spending however much time I have left on this planet without you by my side. I have already wasted too much of it without you. Come back to me, *tesoro mio*. Please?'

Juliette blinked back tears and flung her arms around his neck. 'I never want to be apart from you again. I love you. I've been so sad without you. So miserable and empty and lonely. But we can take our time having another baby. We don't have to rush into it.'

'We will try for another baby after we renew our wedding vows.'

Juliette blinked. 'You really want to do that?'

He grinned. 'Of course. We can even get Damon's cousin Celeste to organise it. It will be a celebration like no other. I'll give her carte blanche.'

Juliette gave a soft laugh. 'You don't have to do that. The simplest ceremony will do me. All I need to hear is you say the words and mean them.'

'I will love and honour and protect you until I take my last breath.' He brought his mouth down to hers in a lingering kiss that contained hope and love and healing. He drew back to gaze down at her once more. 'You have made me happier than I ever thought I could possibly be. I will always feel sad about our baby girl. Always—but that doesn't mean we can't build a wonderful life together. We will support each other during the bad times and celebrate the good ones.'

Juliette hugged him tightly, so full of love and joy it was hard to get her voice to work. 'I can't believe you actually love me. I still think I'm dreaming. That I will wake up and you won't be holding me like this—that I'll be alone again.'

Joe leaned down to kiss the tip of her nose. 'You're not dreaming, *cara mio.* I didn't know it was possible to love someone the way I love you. But if you need any more evidence…' He brought his mouth down to hers, his sexy smile sending a tickly sensation down her spine.

Juliette smiled and stood on tiptoe to meet his lips. 'I'm a big fan of evidence.'

EPILOGUE

April the fifth, the following year...

JOE CRADLED HIS newborn son in his arms and looked down at his beautiful but somewhat exhausted wife. After a mostly trouble-free pregnancy, Juliette had gone into labour the night before his birthday, and at ten minutes past midnight Alessandro Guiseppe Allegranza had been born.

'Isn't he gorgeous?' Juliette said, a dreamy expression on her face.

Joe rocked the little bundle in his arms, his heart feeling as if it was going to explode with love. 'He's amazing, like his mother.'

He stroked a careful finger over the minuscule face—the tiny button nose, the twin wisps of dark eyebrows, the soft downy black hair. It was a miracle to hold new life in his arms. A new life that repaired some of the pain of his own birth that had taken his mother from him. A new life that would help them move on from the loss of their first baby, Emilia. Not as a replacement—no child could ever be that—but as a new chance to experience all the joys and challenges of parenthood.

'Happy birthday, darling,' Juliette said, beaming.

Joe smiled so widely he thought his face would crack. 'I

couldn't have asked for a better birthday present.' He looked down into his baby son's face. 'And you, little guy, couldn't have asked for a better mother.'

* * * * *

The Marakaios Marriage

Kate Hewitt

Books by Kate Hewitt

Harlequin Modern

Kholodov's Last Mistress

The Undoing of de Luca

The Chatsfield

Virgin's Sweet Rebellion

Rivals of the Crown of Kadar

Captured by the Sheikh

Commanded by the Sheikh

The Diomedi Heirs

The Prince She Never Knew

A Queen for the Taking?

The Bryants: Powerful & Proud

Beneath the Veil of Paradise

In the Heat of the Spotlight

His Brand of Passion

The Power of Redemption

The Darkest of Secrets

The Husband She Never Knew

After spending three years as a die-hard New Yorker, **Kate Hewitt** now lives in a small village in the English Lake District with her husband, their five children and a golden retriever. In addition to writing intensely emotional stories, she loves reading, baking and playing chess with her son—she has yet to win against him, but she continues to try. Learn more about Kate at kate-hewitt.com.

To Pippa Roscoe—thank you
for your invaluable feedback on this story.

CHAPTER ONE

'HELLO, LINDSAY.'

How could two such innocuous-sounding words cause her whole body to jolt, first with an impossible joy, and then with a far more consuming dread? A dread that seeped into her stomach like acid, corroding those few seconds of frail, false happiness as she registered the cold tone of the man she'd once promised to love, honour and obey.

Her husband, Antonios Marakaios.

Lindsay Douglas looked up from her computer, her hands clenching into fists in her lap even as her gaze roved helplessly, hungrily over him, took in his familiar features now made strange by the coldness in his eyes, the harsh downturn of his mouth. With her mind still spinning from the sight of him, she said the first thing that came into it.

'How did you get in here?'

'You mean the security guard?' Antonios sounded merely disdainful, but his whisky-brown eyes glowed like banked coals. 'I told him I was your husband. He let me through.'

She licked her dry lips, her mind spinning even as she forced herself to focus. Think rationally. 'He shouldn't have,' she said. 'You have no business being here, Antonios.'

'No?' He arched an eyebrow, his mouth curving coldly, even cruelly. 'No business seeing my wife?'

She forced herself to meet that burning gaze, even though it took everything she had. 'Our marriage is over.'

'I am well aware of that, Lindsay. It's been six months, after all, since you walked out on me without any warning.'

She heard the accusation in his voice but refused to rise to it. There was no point now; their marriage was over, just as she'd told him.

'I only meant that all the academic buildings are locked, with security guards by the door,' she answered. Her voice sounded calm—far calmer than she felt. Seeing Antonios again was causing memories to rise up in her mind like a flock of seagulls, crying out to her, making her remember things she'd spent the last six months determined to forget. The way he'd held her after they'd made love, how he'd always so tenderly tucked her hair behind her ears, cupped her cheek with his hand, kissed her eyelids. How happy and safe and cherished he'd once made her feel.

No, she couldn't remember that. Better to remember the three months of isolation and confusion she'd spent at his home in Greece as Antonios had become more and more obsessed with work, expecting her simply to slot into a life she'd found alien and even frightening.

Better to remember how depressed and despairing she'd felt, until staying in Greece for one more day, one more *minute*, had seemed impossible.

Yes, better to remember that.

'I still don't know why you're here,' she told him. She placed her hands flat on the desk and stood, determined to meet him at eye level, or as close as she could, considering he topped her by eight inches.

Yet just looking at him now caused her to feel a tug of longing deep in her belly. The close-cut midnight-dark hair. The strong square jaw. The sensual, mobile lips. And as for his body…taut, chiselled perfection underneath the dark grey silk suit he wore.

She knew his body as well as her own. Memories rushed in again, sweet and poignant reminders of their one sweet week together, and she forced them away, held his sardonic gaze.

Antonios arched one dark eyebrow. 'You have no idea why I might be here, Lindsay? No reason to wonder why I might come looking for my errant wife?'

Errant wife. So he blamed her. Of course he did. And she knew he had a right to blame her, because she'd left him without an explanation or even, as he'd said, a warning. But he'd forced her to leave, even if he couldn't, or wouldn't, ever understand that. 'It's been six months, Antonios,' she told him coolly, 'and you haven't been in touch once. I think it's reasonable to be surprised to see you.'

'Didn't you think I'd ever come, demanding answers?'

'I gave you an answer—'

'A two-sentence email is not an explanation, Lindsay. Saying our marriage was a mistake without saying why is just cowardice.' He held up a hand to forestall her reply, although she couldn't think of anything to say. 'But don't worry yourself on that account. I have no interest in your explanations. Nothing would satisfy me now, and our marriage ended when you walked away without a word.'

Frustration bubbled through her and emotion burned in her chest. Maybe she hadn't had so many words when she'd finally left, but that was because she'd used them all up. Antonios hadn't heard any of it. 'The reason I'm here,' he continued, his voice hard and unyielding, 'is because I need you to return to Greece.'

Her jaw dropped and she shook her head in an instantaneous gut reaction.

'I can't—'

'You'll find you can, Lindsay. You pack a bag and get on a plane. It's that easy.'

Mutely she shook her head. Just the thought of returning to Greece made her heart start to thud hard, blood pounding in her ears. She focused on her breathing, trying to keep it even and slow. One of the books she'd read had advised focusing on the little things she could control, rather than the overwhelming ones she couldn't. Like her husband and his sudden return into her life.

Antonios stared at her, his whisky-brown eyes narrowed, his lips pursed, his gaze ruthlessly assessing. *In. Out. In. Out.* With effort she slowed her breathing, and her heart stopped thudding quite so hard.

She glanced up at him, conscious of how he was staring at her. And she was staring at him; she couldn't help herself. Even angry as he so obviously was, and had every right to be, he looked beautiful. She remembered when she'd first seen him in New York, with snowflakes dusting his hair and a whimsical smile on his face as he'd caught sight of her standing on Fifth Avenue, gazing up at the white spirals of the Guggenheim.

I'm lost, he'd said. *Or at least I thought I was.*

But she'd been the one who had been lost, in so many ways. Devastated by the death of her father. Spinning in a void of grief and fear and loneliness she'd been trying so hard to escape.

And then she'd lost herself in Antonios, in the charming smile he'd given her, in the warmth she'd seen in his eyes, in the way he'd looked at her as if she were the most interesting and important woman in the world. For a week, a mere seven days, they'd revelled in each other. And then reality had hit, and hit hard.

'Let me clarify,' he said, his voice both soft and so very cold. 'You *will* come to Greece. As your husband, I command you.'

She stiffened. 'You can't *command* me, Antonios. I'm not your property.'

'Greek marriage law is a little different from American law, Lindsay.'

She shook her head, angry now, although not, she suspected, as angry as he was. 'Not that different.'

'Perhaps not,' he conceded with a shrug. 'But I am assuming you want a divorce?'

The sudden change in subject jolted her. 'A divorce...'

'That *is* why you left me, is it not? Because you no longer wished to continue in our marriage.' He bared his teeth in a smile and Lindsay suppressed the sudden urge to shiver. She'd never seen Antonios look this way. So cold and hard and predatory.

'I...' A divorce sounded so final, so terrible, and yet of course that had to be what she wanted. She'd left him, after all.

In the six months since she'd left Greece, she'd immersed herself in the comforting cocoon of number theory, trying to finish her doctorate in Pure Mathematics. Trying to blunt that awful ache of missing Antonios, or at least the Antonios she'd known for one week, before everything had changed. She'd tried to take steps to put her life back together, to control her anxiety and reach out to the people around her. She'd made progress, and there had been moments, whole days, when she'd felt normal and even happy.

Yet she'd always missed Antonios. She'd missed the person she'd been with him, when they'd been in New York.

And neither of those people had been real. Their marriage, their love, hadn't been real. She knew that absolutely, and yet...

She still longed for what they'd shared, so very briefly.

'Yes,' she said quietly. She lifted her chin and met his gaze. 'I want to end our marriage.'

'A divorce,' Antonios clarified flatly. Lindsay flinched slightly but kept his gaze, hard and unyielding as it was.

'Yes.'

'Then, Lindsay,' he told her in that awful silky voice, 'you need to do as I ask. *Command.* Because under Greek marriage law, you can't get a divorce unless both parties agree.'

She stared at him, her eyes widening as she considered the implications of what he was saying. 'There must be other circumstances in which a divorce is permissible.'

'Ah, yes, there are. Two, as a matter of fact.' His mouth twisted unpleasantly. 'Adultery and abandonment. But as I have committed neither of those, they do not apply, at least in my case.'

She flinched again, and Antonios registered her reaction with a curl of his lip. 'Why do you want me to return to Greece, Antonios?'

'Not, as you seem to fear, to resume our marriage.' His voice hardened as he raked her with a contemptuous gaze. 'I have no desire to do that.'

Of course he didn't. And that shouldn't hurt, because she'd chosen it to be that way, and yet it still did. 'Then…'

'My mother, as you might remember, was fond of you. She doesn't know why you left, and I have not enlightened her as to the state of our marriage.'

Guilt twisted sharply inside her. Daphne Marakaios had been kind to her during her time in Greece, but it still hadn't been enough to stay. To stay sane.

'Why haven't you told her?' Lindsay asked. 'It's been six months already, and you can't keep it a secret forever.'

'Why shouldn't you tell her?' Antonios countered. 'Oh, I forgot. Because you're a coward. You sneak away from my home and my bed and can't even be bothered to have a single conversation about why you wished to end our marriage.'

Lindsay drew a deep breath, fighting the impulse to tell him just how many conversations she'd tried to have. There was no point now. 'I understand that you're angry—'

'I'm not angry, Lindsay. To be angry I would have to care.' He stood up, the expression on his face ironing out. 'And I stopped caring when you sent me that email. When you refused to say anything but that our marriage was a mistake when I called you, wanting to know what had happened. When you showed me how little you thought of me or our marriage.'

'And you showed me how little you thought of our marriage

every day I was in Greece,' Lindsay returned before she could help herself.

Antonios turned to her slowly, his eyes wide with incredulity. 'Are you actually going to blame me for the end of our marriage?' he asked, each syllable iced with disbelief.

'Oh, no, of course not,' Lindsay fired back. 'How could I do that? How could you possibly have any responsibility or blame?'

He stared at her, his eyes narrowing, and Lindsay almost laughed to realize he wasn't sure if she was being sarcastic or not.

Then he shrugged her words aside and answered in a clipped voice, 'I *don't* care, about you or your reasons. But my mother does. Because she has been ill, I have spared her the further grief of knowing how and why you have gone.'

'Ill—'

'Her cancer has returned,' Antonios informed her with brutal bluntness. 'She got the results back a month after you left.'

Lindsay stared at him in shock. She'd known Daphne had been in remission from breast cancer, but the outlook had been good. 'Antonios, I'm so sorry. Is it…is it treatable?'

He lifted one powerful shoulder in a shrug, his expression veiled. 'Not very.'

Lindsay sank back in her chair, her mind reeling with this new information. She thought of kind Daphne, with her white hair and soft voice, her gentleness apparent in every word and action, and felt a twist of grief for the woman she'd known so briefly. And as for Antonios…he adored his mother. This would have hit him hard and she, his wife, hadn't been there to comfort and support him through her illness. Yet would she have been able to, if she'd stayed in Greece?

She'd been so desperately unhappy there, and the thought of returning brought the old fears to the fore.

'Antonios,' she said quietly, 'I'm very, very sorry about your mother, but I still can't go back to Greece.'

'You can and you will,' Antonios replied flatly, 'if you want a divorce.'

She shook her head, her hair flying, desperation digging its claws into her soul. 'Then I won't ask for a divorce.'

'Then you are my wife still, and you belong with me.' His voice had roughened and he turned away from her in one sharp movement. 'You cannot have it both ways, Lindsay.'

'How will my seeing your mother help her?' Lindsay protested. 'It would only hurt her more for me to tell her to her face that we've separated—'

'But I have no intention of having you tell her that.' Antonios turned around, his eyes seeming to burn right through her as he glared at her. 'It is likely my mother only has a few months to live, perhaps less. I do not intend to distress her with the news of our failed marriage. For a few days, Lindsay, perhaps a week, you can pretend that we are still happily married.'

'What—?' She stared at him, appalled, as he gave her a grimace of a smile.

'Surely that is not impossible? You have already proven once what a good actress you are, when you pretended to fall in love with me.'

Antonios stared at his wife's lovely pale face and squashed the tiny flicker of pity he felt for her. She looked so trapped, so *horrified* at the prospect of resuming their marriage and returning to Greece.

Not, of course, that they would truly resume their marriage. It would be a sham only, for the sake of his mother. Antonios had no intention of inviting Lindsay into his bed again. Not after she'd left him in such a cold-hearted and cowardly way. No, he'd take her back to Greece for a few days for his mother's sake, and then he'd never see her again…which was what she obviously wanted. And he wanted it, too.

'A few days?' she repeated numbly. 'And that will be enough…'

'It's my mother's name day next week,' Antonios told her.

'Name day…'

'In Greece we celebrate name days rather than birthdays. My family wishes to celebrate it especially, considering.' Grief constricted his throat and burned in his chest. He could not imagine Villa Marakaios without his mother. Losing his father had been hard enough. His father had built the vineyard from nothing; he'd been the brains behind the operation, for better and definitely for worse, but his mother had always been its heart. And when the heart was gone…

But perhaps his own heart had already gone, crushed to nothing when his wife had left him. He'd thought Lindsay had loved him. He'd believed they were happy together.

What a joke. What a lie. But Antonios knew he should be used to people not being what they seemed. Not saying what they meant. He'd had hard lessons in that already.

'We are having a celebration,' he continued, just managing to keep his voice even. 'Family and friends, all our neighbours. You will be there. Afterwards you can return here if you wish. I will explain to my mother that you needed to finish your research.' He knew Lindsay had been pursuing her doctorate in Pure Mathematics, and when she'd left him she'd told him she needed to tie a few things up back in New York. He'd said goodbye in good faith, thinking she'd only be gone a few days. She'd already told him that her research could be done anywhere; she'd said there was nothing for her back in New York. But apparently that, like everything else, had been a lie.

Lindsay's face had gone even paler and she lifted one hand to her throat, swallowing convulsively. 'A party? Antonios, please. I can't.'

Fury beat through his blood. 'What did I ever do to you,' he demanded in a low, savage voice, 'to make you treat me this way? Treat my family this way? We welcomed you into our home, into our lives.' His insides twisted as emotion gripped him—emotion he couldn't bear Lindsay to see. He'd told her he didn't care about her any more, and he'd meant it. He had to mean it. 'My mother,' he said after a moment, when he'd regained his composure and his voice was as flat and toneless as he needed it to be, 'loved you. She treated you like her own daughter. Is this how you intend to repay her?'

Tears sparkled on Lindsay's lashes and she blinked them back, shaking her head in such obvious misery that Antonios almost felt sorry for her again. Almost.

'No, of course not,' she said in a low voice. 'I… I was very grateful to your mother, and her kindness to me.'

'You have a funny way of showing it.'

Her eyes flashed fire at that, and Antonios wondered what on earth she had to be angry about. *She'd* left *him*.

'Even so,' she said quietly, one hand still fluttering at her throat, 'it is very difficult for me to return to Greece.'

'And why is that? Do you have a lover waiting for you here in New York?'

Her mouth dropped open in shock. 'A lover—'

Antonios shrugged, as if it were a matter of no consequence, even though the thought of Lindsay with another man, violating their marriage vows, their marriage *bed*, made him want to punch something. 'I do not know what else would take you so abruptly from Greece.' *From me*, he almost said, but thankfully didn't.

She shook her head slowly, her eyes wide, although with what emotion Antonios couldn't tell. 'No,' she said in a low voice. 'I don't have a lover. There's only been you, Antonios. Ever.'

And yet he obviously hadn't been enough. Antonios didn't even know whether to believe her; he told himself it didn't matter. 'Then there is no reason for you not to come to Greece.'

'My research—'

'Cannot wait a week?' Impatience flared inside him, along with the familiar fury. Didn't she realize how thoughtless, how selfish and cruel she was being?

Even now, after six months of coming to accept and learning to live with her abandonment, he was stunned by how completely she'd deceived him. He had believed in her love for him utterly. But, Antonios reminded himself, they'd only known each other a week when they had married. It had been impulsive, reckless even, but he'd been so *sure*. Sure of his love for Lindsay, and of her love for him.

What a fool he'd been.

Lindsay was staring at him, her face still pale and miserable. 'One week,' Antonios ground out. 'Seven days. And then I intend never to see you again.' She flinched, as if his words hurt her, and he let out a hard laugh. 'Doesn't that notion please you?'

She glanced away, pressing her lips together to keep them from trembling. 'No,' she said after a moment. 'It doesn't.'

He shook his head slowly. 'I don't understand you.'

'I know.' She let out a shuddering breath. 'You never did.'

'And that is my fault?'

She shook her head wearily. 'It's too late to apportion blame, Antonios. It simply is. Was. Our marriage was a mistake, as I told you in my email and on the telephone.'

'Yet you never said why.'

'You never asked,' Lindsay answered, her voice sharpening, and Antonios frowned at her.

'I asked you on the phone—'

'No,' Lindsay told him quietly, 'you didn't. You asked me if I were serious, and I said yes. And then you hung up.'

Antonios stared at her, his jaw bunched so tight it ached. 'You're the one who left, Lindsay.'

'I know—'

'Yet now you are attempting to imply that our marriage failed because I didn't ask the right questions when I called you after you'd left me. *Theos!* It is hard to take.'

'I'm not implying anything of the sort, Antonios. I was simply reminding you of the facts.'

'Then let me remind you of a fact. I'm not interested in your explanations. The time for those has passed. What I am interested in, Lindsay—the *only* thing I am interested in—is your agreement. A plane leaves for Athens tonight. If we are to be on it, we need to leave here in the next hour.'

'What?' Her gaze flew back to his, her mouth gaping open. 'I haven't even agreed.'

'Don't you want a divorce?'

She stared at him for a moment, her chin lifted proudly, her eyes cool and grey. 'You might think you can blackmail me into agreeing, Antonios,' she told him, 'but you can't. I'll come to Greece, not because I want a divorce but because I want to pay my respects to your mother. To explain to her—'

'Do not think—' Antonios cut her off '—that you'll tell her some sob story about our mistake of a marriage. I don't want her upset—'

'When do you intend on telling her the truth?'

'Never,' Antonios answered shortly. 'She doesn't have that long to live.'

Tears filled Lindsay's eyes again, turning them luminous and silver, and she blinked them back. 'Do you really think that's the better course? To deceive her—'

'You're one to speak of deception.'

'I never deceived you, Antonios. I did love you, for that week in New York.'

The pain that slashed through him was so intense and sudden that Antonios nearly gasped aloud. Nearly clutched his chest, as if he were having a heart attack, the same as his father, dead at just fifty-nine years old. 'And then?' he finally managed, his voice thankfully dispassionate. 'You just stopped?' Part of him knew he shouldn't be asking these questions, shouldn't care about these answers. He'd told Lindsay the time for explanations had passed, and it had. 'Never mind,' he dismissed roughly. 'It hardly matters. Come to Greece for whatever reason you want, but you need to be ready in an hour.'

She stared at him for a long moment, looking fragile and beautiful and making him remember how it had felt to hold her. Touch her.

'Fine,' she said softly, and her voice sounded sad and resigned. Suppressing the ache of longing that trembled through him, Antonios turned away from the sight of his wife and waited, his hands clenched into fists at his sides, as she packed up her belongings and then, without a word or glance for him, slipped by him and out of the room.

CHAPTER TWO

LINDSAY WALKED ACROSS the college campus in the oncoming twilight with Antonios like a malevolent shadow behind her. She walked blindly, unaware of the stately brick buildings, now gilded in the gold of fading sunlight, that made this small liberal arts college one of the most beautiful in the whole northeast of America.

All she could think of was the week that loomed so terribly ahead of her. All she could feel was Antonios's anger and scorn.

Maybe she deserved some of it, leaving the way she had, but Antonios had no idea how hard life in Greece had been for her. Hadn't been willing to listen to her explanations, fumbling and faltering as they had been, because while she'd wanted him to understand she'd also been afraid of him knowing and seeing too much.

Their marriage, Lindsay acknowledged hollowly, had been doomed from the start, never mind that one magical week in New York.

And now the time for explanations had passed, Antonios said. It was for the best, Lindsay knew, because having Antonios understand her or her reasons for leaving served no purpose now. It was impossible anyway, because he'd *never* understood. Never tried.

'Where do you live?' Antonios asked as they passed several academic buildings. A few students relaxed outside, lounging in the last of the weak October sunshine before darkness fell. Fall had only just come to upstate New York; the leaves were just starting to change and the breeze was chilly, but after a long, sticky summer of heatwaves everyone was ready for autumn.

'Just across the street,' Lindsay murmured. She crossed the street to a lane of faculty houses, made of clapboard and painted in different bright colours with front porches that held a few Adonirack chairs or a porch swing. She'd sat outside there, in the summers, watching the world go by. Always a spectator... until she'd met Antonios.

He'd woken her up, brought her into the land of the living. With him she'd felt more joy and excitement than she'd ever known before. She should have realized it couldn't last, it hadn't been real.

Antonios stood patiently while she fumbled for the keys; to her annoyance and shame her hands shook. He affected her that much. And not just him, but the whole reality he'd thrust so suddenly upon her. Going to Greece. Seeing his family again. Pretending to be his wife—his *loving* wife—again. Parties and dinners, endless social occasions, every moment in the spotlight...

'Let me help you,' Antonios said and, to her surprise, he almost sounded gentle. He took the key from her hand and fitted it into the lock, turning it easily before pushing the door open.

Lindsay muttered her thanks and stepped inside, breathed in the musty, dusty scent of her father's house. It was strange to have Antonios here, to see this glimpse of her old life, the only life she'd known until he had burst into it.

She flipped on the light and watched him blink as he took in the narrow hallway, made even narrower by the bookshelves set against every wall, each one crammed to overflowing with books. More books were piled on the floor in teetering stacks; the dining room table was covered in textbooks and piles of papers. Lindsay was so used to it that she didn't even notice the clutter any more, but she was conscious of it now, with Antonios here. She was uncomfortably aware of just how small and messy it all was. Yet it was also home, the place where she'd felt safe, where she and her father had been happy, or as happy as they knew how to be. She wouldn't apologize for it.

She cleared her throat and turned towards the stairs. 'I'll just pack.'

'Do you need any help?'

She turned back to Antonios, surprised by his solicitude. Or was he being patronizing? She couldn't tell anything about him any more; his expression was veiled, his voice toneless, his movements controlled.

'No,' she answered, 'I'm fine.'

He arched one dark eyebrow. 'Are you really fine, Lindsay? Because just now your hands were shaking too much for you even to open your front door.'

She stiffened, colour rushing into her face. 'Maybe that's because you're so angry, Antonios. It's a little unsettling to be around someone like that.'

His mouth tightened. 'You think I shouldn't be angry?'

She closed her eyes briefly as weariness swept over her. 'I don't want to get into this discussion. We've both agreed it serves no purpose. I was just—'

'Stating a fact,' Antonios finished sardonically. 'Of course. I'm sorry I can't make this experience easier for you.'

Lindsay just shook her head, too tired and tense to argue. 'Please, let's not bicker and snipe at each other. I'm coming to Greece as you wanted. Can't that be enough?'

His eyes blazed and he took a step towards her, colour slashing his cheekbones. 'No, Lindsay, that is not remotely enough. But since it is all I have asked of you, and all I believe you are capable of, I will have to be satisfied.'

He stared at her for a long, taut moment; Lindsay could hear her breathing turn ragged as her heart beat harder. She felt trapped by his gaze, pinned as much by his contempt as her own pointless anger. And underneath the fury that simmered in Antonios's gaze and hid in her own heart was the memory of when things had been different between them. When he'd taken her in his arms and made her body sing. When she'd thought she loved him.

Then he flicked his gaze away and, sagging with relief, she turned and went upstairs.

She dragged a suitcase out of the hall closet, forced herself to breathe more slowly. She could do this. She *had* to do this, not because she wanted a divorce so badly but because she owed it to Daphne. Her own mother had turned her back on her completely when she'd been no more than a child, and Daphne's small kindnesses to her had been like water in a barren desert. But not enough water. Just a few drops dribbled on her parched lips, when she'd needed the oasis of her husband's support and understanding, attention and care.

'Lindsay?' She heard the creak of the staircase as Antonios came upstairs, his broad shoulders nearly touching both walls as he loomed in the hallway, tall and dark, familiar and strange at the same time. 'We need to leave shortly.'

'I'll try to hurry.' She started throwing clothes into her suitcase, dimly aware that she had nothing appropriate for the kind of social occasions Antonios would expect her to attend. Formal dinners, a huge party for Daphne…as the largest local landowner and businessman, Antonios's calendar had been full of social engagements. From the moment she'd arrived in Greece he'd expected her to be his hostess, to arrange seating for dinner parties, to chat effortlessly to everyone, to be charming and sparkling and always at his side, except when he'd left her for weeks on end to go on business trips. Lindsay didn't know which had been worse: trying to manage alone or feeling ignored.

In any case, she hadn't managed, not remotely. Being Antonios's wife was a role she had been utterly unprepared for.

And now she'd have to go through it all again, all the social occasions and organizing, and, worse, it would be under his family's suspicious gaze because she'd been gone for so long. Her breath hitched at the thought.

Don't think about it. You can deal with that later. Just focus on the present.

The present, Lindsay acknowledged, was difficult enough.

'You left plenty of clothes at the villa,' Antonios told her. 'You only need to pack a small amount.'

Lindsay pictured all the clothes back in their bedroom, the beautiful things Antonios had bought her in New York, before he'd taken her back to Greece. She'd forgotten about them, and the thought of them waiting for her there, hanging in the closet as if she'd never left, made her feel slightly sick.

'I'll just get my toiletries,' she said, and turned to go to the bathroom down the hall. She had to move past him in the narrow hallway and, as she tried to slip past his powerful form, she could smell his aftershave and feel the press of his back against her breasts. For one heart-stopping second she longed to throw herself into his arms, wrap herself around him, feel the comforting heat of his body, the sensuous slide of his lips on hers. To feel wanted and cherished and safe again.

It was never going to happen.

Antonios moved to let her pass and her breath came out in a shuddering rush as she quickly slipped towards the bathroom and, caught between relief and despair, shut and locked the door.

Ten minutes later she'd packed one small case and Antonios brought it down to the hired car he had waiting in one of the college car parks. Lindsay slipped into the leather interior, laid her head back against the seat. She felt incredibly, unbearably tired.

'Do you need to notify anyone?' Antonios asked. 'That you're leaving?'

'No.' Her research, as he'd so bluntly pointed out, could wait. She'd stopped her work as a teaching assistant for introductory classes after her father had died last summer. Only nine months ago, and yet it felt like a lifetime.

It *had* been a lifetime.

'No one will worry about you?' Antonios asked. 'Or wonder where you've gone?'

'I'll email my colleagues. They'll understand.'

'Did you tell them about me?'

'You know I did,' she answered. 'I had to explain why I left my job and house and went to Greece on the spur of the moment.'

His hands flexed on the steering wheel; she could feel his tension. 'It was your choice, Lindsay.'

'I know it was.'

'You said you had nothing left back in New York.'

'It felt like I didn't.'

He shifted in his seat, seeming to want to say more, but kept himself from it.

Lindsay turned her face to the window, steeled herself for the next endless week of tension like this, stalled conversations and not-so-veiled hostility. How on earth were they going to convince Daphne, as well as the rest of his family, that they were still in love?

They didn't speak for the rest of the three-hour drive to New York City. Antonios returned the rental car and took their suitcases into the airport; within a few minutes after checking in they'd been whisked to a first-class lounge and treated to champagne and canapés.

It seemed ludicrous to be sitting in luxury and sipping champagne as if they were on honeymoon. As if they were in love.

Lindsay sneaked a glance at Antonios—the dark slashes of his eyebrows drawn together, his mouth turned downwards in a forbidding frown—and she had a sudden, absurd urge to say something silly, to make him smile.

The truth was, she didn't know what she felt for him any more. Sadness for what she'd thought they had, and anger for the way he'd shown her it was false. Yet she'd been so in love with him during their time in New York. It was hard to dismiss those feelings as mere fantasy, and yet she knew she had to.

And in a few hours she'd have to pretend they were real, that she still felt them. Her breath hitched at the thought.

'Does anyone know?' she asked and Antonios snapped his gaze to hers.

'Know what?'

'That we're…that we're separated.'

His mouth thinned. 'We're not, in actuality, legally separated, but no, no one knows.'

'Not any of your sisters?' she pressed. She thought of his three sisters: bossy Parthenope, with a husband and young son, social butterfly Xanthe, and Ava, her own age yet utterly different from her. She hadn't bonded with any of them during her time in Greece; his sisters had been possessive of Antonios, and had regarded his unexpected American bride with wary suspicion. They'd also, at Antonios's command, backed off from all the social responsibilities they'd fulfilled for him when he'd been a bachelor. A sign of respect, Antonios had told her, but Lindsay had seen the disdain in their covert glances. What they'd done so effortlessly, maintaining and even organizing the endless social whirl, had been nearly impossible for her. They'd realized that, even if Antonios hadn't.

And now she would have to face them again, suffer them giving her guarded looks, asking her questions, demanding answers…

She couldn't do this.

'Is the thought of my family so abhorrent to you?' Antonios demanded, and Lindsay stiffened.

'No—'

'Because,' he told her bluntly, 'you look like you're going to be sick.'

'I'm not going to be sick.' She took a deep breath. 'But the thought of seeing your family again does make me nervous, Antonios—'

'They did nothing but welcome you.' He cut her off with a shrug of his powerful shoulders.

She took a measured breath. 'Only at your command.'

He arched an eyebrow. 'Does that matter?'

Of course it does. She bit back the words, knowing they would only lead to pointless argument. 'I don't think they were pleased that you came home with such an unexpected bride,' she said after a moment. 'I think they would have preferred you to marry someone of your own background.' A good Greek wife…the kind of wife she hadn't, and never could have, been.

'Perhaps,' Antonios allowed, his tone still dismissive, 'but they still accepted you because they knew I loved you.'

Lindsay didn't answer. It was clear Antonios hadn't seen how suspicious his sisters had been of her. And while they *had* accepted her on the surface, there had still been plenty of sideways glances, speculative looks, even a few veiled comments. Lindsay had felt every single one, to the core.

Yet she wasn't about to explain that to Antonios now, not when he looked so fierce—fiercely determined to be in the right.

'You have nothing to say to that?' Antonios asked, and Lindsay shrugged, taking a sip of champagne. It tasted sour in her mouth.

'No, I don't.' Nothing he would be willing to hear, anyway.

His mouth tightened and he turned to stare out of the floor-to-ceiling windows overlooking the runway. Lindsay watched him covertly, despair and longing coursing through her in equal measures.

She told herself she shouldn't feel this much emotion. It had been her choice to leave, and really they'd known so little of each other. Three months together, that was all. Not enough time to fall in love, much less stay there.

She was a mathematician; she believed in reason, in fact, in logic. Love at almost first sight didn't figure in her world view. Her research had shown the almost mystical relationships between numbers, but she and Antonios weren't numbers, and even though her heart had once cried out differently her head insisted they couldn't have actually loved each other.

'Maybe you never really loved me, Antonios,' she said quietly, and he jerked back in both shock and affront.

'Is that why you left? Because you didn't think I loved you?' he asked in disbelief.

'I'm trying to explain how I felt,' Lindsay answered evenly. 'Since you seem determined to draw an explanation from me, even if you say you don't want one.'

'So you've convinced yourself I didn't love you.' He folded his arms, his face settling into implacable lines.

'I don't think either of us had enough time to truly love or even know each other,' Lindsay answered. 'We only knew each other a week—'

'Three months, Lindsay.'

'A week before we married,' she amended. 'And it was a week out of time, out of reality…' Which was what had made it so sweet and so precious. A week away from the little life she'd made for herself in New York—a life that had been both prison and haven. A week away from being Lindsay Douglas, brilliant mathematician and complete recluse. A week of being seen in an entirely new way—as someone who was interesting and beautiful and *normal*.

'It may have only been a week,' Antonios said, 'but I knew you. At least, I thought I knew you. But perhaps you are right, because the woman I thought I knew wouldn't have left me the way you did.'

'Then you didn't really know me,' Lindsay answered, and Antonios swung round to stare at her, his eyes narrowed.

'Is there something you're not telling me?'

'I…' She drew a deep breath. She could tell him now, explain everything, yet what good would it do? Their marriage was over. Her leaving him had brought about its end. But before she could even think about summoning the courage to confess, he had turned away from her again.

'It doesn't matter,' he answered. 'I don't care.'

Lindsay sagged back against her seat, relief and disappointment flooding her as she told herself it was better this way. It had to be.

Antonios sat in his first-class seat, his glass of complimentary champagne untouched, as his mind seethed with questions he'd never thought to ask himself before. And he shouldn't, he knew, ask them now. It didn't matter what Lindsay's reasons had been for leaving, or whether they'd truly known and loved each other or not. Any possibility between them had ended with her two-sentence email.

Dear Antonios,
I'm sorry, but I cannot come back to Greece. Our marriage was a mistake. Lindsay.

When he'd first read the email, he'd thought it was a joke. His brain simply hadn't been able to process what she was telling him; it had seemed so absurd. Only forty-eight hours before, he'd made love to her half the night long and she'd clung to him until morning, kissed him with passion and gentleness when she'd said goodbye.

And she'd known she was leaving him *then*?

He hadn't wanted to believe it, had started jumping to outrageous, nonsensical conclusions. Someone else had written the email. A jealous rival or a desperate relative? He'd cast them both in roles in a melodrama that had no basis in reality.

The reality was his phone call to Lindsay that same day, and her flat voice repeating what she'd told him in the email. Maybe he'd been the one to hang up, but only because she'd been so determined not to explain herself. Not to say anything at all, except for her wretched party line. That their marriage was a mistake.

Disbelief had given way to anger, to a cold, deep rage the like of which he'd never felt before, not even when he'd realized the extent of his father's desperate deception. He'd *loved* her. He'd brought her into the bosom of his family, showered her with clothes and jewels. He'd given her his absolute loyalty, had presented her to his shocked family as the choice of his heart, even though they'd only known each other for a week. He'd shown how devoted he was to her in every way possible, and she'd said it was all a *mistake*?

He turned to her now, took in her pale face, the soft, vulnerable curve of her cheek, a tendril of white-blonde hair resting against it. When he'd first seen her in New York City, he'd been utterly enchanted. She'd looked ethereal, like a winter fairy, with her pale hair and silvery eyes. He'd called her his Snow Queen.

'Did you intend to leave me permanently,' he asked suddenly, his voice too raw for his liking or comfort, 'when you said goodbye to me in Greece?' When she'd kissed him, her slender arms wrapped around his neck, had she known?

She didn't turn from the window, but he felt her body tense. 'Does it matter?'

'It does to me.' Even though it shouldn't. But maybe he needed to ask these questions, despite what he'd said. Perhaps he would find some peace amidst all the devastation if he understood, even if only in part, why Lindsay had acted as she had. Perhaps then he could let go of his anger and hurt, and move on. Alone.

She let out a tiny sigh. 'Then, yes. I did.'

Her words were like a fist to his gut. To his heart. 'So you lied to me.'

'I never specified when I was coming back,' she said, her voice tired and sad.

'You never said you were going. You acted like you loved me.' He turned away from her, not wanting her to see the naked emotion he could feel on his face. She wasn't even looking at him, but he still felt exposed. Felt the raw pain underneath the anger. Still, one word squeezed its way out of his throat. 'Why?'

She didn't answer.

'Why, Lindsay?' he demanded. 'Why didn't you tell me you were planning to leave, that you were unhappy—?'

'I tried telling you the truth but you never heard it,' she said wearily. 'You never listened.'

'What are you talking about?' Antonios demanded. 'You never once said you were unhappy—'

Lindsay shook her head. 'I don't want to go into it, Antonios. It's pointless. If you want an explanation, it's this: I never really loved you.'

He blinked, reeling from the coldly stated fact even as he sought to deny it. 'Why did you marry me, then?' he asked when he trusted his voice to sound even. Emotionless.

'Because I thought I loved you. I convinced myself what we had was real.' She turned to him, her eyes blazing with what he realized, to his own shock, was anger or maybe grief. 'Can't you see how it was for me? My father had died only a few weeks before. I went to New York because I wanted to escape my life, escape my loneliness and grief. I wandered around the city like a lost soul, still feeling so desperately sad and yet wanting to be enchanted by all the beauty. And then you saw me and you told me *you* were lost, and when I looked in your eyes it felt like you were seeing me—a me I hadn't even known existed until that moment.'

She sank back against her seat, out of breath, her face pale, her shoulders rising and falling in agitation. Antonios's mind spun emptily for a few stunned seconds before he finally managed, his voice hoarse, 'And that was real.'

'No, it wasn't, Antonios. It was a fairy tale. It was playing at being in love. It was red roses and dancing until midnight and penthouse suites at luxury hotels. It was wonderful and magical, but it wasn't *real*.'

'Just because something is exciting—'

'Real was coming to Greece—' she cut across him flatly '—and discovering what your life was like there. Real was feeling like I was drowning every day and you never even noticed.' She bit her lip and then turned towards the window; he realized she'd turned to hide her own emotion, just as he'd tried to hide his. The anger that had been a cold, hard ball inside him started to soften, but he didn't know what emotion replaced it. He felt confused and unsteady, as if someone had given him a hard push, had scattered all his tightly held beliefs and resolutions.

'Lindsay…' He put a hand on her shoulder, conscious once again of how small and fragile she seemed. 'I don't understand.'

She let out a choked laugh and dashed quickly at her eyes. 'I know, Antonios, and you never did. But it's too late now, for both of us. You know that, so let's just stop this conversation.'

A stewardess came by to take their untouched champagne glasses and prepare them for take-off. Lindsay took the opportunity to shrug his hand from her shoulder and wipe the traces of tears from her eyes.

When she turned to look at him, her face was composed and carefully blank. 'Please, let's just get through this flight.'

He nodded tersely, knowing now was not the time to demand answers. And really, what answer could Lindsay give? What on earth could she mean, that she'd been drowning? He'd taken her to his home. His family had welcomed her. He'd given her every comfort, every luxury. Just the memory of how she'd responded to his touch, how her body had sung in tune to his, made a bewildered fury rise up in him again. What the hell was she talking about—*drowning*?

And if she truly had been unhappy, why hadn't she ever told him?

CHAPTER THREE

AS SOON AS the sign for seat belts blinked off, Lindsay unbuckled hers and slipped past Antonios. She hurried to the first-class bathroom, barely taking in the spacious elegance, the crystal vase of roses by the sink. She placed her hands flat on the marble countertop and breathed slowly, in and out, several times, until her heart rate started to slow.

Telling him that much, confessing to even just a little of how she'd felt, had depleted every emotional resource she had. She had no idea how she was going to cope with seven more days of being with Antonios, of pretending to his family.

She pressed her forehead against the cool glass of the mirror and continued with her deep, even breathing. She couldn't panic now. Not like she had back in Greece, when the panic had taken over her senses, had left her feeling like an empty shell, a husk of a person, barely able to function.

How had Antonios not seen that? How had he not heard? Maybe her attempts at trying to explain had been feeble, but he hadn't wanted to listen. Hadn't been able to hear. And he still couldn't.

She'd refuse to discuss it any more, Lindsay resolved. She couldn't defuse his anger and she wouldn't even try. Survival was all she was looking for now, for the next week. For Daphne's sake. Her mother-in-law deserved that much, and Lindsay wanted to see her again and pay her respects.

But heaven help her, it was going to be hard.

Taking a deep breath, she splashed some water on her face and patted it dry. With one last determined look at her pale face in the mirror, she turned and headed back to their seats.

Their dinners had arrived while Lindsay was in the bathroom, and she gazed at the linen napkins and tablecloth, the crystal wine glasses and the silver-domed chafing dishes, remembering how they'd travelled like this to Greece. How luxurious and decadent she'd felt, lounging with Antonios as they ate, heads bent together, murmuring and laughing, buoyant with happiness.

Utterly different from the silent tension that snapped between them now.

Antonios gestured to the dishes as she sat down. 'I didn't know what you wanted, so I ordered several things.'

'I'm sure it's all delicious.' And yet she had no appetite. Antonios lifted the lid on her meal and she stared at the beef, its rich red-wine sauce pooling on her plate, and twisted her napkin in her lap as her stomach rebelled at even the thought of eating.

'You are not hungry?' Antonios asked, one eyebrow arched, and Lindsay shook her head.

'No.'

'You should eat anyway. Keep up your strength.'

And God knew she needed what little she had. She picked up her fork and speared a piece of beef, putting it into her mouth and chewing mechanically. She couldn't taste anything.

Antonios noticed, one eyebrow lifting sardonically. 'Not good enough for you?' he queried, and she let out a little groan.

'Don't start, Antonios.'

'I can't help but wonder, when you had every luxury at your disposal, how you still managed to be so unhappy.'

'There is more to life than luxuries, Antonios. There's attention and support and care.' So much for her resolution not to talk about things.

'Are you saying I didn't give you those?' Antonios demanded.

'No, you didn't. Not the way I needed.'

'You never told me what you needed.'

'I tried,' she said wearily. She felt too tired to be angry any more, even though the old hurt still burrowed deep.

'When? When did you try?'

'Time and time again. I told you I was uncomfortable at all the parties, never mind playing hostess—'

His brow wrinkled and Lindsay knew he probably didn't even remember the conversations she'd found so difficult and painful. 'I told you it would get better in time,' he finally answered. 'That you just needed to let people get to know you.'

'And I told you that was hard for me.'

He shrugged her words aside, just as he had every time she'd tried to tell him before. 'That's not a reason to leave a marriage, Lindsay.'

'Maybe not for you.'

'Are you actually saying you left me simply because you didn't like going to parties?'

'No.' She took a deep breath. 'I left you because you never listened to me. Because you dumped me in Greece like another suitcase you'd acquired and never paid any attention to me again.'

'I had to work, Lindsay.'

'I know that. Trust me, Antonios, I know that. You worked all the time.'

'You never acted like it bothered you—'

She let out a laugh, high and shrill, the sound surprising them both. 'You never change, do you? I'm trying to tell you how I felt and you just keep insisting I couldn't have felt that way, that you never knew. This is why I left, Antonios.' She gestured to the space between them. 'Because the way we were together in real life, not in some fairy-tale bubble in New York, didn't work. It made me miserable—more miserable than I'd ever been before—and that's saying something.'

He frowned. 'What do you mean, that's saying something?'

'Never mind.' She'd never told him about her mother, and never would. Some things were better left unsaid, best forgotten. Not that she could ever forget the way her mother had left.

This isn't what I expected.

A hot lump of misery formed in Lindsay's throat and she swallowed hard, trying to dislodge it. She didn't want to cry, not on an aeroplane, not in front of Antonios.

'*Theos*, Lindsay, if you're not going to tell me things, how can I ever understand you?'

'I don't want you to understand me, Antonios,' she answered thickly. 'Not any more. All I want is a divorce. And I assume you want that, too.' She took a shaky breath. 'Do you really want to be with a wife who left you, who doesn't love you?'

Fire flashed in his eyes and she knew it had been a low and cruel blow. But if that was what it took to get Antonios to stop with his questions, then so be it.

He leaned forward, his eyes still flashing, his mouth compressed. 'Do I need to remind you of how much you loved me, Lindsay? Every night in New York. Every night we were together in Greece.'

And, despite her misery, desire still scorched through her at the memory. 'I'm not talking about in bed, Antonios.'

'Because you certainly responded to me there. Even when you were supposedly *drowning*.'

She closed her eyes, tried to fight the need his simply stated words caused to well up inside her. Sex had always been good between them, had been a respite from the misery she'd faced every day. Maybe that made her weak or wanton, to have craved a man who'd hurt her heart, but she had. From the moment they'd met, she had. And some treacherous part of her still craved him now.

She felt Antonios's hand on her knee and her eyes flew open. 'What—?'

'It didn't take much to make you melt,' he said softly, the words as caressing as his hand. His hand slid up her thigh, his fingers sure and seeking. Lindsay froze, trapped by his knowing gaze and his even more knowing hand. 'I knew just where to touch you, Lindsay. Just how to make you scream. You screamed my name, do you remember?'

Heat flooded through her and she had to fight to keep from responding to his caress. 'Don't,' she whispered, but even to her own ears her voice sounded feeble.

'Don't what?' he asked, his voice so soft and yet also menacing. 'Don't touch you?' He slid his hand higher, cupping her between her legs. Just the press of his hand through her jeans made her stifle a moan as desire pulsed insistently through her.

'What are you trying to prove, Antonios?' she forced out, willing her body to stay still and not respond to his caress. 'That I desire you? Fine. I do. I always did. It doesn't change anything.'

'It should,' Antonios said, and he popped the button on her jeans, slid his hand down so his fingers brushed between her thighs, the sensation of his skin against hers so exquisite she gasped aloud, her eyes fluttering closed. Couldn't keep her hips from lifting off the seat.

Lindsay pressed her head back against the seat, memories and feelings crashing through her. He always had known just how to touch her, to please her. He still did, but there was no love or even kindness behind his calculated caresses now. With what felt like superhuman effort she opened her eyes, stared straight into his triumphant face, and said the thing that she knew would hurt him most.

'You might make me come, Antonios, but you can't make me love you.'

He stared back at her, his expression freezing, and then in one deft movement he yanked his hand from her, unbuckled his seat belt and disappeared through the curtains.

Lindsay sagged back against her seat, her jeans still undone, her heart thudding, and swallowed a sob.

Antonios strode down the first-class aisle, feeling trapped and angry and even dirty. He shouldn't have treated Lindsay like that. Shouldn't have used her desire, her body against her.

Shouldn't have been that pathetic.

What had he been trying to prove? That she felt something for him? He stood in the alcove that separated the first class from business and stared out into the endless night. He didn't know what he'd been trying to do. He'd just been acting, or perhaps reacting, to Lindsay's assertion that she didn't love him. That their love hadn't been real.

It had sure as hell felt real to him. But he'd told her he didn't love her any more, and he needed that to be true. He'd made sure it was true for the last six months, even as he'd maintained the odious front to his family that their marriage was still going strong. He'd had to, for his mother's sake as well as his own pride.

Or maybe you were just actually hoping she'd come back. Fool that you are, you still wanted her back. Because you loved her. Because you made promises.

And was that what was driving him now? The desire, the need to have Lindsay back in his life? Back as his wife? Or was it an even more shameful reason, one born of revenge and pride? Did he want to make her hurt the way he had, to pay for the way she'd treated him?

Antonios had no answer but he was resolved to stop this pointless back and forth, demanding answers that he knew would never satisfy him. The reasons she'd given him for leaving their marriage had been ridiculous. Maybe he had been working too hard, maybe he'd even ignored her a little, but that didn't mean you just walked out.

Except to Lindsay it seemed it did, and nothing, no revenge

or explanation, could change that cold fact. His mouth a grim line of resolution, Antonios headed back to their seats.

Lindsay had tidied herself in his absence, her jeans buttoned back up, her face turned towards the window. She didn't move as he slid into the seat next to her. Didn't even blink.

'I'm sorry,' Antonios said in a low voice. 'I shouldn't have done that.' Lindsay didn't answer, didn't acknowledge his words in any way. 'Lindsay…'

'Just leave me alone, Antonios,' she said, and to his shame her voice sounded quiet and sad. Broken. 'It's going to be hard enough pretending we're still in love for your family. Don't make it any harder.'

He watched her for a moment, part of him aching to reach out and tuck her hair behind her ear, trail his fingers along the smoothness of her cheek. Comfort her, when he'd been the cause of her pain and he knew she didn't want his comfort anyway.

'I'm going to sleep,' she said, and without looking at him she took off her shoes, reached for the eye mask. He watched as she reclined her seat and covered herself with a blanket, all with her face averted from him. Then she slid the eye mask down over her eyes and shut him out completely.

Lindsay lay rigid on her reclined seat, her eyes clenched shut under the mask as she tried to will herself to sleep and failed. She felt a seething mix of anger and regret, guilt and hurt. Her body still tingled from where Antonios had touched her. Her heart still ached.

Forget about it, she told herself yet again. *Just get through this week*. But how on earth was she going to get through this week, when being in Greece had been so hard even when Antonios had loved her, or thought he had, when she'd thought she'd loved him?

Now, with the anger and contempt she'd felt from Antonios, the hurt and frustration she felt herself…it was going to be impossible. Something had to change. To give.

She slipped off her eye mask, determined to confront him, only to find him gazing at her, the hard lines of his face softened by tenderness and despair, a look of such naked longing on his face that it stole her breath. She felt tears come to her eyes and everything in her ached with longing.

'Antonios…'

His face blanked immediately and his mouth compressed. 'Yes?'

'I…' What could she say? *Don't look at me like you hate me?* Just then, he hadn't. Just then he'd looked at her as if he still loved her.

But he doesn't. He doesn't even know you, not the real you. And you don't love him. You can't.

'Nothing,' she finally whispered.

'Get some sleep,' Antonios said, and turned his head away. 'It's going to be a long day tomorrow.'

They arrived in Athens at eleven in the morning, the air warm and dry, the sky hard and bright blue, everything so different from the damp early fall of upstate New York. Being here again brought back memories in flashes of pain: the limo Antonios had had waiting outside the airport, filled with roses. The way he'd held and kissed her all the way to his villa in the mountains of central Greece, and how enchanted Lindsay had been, still carried away by the fairy tale.

It wasn't until the limo had turned up the sweeping drive framed by plane trees with the huge, imposing villa and all of the other buildings in the distance that she'd realized she'd been dealing in fantasies…and that she and Antonios would not be living alone in some romantic hideaway. His mother, his brother, Leonidas, his two unmarried sisters, an army of staff and employees—everyone lived at Villa Marakaios, which wasn't the sweet little villa with terracotta tiles and painted wooden shutters that Lindsay had naively been imagining. No, it was a complex, a hive of industry, a *city*. And when she'd stepped out of the limo into that bright, bright sunshine, every eye of every citizen of that city had been trained on her.

Her worst nightmare.

She'd seen everyone lined up in front of the villa—the family, the friends, the employees and house staff, everyone staring at her, a few people whispering and even pointing—and she'd forgotten how to breathe.

Antonios had propelled her forward, one hand on her elbow, and she'd gone, her vision already starting to tunnel as her chest constricted and the panic took over.

She hadn't felt panic like that since she'd been a little girl, her mother's hand hard on her lower back, shoving her into a room full of academics.

Come on, Lindsay. Recite something for us.

Sometimes she'd managed to stumble through a poem her mother had made her memorize, and sometimes her brain had blanked and, with her mouth tightening in disappointment, her mother had dismissed her from the room.

After too many of those disappointments, she'd dismissed her from her life.

This isn't what I expected.

And, standing there in the glare of Greek sunshine, Lindsay had felt it all come rushing back. The panic. The shortness of breath. The horrible, horrible feeling of every eye on her, every person finding her wanting. And she'd blacked out.

She'd come to consciousness inside the house, lying on a sofa, a cool cloth pressed to her head and a white-haired woman smiling kindly down at her.

'It's the sun, I'm sure,' Daphne Marakaios had said as she'd pressed the cloth to Lindsay's head. 'It's so strong here in the mountains.'

'Yes,' Lindsay had whispered. 'The sun.'

Now, as she slid into the passenger seat of Antonios's rugged SUV, having cleared customs and collected their luggage, she wondered if he even remembered how she'd fainted. He'd certainly been quick to accept it as her reaction to the sun, and she'd been too overwhelmed and shell-shocked to say any differently.

And she'd have to face his family again in just three hours. How on earth was she going to cope?

They drove out of Athens, inching through a mid-morning snarl of traffic, and then headed north on the National Highway towards Amfissa, the nearest town to Antonios's estate in the mountains.

With each mile they drove, Lindsay's panic increased. This time she knew what she was facing, and it would be so much worse. Now everyone would be suspicious, maybe even hostile. She could picture his sister Parthenope eyeing her with cool curiosity, her husband by her side and dark-haired, liquid-eyed little Timon clinging to her legs; Leonidas, Antonios's younger brother, giving her one of his sardonic looks; Ava and Xanthe, his younger sisters, eyeing her with sceptical curiosity, as if they'd already decided she didn't belong. And the questions… she would have to answer so many questions…

'Antonios,' she said, his name little more than a croak, and he glanced at her briefly before snapping his gaze back to the road.

'What is it?'

She focused on her breathing, tried to keep it even. 'Would it…would it be possible for me to come to the villa quietly? I mean, not have everyone waiting and… I'd rather not see anyone at first.' *In. Out. In. Out.* With effort she kept her breathing measured and her heart rate started to slow. She could do this. She'd managed to control her anxiety for most of her life. She could do it now. She had to.

'The point,' Antonios returned, 'is for you to see people and be seen. No one thinks anything is wrong between us, Lindsay.'

But they would have guessed. Of course they would have guessed. His siblings weren't stupid, and neither was Daphne. Lindsay had been gone for six whole months and then Antonios had come all the way to New York to fetch her. Everyone would be wondering just what had gone wrong between them.

'I understand,' Lindsay said, her eyes closed as she pressed back against the seat and kept concentrating on those deep, even breaths. 'But I'd rather not have everyone there when we arrive.'

'What am I meant to do? Send them away?'

She opened her eyes as she tried to suppress a stab of irritation or even anger, wondering if he was deliberately being difficult. Or was he just obstinately obtuse, as usual? 'No, of course not. I just don't want them all lined up in front of the villa, waiting to welcome me.' Or not welcome, as the case well might be.

Antonios was silent for a moment, his gaze narrowed on the road in front of them, the sun glinting off the tarmac. 'You mean like last time.'

'Yes.'

'You fainted,' Antonios recalled slowly. 'When you got out of the car.'

So he had remembered. Just. 'Yes.'

Antonios's expression tightened and he turned back to the road. 'I'll see what I can do,' he said, and they didn't speak for the rest of the journey.

Two hours later they'd left the highway for the narrow, twisting lane that curved its way between the mountains of Giona and Parnassus. They came around a bend and Villa Marakaios lay before them, nestled in a valley between the mountains, its many whitewashed buildings gleaming brightly under the afternoon sun.

Antonios drove down the twisting road towards the villa, his eyes narrowed against the sun, his mouth a hard, grim line.

As they drove through the gates he turned to the left, surprising her, for the front of the villa, with its many gleaming steps and impressive portico, was before them. Instead, Antonios drove around the back of the complex to a small whitewashed house with an enclosed courtyard and latticed shutters painted a cheerful blue. It looked, Lindsay thought in weary bemusement, like the villa she'd once imagined in her naive daydreams. A honeymoon house.

'We can stay here,' Antonios said tersely, and he killed the engine. 'It's used as a guesthouse, but it's empty now.'

'What?' Lindsay stared at him in surprise. Last time they'd stayed in the main villa with all the family and staff; only Leonidas had his own place. Since his father's death, Antonios had been appointed the CEO of Marakaios Enterprises and essentially lord of the manor.

Now he shrugged and got out of the car. 'It will make it easier for us to maintain the pretence if we are not so much in the public eye.' He went around to the boot of the car for their cases, not looking at her as he added, 'And perhaps it will be easier for you.'

Lindsay stared at him, his dark head bent as he hefted their suitcases and then started walking towards the villa. He was being thoughtful, she realized. And he'd given credence to what she'd told him, if just a little.

'Thank you,' she murmured and with a wary, uncertain hope burgeoning inside her she followed him into the villa.

CHAPTER FOUR

ANTONIOS PUT THE suitcases in the villa's one bedroom, tension knotting between his shoulders. Coming back to Villa Marakaios always gave him a sense of impending responsibility and pressure, the needs and concerns of the family and business descending on him like a shroud the moment he drove through the gates. But it was a shroud he wore willingly and a duty he accepted with pride, no matter what the cost.

He could hear Lindsay moving behind him, walking with the quiet grace and dignity she'd always possessed.

'Why don't you rest?' he said as he turned around. Lindsay stood in the doorway, her pale hair floating around her face in a silvery-golden cloud, her eyes wide and clear, yet also troubled. 'Everyone is coming for dinner tonight,' he continued. 'I need to see to some business. I'll come back before we have to leave. But I suppose you don't mind me working all hours now, do you?'

The less they saw each other, the better. Yet he still couldn't keep a feeling of bitterness or maybe even hurt from needling him when she nodded, and wordlessly he walked past her and out of the villa.

He walked across the property to the offices housed separately from the family's living quarters, in a rambling whitewashed building overlooking the Marakaios groves that stretched to the horizon, rows upon rows of stately olive trees with their gnarled branches, each neatly pruned and tended, now just coming into flower.

He paused for a moment on the threshold of the building, steeling himself for the demands that would assail him the moment he walked in the door. Ten years after his father had told him of the extent of Marakaios Enterprises' debt, he'd finally brought the business to an even keel—but it had taken just about everything he had, both emotionally and physically.

Now he greeted his PA, Alysia, accepted a sheaf of correspondence and then strode into his office, perversely glad, for once, to immerse himself in paperwork and answering emails and not think of Lindsay.

Except he *did* think of Lindsay; she was like a ghost inside his mind, haunting his thoughts with both the good memories and the bad. The week in New York—that intense, incredible week when they'd shared everything.

And yet nothing, because he was realizing afresh just how much of a stranger she was.

In New York he'd thought he'd known her. She'd told him about her research, and he'd watched how animated she became when she talked about twin primes and Fermat's Last Theorem and Godel's proof for the existence of God. He hadn't really understood any of it, but he'd loved seeing her passion for her subject, intelligence and interest shining in her silver-grey eyes.

She'd told him about her father, too, who had died just a few weeks before they met. She'd cried then and he'd comforted her, drawing her into his arms, fitting her body around his as he'd tenderly wiped the tears from her face.

He thought about the first time they'd made love, how her eyes had gone so wide when he'd slid inside her and she'd said in wonder, 'It's like the most perfect equation,' which had made him laugh even as pleasure overtook them both. With Lindsay he'd felt happier than he ever had before. He'd felt *right*, complete in a way that made him realize just how much he'd been missing.

And then he recalled the emptiness that had swooped through him when he'd talked to her on the phone and she'd told him in that lifeless voice that it was all a mistake.

'Welcome back.'

Antonios looked up from his laptop to see his brother, Leonidas, lounging in the doorway of his office. Fourteen months younger, half an inch taller and a little leaner, Leonidas had been mistaken more than once for his twin. They'd been close as children, united in various boyish escapades, but since Antonios had become CEO the gulf between them had widened, and Antonios's vow of secrecy to his father made it impossible to bridge.

No one is to know, Antonios. No one but you. I couldn't bear it.

'Thank you,' he said now with a nod to Leonidas. He tried to offer his brother a smile, but the memories of Lindsay that had assailed him just now were still too poignant, too painful.

'Good trip?' Leonidas asked, one eyebrow cocked, and not for the first time Antonios wondered how much his brother knew, or at least guessed, about him and Lindsay.

'Fine,' he said briskly. 'Short. I thought about stopping in New York to see the new clients but there was no time.'

'I could do it,' Leonidas offered and Antonios shrugged.

'I'll travel back to New York next week, with Lindsay. I'll see them then.'

Leonidas's expression turned neutral as he gave a careless nod. 'So you're both returning to America in just one week?'

'Lindsay has research to finish.'

'I thought she could do it here.'

Antonios shrugged, hating the deception he was forced to maintain. First with his father, and now this. He'd accused Lindsay of lying to him, but he was the greater liar.

Soon, he told himself. Soon enough he would come clean.

All too soon, when his mother was past knowing. The thought made him close his eyes briefly, and he snapped them open. 'She has to wrap up things with her house,' he said dismissively. 'You know how it is.'

Although of course Leonidas didn't know how it was. He was a determined bachelor and besides his private villa here he kept an apartment in Athens. Their father had appointed him as Head of European Operations before he'd died, and since then Leonidas had spent most of his time travelling to their various clients in Europe, working on new accounts because Antonios didn't want him to see the old ones. Couldn't let him know how close they'd come to losing it all.

'So she'll return when?' Leonidas asked and Antonios forced himself to shrug.

'We haven't decided on a date,' he answered coolly. 'Now, don't you have work to do? I just saw an email from the Lyon restaurant group. They're concerned about their supply.'

'I'm on it,' Leonidas answered, his voice terse, and he turned from the office.

Antonios sank back in his chair, raking his hands through his hair. Maintaining this deception was going to be even harder than he'd realized. And when he came clean…he burned to think of the disbelief and pity he'd face from his siblings.

Burned to think that it had come to this, and why? *Because Lindsay never loved you. And you didn't know her well enough to love her like you thought you did.*

Grimacing, he turned back to his laptop. He'd wasted enough time thinking about Lindsay today.

Lindsay managed to sleep for a couple of hours, waking muzzy-headed and disorientated to the sound of someone knocking on the door.

She stumbled out of bed, reaching for a robe hanging from the bathroom door to cover herself; it had been too warm to sleep in anything but her underwear. A maid whose face she vaguely recognized was standing outside, a man behind her carrying several suitcases.

'What…?' Lindsay began, confused and still only half awake.

'Kyrios Marakaios wanted your clothes to be brought here,' the maid explained in halting English. Lindsay knew only a few words of Greek. 'He asked for me to help put them away.'

'Oh…thank you.' She stepped back to let the woman in, and then watched uncomfortably as the man deposited the suitcases in the bedroom before leaving and the maid began unpacking the clothes she'd barely worn and then hanging them in the walk-in closet.

Lindsay offered to help but the woman insisted she'd do it herself, so she left the bedroom and went to the living area of the villa, gazing through the sliding glass doors that led to a private pool. If she were in the deep end of that thing, she thought disconsolately, she couldn't be more out of her depth.

Dinner, she knew, would be in just a few hours. She needed to get ready, and not just her clothes and make-up. She needed to prepare emotionally. Mentally.

Lindsay made herself some tea and took it outside to the pool area, sitting in one of the loungers and cradling the warmth of the mug between her hands as she closed her eyes and focused on her breathing. She pictured the ornate dining room where the family gathered for more formal meals, imagined each chair, each face, and focused on keeping her breathing slow and even.

Visualization, her therapist had told her, was meant to be helpful when trying to manage new or difficult situations. And she'd become good enough at it that she could picture it all and still stay calm.

It was when she was actually *in* the situation, facing all those people, all their stares and questions, that she started to panic.

'What are you doing?' Lindsay's eyes flew open and she saw Antonios standing by the gate that led out to the drive, his eyebrows drawn together in a frown. 'You sound like you're hyperventilating.'

'No, just breathing.' She felt a blush heat her cheeks and she took a sip of tea. 'Trying to relax.' And not succeeding very well.

Antonios's mouth twisted as he glanced around at the pool, the water sparkling in the bright sunlight, the whitewashed villa looking cool and pristine, everything beautiful and luxurious. Lindsay braced herself for some cutting remark about how difficult she must find it to relax in such a paradise. But to her relief he said nothing, just nodded towards the villa, his mouth tight.

'You should get dressed,' he said as he walked past her. 'We need to be at the main house in an hour.'

The maid had gone when Lindsay went back inside, and she spent a long time in the huge, sumptuous shower, as if she could postpone the inevitable moment when she faced Antonios's family.

He'd told her it was casual, which meant full make-up and a nice dress. The Marakaios family didn't do casual the way she'd ever understood it, and that just added to her stress and tension.

An hour later she stared at her reflection in the bathroom mirror, wiped icy palms down the sides of the lavender linen shift that Antonios had bought for her in New York. She remembered the joy of trying on new clothes, parading them for him, laughing at his deliberately lascivious expressions. An ache of longing swept through her and she leaned her forehead against the mirror. They'd had so much fun together, for such a short while. No matter if it hadn't been real or lasting, she still missed that. Missed him, and missed the woman she'd been with him, before he'd taken her back to Greece. Before everything had gone wrong.

A sharp knock sounded on the bathroom door. 'Are you ready?' Antonios called. 'We need to go.'

'Okay.' Lindsay lifted her head from the mirror and stared at her reflection once more. Her heart was starting to beat fast, her chest to hurt, and she had that curious light-headed sensation that always preceded a full-blown panic attack.

Breathe, Lindsay. You can do this. You have to do this.

She gripped the edge of the sink, focused on her breathing and willed her heart rate to slow.

'Lindsay…' Antonios called, impatience edging his voice, and, after a few more agonized seconds of trying to keep the panic under control, she straightened and opened the door.

'I'm ready,' she said as she walked out of the bathroom. She was feeling light-headed enough to have to focus on her walking, the way a drunk person would. She didn't think she was very convincing because Antonios regarded her silently for a moment. She didn't look at him, just kept her chin held high, her shoulders back. *Breathe.*

'You look lovely,' Antonios said finally. 'I remember that dress.'

'Thank you.' It was hard to get words out of her throat, but she just about managed it. 'Why don't we go?'

She started out of the villa and Antonios followed. She stumbled slightly on the gravel drive and he took her arm, exclaiming as he did so.

'You're freezing.'

She always went cold when she had a panic attack, a result of her blood pressure dropping, but she wasn't about to explain that now. 'I'm fine—'

He stared at her for one long, fathomless moment, his arm gripping hers. He felt warm and steady and strong and the temptation to lean into him was nearly unbearable. She stood straighter.

'Let me get you a wrap. The nights are chilly here.'

'Fine.' Not that a wrap would actually help.

He came back a few minutes later with a matching lavender pashmina and draped it over her shoulders. 'Thank you,' Lindsay murmured, and they kept walking.

The quarter mile to the main villa felt like a trek across the Sahara, and yet Lindsay would have willingly walked it forever rather than face what was inside.

All too soon they had arrived; Lindsay paused before the huge double doors that led to the enormous marble foyer with its sweeping double staircase. Antonios greeted the manservant who opened the front doors, and then several other servants who circulated through the foyer, trays of canapés and glasses of champagne held aloft.

Definitely a casual dinner, then.

Lindsay managed to murmur a few hellos, offer some smiles. After a few minutes Antonios led her into the living room where his family waited; Lindsay saw his brother, Leonidas, by the window, Parthenope sitting on a sofa, her lips pursed and her eyes narrowed as she stared at her. Xanthe and Ava stood together by the window, heads bent together. Lindsay watched as one of them whispered something to the other.

Her chest constricted so much it felt as if she were having a heart attack. She stopped where she stood, flung one hand out to brace herself against the doorway as Antonios walked into the room to greet his family.

'Lindsay,' Daphne Marakaios said and, rising from her chair, she walked towards Lindsay, her arms outstretched.

Lindsay accepted the woman's embrace, felt how much thinner and more fragile she seemed from the last time she'd seen her. 'Daphne,' she murmured, and pressed a kiss against each of her mother-in-law's wrinkled cheeks.

Daphne eased back, her gaze sweeping over Lindsay. 'It's so good to have you back, my dear.' She squeezed her hands. 'I hope it is good to be back?'

The questioning lilt in Daphne's voice made Lindsay wonder just how much her mother-in-law knew about the state of her son's marriage.

'Of course it is,' she murmured. It was good to see Daphne again at least, and she hoped her mother-in-law knew it.

'Come sit by me,' Daphne instructed, and led Lindsay to a sofa in the corner of the room. She was grateful for her mother-in-law's attention; it kept everyone else from besieging her with questions, even if she felt their speculative stares from across the room. Still, she'd got one of the worst parts of the evening over with: the grand entrance that being with Antonios had always entailed, that had always reminded her of those unbearable evenings with her mother's friends.

Daphne chatted with her briefly, asking surprisingly pertinent questions about her doctoral research; in Lindsay's experience most people's eyes glazed over when she started talking about the abstract details of number theory, but Daphne seemed genuinely interested.

And talking about mathematics was the most calming thing Lindsay could have done; explaining the impossible and even mystical beauty of transcendental numbers made her breathing slow and her body relax.

From across the room she caught Antonios glowering at her and her mind blanked.

'I find your work so fascinating, my dear,' Daphne said and Lindsay realized she'd just stopped speaking, maybe even in the middle of a sentence. 'You have such a lively mind, such a fierce intelligence.'

Lindsay smiled, or tried to, because the sincerity in Daphne's voice made her suddenly feel near tears. If she'd stayed, perhaps if she'd just tried harder, she could have developed a relationship with this woman that would have gone a long way to addressing the absence of a mother in her own life since the age of nine. Maybe she would have made friends with Antonios's sisters, rather than having them now staring at her stonily from across the room.

And just like that the panic swamped her again. She pressed one hand to her chest to ease the pain, and Daphne laid a hand on her arm.

'Lindsay, are you all right?'

'I'm fine.' Those two words had become her mantra. Lindsay forced herself to drop her hand from her chest and smile at Daphne. 'Sorry, just tired from the flight. But how are you? Antonios told me—'

Daphne smiled wryly. 'Then you know I'm not so well. But I've lived a good life. I have only a few regrets.'

Which was, Lindsay thought, an extraordinarily honest thing to say. Most people defiantly declared they had no regrets whatsoever.

And as for her? Did she regret marrying Antonios? Loving him, even if it hadn't lasted? Leaving him? All of it?

'Shall we go into the dining room?' Antonios asked. He'd crossed the room without her realizing it and now stood in front of her, his smile perfectly in place although the expression in his eyes was veiled. In his dark suit and crisp white shirt and navy silk tie he looked impossibly beautiful, everything about him reminding her of how happy she'd been with him. For such a little while.

Lindsay stood up and took his arm, grateful for the support even though she could feel Antonios's tension. His forearm was like a band of iron under her hand.

It wasn't until everyone was seated at the dinner table, the first course served, that the questions started. The interrogation.

Antonios's sister Parthenope began it. 'So, Lindsay, how was America?'

'Fine. Cold.' Lindsay dabbed her mouth with her napkin, pressing it against her lips as she took a deep breath.

'You were gone a long time,' Xanthe chimed in, her eyes narrowed, mouth pursed. They were suspicious of her. Angry, too. Antonios might not have told his family what had happened, but they clearly guessed some of it.

'Yes... I had to continue my research.' She forced herself to return her napkin to her lap, pick up her fork. Her knuckles shone white as she clenched it and she made herself relax her grip.

'I thought you could do this research anywhere.' This from Ava, who was the same age as her, twenty-six, yet now looked at her as if she were an alien and inferior species—a wife who had left her husband to do mathematical research. A freak.

'I can,' she answered, her voice seeming to echo in her own ears. Her chest was starting to hurt again. 'But I had a few things I had to wrap up in New York.'

'Then you're finished there? You won't be returning?' Parthenope again, her voice sharper this time, as she shot Antonios a concerned glance.

Lindsay swallowed. And swallowed again. She couldn't think of anything to say. She didn't want to lie, but telling the truth was just as unpalatable an option and would only invite more questions. More disapproval. She could feel everyone's stares on her and her vision started to swim.

'Lindsay's not quite done in New York,' Antonios said, his tone carefully bland. 'But she knows her home is here.'

At this Parthenope nodded approvingly because, unlike Lindsay, she was a good Greek wife and would never even imagine leaving her husband for six whole months.

Lindsay blinked back the dizziness and reached for her wine glass, but her hands were so icy and damp with sweat that the glass slipped from her fingers and fell to the tiled floor, shattering into a million pieces and splashing red wine all over the pristine white tablecloth and her dress.

A ringing silence ensued as a staff member sprang to attention to clean it up. Lindsay stared at the mess in horror, felt her head go light again as everyone's gaze swung to her and the enormity of the situation and just how much of it she couldn't handle crashed over her once again.

'I'm sorry,' she managed through her constricted throat.

'Not to worry, my dear,' Daphne said. 'It could happen to anyone.'

But it happened to me. Lindsay clenched her hands in her lap, dug her nails into her palms and hoped the pain would distract her from the full-fledged panic attack she could feel coming on. Dizziness. Trouble breathing. Chest pain.

She'd tried so many different things to control the attacks while she'd been here. Breathing techniques, reciting prime numbers in her head, the desperate measure of alcohol. Nothing worked, and pain didn't either.

Spots danced before her eyes.

'Excuse me,' she murmured, and rose unsteadily from the table. She could see Antonios frowning at her but she was past caring. If she didn't leave now, she'd embarrass herself—and him—far more than this.

Somehow she made it to the bathroom. She doubled over the sink, rested her cheek against the cool porcelain. Her head spun and her chest hurt.

After a few long moments the dizziness thankfully receded and she started to feel a little better. She washed her face and blotted her dress as best she could. She looked, she realized, terrible. Her dress had a large red stain on the front from the wine. She couldn't go back into the dining room like this.

She sank onto the floor, drew her knees up to her chest and wondered whether she could spend the rest of the night—the rest of her life—in the bathroom.

A knock, an impatient *rat-a-tat-tat*, sounded on the door. 'Lindsay, are you in there?'

Lindsay pressed her face against her knees. 'Go away, Antonios.'

'Open the door.'

She almost laughed at that. He was like a bulldozer, steamrolling over everyone and everything to get what he wanted. She'd been charmed by his determination when they'd met in New York; no one had ever showed such an interest in and desire for her.

Now she just felt tired. 'Please go away.'

'Are you all right?'

This time she did laugh, wearily. 'No.'

Antonios jiggled the door and then pushed his shoulder

against it. The door sprang open, and Lindsay wondered if *anything* could hold out against her husband.

He swore at the sight of her sitting hunched on the floor, and then crouched down so they were at eye level and peered into her face. '*Theos*...what's wrong, Lindsay? Are you ill?'

'No, I'm not ill, Antonios.' She straightened, every muscle aching from the exertion of the panic attack and her own futile resistance to it.

'Then what—?'

And suddenly she was so very tired of it—of him not understanding, of her trying, perversely and at the same time, to explain and to hide. He wanted to know? Fine. He could know. Everything. And she didn't even care whether he believed her or not any more. 'I was having a panic attack,' she told him shortly. She washed her hands and face in the sink, even though she'd already done so once. At least it was something to do.

'A panic attack...' Antonios was staring at her in amazement.

'Yes, a panic attack. I suffer from a social anxiety disorder. Being in strange situations, or being the centre of attention, can cause me to panic.'

Antonios continued to gape at her. 'And you...suffered from this during our marriage?'

'Yes.'

'But you never—'

'Said? I tried, Antonios. I tried to explain, but you never wanted to listen.'

'I would have listened if you'd told me something like that!'

She eyed him wearily. 'Are you sure about that?'

He stared back at her, his expression unreadable. 'Let me make my apologies to my family,' he said finally. 'Will you be all right for a few minutes?'

'I'll be—'

'Fine? I'm not buying that one any more.' His voice was flat, toneless. 'Will you be all right?'

Lindsay let out a shuddering breath. 'Yes.'

* * *

Antonios stalked towards the dining room, fury coursing through him, although what or whom he was angry with he couldn't say. Wasn't ready to think about. He had a terrible feeling it was himself.

Six questioning faces turned to him as he came through the double doors. His mother, his brother, his three sisters, Parthenope's husband. Everyone had witnessed Lindsay stumble out of the room like a drunken bat out of hell, and the ensuing silence had been appalling.

'Lindsay's not feeling well,' he told them all. He kept his voice brisk, his face neutral. 'I'm taking her back to our villa.'

Daphne half rose from her seat, her face drawn in a frown of concern. 'Is there something I can do, Antonios?'

'No. She'll be—' *fine* stuck in his throat '—she needs to rest,' he said instead, and turned from the room.

Lindsay was exactly where he'd left her, in the bathroom, her hands braced against the sink, her hair falling forward to cover her face. 'We'll take a car back,' he said and she shook her head.

'I'm not an invalid. I can walk.'

'Even so.' She looked terrible—pale and sweaty, her hair tangled about her face. Seeing her like this made everything inside Antonios tighten like a giant fist. He wanted to protect her, to take care of her, to shout at her.

Why didn't you tell me?

It was a howl of anguish and anger, of guilt and grief, and he swallowed it all down. There would be time for that later, to ask questions and demand answers. Right now he just needed to take care of Lindsay.

He took her arm and led her from the bathroom, guiding and sheltering her, to the front steps of the villa where the car he'd arranged waited, one of the staff acting as driver.

He opened the door and helped her inside the car; she didn't resist. And then, with neither of them speaking, they drove off into the night.

CHAPTER FIVE

As soon as they were back at the villa, Antonios strode to the en suite bathroom and starting running the tub. Lindsay stood in the doorway of the bathroom, exhausted and emotionally drained, knowing Antonios would expect answers and pretty sure she didn't have the resources right now to give them.

'Have a bath,' he said, and dumped half a bottle of expensive bath foam into the tub. 'Then we'll talk.'

A bath sounded heavenly and Lindsay was grateful for the reprieve from any conversation. Antonios left the room and she stripped out of her ruined dress and sank into the steaming water frothing with bubbles, feeling utterly overwhelmed.

For the three months of their marriage she'd kept it together better than that. She'd hidden it better, at least from his family, and even from Antonios. Now, the very first day, the first occasion she'd had to panic, she had. Utterly. She wondered what Antonios's family thought of her now. What he thought of her. She wished she was too tired to care, but the truth was she hated—had always hated—the thought of him knowing her weakness. It was what had made it so difficult to tell him in the first place. Now she felt a fist of fear clench in her stomach at the thought that he knew, even though it didn't matter. They didn't have a relationship any more.

After half an hour soaking in the tub she felt a little better, although wanting nothing but to sleep, and she got out and swathed herself in one of the huge terrycloth robes hanging from the door. She combed her hair and brushed her teeth and, with nothing left to do, she opened the door, throwing back her shoulders as she went to face Antonios.

He was sprawled on the sofa in the living room, a tumbler of whisky in one hand, the moonlight streaming through the sliding glass doors washing him in silver.

He turned his head to gaze at her fathomlessly as she came into the room; Lindsay braced herself for the questions. The accusations. He spoke only one word.

'Why?'

His voice was so bleak and desolate that Lindsay had to fight back an ache of regret and sorrow. 'Why what?' she asked and he took a long swallow of whisky, shaking his head.

'Why didn't you tell me?'

She sank onto the sofa opposite him. 'I've told you, I tried—'

'I don't recall ever hearing you mention agoraphobia, Lindsay.'

She plucked at a loose thread on the dressing gown. 'Maybe I didn't get that far.'

'And why didn't you? If I'd had any idea of how much you were suffering, I might have understood more. Listened more—'

'Listened more? You didn't listen at all, Antonios. You left for a business trip two days after we arrived in Greece.'

His mouth tightened. 'It was necessary.'

'Of course it was.'

'You never protested—'

'Actually, I did. I asked why you had to leave so soon, and you told me it was important. You practically patted my head before you left. Why didn't you just hand me a lollipop while you were at it?' The words surprised her, yet they felt right. Antonios's gaze narrowed.

'Are you implying that I was patronizing towards you?'

'Oh, well done, you get a gold star. Yes, that's exactly what I'm implying.' The anger she felt now took her by surprise. She was so used to feeling guilty and ashamed about her own deficiency, but this felt cleaner. Stronger. And she needed to be strong.

Antonios was silent for a long moment. 'I didn't mean to be patronizing,' he said at last. 'But I don't see how that has anything to do with you not telling me—'

'Don't you? Can't you see how it might be just a little bit difficult to tell your husband of one week that you have a debilitating condition when all he does is tell you over and over everything is going to be fine, just give it time, and insists you have nothing to worry about?'

'In normal circumstances, that would be true—'

'You think so? You think most wives get whisked off to a country where they don't speak the language—'

'Everyone in my family speaks English.'

'The staff don't. The staff I was meant to *supervise* for a dinner party less than a week after I arrived!'

The skin around Antonios's mouth went white. 'I thought I was giving you an honour, as mistress of the household, to plan—'

'Yet you never asked if I *wanted* to be mistress of your household. Never asked me what I wanted from life, from marriage.' She shook her head, weariness replacing her anger. 'Perhaps I should have spoken up more, Antonios. Perhaps I should have told you the truth more plainly. But I did try, even if you didn't see it.' She swallowed hard. 'I tried as hard as I could, considering how overwhelmed I felt.'

'Drowning,' he reminded her quietly, and she nodded.

'Yes, it felt like I was drowning. Like I couldn't breathe. Couldn't function—'

'And I didn't see this.' He didn't sound disbelieving, more just wondering. 'Did you have panic attacks like the one you had tonight when we were together?' She nodded, and he shook his head. 'How? How could I have missed that?'

'I tried to hide it, from your family. From you.'

'So you were trying to tell me and hide from me at the same time.'

Which made his aggravation understandable. 'I suppose I was.'

He let out a long, weary sigh and then leaned forward, his head bowed as he raked his hands through his hair. 'Tell me,' he said after a moment, his voice low. 'Tell me about your… condition.'

'You saw for yourself.'

'Tell me everything. Tell me how it started, how you've coped…' He looked up, his expression determined even as Lindsay saw an agony in his eyes. She ached for him, for herself, for them. If only things had been different. If she'd been stronger, braver. If only Antonios had listened more…

Or was it absurd to think things could have been different, that a mere action or word could have changed things for the better? The failure of their marriage hadn't happened, she knew, because of a simple lack of communication. It went deeper than that, to who they both were fundamentally and what they'd expected from life, from love.

But, even if their marriage was over, she could still give Antonios the answers he asked for. Maybe it would provide a certain sense of closure for both of them.

'I was always a shy child,' she began slowly. 'Definitely an introvert. I had a bit of a stammer, and I used to get stomach aches over going to school.' Antonios nodded, his gaze alert and attentive, more so than ever before, and she continued. 'My mother came from a family of famous academics. Her father was a physicist who travelled the world, giving lectures, and her mother was an English professor who wrote literary novels, very well received. I think she thought when she married my father, a mathematics professor, that her life would be like that.'

'And it wasn't?'

Lindsay shook her head. 'My father liked his work, but he didn't want to be some famous academic. My mother dropped out of graduate school when she fell pregnant with me, and I think maybe...maybe she resented me for that.'

Antonios frowned. 'Surely she could have gone back to school, if she'd wanted.'

'Maybe she did go back, eventually,' Lindsay answered. 'I wouldn't know. She walked out on me—on us—when I was nine.'

Antonios's gaze widened as it swept over her. 'You never told me that.'

'I suppose there are a lot of things I didn't tell you, Antonios.' Lindsay felt her throat thicken and she blinked rapidly. 'I don't... I don't like to talk about my mother.'

'So you became more anxious after she left?'

'Yes—but I was already suffering from panic attacks before then. She used to hold these sort of literary salons—she'd invite a bunch of academics over to our house and they'd talk about lofty things, books and philosophy and the like. It all went over my head. But she'd always call me into the room before bed and try to show me off, make me recite a poem or something in front of everyone. I think she wanted to prove to them she wasn't wasting her life, being a stay-at-home mother.'

'And you didn't like that.'

'I hated it, but I was also desperate to please her. I'd spend hours memorizing poems, but then when I got in front of everyone my mind would go blank. Sometimes I'd start to hyperventilate. My mother would be so disappointed in me she wouldn't talk to me, sometimes for days.' She still remembered sitting at the kitchen table, swamped in misery, while her mother maintained an icy silence, sipping her coffee.

Shock blazed in Antonios's eyes. 'Lindsay, that's awful. Didn't your father notice?'

'A bit, I think, but he was immersed in his research and

teaching. And I didn't tell him how bad it was because I felt so ashamed.'

'And is that why you didn't tell me?' Antonios asked quietly. 'Because you felt ashamed?'

'Maybe,' Lindsay allowed. Her feelings about her anxiety and Antonios and their time in Greece were all tangled up—frustration and fear, anger and guilt. And, yes, shame. 'I've worked hard as an adult to control my anxiety, and even to accept it as part of me, but I know back then my mother was ashamed of me.' A lump formed in her throat, making the next words hard to form, to say. 'It's why she left.'

Antonios stared at her, his face expressionless even though his eyes blazed—but with what emotion? Anger? Pity? She hated the thought, even now, of him pitying her. 'How can you say that?' he asked in a low voice.

'My father finally noticed things weren't right when I was eight,' Lindsay continued, squeezing the words out past that awful lump. 'He took me to a specialist and had me examined and diagnosed. And he accepted a position in upstate New York, where I live now, far from Chicago, where we'd been living. My mother felt it was a demotion, and she didn't want to live in some poky town.'

'So she left because of that,' Antonios said. 'Not because of you, Lindsay—'

'I suppose it was the whole package really. The town, the house, the husband, the child.' She took a deep breath and met his gaze, the seventeen-year-old memory as fresh and raw as it ever had been. 'She came to New York to look at the house and college. We all went, and I remember how she walked around the empty rooms. She had this terribly blank look on her face and she didn't say anything, not until my father asked her what she thought, and then all she said was, "This isn't what I expected."' Tears stung her eyes, and one slipped down her cheek. Lindsay dashed it away. 'My father and I thought she meant the house, or maybe even the town. But she meant us. Life with us. It wasn't what she'd expected. We didn't make her happy.'

'She said that?' Antonios asked, his voice sharp with disbelief, and Lindsay nodded.

'She spoke with my father that night. I heard them from my bed. She said she couldn't cope, living in a place like this with… with a daughter like me. She said she was leaving.'

'Oh, Lindsay.' She was staring down at her lap by that point so she didn't see Antonios move, didn't know he had until his arms were around her and he'd pulled her onto his lap. 'I'm sorry. So sorry.'

'It was a long time ago,' she said with a sniff, but she couldn't keep the tears back, couldn't keep them from sliding down her face as Antonios wiped them away with his thumbs, just as he had back in New York when she'd told him about her father's death. He'd been so tender with her then, and he was so tender now.

'So you blamed yourself,' Antonios said quietly, one hand still cradling her cheek. 'For your mother's abandonment.' He was silent for a moment, one hand stroking her back. 'Were you afraid I might react the same way?'

'I…' She stilled, her mind spinning with that new and awful thought. Had it not just been shame, but fear, that had kept her from speaking honestly? Had she been afraid Antonios would reject her, even leave her if she told him the truth, the whole truth? Maybe some secret, sad part of her had. 'I don't know,' she said slowly. 'I know some deep-seated part of me hates anyone to know. I don't like you knowing now, even though it doesn't matter any more.' Thoughts and memories tumbled through her mind. 'I suppose I felt with you the same way I did with my mother. Wanting to hide my anxiety because I knew it made her angry, yet desperate at the same time for her to see it, to see *me*.'

'And I never saw you.' Lindsay couldn't tell anything from Antonios's flat tone. 'I only thought I did.'

What they'd felt for each other hadn't been real. It was no more than what she'd been telling him all along, yet it still hurt to hear him acknowledge it. To know how little they'd actually had together.

Antonios was silent for a long moment, one hand still cupping her cheek while the other stroked her hair. 'And so what happened after you moved to New York?' he finally asked.

'Things got worse. I think my father expected them to get better, but with my mother leaving…' She trailed off, then forced herself to continue. 'I started having panic attacks about school—being asked a question, being in a classroom. My father finally withdrew me when I was ten and I was homeschooled. I did all my lessons through a cyber academy, online.' It had been a relief, to leave all the stares and whispers of school, for everyone had realized she was different, that something was *wrong* with her, but it had made for a lonely existence. Her father had tried to be at home as often as he could but he hadn't possessed the resources or sensibility to enrol her in extra classes or activities so she could meet people, make friends. It had just been the two of them, rubbing along together, until he'd died.

'I graduated from high school when I was fifteen,' she continued. 'And started college early, which was hard at first. It made me realize that I had to start coping, that I couldn't hide from life forever. I started therapy and I worked hard to deal with my anxiety. It helped that I was studying mathematics. Numbers have always felt safe to me. They never change.'

'And so you managed for quite a while,' Antonios said. 'Studying and teaching.'

'Academia has always felt like a safe environment to me. I stayed at the same college for my BA and MA and PhD. I taught a few introductory classes, and I was actually okay standing in front of a classroom.'

'And then your father died,' Antonios recalled quietly.

'Yes. He suffered from early-onset dementia and I cared

for him. Life became a bit limited because of that, but I didn't mind.' How could she have minded when her father had given up so much for her? Moved and sacrificed his marriage for her?

'It must have been hard.'

'Yes. And when he died I felt—lost. Adrift. I'd been in the same place for fifteen years but it was as if I didn't know anything any more. So I went to New York to escape everything, even myself, and I met you.'

'And I,' Antonios said after a moment, 'was the ultimate escape. The perfect fairy tale.'

'Yes.'

They were both silent, the only sound the draw and sigh of their breathing. 'I'm sorry I didn't know all of this before,' Antonios said finally. 'I'm sorry you didn't feel you could tell me.'

'I don't know if it would have made a difference, Antonios.'

He turned her on his lap so he could look her in the face. 'How can you say that? You were suffering—'

'I never should have married you,' Lindsay told him, even though it hurt to say it. 'I never should have come to Greece with you. I should have realized it wasn't real. That it couldn't work.'

Antonios didn't answer, and Lindsay wondered if he agreed with her. If she wanted him to agree with her. She felt tired and sad, the relief of having told him the truth coupled with a weary resignation that it didn't, after all, change anything.

'It's late,' he finally said. 'You should get some sleep.' He slid his hands up to cradle her face and pressed a kiss to her forehead. Lindsay closed her eyes, willing yet more tears away. It had been far easier to convince herself she'd never loved Antonios when he was arrogant and dismissive. It was much harder when he was so gentle. 'Thank you for telling me now, Lindsay,' he said softly and wordlessly she nodded. She was afraid if she spoke she would cry. Again.

He stared at her for a long moment, and then he tucked a stray tendril of hair behind her ear. He smiled sadly and Lindsay tried to smile back, but her lips wobbled and, knowing she was far too close to losing it completely, she slid off his lap and hurried from the room.

Antonios stayed in the living room, drinking far too much whisky as Lindsay got ready for bed. He could hear her in the bedroom, opening and closing drawers, the sensuous slide of material as she took off the robe.

He could imagine her, her alabaster skin, so creamy and smooth, the full, high breasts he'd held in his hands and taken into his mouth. Her slender waist and slim hips, those long legs she'd once wrapped around his waist. Her hair as soft and blonde as corn silk, spread out across his bare chest.

They'd been happy together, damn it, even if just for a little while. And yet now he could no longer live in the little bubble of his own certainty. He'd been so damnably certain about how right he was. How *wronged* he'd been. He'd blamed Lindsay for everything, when he hadn't even noticed that she'd been struggling. Suffering.

Drowning.

He poured himself another whisky and tossed it back, needing the burn of alcohol against the back of his throat, in his gut. Craving the oblivion. He'd been blind before, of course. He'd been ridiculously, wilfully blind when it came to his father. He'd refused to see that anything was wrong, that Marakaios Enterprises was struggling. Just as he had with his marriage.

What the hell was wrong with him? Why couldn't he see what was right in front of his face?

Because you didn't want to see it. Because you were afraid.

Looking back, he could remember moments that should have given him pause. Moments he'd pushed aside because it had been easier. Lindsay claiming she had a headache, her eyes puffy and red. Excusing herself from a party or dinner table with sudden urgency. Yes, looking back, he could see that she'd been unhappy. He just hadn't wanted to see it at the time.

And now? What could he do now to make it better? He'd brought Lindsay back to Greece, back into the spotlight she despised. At least now he could try to make things easier for her. She might need to be here for his mother, but she didn't need to play hostess or be the centre of attention. He'd make sure of that. It was, considering all that had happened before, the least he could do for her.

It was nearing two in the morning by the time he finally made it to bed, his head aching from the endless circling of his thoughts as well as far too much whisky. He stopped in the doorway of the bedroom, his heart suspended in his chest as he watched Lindsay sleep. Her hair was spread out across the pillow, the colour of a moonbeam. She wore a white cotton nightgown with thin straps of scalloped lace, and Antonios could see the round swell of her breasts above the thin material as her chest rose and fell in the deep, even breaths of sleep.

Desire shafted through him, along with an almost unbearable sorrow. It was too late now. Too much had happened, too much hurt and misunderstanding. Their marriage really was over. Lindsay had made that clear.

Wearily, Antonios stripped down to his boxers and slid into bed. It was a wide king-sized bed but it felt too small as he lay on his back, trying not to touch Lindsay even though everything in him ached to pull her into his arms, remind her just how good it had been between them. That, he knew, would be a very stupid thing to do.

Eventually both the whisky and exhaustion overcame him, and he slept.

Lindsay awoke just before dawn, a pale greyish-pink light filtering through the bedroom curtains. She blinked, closing her eyes again as she sank back into the soft, sleepy cocoon of a feather duvet—and a hard body pressed against her own.

Her senses jarred awake even as her mind remained fogged

with sleep. She could feel a masculine, muscular leg between her own, a hard chest squashing her breasts. *Antonios.*

Her body went on delicious autopilot, her arms sliding around Antonios's neck as she arched closer to him. Felt the hard press of his arousal against her thighs.

Memories rippled through her mind like reflections in water. Laughing with Antonios. Hugging him, feeling safe and protected and cherished. Making love with him.

She felt one large hand slide from her hip to the dip of her waist to finally, thankfully cup her breast, his thumb moving over the already taut peak.

She gave a breathy sigh of pleasure and Antonios moved her onto her back, his hands seeking her urgently now, lifting her nightgown, finding her flesh. One hand slid between her legs and she moaned and lifted her hips in invitation, wanting and needing to feel him inside her, to experience that wonderful sense of completion and wholeness again.

He was above her, braced on his forearms, poised to slide so deliciously inside her, when the alarm bells that had started to clang distantly in her mind broke into furious peals.

She opened her eyes, stared straight into Antonios's face. He was staring at her with the same expression of appalled realization that she knew she must have on her own.

This shouldn't be happening.

She could feel the tip of his arousal brushing against her and it took everything she had not to arch her hips upwards in invitation.

With a groan Antonios flung himself away from her, rolled onto his back, one arm covering his eyes. Lindsay lay there, her nightgown rucked up to her waist, everything in her aching, demanding satisfaction. With a shuddering breath she pulled down her nightgown and rolled onto her side.

'I'm sorry,' she said hesitantly.

'Don't be.' Antonios lowered his arm and gazed up at the ceiling. 'We both got carried away.' He sat up, throwing off the sheets, and strode, magnificently naked, towards the en suite bathroom. 'We're due at the main house for breakfast with my family,' he said over his shoulder, his tone flat. 'But if it's easier for you, we can have breakfast here and then visit my mother privately.'

His thoughtfulness only hurt her more. 'I think I can manage breakfast.'

He turned to look at her, his eyes narrowed. 'Don't push yourself, Lindsay, on my account.'

'It's fine, Antonios. I know what I'm capable of.'

He nodded in wordless acceptance and disappeared into the bathroom. Lindsay sank back against the pillow. If Antonios had been this sensitive and understanding before, would their marriage have survived? It was a hard question to ask, and an impossible one to answer.

The morning when she'd decided she was going to leave him, her body had felt like a leaden weight, her mind nothing but buzzing emptiness. At that point, after enduring three months of near-constant scrutiny from his family while being routinely ignored by her husband, her anxiety had been nearly all-consuming.

She'd barely been able to drag herself to luncheons and dinners, parties and receptions, all planned for Antonios to introduce his new wife to the local community, to his world. All the while she'd tried to hide the stress-induced eczema on her hands and eyelids, the nausea that had her rushing to the bathroom at inopportune moments, the migraine headaches that came out of nowhere, the light-headedness and shortness of breath that had plagued her every time Antonios took her somewhere public.

The attacks had been worse than anything she'd ever experienced before; she'd been in a strange environment and, far worse, with a man she thought she'd loved but who suddenly seemed like a stranger. She'd been lonely and lost and utterly miserable.

Escaping had felt like her only option for survival. She'd

woken that morning and known she no longer possessed the strength, either physically or emotionally, to continue. She couldn't drag herself to one more lunch or dinner, couldn't try to have one more fruitless conversation with Antonios. It had all felt, quite literally, impossible.

And so she'd left. Not telling him she was leaving had been the coward's way out, Lindsay knew, but she simply hadn't had the strength to explain anything any more. She'd told him she needed to return to New York to wrap up some things with her father's house. Antonios had asked her how long she'd be gone and she'd prevaricated, telling him she'd book a return ticket when she was done. He thought she'd be gone a week.

On the plane back to New York she'd felt like a zombie, an empty shell. She'd barely heard the stewardess asking her if she wanted something to drink or eat. She'd simply stared straight ahead, her mind and body going into a kind of emotional and mental hibernation.

Then she'd stepped across the threshold of her father's house; she'd still been able to smell the scent of his pipe and suddenly she'd burst into tears. She wasn't even sure what she was weeping for: her failed marriage, her father, dead just four months, her own weakness that had wrecked so much in her life. Everything.

With a heart that felt like a dead weight inside her she'd typed out the pithy email to Antonios, telling him their marriage was a mistake and she wasn't coming back. He'd called that afternoon and she'd heard the bewilderment and anger in his voice, had felt it when he'd hung up on her. At least she'd chosen to leave, she'd told herself, and then she'd curled into a ball on her bed and slept for fourteen hours straight.

And waded through the next few weeks, trying to summon the strength to rebuild her life. And she had, or at least she'd started to. She'd started therapy again and returned to her research. She'd met up with a few friends who hadn't asked too many questions about her brief failed marriage, and she'd told herself it was enough.

It had to be enough.

Lindsay rolled onto her back and stared up at the ceiling as she heard the sound of the shower being turned on. She imagined Antonios naked under the spray, rivulets of water streaming down the taut perfection of his body.

The body she'd almost just taken into her own, the body she knew as well as her own. The body she missed so much.

Because the little life she'd built for herself back in New York hadn't been enough. Not remotely, not when she'd tasted true happiness with Antonios.

It wasn't real, she reminded herself. *It didn't last.* Letting out a long weary sigh, Lindsay rolled out of bed.

They got ready for breakfast without speaking or even looking at each other. Lindsay showered and changed into a pale green sundress and sandals, plaited her hair into a French braid.

Antonios was wearing chinos and a white linen shirt open at the throat, the light-coloured clothes making his skin and hair seem even darker. He looked magnificent and the sight of him freshly showered, the scent of his aftershave, made desire spiral dizzily inside her again.

Desire she would have to control. Neither of them could afford another encounter like the one they'd had this morning.

His gaze flicked over her as she emerged from the bedroom but he said nothing and they walked in silence to the main villa.

Just as before, everyone was assembled in the dining room as they arrived, and six pairs of eyes trained on Lindsay as she walked into the room. She felt the speculation, even the censure, and once again her chest went tight.

This time, though, Antonios didn't stride ahead, oblivious. He reached for her arm, steadied her elbow, his body half shielding her from the stares of his family. She glanced up at him in surprise and saw him gazing back at her with that steady strength that had drawn her to him when they'd first met. Antonios had felt like the rock she could cling to in the drowning sea of her own fears and anxieties. He felt that way now, and she was touched by his sensitivity. Despite everything that had happened last night, she hadn't expected it.

After a few seconds her breathing returned to normal and with a little nod she walked forward; Antonios dropped his arm and went to pull out her chair.

'I hope you are feeling better this morning, Lindsay?' Daphne asked as one of the staff poured Lindsay some of the thick Greek coffee she'd learned to drink and even like while she was there before.

'Yes, I think so. Really, I was just tired.'

Ava and Parthenope shot each other significant looks and Lindsay wondered why that remark would set Antonios's sisters off. Deciding not to care, she focused on eating her breakfast of fresh fruit and yogurt with honey, and thankfully the conversation swirled around her without her needing to contribute to it.

'Would you like to go back to the villa?' Antonios asked as they left the dining room. 'I need to work this morning.'

'I suppose.' She could check her email and do some work on her research. She glanced at Antonios, wished she knew what he was thinking about everything. What she'd shared last night. What they'd nearly done together this morning.

Clearly none of it had changed anything between them—but had she wanted it to? The question jarred her because she didn't want to ask it, much less answer it.

'You'll be all right?' Antonios asked when he'd dropped her back off at the villa.

'I have an anxiety disorder, not a life-threatening illness,' Lindsay answered a bit sharply. 'You don't have to coddle me, Antonios.'

'I'm just trying to be considerate,' he returned. 'Since I wasn't before.'

His thoughtfulness made guilt twist inside her. 'I'm sorry,' she said. 'This is hard for me.'

'I know, Lindsay. And I'm trying to make it easier.'

'I don't mean that. I mean having you know about my condition. I hate seeming weak.'

He raised his eyebrows at that. 'You think you seem weak? I think you're strong. Amazingly strong, to have managed as much as you have, and coped for so long.' He smiled with a painful wryness. 'I think you're strong for having been able to hide so much from me, but maybe I was just too blind to see it.'

'I think we were both to blame, Antonios.'

'Maybe so.'

They stared at each other for a moment, regret etched on both of their faces. Then, her heart aching, Lindsay turned to go inside.

She fetched her laptop from her carry-on bag and Antonios retrieved his phone and shrugged on a blazer before heading out once more.

'I'll see you later,' he said and Lindsay watched him go, wishing all over again that things were different between them… and knowing they never could be.

CHAPTER SIX

ANTONIOS SPENT THE morning working in his office but he had trouble focusing on anything. His mind once more was on Lindsay, and all the things she'd told him last night.

As well as what had happened this morning. Dear heaven, but it had felt so good to have her in his arms once again. It had taken every ounce of his control not to slide inside her, not to take his pleasure and give her her own.

And yet what a paltry pleasure it had turned out to be. Good or even incredible sex wasn't enough to make a marriage. And he accepted now that their marriage had made Lindsay miserable. Guilt and grief weighed heavily inside him at the thought.

After Lindsay left him, he'd been so consumed with self-righteous anger. So certain it was all her fault, that he'd done everything in his power to make her happy. He'd bought her clothes and jewels, had showered her with physical affection, had brought her into his home and his family, and he'd thought that had been enough. He knew now it hadn't been, and never could be.

He attempted to focus on work for another hour but thoughts about Lindsay were bouncing around his brain like the little ball in a pinball machine and he finally gave up and headed out into the sunshine of a fall afternoon. He walked back to the villa with no clear goal in mind other than seeing Lindsay again. What he would say to her, he had no idea. What was there left to say?

He came into the cool shelter of the villa, stopping in the doorway to watch Lindsay unobserved. She was sitting on the sofa, her slender legs propped up on the coffee table, her computer on her lap. She was frowning at the computer screen, utterly intent, a few tendrils of hair having escaped her plait to frame her face in white-blonde curls. She was, he saw with a sudden surge of affection, mouthing something silently.

'You look incredibly engrossed in what you are doing,' he said and, startled, she jerked her head up, her body tensing as she caught sight of him.

'Just some research.'

She'd told him a bit about her research before, but Antonios hadn't really understood it. Hadn't tried to, he supposed, because he'd been showing her his life, not having her show him hers. He'd been incredibly selfish, Antonios thought with a fresh bout of recrimination. Incredibly self-centred and arrogant, assuming Lindsay could just drop her life and friends without a thought. He'd felt, he realized, as if he were rescuing her, and he'd liked that, liked feeling like someone's salvation. And instead he'd caused the destruction of her happiness.

'Tell me about it,' he said now, and he came to sit on the edge of the coffee table. He had an urge to reach out and touch her, wrap a hand around the slender bones of her ankle. He resisted.

Lindsay looked up at him warily, her gaze narrowing. 'Do you really want me to?' she asked.

'I wouldn't have asked otherwise.'

'Okay, but you never…' She stopped, shrugging, and then explained, 'At the moment I'm working on maximal prime gap function.'

'Okay,' Antonios said, although he didn't actually know what that meant. Lindsay gave him a lopsided smile, as if she guessed as much, and he smiled back and shrugged.

'I might need you to explain this in plain English.'

'It's all Greek to you?' she teased softly and his smile widened. He was enjoying their light banter. It certainly made a change from the endless arguments they'd had lately.

'Something like that. You must be used to people not understanding your research.'

She gave him a rueful nod and smile. 'Most people don't.'

'So…maximal prime gap function. Give me the low-down.'

She laughed softly, and the sound was the sweetest music to Antonios's ears. He'd missed her laugh, her happiness. Knowing he was causing it now, if just a little, was a balm to his soul. To his heart. Maybe he could use this week to make up for the unhappiness he'd caused her during their marriage. If he could make her laugh again, or even smile…

'Well, you know what prime numbers are?' she said, and he had to think for a moment to dredge up the arithmetic he'd learned as a child.

'A number that is only divisible by itself and one.'

'Yes. The prime gap is the difference between two prime numbers. A maximal gap is the greatest difference.'

'So, for example, the difference between three and seven.'

'Yes, although I'm working with numbers far higher than that—numbers that have yet to be determined if they're in fact prime.'

'And have you drawn any conclusions?'

She shook her head. 'Not yet. I'm still gathering data. But when I have enough I'll start to look for patterns.'

'What kind of patterns?'

'Similar gaps between primes mainly.'

'And what will that tell you?' Antonios asked. 'About…anything?'

She let out a laugh, no more than a breath of sound, her smile turning rueful. 'I know—it seems completely useless to you.'

'Not useless,' he replied. 'But I must admit, as a businessman, I prefer to deal in practicalities.'

'Understandable.'

'So what will the patterns tell you?'

'Well…' Her fingers splayed over her keyboard, a faint frown puckering her forehead. 'Maybe nothing; maybe everything. That, really, is what draws me to number theory. The more research scientists do in physics and mathematicians in number theory, the more they realize how much we don't understand. But the research provides little glimpses into a world of knowledge—a world defined by numbers, and to me it is both mystical and beautiful.' She smiled self-consciously, but Antonios was intrigued.

'Defined by numbers?' he repeated. 'What do you mean?'

'Well, for example, cicadas.'

'Cicadas?'

'Yes, you know, like grasshoppers?' She smiled, her eyes dancing with amusement, turning to silver.

'What do cicadas have to do with prime numbers?'

'In the eastern US they only appear after a prime number of years. For example, in Tennessee cicadas have a thirteen-year life cycle. In other places they only appear every seventeen years.'

'And you think there is a reason for this?' Antonios asked, mystified.

'Science has shown us again and again that things in nature are rarely arbitrary. In the case of cicadas, having an irregular life cycle means they're avoiding their natural predator population cycles. So cicadas on a thirteen-year life cycle are less likely to be gobbled up by a frog.'

'How would they know that?'

She shrugged, smiling. 'They wouldn't, necessarily. It's most likely part of natural selection. But I certainly find it interesting. Why have cicadas adapted and other insects haven't?'

'Maybe they're smarter than we think.'

Her eyes danced some more. 'Maybe.'

'Fascinating,' he said, and meant it. 'But the research you're doing, with these huge prime numbers. How does that apply?'

'It doesn't, yet. But with the advances being made in technology and quantum physics, it could in years to come. Understanding the relationships between numbers could be the key to unlocking the universe.'

Her mouth curved in a teasing smile and Antonios chuckled. 'You think so, huh?'

'Actually, I do, in a manner of speaking. But it probably sounds weird to you.'

'Not as weird as it did.'

She laughed and closed her laptop. 'Then my job here is done.'

'Good,' Antonios said. 'Because I thought we could go for a walk.'

She raised her eyebrows, searched his face, wondering, no doubt, why he was being so friendly. He'd been angry for so long. Too long. But he'd enjoyed the last twenty minutes and he wanted to spend more time with Lindsay. Wanted to make her smile again.

'Okay,' she said, and Antonios rose from where he'd been sitting.

'You should put on sunscreen and take a hat.'

'Where are we going, exactly?'

'To the olive groves.'

As a child he'd loved the olive groves that spread across the hillside, all the way to the horizon. He loved the twisted, gnarled trunks of the olive trees, and the pungent smell of their fruit as it ripened. He loved the crumbly earth beneath his feet and the high, hot sun above. And most of all he'd loved walking with his father, feeling important as his father had pointed out the different trees and flowers.

Until everything had changed.

He knew, just as Lindsay did, how a parent could make you feel confused and ashamed. Unloved and rejected.

They walked through the complex of buildings that made up Villa Marakaios, passing the main villa as well as Leonidas's, the staff housing and the central office, before coming to the wrought iron gate with *Marakaios* worked into the iron in curling script above them, in both Greek and English. Antonios opened the gate and ushered Lindsay into the grove.

'So how did your family get into the olive oil business, anyway?' she asked as they walked between neat rows of trees, their grey-green leaves rustling in the wind, the tight cream-coloured buds of their flowers raised to the sun.

'It was my father,' Antonios said, and heard both the tension and pride enter his voice. He had such conflicting feelings when it came to his father. Respect and disdain. Anger and grief. Love and hate. 'He came from nothing,' he told Lindsay. 'His father lived in Athens and worked as a dustman. But my father had dreams and ambition, and he loved the earth. He sweated blood to buy some land, and over the years he expanded it. He decided to grow olive trees for oil because he felt it was something that would always be in demand.'

'And he was very successful.'

'Yes,' Antonios said, 'although not at first. It can be very expensive to make olive oil unless you make it in large quantities using efficient methods. My father struggled at first, but then he was able to buy more land and plant more trees.'

'And so you inherited an empire.'

Antonios's insides tightened with memory. 'Yes,' he agreed. He had sworn never to tell anyone about how the Marakaios empire had been crumbling beneath his feet when he'd been summoned home after his father's heart attack. He wouldn't tell Lindsay. He'd protect his father's memory as he always had, even though it sometimes felt as if he were selling his soul to save his father's.

He still remembered coming home after starting a job in Athens—a job his father had insisted he start because he hadn't wanted him near the family business. Hadn't wanted him to figure out just how badly things were going. Antonios hadn't realized that at the time, though. He'd just felt the rejection.

Just like he had with Lindsay. God help him, he didn't want to be blind any more. He wanted to see what was happening around him, and to help. And he would this week with Lindsay.

'What are you thinking about?' Lindsay asked and Antonios snapped his gaze back to her.

'Nothing.'

'You're frowning.'

He shrugged. 'I was just thinking about all there is to do.'

'Taking time out to go to New York was costly, I suppose.'

'But necessary.'

Lindsay didn't answer and they walked on for a bit, the sun hot on their heads and shoulders even though the air was still cool and crisp. The aromatic scent of the olive flowers wafted up from where they trod over fallen buds.

The grove stretched in every direction, a sea of land and trees that gave him a fierce, almost painful sense of satisfaction. He'd held onto it all, if only just. He might have sold his soul, but at least he'd saved this. Lindsay turned to him with a small smile.

'You look like a king surveying his domain.'

'I suppose I feel a bit like one,' he admitted. 'I am very proud of what my father built from nothing.' And what he'd kept, if only by the skin of his teeth.

Lindsay laid a hand on his wrist, her fingers cool and soft. 'I'm glad you showed me all of this, Antonios. It helps me to understand you.'

He gazed at her, conscious of her hand still on his wrist, her lovely grey eyes so wide and clear. 'And do you want to understand me?' he asked quietly.

Her eyes clouded and she withdrew her hand from his arm. Antonios felt the loss. 'I…' she began, and then shook her head. 'I suppose there isn't much point, is there?' she said, her lips twisting in a sorrowful smile. 'But I'm still glad.'

Antonios just nodded. He felt emotion burn in his chest, words rise in his throat and tangle on his tongue. Too many memories, too close to the surface. Too much hopeless longing and unsatisfied desire.

Their marriage, he reminded himself grimly, was over.

'We should get back,' he said. 'My mother is hoping to have us over to the main villa for lunch.' He glanced at her sideways. 'Just the two of us. Will that be all right?'

'Fine,' Lindsay assured him. 'I'm all right in small groups of people. And I like your mother, Antonios. I like being with her.' Her expression clouded once more as she turned to him. 'I'm so sorry about her illness.'

He nodded, his chest tightening once more. 'I am, too.'

'I'm… I'm sorry I wasn't there for you when she was diagnosed.' She bit her lip. 'I know I should have been.'

Antonios struggled for words for a moment; the emotions that swooped through him were too powerful and overwhelming for speech. He couldn't untangle one from the other: gratitude and compassion, hope and sorrow. He wished she'd been there. He wished she'd wanted to be there, had been happy there.

'You're here now,' he said. 'That's what matters.'

They started walking back the way they'd come. 'When will you tell your family that we're getting divorced?' Lindsay asked and Antonios tensed.

'When the moment is right. Are you in such a rush?'

'No, but are you really going to keep up the deception for the rest of your mother's life?'

'That won't,' he answered, 'be all that long. The doctors have only given her a few months or maybe even weeks. The cancer has spread, and she doesn't wish to undergo invasive treatment again.'

'Do you want me to tell her?' Lindsay asked quietly. 'I owe you that much, at least.'

'No.' His voice came out too loud, too hard. 'It would only hurt her. Why can't we let her die happy, believing we're happy?'

Lindsay nibbled her lip. 'I don't like lying.'

'I don't either.' And God help him, he'd been doing it for too long. But for a greater good, just like now. 'It would be a mercy for her, Lindsay,' he said quietly. 'Why trouble her in the short time she has left?'

Lindsay gazed at him, her eyes shadowed, and then slowly she nodded. 'All right. But what about your sisters and brother, Antonios? They seem suspicious already—'

'After,' Antonios said, his voice hoarse and raw. 'I'll tell them after she dies.'

Lindsay's face crumpled and she reached out for Antonios's hand, seeming to surprise both of them. She squeezed his hand, her face filled with compassion. 'I'm so sorry, Antonios. Daphne has been more of a mother to me than my own ever was.'

'We'll both miss her,' he agreed, his voice still hoarse. He didn't want to let go of her hand. Didn't want to resort to this careful politeness and wary friendship. Maybe what they'd had before hadn't been real, but it had been good. And maybe they could build something real now.

The thought was like a dagger slipping inside him, slyly finding his heart—and hurting. Because he knew he couldn't suggest such a thing to Lindsay. Not when being here with him had only caused her unhappiness. He owed her her freedom, at the very least.

Lindsay followed Antonios out of the olive grove, reluctant to leave behind the surprising camaraderie they'd shared. She'd enjoyed chatting with him, teasing and sharing, learning about one another. It was more than they'd ever done before during the three months of their marriage. The week in New York had been one of sensual rather than emotional discovery, and then during those months in Greece they'd been like strangers unless they'd been in bed. But today they'd actually felt like friends.

It made her feel both sad and happy at the same time, because while friendship with Antonios was better than the hostility she'd experienced over the last few days, it still made her ache with regret and longing.

They walked to the villa in companionable silence, and then Lindsay went into the bedroom to change. She exchanged her sundress for a pair of linen trousers and a matching sleeveless top, and touched up her make-up and hair.

Antonios was waiting for her in the living room when she emerged and his gaze fastened on her as soon as she opened the door.

'You look lovely,' he said, his voice full of warm sincerity as his gaze swept over her.

She blushed, although she wasn't sure why. He'd told her she'd looked lovely before, had showered her with compliments, but this felt different. And then Lindsay knew why. Because for the first time Antonios truly saw her…and he still thought she was beautiful.

The realization made her understand afresh why she hadn't told him about her anxiety. She really had been filled with shame and fear, terrified that he would reject her or even leave her. She'd convinced herself that she'd tried her best to tell him, but she really hadn't. She hadn't wanted to.

'Lindsay?' He came forward, one strong hand cupping her elbow. 'Are you okay?'

'Yes—'

'You look pale.'

She shook her head. 'I was just realizing how unfair I was to you, Antonios, not telling you the truth. I told myself I'd tried as hard as I could, but I know I really didn't. Because I really didn't want you to know.'

'Between a rock and a hard place,' Antonios surmised with a small sad smile. 'We were doomed, weren't we?'

'I suppose we were.' Which made her feel like bursting into tears. Wanting to hide her emotion, she turned away from him, making a pretence of straightening her top. 'We should go. Your mother will be waiting.'

They walked over to the main villa where Daphne was waiting for them. Lunch had been set out for the three of them in one of the villa's smaller dining rooms, with French windows overlooking a small walled herb garden. Lindsay had never been in the room before and its cosy proportions and atmosphere put her immediately at ease, as did Daphne.

'How are you settling back into life in Greece?' she asked as she took Lindsay's hands in her own thin ones. 'Is it very hard?'

Lindsay swallowed, hating to deceive her, yet knowing as Antonios had said it was both a mercy and kindness. 'Not too hard.'

'And I hope you're treating her right,' Daphne said with a stern look at her oldest son. 'Antonios works too hard,' she told Lindsay. 'He's just like his father that way.'

Lindsay felt the shudder of tension go through Antonios's body and wondered at it. She slid him a glance, but his face was impassive as he held out a chair for his mother.

Daphne took a seat, smiling up at Antonios. 'Evangelos was always working. I used to come into his office and sit on his desk.'

Lindsay let out a choked laugh and Antonios's eyebrows shot up. 'I didn't know that, Mama.'

'Why would I tell you?' she asked with a surprisingly pert look. She turned back to Lindsay. 'But it was the only way to make him stop working.'

'Maybe I should have tried that,' Lindsay joked, then bit her lip as she registered the past tense. Her gaze locked with Antonios and she knew he'd registered it, too.

'It would make for an entertaining change from what's usually on my desk,' he said smoothly. 'Let me pour you some water, Mama.'

This was going to be so hard, Lindsay thought, busying herself with spreading her napkin in her lap. Pretending at a party was one thing, but to someone's face, someone she cared about…

'Let me call for the first course,' Daphne said. 'I'm afraid I don't last for more than a few hours before I need a nap these days.' She smiled apologetically and Lindsay touched her hand.

'I'm sorry…' Lindsay began. 'If there's anything I can do…'

'There is no need for you to be sorry,' Daphne said. 'I've lived a good life, and I'd rather no one made concessions to my condition now. I want to live life as fully as I can for as long as I can.'

One of the staff came in to set the first course before them, a fruit salad with grapes and succulent slices of melon.

'Tell me, Lindsay,' Daphne asked as soon as the staff member had quietly left again, 'do you miss America very much? Did you leave many friends behind?'

Lindsay couldn't help but glance at Antonios, whose face was carefully expressionless. 'Not so many,' she said.

'And your research? Will you be able to finish it here? You are not far from achieving your doctorate, are you?'

'I have a few more months of work at least,' Lindsay answered. 'Most of the research can be conducted from anywhere, as long as I have my laptop.'

'I'm sure you will have to make some trips back to America,' Daphne said, and Lindsay nodded in relief.

'Yes, I will.'

'Not too many, though,' Daphne continued. 'A man and a wife belong together.' She speared a slice of melon, her gaze suddenly seeming almost shrewd. 'Six months apart is a very long time.'

Lindsay threw a panicked gaze at Antonios, not sure how she should answer.

'Lindsay had some business to deal with, back in America,' he said, his voice as smooth and controlled as ever. 'With her house and such things. Her place is here now, Mama, with me.'

'And why couldn't your place be with her?' Daphne countered, a playful smile curving her mouth. 'In America?'

Antonios's composure slipped for a second as he stared at his mother, slack jawed. 'Because I can't run Marakaios Enterprises from America,' he said finally.

Daphne nodded, her playful smile turning down at the corners. 'No,' she agreed softly, 'you can't.'

Antonios pushed his plate away, wishing this meal could be more pleasant for all of them. Deceiving his mother so directly was far more difficult than he'd envisioned, and he could tell Lindsay was finding it hard, too.

As for his mother's suggestion he leave Villa Marakaios… the idea was absurd. He'd poured his soul into the family business, had sacrificed all semblance of a normal life to keep things afloat. He couldn't walk away from it, even if he wanted to.

Thankfully, Daphne moved the conversation to more innocuous matters as they ate their way through three courses, and Antonios was glad to leave contentious matters aside as they chatted simply. He liked watching Lindsay, the way her eyes sparkled when she was amused, the way she tilted her head to one side when she was considering a point. The clear peal of her sudden laugh made him long to make her laugh again. Make her happy again, even if just for this week.

By the time dessert had been cleared Antonios could see that his mother was fading and so he made their excuses, kissing her on both cheeks, as Lindsay did after him, before they left the main villa to head back to their own.

The afternoon air was still and drowsy, the grounds silent and empty in this hot part of the day.

'Are there any more engagements today?' Lindsay asked and Antonios shook his head.

'No, but there will be preparations for the party tomorrow, and then the actual celebration the day after.' He glanced at her, wanting to be considerate but knowing she would resist being coddled. 'Will that be all right for you?'

'I think so.'

'I want to make things easier for you,' he said, his manner stilted yet sincere, the awkwardness of it making him cringe inwardly. 'But I know you don't want me to treat you differently, either.'

'You're being very kind, Antonios. I appreciate all you're doing for me.' For a moment she looked as if she wanted to say something more and Antonios felt his heart lurch with fear and hope. Then she shook her head, her eyes shadowed as she touched his hand. 'Thank you,' she said, and walked on to the villa.

CHAPTER SEVEN

LINDSAY TILTED HER face to the sun and closed her eyes, enjoying the warmth—as well as the respite from the preparations for Daphne's party. Even though Antonios had insisted she didn't need to, she had joined his sisters in the villa's main salon to help with the decorations.

Antonios was so clearly making an effort to help her, she felt she could do no less and help him. And if they'd had this kind of understanding before, would it have made all the difference? Could their marriage have survived, or even flourished?

Restlessly, she shifted in her seat, plucked a blossom of bougainvillea that twined its way up the stone wall. That question had been tormenting her in one form or another since she'd told Antonios about her anxiety. Maybe they'd needed to come to the brink of disaster to truly start listening and understanding each other. Maybe they'd needed the heartache and separation to come to a place where they could build something strong and true.

And maybe you're just spinning another fairy tale. Another fantasy.

She pressed the blossom to her cheek and closed her eyes once more. Even if she and Antonios understood each other now, even if they became friends, a marriage still couldn't work between them. She couldn't be the kind of wife Antonios needed, the social hostess and organizer. No matter how much she managed to control her anxiety, the endless social engagements his career as CEO demanded would still defeat her. And what of her own research? She'd told Antonios she could do her research anywhere, which was true. But her PhD would be finished in a few months and she'd already started looking for professorships. Staying here in Greece meant kissing her career goodbye.

Something she hadn't cared about or even considered when he'd asked her to marry him, to come with him to Greece. She'd been so desperate then—desperate to be happy, to leave the sadness of her life behind. But, nine months later, she could acknowledge how incompatible their life goals really were.

Antonios had stated plainly he would never leave Greece. Even if he wanted to restart their marriage, it would mean staying here, doing her best to be the wife he needed, playing hostess and socialite. Roles she couldn't bear.

'May I join you?'

Lindsay opened her eyes to see Daphne standing in front of her, offering her a kindly smile.

'Of course.' She shifted on the bench to make room for her mother-in-law.

Daphne sat down with a sigh of relief. 'Everything aches,' she said quietly, her gaze on the mountains cutting a jagged line out of the horizon. 'I think, when it is my time, I will be ready for the aching to stop.'

'I'm sorry,' Lindsay said quietly. She felt inadequate for the moment, especially in the light of Daphne's grace in the face of so much suffering and sorrow.

'Knowing you are going to die shortly is, in some ways, a gift,' Daphne said after a moment, her gaze still on the mountains. 'It gives you a chance to set your affairs in order and say things you might have resisted before.' She turned to Lindsay, a surprising humour lighting her eyes. 'Speak the truth of your heart, because it doesn't really matter if you ruffle a few feathers.'

'I suppose,' Lindsay agreed after a second's pause. She had a feeling Daphne was going to speak a few truths now and she had no idea what she'd say in return.

'I know,' Daphne began, choosing her words with care, 'that things went wrong between you and Antonios.'

Shock blazed through her, followed by a deep unease. If she admitted the truth, would Antonios be angry? Was she to lie even now?

'I also know,' Daphne said, patting her hand, 'that Antonios doesn't want me to know. He tries to protect me from so much.'

Lindsay swallowed hard, searched for words. 'He loves you very much.'

'And I love him. I want him to be happy.' Daphne was silent for a moment. 'I think you can make him happy, Lindsay.'

Lindsay shook her head, the movement instinctive and utterly certain. 'I can't. I know I can't.' Too late she realized how much she'd admitted, but her mother-in-law seemed unsurprised.

'Why don't you think you can?'

'Because I'm not what he needs. I can't be the kind of wife he needs.'

'I think,' Daphne answered, 'Antonios doesn't know what he needs.'

Curious now, Lindsay asked, 'What do you think he needs?'

'A wife who loves him. Who believes in him. You love him, don't you?'

'I…' Lindsay shook her head. 'I don't know. I thought I did, and then I thought I didn't. And now…now it doesn't matter.'

'Why not?'

Lindsay bit her lip. She'd said far too much. She'd been startled into more honesty than she'd ever meant to share. 'I only mean because we're already married,' she said feebly and Daphne smiled, as if she knew what a pathetic pretence this was.

'You weren't happy here,' she said after a moment. 'Were you?'

'No,' Lindsay admitted after a second's pause. 'But that was as much my fault's as—'

'A husband's duty is to make his wife happy, no?'

'I suppose a husband and wife should try to make each other happy—'

'Let me say again,' Daphne corrected. 'If a wife is unhappy, a husband needs to address her unhappiness.'

Lindsay swallowed hard. 'Antonios didn't know I was unhappy.'

'Exactly. I could see it and he could not. Because he is just like his father, Lindsay. He only sees what he wants to see.' Daphne let out a long weary sigh. 'Evangelos was a good man and I loved him dearly. But he worked himself to the bone for his business and he closed his eyes to any problems because he could not bear to think of them. Just as Antonios closed his eyes to your suffering because he could not bear it.'

Lindsay blinked, taking this in. It was an entirely new thought, and one she had to sift over for a few moments before replying. 'His eyes aren't closed now,' she said, half-amazed at how honest she was being. 'We've talked about it since I've returned. He knows everything. I'm not sure it makes much difference.'

'Because you still are not happy here,' Daphne said quietly. She sounded sad.

'Because, I told you,' Lindsay said sadly, 'I can't be the wife he needs.'

'And I told you that what he needs is to love and to be loved. That is all anyone needs.'

'You make it sound so simple.'

'No, not simple. Endlessly complicated and difficult.' Daphne smiled, resting one bony hand on top of Lindsay's. 'But worth it, if you both resolve to try. To learn.'

Lindsay swallowed and nodded. She wanted to believe

Daphne, wanted to believe love could be that easy. But the question remained: did she want to try again? And, more importantly, did Antonios?

Antonios stared at his brother and tried to mask his shock. 'So you kept this from me?'

'I wanted to make sure it was a definite go,' Leonidas answered, his voice level. The brothers stared at each other, tension simmering in the air.

Antonios glanced back down at the file folder of information Leonidas had presented to him ten minutes ago, much to his stunned amazement. The neat rows of figures and the printed transcript of correspondence showed his brother had been planning this investment in providing luxury bath products to a chain of hotels for a long time. Without telling him a damned thing.

'And it never occurred to you,' he asked, an edge entering his voice, 'to tell me you were thinking about doing this?'

'No, it didn't,' Leonidas answered flatly. Antonios jerked back.

'Do I need to remind you that I'm the CEO of this company?'

'No,' Leonidas interjected, 'you certainly don't.'

Antonios stared at his brother, felt a ripple of shock at the anger he saw there. 'What is that supposed to mean?'

'Exactly what I said. You remind me every day that you're the boss, Antonios. That's why I didn't approach you about this plan. I knew you'd want to take it over.'

Antonios's gaze narrowed. 'As CEO, it's necessary that I—'

'Have your fingerprints on everything? And why is that, Antonios? I am your second-in-command, the Head of European Operations, a Marakaios.' His mouth twisted bitterly. 'He was my father, too.'

Antonios slapped his hand on the desk, the sound loud in the taut stillness of the office. 'Damn it, I do not need this now.'

'Fine. We won't discuss it. Just sign off on the deal and I'll go to our investors.'

'No.' The word came out in a sudden, sharp cry. Leonidas raised his eyebrows. Antonios's jaw tightened. He had, he knew, kept his brother on a short rein because he'd been hiding the extent of the debt their father had amassed. He'd cleared it now, but if Leonidas went to their investors, if he looked at their bank statements or credit history, he would know in an instant how bad things had been. How their father had failed.

And Antonios had promised never to let anyone know.

He'd kept Leonidas busy wining and dining new clients, visiting factories and restaurants, drumming up new business. He'd always handled the money side, but now Leonidas had gone behind his back, set up an entire new deal that he, quite naturally, wanted to close.

And Antonios couldn't let him.

'I'll sign off on the deal,' he said tersely, 'and I'll contact the investors.'

Leonidas's mouth twisted. 'Taking the glory, as usual.'

As if he concerned himself with glory. As if there was anything *glorious* about the debt and despair his father had fallen into, the life Antonios had lived for far too long. 'You can have your name on it,' he said shortly. 'I'll give you credit. But I'll handle the finances and paperwork.'

Leonidas stared at him for a long moment, his face taut with fury. 'Don't you trust me?'

'This isn't about trust, Leonidas.' At least not the kind his brother thought.

'Then why won't you give me more responsibility, Antonios? Damn it, I deserve it. I've worked hard these last ten years—'

'What responsibility do you want?' Antonios snapped, irritation masking his guilt. 'To sign some tedious paperwork, go over a few boring columns?'

'If it's so boring, why won't you let me do it?' Leonidas countered.

Antonios stared at him, hating that they were having this confrontation and yet knowing it had been a long time coming. Fearing he couldn't hide forever. And wouldn't it feel good to come clean, to admit what he'd been covering up, sharing the burden? Lindsay had been honest about her own fears and secrets. Why couldn't he be honest about his?

The desire to unburden himself was so strong he nearly trembled with the force of it. Longed to give Leonidas all the responsibility he craved and more, to walk away from it all, finally free of the shackles of Marakaios Enterprises that had bound him for so long…

Theos, what was he thinking? Appalled, Antonios took a step back, as if he could distance himself from his own thoughts. He could not betray his father that way. It would be a betrayal of himself, of his sense of duty and honour that was at the core of who he was.

'Be happy with what I've offered,' he told Leonidas flatly. 'Because it's all I ever will.'

With a muffled curse Leonidas strode from the room. Antonios pushed back from his desk, striding to the window that overlooked the olive groves. His mind seethed with too many thoughts.

He had never seen his brother so angry before, seeming so resentful of the control Antonios exerted. He'd sensed it, but Leonidas had never spoken so plainly before. Or maybe he hadn't wanted to acknowledge how unhappy his brother was, just as he hadn't wanted to acknowledge how unhappy Lindsay had been. Blind, wilfully blind, as always.

Antonios pressed a fist to his forehead, longing for so much to be different. For his father not to have sworn him to secrecy. For him to have realized the unhappiness around him and sought to change it.

And if only he could change things now. Change things with Leonidas. Change things with Lindsay.

Wearily, he dropped his fist and turned back to his desk. Sometimes change was impossible.

After talking with Daphne, Lindsay went back into the villa, determined to make one more attempt to help with the party preparations. Parthenope and Xanthe were in the salon, debating where to put a display of photographs; Lindsay watched them for a moment before coming over to examine the photos of the Marakaios family throughout the years.

She could pick out Antonios easily—a dark-haired, solemn little boy. For a second she imagined what their child might have looked like and felt an unsettling twist of longing for something she hadn't even truly considered before.

Antonios had wanted to start trying for children right away, but Lindsay had put him off. Attempting to cope with her new life in Greece had been hard enough without adding pregnancy to the mix.

And it was still hard. Too hard to continue. Too hard to try again.

She turned to watch Xanthe and Parthenope continue to wrangle over the display board, their voices raised, their hands moving wildly.

Xanthe caught her looking and put her hands on her hips. 'Do you have a suggestion, Lindsay?' she asked, a faint note of challenge in her voice. Parthenope turned to look at her, too, and even though it was just the two of them Lindsay felt a sweat break out between her shoulder blades.

Damn it, she did not want to go into panic mode right now.

'I'd put it in the corner,' she said, and Xanthe's eyebrows shot higher.

'People won't see it there.'

'It will be in the way anywhere else,' Lindsay countered quietly, 'and a person's gaze is generally drawn to the vertex of an angle, especially a right angle.' She saw the look of incomprehension on the two women's faces and felt herself flush. 'The walls of the room form an angle,' she explained in a half mumble. 'A right angle, with the corner as its vertex.'

They just stared at her, completely nonplussed, and Lindsay turned away. 'Never mind,' she muttered, and everything in her jolted with surprise when she heard Antonios's voice.

'A mathematical proof for putting photographs in the corner. Brilliant.' He came into the room, his smiling gaze trained on Lindsay, rooting her to the spot. 'I knew I needed a reason to have the photo of me as an eight-year-old with knobbly knees put in a dark corner.'

'You could backlight the display board,' Lindsay offered, pleasure rippling through her as Antonios joined her, looping one arm around her shoulders. 'Your knobbly knees could still be on view.'

'You did have knobbly knees, Antonios,' Parthenope remarked as she peered at one of the photos. 'Are they still so knobbly? You always wear business suits now.'

'I'll never tell,' Antonios answered, and slid Lindsay a teasing glance. 'And I trust my wife will keep my secret.'

'My lips are sealed,' Lindsay promised, but inwardly she reeled. Why was Antonios acting so...*lover-like*?

Then it hit her. He was pretending, for his sisters' sake. *Duh.* How could she have forgotten it for even a moment? How could she have wanted something real?

She slipped out from under Antonios's arm. 'I don't think my mathematical proofs are really needed here,' she said with an apologetic smile for Parthenope and Xanthe. 'I'll just head back to our villa.'

'I'll join you,' Antonios answered smoothly. 'I'd like to rest before dinner.'

Lindsay saw Xanthe and Parthenope exchange knowing looks and inwardly cringed. Outside, she started walking quickly towards the villa and Antonios easily matched her pace.

'It's too hard, Antonios,' she burst out. 'Pretending to everyone. It feels wrong.'

'I know.'

This stopped her short. 'Then shouldn't we come clean? Wouldn't it be easier?'

'For whom? Us? Think of my mother, Lindsay.'

Lindsay bit her lip. 'I think your mother knows. Or at least guesses.'

Antonios turned to her sharply. 'Why do you say that?'

'Because she spoke to me this morning. Privately. And some of the things she said made me think she knows. She knew I was unhappy, anyway.'

Antonios's mouth thinned. 'Which was more than I knew.'

Lindsay stopped to lay a hand on his arm. 'What happened before, we should both put behind us, Antonios. I know we were both to blame. We can accept our guilt and move on.'

Something flared in his eyes. 'Move on?'

'I mean, you know...move on with our lives,' Lindsay stumbled through the explanation. A blush heated her cheeks as she thought what Antonios might have assumed she meant. To move on together.

Antonios didn't answer, just stared at her for a long moment, his gaze seeming to both test and assess her. 'Have dinner with me tonight,' he said suddenly.

Lindsay stared at him in surprise. 'I thought we were having dinner with everyone, at the main villa—'

'No. Have dinner with just me. Alone.' She searched his face, saw how intent and determined he looked. As determined as he had when he'd asked her out in New York, his playful banter not quite disguising his utter intent to have her go out with him, to have her fall in love with him. And she had. Oh, she had. She'd fallen for him so hard and fast her head had still been spinning a week later, when they'd landed in Greece.

And what did he want now? What did she even want him to want?

'Antonios...'

'Please,' he said softly, and she was lost. As lost as she'd been when he'd given her that achingly whimsical smile of his and said, *What would it take for you to have coffee with me?*

And she'd grinned and said, *A simple please would do.*

And so he'd said it. Tears stung her eyes and she blinked them back, everything in her aching for what they'd had and lost.

And what they could have again?

Hope was such a dangerous thing.

'All right,' she whispered and Antonios's answering smile reached right into her soul.

Antonios paced the living room as he waited for Lindsay to emerge from the bedroom for their dinner. Nerves coiled in his belly and anticipation sang in his blood. He'd planned everything, from the food they'd eat to where they'd eat it, the music that would be playing and the flowers on the table. He wanted this evening to be perfect, and focusing on all the details had kept him from thinking about all the things that could go wrong.

Like Lindsay telling him no.

But that wouldn't happen. He wouldn't allow it to happen. He'd pulled himself back from the brink once before, by sheer force of will and a hell of a lot of hard work. He could do it again. He was, he knew, willing to work hard for his marriage. And it would begin tonight.

'I'm ready.'

He turned to see Lindsay standing in the doorway, looking both uncertain and beautiful. She was dressed in a silvery, spangled sheath dress, her hair loose and tousled about her shoulders.

'You look like a moonbeam,' Antonios said and came forward to take her hands in his. 'Or a Snow Queen, perhaps.'

She gave him a faint smile, and he knew she remembered him calling her that when they'd met in New York. His Snow Queen. For she would, God willing, be his still.

'Where are we eating?' she asked as she glanced around the empty, darkened villa.

'Somewhere private. I made arrangements earlier. It's only a short walk away. Do you have a wrap?'

She held up a scrap of spangled silk and Antonios took her arm in his.

Outside, the night was dark, the air crisp, the sky scattered with stars like a thousand diamond pinpoints in a cloth of black velvet. Lindsay took a deep breath.

'I love the smell of the air here,' she said. 'So fresh and clean. It smells like pine.'

'From the trees on the mountains,' Antonios told her. 'The villagers used to harvest the pine resin.'

'The resin? For what?'

'Well, it's edible,' Antonios told her, 'but I wouldn't advise eating all that much of it. Mainly it was used to make pitch and other adhesives.'

She slid him a smiling glance. 'And you didn't think about going into the resin business?'

'I'm not sure pine resin has all that much value these days, with all the chemical adhesives available now.'

'Did you always want to take up the family business?' Lindsay asked after a moment, and Antonios tensed.

'It was never a question of want.'

'You mean your father expected you to?'

'Of course. He built an empire. He wanted to hand it down to his sons.' And he hated talking about this, about the lies that he knew he'd get tangled up in.

'So you've always worked for Marakaios Enterprises?'

'I worked for an investment management company in Athens briefly, when I was younger. My father wanted me to have some other experience.' That, at least, had been what Evangelos had told him. The truth had been he'd wanted him out of the way.

'And did you enjoy that? The investment management?'

'Yes, I did,' Antonios said, and heard the note of surprise in his voice. He'd never really thought about the work he'd done in Athens, only the hurt he'd felt about being sent away. But the truth was he'd enjoyed it very much. Enjoyed the analysis coupled with risk-taking, and the freedom of not having another man's burden on his shoulders.

'What about you?' he asked. 'Your father was a mathematician. You taught at the same university he did. Did you ever think about doing something else?'

'No. Never,' she answered. 'Mathematics has always been my passion, and I've never been very good at starting somewhere new.' She swallowed and looked away and it occurred to him afresh how difficult it must have been for her to come to Greece, an entirely new place, with him.

And he hadn't made it one iota easier for her. But he would this time. He'd make sure of it.

'Here we are,' he said and, taking her elbow, he guided her into the extensive walled gardens of the estate. They walked in silence along several twisting paths, the gravel crunching under their feet, until they came to a private little garden surrounded by stone walls climbing with bougainvillea, a fountain in its centre, the water gleaming under the moonlight.

Lindsay stopped as she took in the preparations Antonios had made: the table set for two with fine china and linen, candlelight flickering over the silver chafing dishes. A bottle of champagne was waiting on ice in a silver bucket and a recording of a double concerto for violin and cello was playing softly in the background.

'Brahms' Concerto in A Minor,' Lindsay said softly. Remembrance suffused her face; they'd seen the New York Philharmonic play this at Carnegie Hall in New York, after Lindsay had told him it was one of her favourite pieces of music. 'The musical A-E-F is a permutation of F-A-E,' she'd explained to him, amusing him with her mathematical way of looking at everything. 'It stands for his personal motto: *Frei aber einsam*.' Her mouth had twisted as she'd translated, 'Free but lonely.'

Now he understood how those words must have resonated with her. And with him, too, he thought now—working so hard to save Marakaios Enterprises, hiding the truth from everyone. Until he'd met Lindsay and felt his soul start to soar.

And it would soar again. Both of theirs would. He could make it happen.

'This is very thoughtful, Antonios,' Lindsay said quietly. 'And very romantic.'

'That was my intention,' he answered as he pulled out her chair. She sat down with a whisper of silk and he laid the napkin on her lap before sitting down opposite her.

Lindsay's gaze was shadowed as she looked at him. 'This is lovely, Antonios,' she said. 'So lovely, but…'

'But why am I doing it?' he filled in before she could say anything more.

She nibbled her lip, her eyes wide. 'Yes.'

'Because I want to,' he answered her simply. He took a deep breath, meeting her gaze, knowing his heart was in his eyes. 'Because I still love you, Lindsay, and I want you to stay in Greece.' He smiled, or tried to, for her expression hadn't changed. 'I want us to stay married.'

CHAPTER EIGHT

LINDSAY STARED AT ANTONIOS, saw sincerity blazing in his eyes as his words echoed through her. *I want you to stay in Greece... I want us to stay married.*

I want. I want.

And nothing about what she wanted. What she needed. What she'd felt, all those weeks in Greece. She took a deep breath, felt sorrow sweep through her; she was too tired and sad to be angry. She felt only disappointment at the realization that, as much as he was trying, Antonios still hadn't changed. Still couldn't see.

And yet she wanted him to. Wanted this to work, even though she knew it couldn't. *She* couldn't.

'You're speechless?' Antonios said with a little laugh. 'Say something, Lindsay.'

'I don't know what to say.'

'Say you want that, too, then,' Antonios answered. He was trying to speak lightly, but she could hear an edge entering his voice, signifying what? Irritation? Impatience? She wasn't falling all over herself to say yes.

'Oh, Antonios,' she said finally. She shook her head, and his mouth tightened. 'It's not that simple.'

'I think it seems quite simple. I love you. Do you love me?' He tilted his chin a bit, as if bracing himself for a hit.

Lindsay stared at him miserably. 'I don't know,' she said finally, but she knew it was a lie. She wouldn't feel this terrible, this torn, if she didn't love him. 'I do love you, Antonios,' she said, the words drawn from her reluctantly because she knew they would only make him insist all the more. 'But it's not enough.'

'Of course it's enough.' Triumph blazed through his voice and Lindsay closed her eyes briefly.

Daphne's words had been rattling around in her head all afternoon. *To love and to be loved...is all anyone needs.*

If only that were true. But she was all too afraid it wasn't, at least not for them. Not for her.

'I know what you're thinking,' Antonios said and Lindsay's eyes flew open.

'Do you?' she asked.

'You're wondering how it will work, with your condition.'

She stilled, wondering just how he intended to fix this. Control it, because that was what Antonios did with everything.

'A bit,' she allowed.

'I've thought about that,' Antonios continued, leaning forward, the untouched meal before them momentarily forgotten. 'We can make concessions, Lindsay.'

'Concessions,' she repeated, and knew she hated that word.

'Adjustments,' he amended. 'We'll curtail your appearances at public events. We can live separately from everyone else, in our own villa. We can even limit family engagements, although I hope in time you might come to accept—'

'Stop, Antonios—' she cut him off, unable to listen any more '—just stop.'

He sat back, confusion and irritation chasing across his features. 'I thought you'd be pleased.'

'That you're willing to make so many *concessions*?' she finished and his mouth tightened.

'It's just a word.'

'No, it's not.' She shook her head, slumping back in her seat.

'I don't want you to make concessions, Antonios. I don't want you to have to put up with me.'

'I'm not putting up with you—' he cut her off, his voice sharp '—I told you I loved you. I want this, Lindsay. I'm trying to be considerate.'

'I know you are,' Lindsay said. 'But it's not enough, Antonios. I'd only make you unhappy because I'm not what you want, not really.'

'Maybe you should let me decide what I want.'

'And you really want a wife who hides in the shadows, who can't be by your side?'

'In time—' he began and she shook her head almost frantically.

'No. No. I don't want you to try to *fix* me, Antonios.'

'You said yourself you've worked hard to control your anxiety. I just want to help you.'

Lindsay closed her eyes. 'So I can fulfil a role I never even wanted or asked for.' He was silent at that and she opened her eyes. 'In any case, you'd only become frustrated and disappointed. Because I'd never be good enough.'

'Let me decide that.'

'No, I won't, actually. I won't agree to a half life here that dwindles away to nothing when you decide you're done with me—'

'I wouldn't,' he shot back, his voice rising to a roar. 'I would never abandon a marriage.'

'Like I did?' The hurt spilling from her didn't make sense. She was so angry and so sad, and it felt as if nothing could make things better.

'Like your mother did,' Antonios answered. 'Because life wasn't what she expected. Was that why you left, Lindsay? Because life wasn't what *you* expected?'

She felt the blood drain from her face, empty from her head. 'I can't believe you said that.'

'Damn it, I'm trying to fight for our marriage. To find a compromise. What is so wrong about that?'

'Because the compromise rests on the assumption that I have to stay here in Greece and try to be your perfect little wife,' Lindsay snapped. 'And you never even asked if I wanted that.'

'I'm a traditional man,' Antonios answered tightly. 'Naturally I would expect my wife to have her place with me. And you told me you wanted to go to Greece, that there was nothing left for you in New York.'

'And I've told you since then,' Lindsay reminded him, 'that I was feeling particularly lonely and vulnerable when you asked me. But the truth is, Antonios, I did have a life in New York. Maybe it was a small one, with just a few friends, a little job. But I liked it. I don't want to give that all up just to be a shadow of the woman you want.'

They stared at each other, the anger and tension between them palpable in the cool night air. Antonios threw down his napkin on the table.

'*Theos*, I don't know what I can do,' he muttered, raking a hand through his hair.

Lindsay stared down at her plate as she blinked back tears. Maybe she was being unreasonable. Unfair. Antonios had created this lovely romantic dinner, was trying to find ways to make her—*their*—life in Greece possible. And she just kept insisting it wouldn't—couldn't—work.

Maybe she needed to give a little. Find a way to make their marriage, their life together possible. Antonios was willing to be flexible; surely she could be, too. She could look into professorships at universities in Greece, or even do some private tutoring. Something. If she loved him she would try, wouldn't she?

Try to be someone you really aren't? Was that what love was?

'I never considered that coming to Greece would be difficult for you,' Antonios finally said, the words drawn from him slowly. 'I was so eager to bring you here, to have you share in my life. Because I was lonely, too, Lindsay. I needed you, even if you didn't think I did.'

Lindsay's throat had thickened so it hurt to get the words out. 'Antonios…'

'And I want you to want to share it,' he continued. 'But you don't.'

Lindsay felt a tear slide down her cheek. 'It's not that simple.'

'Isn't it?' He gazed at her bleakly. 'Isn't it, Lindsay? You don't even want to try.'

Because I'm afraid of failing. Because I'm afraid you'll reject me, hurt me, leave me.

The realization was painful in its clarity. This wasn't even about expectations, or living here, or whether she could teach in Greece. It was about fear—a fear she'd held on to since she was nine years old and her mother had walked out on her because she hadn't been enough.

She was so afraid of that happening again. More afraid than she'd ever admitted to herself.

She remembered when Antonios had asked her to marry him, to go with him to Greece.

They'd been lying on the huge king-sized bed in his suite at the Plaza, their legs tangled together, their hearts still beating fast from the lovemaking they'd just shared.

Antonios had twined his fingers with hers, ran his other hand up her bare thigh, resting it on the curve of her hip. 'I never thought I'd fall in love like this,' he'd told her, his voice husky with emotion. 'I never thought I'd be so lucky.'

Lindsay had blinked back tears as she'd answered, 'I never thought I would, either.'

'We're the luckiest people in the world,' he'd said with a smile before kissing her softly. And she'd agreed with him. She'd felt as if she'd won the lottery when she'd met Antonios. She'd felt like the most loved, adored and cherished woman in the world. After her lonely life, it had been the most incredible feeling.

And it had felt even more incredible when he'd risen onto

his knees and taken her hands in his. 'I love you, Lindsay, more than anything. Will you be my wife?'

She'd seen the love shining in his eyes, felt it in herself. She hadn't had to think for so much as a millisecond before answering. 'Yes, Antonios. I'll marry you.'

They'd got married the next day, at a register office by special licence. It had been crazy and impulsive, and maybe that was because they'd both known that if they'd told people, Lindsay's colleagues or Antonios's family, someone would have talked them out of it. Advised them to wait.

And if they had waited?

Maybe they wouldn't be married after all.

But they were married, and they did love each other. And maybe that really could be enough.

'I never felt like I was good enough for my mother,' she told him slowly, haltingly. 'I felt like I always disappointed her, and that made me more anxious than anything else. She used to give me the silent treatment after I'd let her down. Once she didn't talk to me for a week.'

Antonios's face twisted with both sympathy and grief. 'And that was terrible, Lindsay. A terrible, terrible thing to endure.'

'And it affected me more than I'd ever let myself realize,' Lindsay continued. 'But I know now I can never let myself feel that way again. I can never let someone make me feel that way again.'

Antonios's expression darkened. 'And I would never do that to you.'

'But don't you see, Antonios, how it is?' Desperation edged her voice and her hands curled into fists at her sides. 'I don't fit in here. I can't be the kind of wife you need—'

'Maybe you should let me decide that.'

'I don't want you to have to make *concessions*—'

'It was just a word, Lindsay, just a stupid word!' He rose from his chair, took a step towards her. 'I love you. I fell in love with you in New York, on a snowy afternoon. Maybe it was fast and crazy but it was real, no matter what you said or tried to convince yourself of. What I felt for you, what I feel for you now, is *real.*' His voice throbbed with sincerity, the low growl of it reverberating through Lindsay's chest. 'And my love—our love—will be enough. I'll make sure of it. I won't let you down, I swear. I'll listen. I'll *see.*'

He looked so earnest and determined, and she wanted to believe him so badly. Was fear going to keep her from finding her happiness with this man? Would she let it?

'Lindsay.' He rose from his chair, came and dropped to his knees in front of her as he took her hands in his. 'Trust me. Please.'

Trust him. Trust him with her happiness as well as with her fear. With her heart and with her soul.

'You're asking a lot, Antonios,' she whispered.

'And I'll give a lot. I promise.' His hands tightened on hers.

She stared down at him, this proud, passionate man who was on his knees, begging for her. For her to love him. Her throat was so tight she could barely get the single word that she knew she meant, even if she was still afraid.

'Yes.'

He looked up at her, a fierce light of hope dawning in his eyes. 'Yes…?'

'Yes, Antonios, I'll try.'

With his eyes still blazing he pulled her face towards his, catching her up in his arms and then kissing her as if he would never stop.

And she never wanted him to.

CHAPTER NINE

AS ANTONIOS'S MOUTH crashed down on Lindsay's, he realized how long it had been since he'd kissed his wife. They hadn't kissed yesterday morning when they'd almost made love. They hadn't kissed, he realized as his tongue plundered the silky depths of her mouth, since she'd said goodbye to him in Greece.

And now she'd said yes. Yes to their marriage, to their love. Yes to him. Triumph and need surged through him and he deepened the kiss, turned it into a demand. He wanted her to give him everything now, not just a hesitant yes from her mouth but a passionate cry from her body. Yes. *Yes.*

In one fluid movement he pulled the silvery dress up and over her head. She gasped softly, her skin pale and pearl-like in the wash of moonlight.

'Antonios…' she whispered, and his name ended on a soft moan as he kissed her again, his hands sliding over her body, remembering the wonderfully familiar feel of her. From the moment he'd first touched her, he'd felt how they fitted, two halves of a whole beautifully joined. Now, as he drew her slender curves towards his, he felt it again, that inalienable rightness of the two of them together. And Lindsay must have felt it, too, for she returned his kiss, her body yielding to his in every way possible.

She shuddered under his touch, his fingers finding her secret places as her head fell forward in surrender, her hair gleaming in the moonlight.

'You love me,' Antonios said fiercely and she let out a trembling laugh.

'I already told you I did.'

'Say it again,' Antonios demanded, needing to hear it. To believe it.

'I love you,' she told him, her voice choking. 'I love you, Antonios.'

And, with triumph roaring through him, Antonios kissed her again.

If he was trying to prove to her how much she loved him, Lindsay thought hazily, he was wasting his time. She knew she loved him. And he set her body on fire. There had never been any question of that.

Already sparks were spreading out from her centre as Antonios kissed his way down her body, his hands cupping her breasts, thumbs teasing the already taut peaks. Need coiled tightly inside her, everything in her straining for the satisfaction only he could give her.

She gasped his name as she pulled at his shirt, craving the feel of his bare skin against hers. Fingers fumbling, she unbuttoned his pants, tugging them down from his hips.

Antonios pulled her onto his lap and she straddled him, his arousal pressing against the soft juncture of her thighs.

The desperate need to have him inside her overwhelmed her, drove out any rational thought. She sobbed his name as he positioned her above him and then drove into her, her legs wrapped around his waist, his name a ragged cry torn from her lips.

Afterwards they remained wrapped around each other, Antonios braced against the stone fountain, Lindsay cradled in his lap with her legs around his waist.

'We look like a Lissajous curve,' she murmured against his shoulder and Antonios eased back to smile wryly at her.

'A what?'

'A figure eight, I suppose,' Lindsay explained. She gestured to their legs: his stretched out and hers pretzeled behind his back. 'A Lissajous curve is the graph of parametric equations that describe complex harmonic motion. It looks a bit like a figure eight.'

'Complex harmonic motion,' Antonios repeated thoughtfully, lightly rocking his hips against hers. 'That sounds about right.'

Lindsay laughed softly and rested her head against his shoulder, breathing in the tangy masculine scent of him. She felt utterly sated, both physically and emotionally. *Complete*. The resistance she'd kept up for so long had been swept away, just as Antonios had swept her away in New York.

She had no idea what the future would look or feel like, and dwelling too long on the possibilities and pitfalls made fear clench her belly. But, no matter how afraid she might feel, she no longer fought against the future. Against Antonios and her love for him. His love for her.

What they shared, she thought as she pressed a kiss against his bare shoulder, was impossible to fight.

Antonios adjusted their bodies so he could look into her face. His eyes blazed with ferocity and yet his smile was tender. 'No regrets?' he asked softly and she smiled back.

'No. Some reservations, maybe. But no regrets.'

'It will work out, Lindsay. I swear it.'

And she knew that Antonios was the kind of man who would refuse all obstacles. Who would make things happen by sheer force of will. And maybe, for once, that was a good thing.

Tenderly, Antonios scooped her up from the fountain and carried her back to the table.

'Our dinner awaits.'

'I'm naked,' she pointed out, and Antonios gave a negligent shrug.

'I don't mind.'

She laughed, happiness rising inside her like a bubble. 'I'm also cold.'

He let out a theatrical sigh. 'Well, if you must,' he said, and scooped up her underwear and dress. Instead of handing them to her, he dressed her himself, slowly and lingeringly, so by the time he'd tugged up the zip on her dress Lindsay was nearly melting again with desire. 'Later,' he promised, and with one last soft kiss he led her back to the table and, with her heart brimming with happiness, Lindsay sat down to eat. She found she was suddenly starving.

Antonios left the bed, sunlight streaming over Lindsay as she lay tangled amidst the silken sheets, her hair spread over the pillow like a moonbeam. In sleep she looked relaxed and happy, her mouth curved in a small smile, one hand flung, palm upwards, by her face.

Antonios luxuriated in the simple pleasure of watching her and knowing she was his. Finally. Again. *His.*

Last night, after they'd made love, they'd spent several pleasant hours eating their delayed dinner and chatting in an easy way that he wasn't sure they'd ever experienced before, not even in those heady days in New York, when everything had been an odyssey of discovery. Certainly not in Greece, which in hindsight he could see had been marked by strain and silence. This was new, and all the more precious because of it.

They were building something good now, he told himself. Something new and strong. And he would make sure it worked. His mouth hardening in a line of resolve, he turned from Lindsay lying asleep in their bed.

The sun was rising in a bright blue sky, the olive groves sparkling under its light. He wanted to wake Lindsay up before he left for work, make love to her again, but he knew he needed to get to the office. He had a staff meeting in a few hours, and he still needed to talk with Leonidas.

Just the thought of his brother had Antonios's insides tightening in a familiar and unwelcome way. For ten years he'd lived with that tightening, the unrelenting pressure of leading his father's business away from the precipice of disaster while keeping it all from his family.

When he'd met Lindsay in New York and fallen in love with her, it had felt like the first time he'd truly relaxed or been happy. And even though he now had that again he couldn't ignore the tension that ratcheted inside him as he scrawled her a note and walked across the estate to Marakaios Enterprises' offices.

He needed to talk to Leonidas. He hadn't realized the extent of his brother's resentment. They'd been close growing up, getting into similar scrapes on the estate, sharing the usual boyish escapades. United, perhaps, in the alienation they'd felt from their father, who had been consumed by the business he'd eventually run into the ground.

Thinking about his father made Antonios's chest hurt. He loved his parents, his family, and as any Greek man he was fiercely loyal to them. Even acknowledging his father's faults to himself felt like a betrayal and he forced down the stress that felt as if it had a stranglehold on his soul.

'You're late,' Leonidas remarked, unsmiling, as Antonios came into the reception area of the office. Antonios suppressed a flicker of irritation as he walked past his brother into his office, its floor-to-ceiling windows overlooking the olive groves now dazzling in morning sunlight.

'I didn't realize you were waiting for me,' he said. He dropped his briefcase by his desk, shed his suit jacket and sat down before opening up his laptop.

Leonidas stood in front of his desk, arms folded and chin jutting. 'I want more control, Antonios.'

Antonios didn't look up from his laptop. He wasn't surprised by Leonidas's demand, but he still didn't know how he was going to deal with it. 'You're Head of European—'

'Don't fob me off with that,' Leonidas snapped. 'I'm not a

dog to be tossed a bone. In the ten years since you took over, I've never had access to financial information. I've never had any true authority. I'm nothing more than a front man who's meant to do the fancy talk.'

'And you're so good at it,' Antonios pointed out, spite spiking his voice even though he'd meant it to be flattery.

'Well, I'm done with being patronized,' Leonidas stated. 'You either give me more control or I leave.'

Anger surged through Antonios and he rose from his chair, one hand flat on the desk as he glared at his brother. 'Are you threatening me?'

'Simply stating a fact.' They glared at each other and in some distant corner of his brain Antonios wondered how it had come to this.

Because your father made it happen.

'I wonder,' Leonidas continued coolly, 'why you insist on hiding the financial information, Antonios.'

'Our accountant is completely up to date—'

'And you never let me in on those meetings. You've never let me so much as look at a spreadsheet. What are you hiding, I wonder?'

It took Antonios a stunned second to realize what his brother was implying. That he was cooking the books, skimming money off the top. It was so far from the truth that for a moment he couldn't speak.

'Don't *ever*,' he finally warned Leonidas in a low voice, 'make such a despicable insinuation again. I've given my life, my soul, to Marakaios Enterprises.'

Leonidas stared at him for a long moment, his jaw tight. 'You're not the only one,' he finally said, and walked out.

Antonios sank into his chair, his mind still spinning, and pulled his laptop towards him. Grimly he clicked the mouse to download his emails and refused to think about what Leonidas had just said.

A couple of hours later he heard voices in the reception area and lifted his head to see Lindsay coming through his door. A wave of relieved joy broke over him at the sight of her; she wore a floral sundress and her hair tumbled loose about her shoulders. She offered him a shy smile as she came in the room and Antonios rose from behind his desk, barely restraining himself from striding across the room and pulling her into a desperately needed embrace.

'I thought I'd see how you are,' she said with a little smile. 'And where you work. I hope you don't mind.'

'I don't.' Emotion bottled in his chest, making his voice sound abrupt. Lindsay frowned.

'Is everything all right, Antonios?'

'Fine. Everything's fine, now that you're here.' Her frown deepened at this but Antonios didn't care. He just needed to touch her. He came round from his desk and pulled her into his arms, fitting her against him, needing her there.

She pressed her hands to either side of his face, twisting to look up at him. 'You seem angry.'

'Just a little stressed. Nothing to worry about.' And to silence any further questions he kissed her, revelling in the honeyed sweetness of her mouth, the instant melting of her response.

He slid his hands down her body to cup her bottom and fit her even more snugly against his growing arousal. She let out a choked laugh.

'Antonios…'

'You know something I've never done in my office?'

'I think I can probably guess.'

He slid his hands under her sundress, fingers finding sweet, warm flesh. He rejoiced at the way she shuddered under his touch, her head falling onto his shoulder.

'Your PA is right outside…' she murmured, but offered no other resistance.

'The door is closed and incredibly soundproof.'

'How do you know?'

He didn't, but at this point he didn't care. 'Trust me,' he said, and hoisted her onto his desk. Lindsay's lovely eyes widened as he spread her legs and got rid of her underwear with one swift tug. They widened further when he stepped between her legs, stroking her softly as she moaned her response.

'This is crazy,' she murmured, and Antonios slid inside her.

'Crazy,' he agreed, 'and incredible.'

And Lindsay obviously agreed as her body arched under his and she wrapped her legs around his waist to pull him even more deeply inside her.

Afterwards he still didn't let her go, savouring the feel of her, already wanting her again. 'What do you think about going into Amfissa for lunch?' he asked.

Suddenly the thought of escaping the office, the entire estate, seemed like a wonderful and even necessary idea.

'Now?' She peered up at him again. 'But the party's to-night…'

'Right. Of course.' The hope that had seized him for a moment trickled away. He needed to stop by the villa, make sure the preparations were going well, check on his mother. His sisters would expect it. His family needed it.

Lindsay searched his face for a moment, a slight frown puckering her forehead. 'I suppose we could,' she said after a moment. 'For a few hours. I was just in the villa, trying to help your sisters. I think I'm more help to them by just staying out of the way.'

'They can be a bit officious when it comes to party planning,' Antonios conceded with a smile, and Lindsay gave a rueful nod.

'Why don't we go?' she suggested softly. 'Have a date? They can do without us for an hour or two, surely.'

An hour or two snatched from a packed schedule. They'd had even less the last time they'd been together in Greece, Antonios acknowledged. Work had consumed him and he'd expected, wrongly, for Lindsay to simply slot herself into all that was going on around her.

He wouldn't make that mistake again.

'Let's go,' he said and, taking her by the hand, he led her out of the office.

Lindsay followed Antonios from the office, blinking in the bright sunlight. Ten minutes later they were in his SUV, speeding down the mountain towards Amfissa, the town no more than a cluster of red-roofed, whitewashed buildings huddled against the mountainside.

'I haven't even been in Amfissa before,' Lindsay said a bit ruefully, and Antonios shot her just as regretful a glance.

'I know. I was realizing again how little we actually did together before. That undoubtedly made things even harder for you.'

'Yes. You were busy, though, with work. I understood that.' At least, she'd tried to. But she knew her anxiety had been made worse by Antonios's absence, his total focus on work as soon as they'd returned to Greece.

Antonios flexed his hands on the steering wheel. 'I should have made time. We should have had a honeymoon.'

'Our meeting was our honeymoon,' Lindsay joked and Antonios shook his head.

'We'll have a proper honeymoon after my mother's party. When I can get away.'

'And when will that be, do you think?' Lindsay spoke lightly even as realization was slipping through her in an unwelcome rush. No matter what Antonios had said about things being different now, they surely couldn't be that different. He was still CEO of a company that demanded much of his time and energy. When she'd come into the office this morning he'd looked so grimly focused, so unhappy.

It had surprised and unsettled her, and it made her wonder if Antonios really could work less. If their marriage could work.

Plenty of women had workaholic husbands, she reminded herself. It didn't have to be a deal-breaker.

'Don't,' Antonios said softly, and reached over to link her hand with his.

She turned to him. 'Don't what?'

'Don't start worrying already. We'll make this work, Lindsay, I swear it. We both want it to work, don't we?'

'Yes—'

'Then it will.'

He sounded so confident, so sure, as sure as he had when he'd asked her out, when he'd asked her to marry him. She'd believed in him then, and she chose to believe in him now. At least for an afternoon when they could simply revel in each other's company, an afternoon out of time, out of reality.

And when you return to Villa Marakaios? When life catches up with you, with all of its expectations and demands?

She'd think about that later, Lindsay told herself, and pushed the questions to the furthest reaches of her mind. Today she just wanted to enjoy herself—and enjoy being with Antonios.

Once in Amfissa they strolled down the town's wide main boulevard, taking in the many different shops. Antonios was recognized by many of the townspeople and he stopped and spoke to them all, introducing Lindsay. She could handle small groups of people and everyone seemed so friendly, so interested, that the initial anxiety she felt melted away and she chatted with the different people easily, or as easily as she could considering they spoke different languages.

'Is it all right, meeting all these people?' Antonios asked as they walked away from a local joiner and his wife who had been shopping in the market, and had welcomed Lindsay with kisses on both of her cheeks.

'It's fine,' she answered, and meant it. 'I'm not anxious.' It was different, she realized, having Antonios by her side, concerned and supportive. Different when she didn't have the weight of expectation and potential disappointment on her. Not a magical cure by any means, and she knew she would still be dealing with her anxiety for years to come. But it was better. She felt stronger.

'Let's have some lunch,' Antonios said, and led her down a side street to a small taverna tucked away from prying eyes.

The inside of the restaurant was dim and quiet, with only a few patrons who barely looked up from their meals as they entered. Antonios spoke rapidly in Greek to the owner of the place, and within minutes he was ushering them to a private table at the back of the restaurant. The owner brought them menus, a bottle of spring water and two glasses before quietly disappearing.

'A little privacy never goes amiss,' Antonios said.

'I was fine,' Lindsay protested.

'I know you were. I was proud of you, Lindsay. But I want you to myself now.' He gave her a teasingly lascivious smile and she laughed and shook her head.

'You're insatiable.'

'Only when it comes to you.'

Which felt like some kind of miracle. She'd spent so much of her life feeling deficient and unworthy. Yet Antonios looked at her and saw someone strong, someone beautiful. Someone he loved.

'You know,' she said slowly, 'I think part of the reason I didn't tell you about my anxiety is because I didn't want you to look at me differently.' Antonios waited, eyebrows raised, clearly sensing she had more to say. 'When we met in New York you made me feel so special and beautiful and strong. And I was afraid you'd stop looking at me that way if you knew.'

'I wouldn't—'

'I know that now, Antonios, because you didn't. Because you know the truth and you still love me. You still make me feel special.' She blinked back tears of emotion as she reached for his hand. 'Even more special because you know me completely. I'm not hiding anything from you.'

He squeezed her hand. 'And I pray you never do or feel you have to.'

'I won't.'

They ordered then, and spent the next hour tasting each other's dishes and chatting companionably. Afterwards they strolled through the town, hand in hand as the cares fell away from them both.

Lindsay noticed how much more relaxed Antonios seemed, away from Villa Marakaios—or was it their renewed relationship that had smoothed away the lines of strain from his nose to his mouth and brought the sparkle back to his whisky-coloured eyes?

'I feel like I did back in New York,' she confessed as they sat on one of the stone walls that overlooked the valley, on one of the town's higher winding streets. 'When we first met.'

'That's a good thing, I hope?' Antonios answered, his eyebrows raised, and Lindsay smiled and nodded.

'Yes. Definitely. You seem more like you did in New York.'

'And how is that?'

'More relaxed. Happier.' She paused then asked cautiously, 'Sometimes it seems like work doesn't make you happy, Antonios. Like it's a huge strain.' She waited for him to say something in response but he didn't, just gazed out at the valley with his eyes narrowed.

'I suppose in New York I was free from the concerns of work and daily life,' he finally said, his gaze still on the view. 'It was, as you said before, a time apart.'

'So we need to figure out how to make things work amidst those concerns.'

'And we will,' Antonios said with the same confidence he'd shown in the restaurant. 'All that matters is that we love each other, Lindsay. The rest will work itself out.'

He raised her hand to his lips and kissed it, and Lindsay smiled and said nothing. She wanted to feel as confident as Antonios seemed to be, but worries still nagged at her, made her wonder just *how* things were going to work themselves out. Would Antonios work less? Would he entertain less? How were they actually going to manage the day-to-day of their joined lives?

A short while later they headed back to the car and drove in silence back to Villa Marakaios. Lindsay slid a sideways glance at Antonios as they approached the estate, silently noting how his eyes narrowed and his mouth hardened the moment they drove through the gates.

At their own villa he left her with a quick distracted kiss, telling her he needed to return to the office before the party that night. Reluctantly, Lindsay headed over to the main villa to see if she could help with the preparations. Antonios's sisters seemed to have affairs well in hand but she wanted to be seen to make an effort, even if she still found her relationship with her sisters-in-law to be one of tension and suspicion.

'Oh, Lindsay, where have you been? Was Antonios with you? Ava's been looking for him—'

'We went out for a bit,' Lindsay answered. 'Is everything all right?'

'Parthenope's been tied up all afternoon with Timon,' Xanthe explained. 'And Ava has decided she can't wear anything she owns and has gone shopping, of all things.' Xanthe rolled her eyes in exasperation.

'Is Timon all right?'

'Just a bit of cold,' Xanthe dismissed. 'But Parthenope was meant to deal with the caterers, where to have them set up, all of that. I've been busy myself with the decorations—'

'I could help,' Lindsay offered and Xanthe looked, perhaps rightly, sceptical. Lindsay straightened, threw back her shoulders. 'What do you need me to do?'

'Well…' Xanthe nibbled her lip. 'The housekeeper Maria is sorting them out in the kitchen, but she's in a flap because she wanted to do the cooking herself. Mama said no, because it was too much. Maria is not as young as she once was.'

'I see,' Lindsay said. 'So you want me to talk to Maria?'

Xanthe nodded in relief. 'Yes, and then show the caterers what to do.' Xanthe turned back to the table she was festooning with large silk bows, clearly itching to keep going with her own work. 'Do you think you could do that?' she tossed over her shoulder.

'Yes, of course,' Lindsay said with more confidence than she felt. She didn't even know where the kitchen was.

She watched Xanthe for a moment, fussing with one of the bows, and then turned and made her uncertain way to the kitchen, opening a few random doors until one of the house staff pointed her towards the large, light room at the back of the house.

The caterers were bringing in large plastic-wrapped trays of hors d'oeuvres, watched over by a silent and surly Maria. Lindsay had seen the housekeeper in passing and had probably been introduced to her on that first awful day, but they'd never had a conversation.

She took a deep breath and approached her. '*Herete*, Maria,' she said as cheerfully as she could. 'Is everything all right?'

Maria just looked at her blankly, and Lindsay realized the older woman did not speak English. And she, unfortunately, had no more than a few words of Greek.

She gestured to the caterers and raised her eyebrows in query, asking haltingly, '*Ti kanete?*' How are you?

In answer Maria let out a torrent of Greek that Lindsay could not begin to understand, but she certainly got the gist of Maria's bitterness at having strangers invade her kitchen. Making soothing noises, she led the woman over to the table in a sunny alcove, and listened with all signs of interest and attention as Maria continued to lament in a language she didn't speak.

Fifteen minutes later, having vented her spleen, Maria seemed somewhat appeased, and with gestures and an absurd amount of miming Lindsay suggested she organize the hors d'oeuvres. The caterers could have a respite from Maria scowling at them, and the housekeeper would hopefully feel she was being consulted.

Twenty minutes later things were going smoothly, and Lindsay felt rather ridiculously proud of herself for coping with it all. She was smiling as she came back to the front house, stopping when she saw Antonios come through the door of the living room, scowling.

'Is everything all right?' she asked, and Antonios jerked his gaze towards her, his face clearing, Lindsay suspected, by sheer force of will.

'Fine. Are things in hand in the kitchen? I just got an earful from Xanthe.'

'Yes, I think so. I was just down with Maria.'

'Were you?' Antonios's eyebrows rose at that, and Lindsay smiled self-consciously.

'I didn't realize she didn't speak English, but we managed all right.'

'That's very good to hear.'

'Shall we go back to the villa?' she asked, and Antonios nodded. Lindsay could still see lines of tension bracketing his mouth and eyes and she stopped in front of him, reaching up to cup his cheek. 'Are you sure you're all right?' she asked quietly.

Antonios closed his eyes briefly, seeming to take strength from her small caress. 'I'm fine,' he said, and Lindsay heard the note of implacability enter his voice. He sounded, she thought, like she used to, claiming things were fine when they clearly weren't.

As she followed Antonios out of the villa, she wondered if he would be as honest with her as she had learned to be with him, and tell her what was going on.

CHAPTER TEN

ANTONIOS STOOD ON the edge of the living room, watching as guests chatted and circulated amidst the staff holding trays of hors d'oeuvres. His mother sat on a chair in the centre of the room, looking weary and yet happy as she held court over all the family, friends and neighbours that had been invited to her name day party.

His gaze moved to the opposite corner of the room where Lindsay stood, looking pale and lovely and amazingly poised, chatting with a guest, a smile making her seem radiant. She was, Antonios thought, the most beautiful and elegant woman in the room.

While they were getting ready, back at their own villa, he'd assured her that she wouldn't need to be the centre of attention and could leave if she felt uncomfortable. Invariably, though, Lindsay attracted attention. She was beautiful, and she was his wife. People wanted to meet her, talk to her, and Antonios had responsibilities of his own. As much as he wanted to, he couldn't hide in the corner, protecting his wife.

Not, he acknowledged with a small wry smile, that Lindsay needed protecting. She'd been more than holding her own so far tonight, chatting with people as they approached her, smiling and laughing. Pride surged through him, mixed with love. She was everything he'd ever wanted in a wife, a partner.

His gaze narrowed as he watched Leonidas come up to her. He still hadn't agreed to give Leonidas access to any of the company's financial information, and he didn't think he ever could, not without betraying his father.

He'd thought, more than once, about telling Leonidas the truth. Sharing the burden. But it wasn't his secret to share. He'd made a promise. A vow. If he couldn't honour it, what sort of man was he?

One whose family is being torn apart by secrecy.

Now, as he watched Leonidas talk to Lindsay, he wondered if his brother intended to put pressure on his wife. Leonidas was so angry and bitter that Antonios wouldn't put such an underhand tactic past him at this point.

Lindsay frowned at Leonidas and every protective instinct in Antonios reared up. The last thing he needed or wanted was his brother breathing his bitter poison into his wife's ear. His mouth set in a grim line, he headed towards his brother and his wife.

Lindsay had been trying to answer Leonidas's questions in a relaxed manner but the more he talked, the harder it was to ignore the edge to his voice.

Are you happy to be back at Villa Marakaios? It's all marital bliss, is it? You and Antonios have everything you want, I suppose? He certainly does.

Lindsay couldn't tell if Leonidas knew the truth of their earlier troubles or if he was simply bitter about what he perceived as his brother's good fortune. What was coming through, loud and clear, was the resentment and animosity he felt towards Antonios.

'Everything all right here?' Antonios asked as he strolled up to them. His voice was pleasant but his gaze had snapped to Lindsay, and she could see the question in his eyes.

'Fine,' Leonidas answered for both of them. 'Just getting

to know my sister-in-law. Wondering what she sees in you.' Lindsay thought Leonidas had meant this as a joke, but it fell rather flat.

'I wonder myself every day,' Antonios answered, his voice light but his face unsmiling. 'Lindsay, there are some people who would like to meet you. The Atrikes family. They're local business owners. Why don't you come with me?' He held out his hand and, with a moment's hesitant glance at Leonidas, whose expression had ironed out to bland boredom, she took it.

'What's going on between you and Leonidas?' she asked when they were alone in a private alcove off the library.

'What do you mean?'

'You clearly don't get along,' Lindsay said bluntly. 'And yet you work together.'

Antonios twitched his shoulders in an impatient shrug. 'Nothing more than a little brotherly competition.'

'Over what?' He just shrugged again, not answering, and frustration fired through her. 'Antonios, can't you tell me? You didn't like it when you were in the dark about how I was feeling, but now you're the same—'

'It's just a business matter—' he cut her off, his tone dismissive '—it will sort itself out.'

'What kind of business matter?'

'Nothing you need to concern yourself about.' He'd kept his voice mild but Lindsay still felt the rebuke. Nothing he wanted to concern her with, he'd meant.

'You're doing so well tonight, Lindsay,' he continued, and dropped a kiss onto her forehead. 'You're the most beautiful woman in the room, the most elegant and poised. I'm proud of you.'

She smiled and turned her face so he could kiss her on the mouth. He did so, lingeringly, and Lindsay knew both of them were thinking about later that evening, after the party, when they could be alone.

'I'm proud of you, Antonios,' she told him. 'You've led your family and your business so well in the absence of your father. So many people have been telling me how you've taken the helm of Marakaios Enterprises without a single misstep.'

Antonios smiled at this, but it was a small, tight smile that didn't reach his eyes.

'We should go. The Atrikes family are waiting.'

A little while later they headed back to the living area, where Xanthe and Parthenope were ushering people towards the dining room, where platters of food were laid out.

Daphne rose from her chair, her hands outstretched towards Antonios. 'Antonios, Lindsay. Come celebrate with me.'

Lindsay came forward and took Daphne's hand, feeling how fragile it was in hers, the skin papery, the bones seeming hollow, like a bird's.

Daphne smiled wryly, as if she noticed Lindsay's awareness, and squeezed her hand. 'Tonight is for happiness,' she said quietly, and her gaze moved to Antonios. 'Yes?'

'Yes,' Lindsay said firmly and gently squeezed her mother-in-law's hand back.

The party lasted until well after midnight, even though Daphne excused herself earlier, tired as she was. By the time she and Antonios returned to their little villa, Lindsay was exhausted, her feet aching.

'I think it was a success,' she said as she kicked off her heels with a sigh of relief. She hadn't had a single moment of true anxiety, at least in part because Antonios had been aware of when she needed to take a step back, have a moment's space and peace.

'I think so,' Antonios agreed. He shrugged out of his suit jacket and undid the knot of his tie. Even though he'd been his charming, confident self throughout the whole evening, Lindsay had sensed his restlessness and tension and it felt like a thorn in her side, in their marriage.

'Are you sure everything is all right, Antonios?' she asked. 'Between you and Leonidas?'

'It's fine,' he dismissed and took her into his arms. 'And the last thing I want to talk or even think about now is my brother. Do you know how beautiful you look in that dress?'

Lindsay glanced down at the pale blue evening gown she wore, the silk rippling in a shimmering sheet to the floor, reminding her of water. She'd never cared much about clothes one way or the other, but she loved the look on Antonios's face when he saw her in something beautiful. When he so clearly thought *she* was beautiful.

'You look gorgeous,' Antonios said in a growl as he pulled her to him. 'But I couldn't stop thinking about peeling it off you all evening.'

Lindsay laughed softly, already breathless with anticipation. 'And will you make that a reality, do you think?'

'I intend to right now.' His gaze blazed into hers as he reached around to her back and slowly, sensuously, tugged the zip all the way down to her hips. The dress fell from her shoulders and, with one tiny shrug, it slid down to her waist.

The style had precluded the wearing of a bra and Lindsay wasn't so generously endowed that she needed one, so now she stood before him, completely bare to the waist, basking in the admiration, the *adoration* she saw in his eyes.

A lump of emotion rose in her throat and Antonios tugged her towards him by the hand. 'What are you thinking?' he asked hoarsely. 'You look as if you're about to cry.'

'I was wondering how I ever could have left you,' Lindsay whispered, her voice catching. 'Even for a moment.'

He pulled her towards him, her breasts colliding with the crisp cotton of his shirt, the friction sending shivery arrows of pleasure ricocheting through her. 'Never again,' Antonios whispered against her hair as he slid his hands up her bare back to cradle her face. 'Never leave me again, Lindsay. Promise. I couldn't bear it.'

'I promise,' she whispered, and then lost herself to Antonios's passionate, desperate kiss.

* * *

The next few weeks seemed to pass in a golden blur of contentment and joy: days spent working on her research or walking through the countryside, taking the first steps in getting to know Antonios's family. His sisters were still a little guarded, but they'd thawed when Lindsay had, at Antonios's urging, explained about her anxiety.

Parthenope's face had fallen and she'd pulled Lindsay into a spontaneous hug. 'You should have told us. It would have made such a difference.'

'Parthenope thought you were a snob,' Ava confided and Parthenope pulled away from Lindsay, blushing.

'Ava!'

'Because you're so smart,' Ava continued, shooting her sister a mischievous glance. 'She's jealous, really. I'm the only one who went to university.'

'I got married instead,' Parthenope said, her cheeks bright red.

'I'm not sure a doctorate in number theory is something to be jealous of,' Lindsay said wryly. Her mind reeled from her sisters-in-law's admissions. 'It's not very useful.'

'Antonios told us it was,' Xanthe piped up. 'He said it would help with all sorts of advancements in technology and science.'

'Well, maybe,' Lindsay allowed. The thought that Antonios had championed her research sent a tingling warmth through her.

'We did wonder if you thought you were too good for us,' Parthenope admitted, her face still flushed, and Lindsay's jaw nearly dropped.

'I never thought that,' she said. 'Not once.'

They all smiled at each other, awkwardly and yet with affection, and while Lindsay knew she might not have been what Antonios's sisters had been expecting or even wanting for his wife, she knew they accepted her. A few weeks ago their acceptance would have made her feel guilty, wondering yet again if she should have been honest about her issues when she'd been in Greece before. Now she recognized that she couldn't have been, that both she and Antonios were different people now, capable of different things.

A week after Daphne's birthday party Antonios had asked her if they could move into the main villa. 'My mother would like us there,' he said. 'And I would like to be there. We'll have our own wing, and you can redecorate as you like—'

His thoughtfulness nearly brought tears to her eyes. 'Of course we can move back to the main villa,' she said.

Yet it was a little strange to be back in the house where she'd once been so unhappy. She walked down the upstairs corridor, her footsteps muffled on the thick carpet, and remembered how she'd run up these stairs, spots dancing before her eyes, everything in her aching, as she'd excused herself from yet another endless social function, Antonios so wilfully oblivious.

In the huge sumptuous bathroom she remembered how she'd locked the door and curled up against the marble tub, hugging her knees to her chest and rocking back and forth as she'd tried to calm her racing heart.

And in the bedroom she remembered how Antonios had brought her such incredible pleasure, and how she'd left him one chilly morning, the grey light of dawn filtering through the curtains as she'd kissed him goodbye and felt her heart break.

So many memories, and she didn't want to linger on them for too long. She wanted to make new memories, have new dreams. Inadvertently, Lindsay pressed her hand against her stomach. They hadn't used protection in the last few weeks, something that made her insides lurch with both excitement and alarm. She knew Antonios had wanted to start a family right away; she'd been more cautious. But now she thought about a baby—Antonios's baby—and a smile spread across her face at the possibility.

Antonios came into the bedroom, resting his hands on her shoulders as he stood behind her. Both of them were silent, gazing at the wide bed with its cream silk duvet, the shutters of the windows open to the view of the mountains.

Lindsay knew they were both remembering, reliving those last moments. Her final farewell. Then Antonios brushed a kiss against the nape of her neck and it felt like a benediction. They were both moving on from the past.

'I have something to show you,' he said, his breath fanning her skin and making her shiver.

'You do?'

'Come.' He tugged her by the hand down the corridor of their private wing, towards a room Lindsay hadn't been in before. He pushed open the door and then stepped aside so she could enter.

Her breath caught in her chest as she took in the spacious sunlit room: the wide oak desk with the top-of-the-line desktop computer, the comfortable chair, the bookshelves and the huge dry-erase board, just like she'd had in her office back in New York.

'For your research,' he said simply. 'If there's anything else you need, just let me know and I'll get it for you.'

She turned and threw her arms around his neck. 'There's nothing else I need,' she told him as she kissed him. 'Nothing else at all.'

Another week slid by, a week blurred by pleasure and love, and yet not without its moments of disquiet. Antonios still spent all his days and many of his evenings at work, and Lindsay couldn't ignore the strain that etched lines on his face and made him quiet and irritable whenever she asked him about it.

Love was complicated, she reminded herself. *Life* was. Whatever Antonios was dealing with, he'd tell her in his own time. They could deal with it.

But one night she woke up to an empty bed and, with unease crawling along her spine, she rose and went to their adjoining living area, stopping in the doorway when she saw Antonios standing by the window, one hand braced against the glass.

'Antonios…'

He didn't turn at the sound of her voice. 'I couldn't sleep,' he said, his voice flat and toneless.

'Is everything all right?' she asked. It was the same question she'd asked before, over and over, and as usual Antonios gave the same answer.

'It's fine.'

'Something's going on, Antonios,' Lindsay protested. 'I can feel it. You're unhappy—'

'Just a little stressed,' he corrected, but Lindsay felt it was more than that, deeper than that.

She also knew she wouldn't get any answers from Antonios now. Wordlessly, she went back to bed, lay flat on her back and stared up at the ceiling.

Why wouldn't Antonios tell her what was going on? He'd been hurt that she'd kept so much from him, and he'd never ever noticed she was unhappy. Yet now she was noticing and Antonios didn't seem to want her to.

Sighing, Lindsay told herself yet again to be patient. To trust. They could get through this. She had to believe that.

A month after Daphne's name day party Lindsay received an email from a university in New York City, offering her an assistant professorship of Pure Mathematics. She stared at it in surprise, knowing she shouldn't be so shocked since her supervisor had hinted that her research was being well received by academia in general. But that had been a lifetime ago, when she'd only had her research to think about, to keep her company…

And now? She felt a treacherous flicker of doubt and yearning. She loved being with Antonios, was enjoying this time in Greece…*but for the rest of her life?*

She looked up from her computer and gazed unseeingly out at the pine-covered mountains. She and Antonios had been enjoying a honeymoon period to their marriage, she realized. But even the honeymoon had its bumps, with Antonios's stress over work. And when that phase wore off, when he worked even harder, when the stress and strain of that work took an even greater toll?

Antonios had made it clear he couldn't leave Greece. But what if he needed to? What if working for Marakaios Enterprises, for whatever reason he refused to name, was killing him, destroying his happiness?

What if he needed something different as much as she did—or even more?

The thought was so incredible, so revolutionary, that Lindsay couldn't take it in fully. And maybe it was just wishful thinking because she wanted Antonios's plans to fit in with her own. But she'd tied herself to him and promised to try life in Greece again. She couldn't suggest something else now, not even for his sake. Antonios wouldn't countenance it for a moment.

And, really, she couldn't imagine Antonios anywhere else. This was his home, his kingdom. Yet she also knew she missed the excitement of teaching a class, discussing number theory with students and professors. Being part of a community, however small, of people who were as passionate and excited about mathematics as she was.

Restless and more than a little anxious, Lindsay closed her laptop and headed outside. It was a glorious fall day and the estate gardens were still in full flower. She walked down the winding brick paths that led to different gardens: the walled herb garden where she'd talked to Daphne, the courtyard with the fountain where she and Antonios had reconciled and made love. Just looking at the stone lip of the fountain where she'd wrapped herself around his body made her blush and smile.

She sank onto a stone bench, staring at that fountain, trying to untangle all the feelings that had become twisted up inside her. Hope and fear. Frustration and joy. Anxiety—not for herself, but for Antonios.

'Li-li!' Lindsay turned around to see two-year-old Timon toddling towards her. He'd started calling her Li-li a few days ago, much to everyone's amusement. Now Lindsay reached out and grabbed him by his chubby hands.

'Have you escaped, young man?' she asked, and Timon grinned up at her uncomprehendingly; he was learning both English and Greek, but he understood Greek much better.

'Timon!' Parthenope appeared around the corner, worry replaced by exasperation as she caught sight of her son. She let out a stream of scolding Greek but the little boy just giggled. Rolling her eyes at Lindsay, Parthenope gathered her son up on her lap and sat next to her on the bench.

'You are well?' she asked, a frown settling between her straight brows, and Lindsay laughed lightly.

'Do I not look well?'

'You look worried.' She hesitated then asked cautiously, 'Are things all right between you and Antonios?'

Lindsay stiffened at the implication that Parthenope, and who knew who else, suspected they weren't. 'Yes, of course.'

'Because, you know, when you left for New York he walked around like a raging lion. He pretended he was fine; he wouldn't tell us a thing, but we all knew better.'

Lindsay fought a flush as Parthenope subjected her to a searching gaze. 'Well…things are a lot better than that,' she said after a moment. 'We're working out our problems.'

At least, she hoped they were.

Parthenope laid a hand on her arm as Timon squirmed out of her lap. 'Marriage is not always easy.'

'No, that's what your mother said,' Lindsay said with a small smile. '"Endlessly complicated and difficult" were her exact words.'

Parthenope let out a little laugh. 'Perhaps not quite that bad. But if you both try, it will be good, yes?'

Lindsay saw the hope and concern in Parthenope's eyes and slowly nodded. She sincerely hoped trying was enough. But was Antonios even trying? If he was, surely he would share some of his concerns with her. Maybe, Lindsay thought, she needed to ask him more bluntly. Demand, even, out of her love for him.

She smiled at Parthenope, not wanting to burden her sister-in-law with her private concerns. 'Yes,' she said, 'it will be good.'

That night Antonios stayed late at work, which left Lindsay alone in their bedroom, waiting for him and thinking far too much. At nearly eleven o'clock at night she finally broke down and headed out into the night to look for him.

The air was cool and crisp and she shivered in just her light sweater and jeans as she walked down the deserted drives towards the office building; she could see a single light burning inside.

The front door was open and she slipped silently inside, her heart starting to beat hard. She walked towards Antonios's office; his door was ajar and she stood at the threshold, peeked inside.

At the sight of him her heart lurched with fear, swooped with sorrow. He looked so despairing, his head cradled in his hands, his shoulders bowed.

'Antonios…' she whispered and he jerked up straight, anger blazing in his eyes.

'What are you doing here?'

'I was looking for you.'

'You shouldn't have. You knew I was working.'

She knew his anger was a defence mechanism but it still stung. 'It's nearly midnight, Antonios.'

'I have a lot going on at the moment.'

She took a step into the room, glanced at the computer screen that had been left up, with its many columns of numbers. 'What are you doing?'

He slammed down the lid of his laptop. 'Don't. Don't look at that.'

Lindsay felt herself go cold at the implacable note in his

voice. 'Why not?' she asked as reasonably as she could. 'It's only numbers.'

'And you're so good at numbers,' Antonios shot back.

Lindsay jerked back at the sneer in his voice. 'Antonios, what is going on? Why are you acting this way, hiding—'

'I'm not hiding,' he returned in a near roar. '*Theos*, Lindsay, just let me be.' He rose from his chair, pacing the room like a caged lion, one hand clenching in his hair. He looked, Lindsay thought, like a man in torment.

'I don't understand what's going on,' she said quietly. 'And I think I need to.'

Antonios didn't even turn around. 'Trust me, you don't.'

'Does this have to do with Leonidas?' Antonios didn't answer and, filled with frustration, Lindsay walked up to him, put her hands on his taut back. 'Damn it, Antonios, stop hiding things from me. You're making a double standard for our marriage and it's not fair.'

'Don't talk to me about what's fair,' Antonios answered bleakly, and she shook her head.

'I don't understand.'

'I don't want you to understand.' He turned around, clasping her cold hands in his. 'Lindsay, you're right. I am hiding something from you, but I have to.' Anguish lit his eyes and twisted his features. 'Please believe me. This has nothing to do with you, with us. It's just business. Naturally, there are some confidential matters I can't discuss—'

'Confidential matters that are tearing you apart, making you look haunted?' Lindsay finished. 'Making you seem like someone else entirely. Antonios, you're wrong. This has everything to do with us.' She stared at him, watched as his mouth thinned and his eyes hardened. She knew he wouldn't tell her anything now.

Wordlessly, she slipped her hands from his and walked from the room.

CHAPTER ELEVEN

ANTONIOS LISTENED TO the front door of the office close and with a groan he sank back in his chair, raking his hands through his hair. *Theos*, what had he been about to do?

He flipped up the screen of the laptop and watched as the financial figures of Marakaios Enterprises filled the screen. Figures he'd been contemplating doctoring to hide his father's shame—and add to his own. He couldn't believe he'd been contemplating doing something illegal for his father, or at least his father's memory. His father had done his fair share of tinkering with numbers, and Antonios had felt nothing but a sickening disdain. Yet now he'd been about to do the same thing.

He rose from his chair and restlessly paced the length of his office. He felt a need to escape not just the confines of the room, but of his life. Of the promise he'd made to his father, and the shackle Marakaios Enterprises had become to him.

He'd alienated his brother by hiding the truth of his father's actions, and now he'd done the same to Lindsay. He groaned aloud, shaking his head. Somehow this had to stop before it was too late. But maybe it was too late already.

A little after two in the morning Antonios headed back to the villa. Lindsay was already asleep, curled on her side, her knees tucked up to her chest like a child's. Antonios doubted he'd be able to sleep. It had eluded him most nights these last few weeks. Leonidas was barely talking to him, and the tension in the office was palpable, not just to him but to all the staff. And he still didn't know what to do.

He was still staring gritty-eyed at the ceiling when, an hour later, a light yet urgent tapping at the door of the bedroom had every sense springing to alert. Antonios rose from the bed, careful not to disturb Lindsay, and went to answer the door.

'Xanthe—'

'Antonios, it's Mama.' His sister's face was pale and pinched, tears shining in her eyes. Antonios felt as if his heart had stilled for a moment before beginning to thud with hard, painful beats.

'What has happened?'

'She woke up in the night, moaning and in pain. Maria has called the doctor. But she seems…it seems…' Xanthe couldn't go on, tears spilling down her cheeks, and Antonios hugged her briefly, murmuring meaningless words of consolation before he strode down the corridor.

His mother's room was lit only by a bedside lamp and its pale glow threw her features into shocking relief. Antonios knew his mother had been getting more tired and frail in the last few weeks, but the reality of it and her illness hit him now with painful force. The skin of her face was drawn tightly over her bones and she lay back on the pillows, her eyes closed, her breathing shallow.

Swallowing hard, Antonios approached the bed and perched carefully on its edge. '*Yeia sou*, Mama,' he said softly.

Daphne's eyelids fluttered but that was all. Antonios felt a swooping sensation in his chest, like missing a step. He reached for her hand, noticing how thin her wrist had become, her fingers claw-like. He didn't know what to say; everything felt like a platitude or a lie, so he just held her hand.

After a few minutes the doctor arrived and Antonios stood up, watching as the man checked his mother over, took her pulse and blood pressure.

'Well?' he bit out when he could stand it no longer.

Spiros Tallos straightened slowly and turned to face him. The older man had been the family doctor for two generations; he had set Antonios's leg when he'd broken it, falling out of a tree when he was six.

'She's dying, Antonios,' Spiro said gently. 'But we all knew that.'

'She has not been like this before,' Antonios answered, his voice terse.

'She is closer to the end.'

Everything in him roared in denial. 'How long?'

'It is impossible to say.'

'Guess,' Antonios snapped, and Spiros sighed sadly.

'It could be days, or it could be weeks. There will be good days and bad days, but continued decline.' He gave a little shrug, spreading his hands. 'I am sorry.'

Antonios turned away so the doctor would not see the naked grief on his face; he felt the burn of tears behind his lids and blinked them away rapidly. 'Thank you,' he finally said, when he trusted himself to speak. He cleared his throat. 'Can you… is there anything you can give her, for pain relief?'

'Of course,' Spiros said, and turned back to Daphne. Antonios turned to Xanthe, who was crying quietly. Wordlessly, he drew her into a hug and Xanthe took a shuddering breath, her cheek pressed against her shoulder.

'I know it shouldn't be a shock,' she whispered haltingly, 'but it is.'

Yes, it was. A terrible shock, a grim reality. Antonios closed his eyes, wished Lindsay were here with him. He longed for her quiet, comforting presence, the steadiness and strength he'd always appreciated in her. And yet he didn't want to have to tell her how Daphne had declined.

'Antonios.'

Xanthe jerked out of his arms and he hurried to his mother's bedside. 'Mama…'

'I want…' Daphne swallowed convulsively, her breath coming in shudders and gasps. Xanthe pressed a fist to her lips and Antonios took his mother's hand.

'Don't speak, it's too much for you now—'

She shook her head, the movement violent. 'I want… Leonidas,' she finally managed.

'I'll get him,' Xanthe offered and Antonios nodded his thanks.

Ten taut minutes later Leonidas was striding into the room, his hair dishevelled, his shirt untucked from the jeans he'd hastily put on before coming from his own villa to here.

His gaze snapped to Antonios and then back to his mother and, without a word of greeting for his brother, he sat on the opposite side of the bed and took his mother's other hand.

'Mama.'

Antonios began to rise. 'I'll go,' he murmured. 'You can have privacy…'

Daphne shook her head again. 'No. The two of you here. That is what I want. Together.' Neither Antonios nor Leonidas spoke and with effort Daphne drew her hands together so their hands, clasped in hers, were touching.

'There is too much pain and bitterness between you,' she said, her words coming slowly, her breathing laboured. 'You must make peace with each other now, before it is too late.' A tear snaked its way down her withered cheek. 'Before I am gone.'

Leonidas's hand twitched against Antonios's. They were both, he suspected, itching to pull their hands away, yet they wouldn't for the sake of their mother.

'We're fine, Mama,' Leonidas said placatingly, and Antonios's mouth tightened. *Fine*. He was beginning to hate that word. They were not fine. Lindsay had not been fine. In that moment, nothing, about anything, felt *fine*.

Daphne must have agreed for she shook her head, her hands tightening on her sons'. 'No,' she rasped. 'You have been angry and bitter with Antonios for too many years, Leonidas. It must stop now.'

Years? Antonios blinked, shooting his brother a sideways glance. Leonidas's jaw was tight but he said nothing.

'Don't worry about Antonios and me,' Leonidas finally bit out and Daphne let out a soft cry that tore at Antonios's heart.

'Of course I worry about you,' she answered, her voice choking. 'I know what Evangelos has cost both of you...'

Antonios's whole body tensed and he strove to keep his voice even as he asked, 'What do you mean, Mama?'

She turned her anguished face towards him. 'Making you the CEO—'

'You think he shouldn't have?' The words were out before Antonios could think better of them.

'Oh, Antonios, it doesn't matter what I think,' Daphne said, the words so soft Antonios had to lean forward to hear them. 'What matters is what it has done to you—'

'Done to me—'

'And Leonidas.'

Antonios simply sat and stared, his mind spinning. At least, he thought numbly, his mother hadn't known about his father's debt. For a moment, he'd been afraid she had.

'You must reconcile,' Daphne insisted. 'And be at peace with one another.'

'I—' Antonios began, but Leonidas cut across him.

'We will reconcile, Mama,' he said. 'We will be as brothers should be.'

This seemed to be exactly the right thing to say, for a beatific smile transformed Daphne's tired face and then she sank back against the pillows and closed her eyes. Just seconds later she was asleep.

Antonios and Leonidas remained on either side of her for a moment until, by silent, tense agreement, they rose and retreated to the far side of the room.

'What did the doctor say?' Leonidas asked.

'He said she would continue to decline. It could be days or weeks.'

'But not months.'

'No.'

They were both silent and, despite Leonidas's promise to their mother, neither of them, Antonios noted, was making any attempt to reconcile. Damn it, he hadn't even realized they'd needed to reconcile, at least not before the whole thing with Adair Hotels had blown up.

Leonidas glanced at their mother, lying asleep in bed. She looked peaceful, despite the agitation she'd shown them both just moments ago.

'Someone should stay with her,' he said.

'I will,' Antonios answered. Leonidas gave him one long, considering look and then nodded. 'Fine. Wake me if…if anything changes.'

Antonios nodded and Leonidas left. He turned back to Daphne, feeling weary in body and soul. Knowing he would not sleep that night, he pulled a chair up to the side of the bed and sat down.

Antonios wasn't in bed when Lindsay woke before dawn. Normally she wouldn't have woken up properly, but the cool expanse of sheet she encountered when she stretched her legs made her whole body jolt with shock.

Then she remembered their argument last night and her heart sank. Had he stayed in the office all night? And how were they going to get past this?

Too awake now even to consider going back to bed, Lindsay paced the elegant confines of the bedroom for a while before curling up in a chair by the window and watching the sun's first pearly rays peek over the mountains, touching the dense forest of pine trees with gold. She wondered where her husband was.

At half past eight the door to the bedroom finally opened and Lindsay sprang from her chair.

'Where were you?' she demanded, her voice coming out in a harpy's shriek.

Antonios looked at her wearily, his face haggard, his eyes shadowed. 'Daphne,' he said simply, and all of Lindsay's petty concerns faded in light of this far greater worry.

'What happened—is she all right?'

Antonios shook his head. 'I need a shower,' he said and, without another word for Lindsay, he disappeared into the bathroom, closing the door behind him.

Lindsay paced the bedroom once more, fresh anxiety eating away at her. She feared for Daphne, for Antonios, who would feel the loss of his mother so keenly, and for their marriage, which suddenly seemed a fragile and untested thing, its foundation rocked by every silence, each argument.

Ten minutes later Antonios came out of the shower, his hair damp and spiky, a towel slung low around his hips. Lindsay stood up from where she'd sunk onto the bed and stared at him, her heart starting to pound.

Wordlessly, Antonios strode towards her and then pulled her, suddenly and urgently, into a tight embrace, his face buried in her neck. Lindsay put her arms around him, hugging him back just as tightly. Neither of them spoke for a long moment, just absorbed each other's uncertainty and pain. This was all the reassurance she needed, she told herself, that Antonios loved her. They would weather these storms.

Finally Antonios eased back, his face bleak. 'It won't be long.'

A lump formed in Lindsay's throat and she blinked back tears. 'Oh, Antonios, I'm sorry.' He nodded, and she sniffed. 'I don't know why it feels sudden—'

'Death is always a shock.' He rubbed his face, clearly exhausted from his night spent in Daphne's room. 'I'm sure she'd like a visit from you.'

'Of course,' Lindsay answered quickly. 'Is she…is she lucid?'

'At times. She spoke, for a little while, to me and Leonidas.' Antonios's mouth hardened at that and his gaze flicked away.

'What did she say?' Lindsay asked quietly, and Antonios shook his head.

'It doesn't matter.'

Lindsay didn't answer because whatever Daphne had said to her two sons was personal, private, and yet…it did matter. Of that she was sure. It was just one more thing Antonios didn't want to tell her. Anxiety churned inside her and Antonios turned away.

'I should get to the office.'

'You haven't even slept—'

'There are things to be done.'

'And what about you and Leonidas?' she blurted.

Antonios swung back towards her, his gaze narrowed. 'What about us?'

Lindsay took a deep breath. 'Antonios, I know you're keeping something from me. Something that is hurting you. I kept something from you, and when I told you it was such a relief. Won't you tell me?'

His face contorted briefly and then he shook his head. 'No. I'm sorry, Lindsay, but I can't. Not…' He took a breath, let it out slowly. 'I can tell you that Leonidas is angry with me, and has been for years.'

'Why?'

'Because our father appointed me CEO. Because I have the authority he wants.' He let out a weary sigh. 'Our mother wants us to reconcile.'

'And have you?' Lindsay asked quietly. Antonios shook his head.

'No, Leonidas left after Mama was settled. And I'm not sure Leonidas and I will ever see eye to eye.'

'And will we?' Lindsay asked softly.

Antonios frowned. 'I told you before. This doesn't affect our marriage.'

'Of course it does,' Lindsay cried. 'All of it does. You think the tension and anger I see in you every day, the bitterness between you and your brother, doesn't affect us?'

Antonios folded his arms, his expression implacable. 'I can't tell Leonidas.'

'Why not?'

'Because I made a promise to my father.'

Lindsay stared at him searchingly, wishing she knew what to say, how to reach across this impasse. Perhaps now, with his mother so near death, was not the time to push.

Slowly she nodded, swallowing hard. 'All right.'

Antonios's expression softened and he pulled her into a hug. 'Thank you for understanding,' he said softly, pressing a kiss against her hair, and Lindsay closed her eyes. She was afraid her understanding wouldn't be enough…for either of them.

Daphne died three days later. Lindsay had been to see her several times, sitting by her bed and talking to her even though Daphne slipped in and out of lucidity. Xanthe, Parthenope and Ava came, too, brushing their mother's thin white hair, holding her hand, singing songs from their childhood.

The process of saying farewell, Lindsay thought, was so important. She'd missed it with her own mother, who had left and never returned, never reached out even once. It had been as if she'd died, or perhaps even worse.

This slow goodbye was painful but necessary, for her as well as for Antonios and his family.

And yet even as the end loomed nearer, and Daphne slipped deeper and deeper into unconsciousness, death was, as Antonios had said, a shock.

Lindsay was in her study, trying and failing to focus on the research she'd ignored for days, when Antonios came to tell her. She'd pulled up the email from the university and had drafted the first stilted sentences of a reply:

Thank you very much for your email. I have greatly enjoyed my time in the Mathematics Department and am honoured to...

To what? ...have been asked? ...accept? Her mind churned with possibilities, fears and desires.

'Lindsay.'

She turned from her laptop, her heart lurching into her throat at the bleak and haggard look on Antonios's face.

'Not—'

'Yes.' His mouth compressed and he took a quick steadying breath. 'I was there. So was Parthenope.'

'And the others?'

He shook his head. 'We've been taking it in turns to sit with her.'

'Oh, Antonios.' She rose from her desk and put her arms around him. Antonios pulled her to him as he had before, fitting her body to his. 'I'm so sorry.'

'I know.'

They remained in a silent embrace, needing no words. Then Antonios eased back. 'I'll need to start making arrangements for the funeral.'

'Of course. If there is anything I can do—'

He shook his head and left. Lindsay glanced back at her laptop.

Thank you for your email. I am honoured to...

With a sigh, she closed the laptop and went to find Antonios's sisters.

The funeral was two days later, at the Orthodox church in Amfissa, with a large crowd of townspeople along with all of the family, staff and employees of Marakaios Enterprises. Lindsay saw how Antonios and Leonidas stood apart from each other, their sisters like a barrier between them, as the coffin was lowered into the hard, stony earth.

There was a sombre reception back at the house, painfully reminiscent of Daphne's name day party, yet without her holding court in the centre of the room.

Lindsay helped organize things in the kitchen, glad to be out of the spotlight and knowing Antonios and his siblings needed time together. Her husband, she saw, was still not talking to Leonidas, never mind attempting some kind of reconciliation.

By the end of the day she was exhausted and aching in body and spirit, grateful to retreat up to their private wing. She hadn't seen Antonios for the last hour and had assumed he was closeted somewhere with his siblings.

He opened the door to their bedroom before her hand had touched the knob, causing her to give a small gasp of surprise.

'I didn't realize you'd come up—'

'Yet here I am.' Antonios's voice was clipped, his expression grim. Lindsay closed the door behind her.

'Is everything…' she began, only to have Antonios fill in unpleasantly,

'All right? No, Lindsay, it is not. It is not all right. It is not *fine*.' The last word was spoken in a sneer, a mockery of the times she'd insisted she was.

Lindsay shook her head. 'Antonios, what—'

'When,' he asked, his voice turning savage, 'were you going to tell me?'

Lindsay blinked as he glared at her, his whole body taut with fury, his fists clenched at his sides.

'What…'

'You haven't forgotten, have you?' he enquired silkily. 'The job offer you're so *honoured* to accept?'

Her jaw dropped. 'You read my email—'

'You left it up on the screen. And I'm not going to apologize for some imagined invasion of your privacy when you've been keeping such things from me.' He shook his head, his features twisting with bitterness. 'When were you going to tell me you were leaving, Lindsay, or were you just going to slip away again?'

CHAPTER TWELVE

Everything in him hurt. Antonios heard his own ragged breathing as he stared at Lindsay and saw the truth in her face. She had deliberately kept the job offer from him.

And why? It felt painfully obvious: because she'd been intending to take it up, to leave him.

Lindsay had gone pale, her breathing shallow. 'Don't have a damned panic attack now,' Antonios growled. 'I won't have an ounce of sympathy for you if you do.'

Her mouth compressed and she swallowed. 'Good to know.'

'Why?' he asked, and heard a world of hurt in his voice, making him cringe inwardly even as fury fired through him. *Theos*, but he'd been here before. Only this time it felt a thousand times worse.

'Why what, Antonios?' Lindsay asked quietly. She had composed herself, and even that infuriated him. She seemed unaffected by his own agony, but then he hadn't been able to read her before, had had no inkling of the anguish she'd tried so hard to hide.

Perhaps he hadn't changed as much as he'd thought and hoped he'd had.

'Why,' he clarified, 'did you not tell me you had a job offer from a university in New York? A job offer you were thinking of accepting—'

'I haven't accepted it.'

'You're thinking about it, though, aren't you?' Antonios returned. 'In the email you haven't finished the sentence about just what you're *honoured* to do, and why was that? Because you aren't sure.'

Lindsay's face was pale but when she spoke her voice came out calmly. 'No,' she agreed, 'I'm not.'

And somehow her calm admission hurt all the more, and turned his anger into despair. His shoulders sagged and he felt an unbearable weariness sweep through him, making every muscle he had ache. 'And you couldn't even tell me that.'

'I was going to.'

'When?' He shook his head. '*Theos*, what kind of marriage do we have, if we cannot be honest with each other?'

'I don't know.' Lindsay took a deep breath. 'But I'll be honest now, Antonios. I'll tell you exactly what's in my heart because if I don't, I don't think we have a marriage. I don't think there's much point in going on.'

'You always are quick to give up, aren't you?' he said, the words coming out before he could stop them and hitting Lindsay where it hurt.

He saw her flinch but then she composed herself, straightened her shoulders and lifted her chin. 'I'm not giving up. And being honest with you feels like fighting for my marriage, Antonios. For us. It would be easier in some ways to just ignore the things that are hurting you, pretend everything is fine. I did it before, and I'm not going to do it again. Because I love you. Because I want our marriage to succeed.'

He shrugged her words aside, too raw to do anything else. 'So, tell me then. Be honest about whatever it is you have to say.'

'Receiving that email made me realize that I do miss being part of an academic community,' she began. 'Teaching seminars, talking to people who are excited about what I'm doing.

But I also knew that I'd committed myself to you, and your life is here in Greece.'

'Such a dilemma,' he cut in, his voice sharp with sarcasm, and she stared at him.

'Are you even going to try to understand?' she asked, and inwardly Antonios cringed.

He was lashing out because he was afraid Lindsay was going to leave him. Just as she'd once been afraid he would leave her. *Theos*, the things you did out of fear.

'I'm sorry,' he said. 'I shouldn't have said that. Please, continue.' He swallowed hard, jammed his hands in his pockets and forced himself to listen without speaking. But if she told him, in that calm and cool way of hers, that she was *leaving…*

'When you brought me to Greece, Antonios,' Lindsay said quietly, 'I was unhappy. So unhappy I didn't notice, didn't even consider, that you were unhappy, too.'

He stiffened, thrown by the sudden change in subject. 'What are you talking about—?'

'I'm talking about how you don't sleep at night. How the moment you drive through the estate gates your whole body tenses and a shadow comes over your face. How you work so hard but you don't even seem to enjoy it.'

Each word felt as if she were stripping him bare, flaying him. He stared at her, shaking his head. 'You're reading too much into something that is temporary…'

'What's temporary, Antonios? This bitterness between you and Leonidas? That's been going on for years. The stress and strain of your job? I see it now and, looking back, I should have seen it before. You weren't just blind to my anguish, Antonios. I was blind to yours.'

Anguish. The word captured him, felled him. Because he knew she was right and he hated it. Hated it because it meant he'd failed.

'I don't see what any of this has to do with your job offer,' he said finally, his voice flat.

'Because when I read that email I thought of you. I thought of us and how maybe we would be happier, you would be happier, away from here. Away from Marakaios Enterprises.'

Emotion leapt inside him but he refused to name it. 'That's a very convenient justification for following your own desires.'

'Tell me you're happy here, Antonios,' Lindsay answered. 'Tell me you don't want to leave. Tell me this is what you want for the rest of your life.'

'I have no choice,' he said, the words torn from him. 'Don't you see that? My father named me as his successor. This is what I was born to do, what I have to…' He broke off, his chest heaving, his fists clenched.

'Who says?' Lindsay said quietly. 'Why can't you control your own destiny, choose your own life? And choose one that makes you happy?'

'There is such a thing as duty.'

'There is also such a thing as your brother,' Lindsay reminded him. 'Someone who wants more authority, who is already working for—'

'*Theos*, enough.' He flung out a hand to stop her from saying any more. 'Happy or unhappy, my life is here. It has to be here. But if you choose not to share it, then tell me so.'

'I want to share it,' Lindsay answered, her voice trembling. 'Of course I want to, but you don't want to share it with me.'

'Not this again—'

'Of course *this* again! You're unhappy, Antonios, but you won't tell me why. You won't tell me what is going on with your brother, or what happened with your father, or anything. How can I help? How can I be your wife, supporting and loving you, when you deliberately shut me out?' He couldn't answer and she stepped towards him, grabbing him by the shoulders. 'I love you,' she told him fiercely, her voice choked with emotion. 'I love you enough to risk everything because I know you can't go on like this. We can't go on. Please, Antonios.' She stared at him, tears running down her face, and the certainty he'd shielded himself with for so long started to crack.

Lindsay had kept a secret from him and he'd felt angry and hurt. Betrayed—as betrayed as when his father had kept the wretched state of the business from him. How could he keep anything from her? How could he perpetuate this life of secrets and lies?

But it's not my secret to tell.

Yet had it been his to keep?

'When I took over the business,' he told Lindsay, the words coming haltingly yet with growing determination, 'I didn't realize—no one realized—that it was in debt. Utterly in debt. My father had a heart attack because he was faced with losing it all.' Lindsay gaped at him and Antonios smiled grimly. 'A shock, no?' he said and she nodded.

'And you didn't tell anyone about this?'

'My father asked, *begged* me not to. Some of his dealings had been…illegal. Criminal.' He drew a shuddering breath. 'Telling my family would have brought such shame to my father. My mother loved him, and my siblings, too. I couldn't bear for their feelings to change, and I knew it would destroy my father. So I worked to get the business back on an even footing.'

She cocked her head, her luminous gaze sweeping slowly over him, and he braced himself to hear recrimination. Rebuke that he hadn't told anyone, that he'd kept it to himself.

'Oh, Antonios,' she said softly, her voice filled with so much love and compassion, 'that must have been so very hard for you. Keeping such a secret for so long, and working so hard.' She shook her head, more tears spilling down her cheeks, and her understanding just about undid him.

'Lindsay, I love you,' he said as he reached for her. 'I know there are a lot of unknowns, a lot of complications, but that is one thing that I know. One thing that it is certain. It is my rock.'

Another tear snaked down her cheek. 'It's my rock, too,' she whispered. 'Loving you. Knowing you love me.'

He drew her to him, needing to feel her soft, slender body against his. 'Then we'll work the rest out,' he murmured against her hair. 'Somehow we'll work the rest out.'

'Antonios.' She pulled away from him. 'It's not that simple.'

'It can be—'

'No,' she answered, 'it can't. I wish it could because it would make things so simple. Just sail along on the certainty of our love.' Her mouth twisted wryly. 'But it's not simple, Antonios. Your mother said it was endlessly complicated. And love is hard work.'

He stiffened, not wanting to hear this and yet knowing in his gut she was right. 'So what are you saying?'

'I'm saying you need to talk to Leonidas. You need to think about what would make you happy, and how our marriage can thrive.'

He tensed, withdrawing from her. 'Is that an ultimatum?'

She stared at him sadly. 'Does it need to be one?'

'This is about your job offer, isn't it?'

'No, Antonios.' Lindsay shook her head. 'It's about so much more than that.'

Anger fired through him, coming so quickly on the heels of the love and gratitude he'd felt. 'Lindsay—'

'I'll refuse the offer if you want me to,' she told him quietly. 'This is about you. And me. *Us*.' She stared at him steadily. 'I wish you could see that.'

And he could see it, Antonios realized. Of course he could. He just hated the thought. He stared at her, the sadness turning down her mouth, the love still shining in her eyes. He hated that he'd made her so unhappy. Again.

'I need to be alone,' he said abruptly and turned from the room.

He walked the length of the estate, ending up in the olive groves, memories of his childhood dancing through his mind. Memories of walking there just a few short weeks ago with Lindsay, when they'd forged this new and fragile foundation of their marriage. He'd fallen in love with her all over again these past few weeks. She'd made coming back here, dealing with Marakaios Enterprises, bearable.

And do you want more from your life than bearable?

Antonios pressed a fist to his forehead and closed his eyes. Lindsay was right. Marakaios Enterprises had been slowly strangling him for a decade. Not just the secret he'd kept from his family, but the whole of it. He was reaching his breaking point and only Lindsay had seen it. Had possessed the courage to confront him.

He would be no less brave. Resolutely, he went in search of Leonidas.

His brother was not in the main villa or his own house; it took Antonios a few stunned seconds to realize Leonidas had gone to the office, on today of all days.

It was dark, twilight having descended without his even being aware of the descent into night, and a few stars glimmered close to the horizon.

A single light shone from the office building. Antonios thumbed the key code and stepped inside. He paused on the threshold of Leonidas's office, taking in his brother's bent head, one hand raked through his hair, the determined yet slumped set of his shoulders.

'It's a little late to be working,' he said quietly and Leonidas looked up, startled, before he gave a shrug.

'The world doesn't stop, even for a funeral.'

For a second Antonios wanted to berate his brother for his callousness, but then he saw the grief in Leonidas's eyes and realized this was how he coped. He was, Antonios thought wryly, starting to see people a little more clearly, thanks to Lindsay.

He took a step into the room. 'I want to talk to you.'

'Oh?' Leonidas eyed him warily. 'About what?'

'About Father.'

He'd spoken quietly, but the two words seemed to bounce

around the room, echo in the stillness. Leonidas glanced down at the papers he'd been studying, needlessly rearranging a few.

'What about him?' he asked finally.

Antonios took a deep breath, then plunged. 'Father was deeply in debt, Leonidas. He'd nearly lost it all when he had the heart attack.'

Leonidas's jaw dropped, just as Lindsay's had done. Wearily, Antonios explained it all again: the debt, the shame, the secret.

After a long, taut moment Leonidas pushed away from the desk, turned towards the window. 'You should have told me.'

'I didn't feel I could.' He sounded, Antonios realized, just as Lindsay had when she'd explained why she'd left without an explanation. They were so alike, and yet in such different ways. And they'd taught each other so much. Helped each other so much. 'I realize now,' he told Leonidas, 'I may have been wrong.'

'May have been?'

Temper flared at his brother's obvious sarcasm, but he suppressed it. 'Leonidas, Father made me promise not to tell. He was deeply ashamed that he'd let it get so far. Telling anyone would have felt like a betrayal. It still feels like one now but I recognize that you deserve to know, perhaps more than anyone.' And at least, Antonios thought, his mother had been spared the knowledge of her husband's criminal folly. It was a small mercy.

'I wish he'd told me,' Leonidas said after a long moment. His voice sounded thick. 'I wish he'd seen how much I loved the business, how much I wanted to share it with him. I wish he'd trusted me with that burden.'

'I wish it, too,' Antonios answered. 'I wish there had been no secrets between anyone, ever.'

They were both silent, and then Leonidas looked up and asked, 'So what now? Things will continue on as usual? You'll give me a little more freedom?'

He sounded so cynical, so jaded and yet also despairing, and

Antonios knew it was his fault his brother was like that. He'd given him a very short leash.

'No,' he said slowly, and Lindsay's words echoed through his mind. She'd understood him better than he'd ever understood himself. 'That's not what's going to happen.'

Leonidas let out a bitter laugh. 'I see.'

'No,' Antonios said, 'I don't think you do.' He took a deep breath. 'What would you think,' he asked, 'if you became CEO?'

Lindsay paced her bedroom for an hour, until she feared she'd wear down the carpet with her restless tread. It was evening, and everyone from the reception after the funeral had gone. Parthenope would be leaving to return home tomorrow, and the house, Lindsay supposed, would settle into a new and unwelcome normal.

And what about her and Antonios?

She had no idea if he'd accepted or understood what she'd said. No idea if their marriage was teetering on a precipice or about to take off and fly.

She would refuse the job offer, she told herself, as a sign of her faith in him and their marriage. It had been unreasonable of her even to consider it.

Yet her heart still felt heavy as she headed to her study and opened her laptop. The unfinished email was still on the screen where she'd left it, where Antonios had read it. Lindsay scanned the two sentences and then started writing.

I am honoured that you have considered me for this position, but I am afraid that I cannot accept...

'You're not turning down that job, are you?'

Lindsay's hands stilled on the computer keys and then she turned around in her chair, saw Antonios standing in the doorway of her study. He looked both weary and wonderful, and his mouth curved in a slow, tired smile as he took a step forward. 'Because I wouldn't do that, if I were you.'

Lindsay frowned, uncertainty and hope warring within her. 'You wouldn't?'

'No.'

'But…'

'You were right, Lindsay, about everything. About me. About Leonidas. And, most importantly, about us.'

An incredulous smile started blooming across her face. 'What's happened?'

'I told him the truth.'

'Oh, Antonios.' Her smile widened even as she felt the sting of tears. 'I'm proud of you. That must have been hard.'

'It was. But it was also a relief. I suspect you know what that feels like.'

'Yes.' She nodded and he took her hand, drew her up from her chair. 'Thank you for being patient with me,' he whispered against her hair. 'Thank you for loving me the way I needed, even when I didn't think I did.'

'Oh, Antonios.' Her voice was too choked to say anything more, so she just put her arms around him. He held her, stroking her hair, and she pressed into him, revelling in how he managed to make her feel both strong and small.

'So about that job,' Antonios said with a nod towards her laptop. 'What was it exactly, anyway?'

She eased back to eye him warily. 'It doesn't matter—'

'I think it does.'

Unsure of where he was going with this, she gave a little shrug. 'Assistant professorship of Pure Mathematics.'

'Sounds right up your alley.'

'I suppose.' Actually, it involved teaching an advanced seminar on her research topic, but she didn't need to tell Antonios about that. 'I was just about to refuse,' she told him, stopping when she saw he was shaking his head.

'And I told you I wouldn't do that if I were you.'

'Why not?'

'Because I think I fancy the idea of living in America.'

Lindsay's jaw dropped. 'What?'

'Leonidas is now the CEO of Marakaios Enterprises.'

'But…' Lindsay's head spun. No matter what she'd told Antonios earlier, she'd never actually believed he would resign.

'I offered him the position,' Antonios explained. 'I realized you were right, Lindsay. Being CEO of Marakaios Enterprises has never made me happy, and I know it's what Leonidas has wanted. He deserves a chance, and I deserve a chance to try something else. To be happy…with you.'

'You've put so much into it, Antonios,' Lindsay said, marvelling at how much he was willing to give up. 'You *saved* it—'

'And now I'm handing it over to Leonidas. But I'm not leaving completely.' He gave her a crooked smile that felt like a fist reaching down and taking hold of her heart. No matter what the future held, she loved this man. She wanted to be with him. 'I've accepted a newly created position with Marakaios Enterprises,' he explained. 'Head of North America and Investment Management.'

'North America…' she repeated slowly, her mind whirling. 'Investment Management—but I didn't think Marakaios Enterprises even did that?'

'They didn't, but they will, starting with me. I'm opening a new branch of the corporation in finance, in North America. Based in New York.'

She blinked rapidly, shaking her head in disbelief. 'You'd do that for me?'

'I'm doing it for us. Just like you fought for us by confronting me. I didn't want to admit how unhappy I was here. It felt like a betrayal of my father, of my own sense of honour and duty. But you woke me up, Lindsay. You made me realize what I was afraid to acknowledge to myself.'

'Antonios…' Lindsay shook her head, her eyes shining with tears. 'I don't know what to say.'

'Then say yes. Say yes, I'll take the job, I'll go with you, I'll start this grand adventure.' He squeezed her hands. 'Say yes because you love me and I love you and that really is all that matters.'

Just like Daphne had said. Lindsay could almost feel her mother-in-law's presence, imagined her beaming smile. She squeezed Antonios's hands back.

'Yes,' she said.

* * * * *

Keep reading for an excerpt of
An Honourable Seduction
by Brenda Jackson.
Find it in the
Heroes Blockbuster 2024 anthology,
out now!

PROLOGUE

The Naval Amphibious Base
Coronado, San Diego, California

"WHAT KIND OF trouble have you gotten into?"

David Holloway, known to his Navy SEAL teammates as Flipper, glanced at the four men surrounding him. They were like brothers to him. More than once they'd risked their lives for each other and they would continue to have each other's backs, on duty or off. That bond was what accounted for the concerned looks on their faces. He wondered how they'd known he'd been summoned to the admiral's office.

"Let's hope I'm not in any trouble, Mac," Flipper said, rubbing a hand down his face.

He had to admit he was wondering what was going on, just like they were. Usually, you were only summoned to a meeting with the admiral when you were getting reprimanded for some reason, and he never got into trouble. At least he *rarely* did. As the son of a retired SEALs commanding officer and the youngest of five brothers—all Navy SEALs—he knew better.

"Maybe there's an event on the base and he wants you to escort his daughter now that you're the single one among us," Coop said, grinning.

Flipper didn't grin back. They'd seen Georgianna Martin, the admiral's twenty-three-year-old daughter. She was beautiful, but they'd heard the horror stories from other teammates who'd been ordered to take her out on dates. According to them, those evenings had been the dates from hell. The young woman was spoiled rotten, selfish as sin and had an attitude that sucked. That's why Flipper didn't find Coop's comment at all amusing. He hoped that wasn't why the admiral wanted to see him.

It didn't surprise Flipper that it was Mac who'd asked if Flipper had gotten into trouble. Thurston McRoy—code name Mac—was older than the other four men on the team, who had all started their careers as SEALs around the same time. Mac had been a SEAL five years before the rest of them. Mac seemed to like to think he was the big brother looking out for them, almost like he figured they couldn't take care of themselves. He was forever giving them advice—even when they didn't ask for it.

In addition to Mac and Flipper, their SEAL team included Brisbane Westmoreland, code name Bane; Gavin Blake, whose code name was Viper; and Laramie Cooper, whose code name was Coop.

Flipper checked his watch. "Since I have a couple of hours to spare before meeting with the admiral, let's grab something to eat," he suggested.

"Sounds good to me," Bane said.

Less than an hour later, Flipper and his four teammates shared burgers, fries and milkshakes at one of the most popular eating places on base. They decided to sit outside at one of the café tables in the front instead of inside where it was crowded since it was such a beautiful May day.

No one brought up his meeting with the admiral again or the notion of him taking the admiral's daughter on a date. He was glad. Instead, the guys had more important things to talk about, namely their families.

Bane's wife, Crystal, had given birth to triplets last year and he had new photos to share, so they passed Bane's cell phone around.

Viper's wife, Layla, was expecting with only a few months to go before Gavin Blake IV would be born. Viper was excited about becoming a father, of course.

Like Bane, Mac had plenty of photos to share; he was married and the father of four.

And Coop had a two-year-old son he hadn't known about until he'd run into his old girlfriend about six months ago. They'd reconnected, gotten married and were now a happy family.

Earlier in the week, the teammates had gotten word from their commanding officer that next week was the start of a four-month leave. For Flipper, that meant heading home to Dallas and he couldn't wait. His mother had a birthday coming up and he was glad he would be home to celebrate.

"I don't care what plans you all are making for your leave, just as long as you remember my mom's birthday celebration. I understand you not showing up, Viper, with a baby on the way. The rest of you guys, no excuses."

"We hear you," Bane said, grinning. "And we will be there."

When Viper ordered another hamburger, everyone teased him about being the one to eat for two instead of his wife. And then everyone talked about what they planned to do with their four months off.

It was two hours later when Flipper walked into the admiral's office. He was surprised to find Commanding Officer Shields there as well. Flipper saluted both men.

"At ease. Please have a seat, Lieutenant Holloway."

"Thank you, sir," he said, sitting down. He was used to being under his commanding officer's intense scrutiny, but there was something in the sharp green eyes of Admiral Norris Martin that was making him feel uncomfortable.

"You come highly recommended by your commanding officer here, Lieutenant Holloway. And the reason I asked to meet with you is that we need you. Your country needs you."

Flipper was happy to step up. He was a Navy SEAL, and the reason he'd enlisted, like his father and brothers, was to protect his country. "And what am I needed to do, sir?" he asked.

"Our investigators have provided intelligence and a preliminary report that says acts of espionage are happening in Key West. Someone is trading valuable government secrets to China."

Flipper didn't respond immediately.

The one thing he hated was a traitor, but he'd discovered that for the right price, a number of American citizens would perform acts of treason. He understood that. However, what he didn't understand was why he'd been singled out for this meeting. He was part of a SEAL team. He didn't work in naval intelligence.

Confusion must have shown on his face because Admiral Martin continued, "The report was given to me, but I don't believe it."

Flipper raised a brow. "You don't believe a report that classified documents are being traded in Key West, sir?"

"Oh, I believe all that, but what I refuse to believe is that this suspect is guilty of anything."

"Is there a reason why, sir?"

"Here is the information," said Commanding Officer Shields, speaking for the first time as he handed Flipper a folder.

Flipper opened it to find a picture of a very beautiful woman. She looked to be around twenty-four, with dark, sultry eyes and full, shapely lips. Then there was her mass of copper-brown spiral curls that flowed to her shoulders, crowning a cocoa-colored face. A pair of dangling gold earrings hung from her ears and a golden pendant necklace hung around her neck.

He knew he was spending too much time studying her features, but it couldn't be helped. The woman was strikingly beautiful.

Reluctantly he moved his gaze away from her face to check out the background of the photo. From the tropical vegetation captured by the photographer, she seemed to be on an island somewhere. She stood near a body of water that showed in the corner of the eight-by-ten photo. Scribbled across the bottom were the words:

Miss you, Godpop 1

Love, Swan

Swan? It was an unusual name, but it fit.

He moved to the next document in the file. Attached to it was a small family photo that showed a tall Caucasian man with sandy-brown hair and brown eyes standing beside a beautiful woman who closely resembled Swan. Her mother. In front of the couple was a beautiful little girl who looked to be around eight.

Flipper studied the child's face and knew that child had grown up to be the gorgeous woman in the first photo. The shape of her face was the same, as were her eyes. Even as a child, she'd had long curly hair.

The family photo was clipped to a profile of the young woman. As he'd guessed, she was twenty-four. Her name was Swan Jamison. She was an American, born in Key West. Presently, she owned a jewelry store on the island. That was all the information the document provided.

Flipper lifted his gaze to find his commanding officer and the admiral staring at him. "I assume this is the person naval intelligence believes is the traitor."

"Yes," Admiral Martin said. "She's my goddaughter. I am Godpop 1."

"She's my goddaughter as well," added Commanding Officer Shields. "I am Godpop 2."

Flipper's gaze moved from one man to the other. "I see, sirs."

Admiral Martin nodded. "Her father was part of our SEAL team and our best friend. His name was Andrew Jamison."

Flipper had heard that Commanding Officer Shields and

Admiral Martin were part of the same SEAL team a number of years ago.

"Andrew was the best. He lost his life saving ours," said Commanding Officer Shields. "He didn't die immediately, and before he died, he made us promise to look after his wife, Leigh, and his daughter, Swan." The man paused and then said, "Over twenty-eight years ago, when we were taking some R & R in Jamaica, Andrew met Leigh, who was a Jamaican model. They married a year later, and he moved her to Key West, where our team was stationed. After Andrew was killed, Leigh returned to Jamaica. When Swan graduated from high school, she returned to the Keys and moved into her parents' home."

"How old was she when her father was killed?" Flipper asked.

"She was fifteen," Admiral Martin said. "Swan was close to her dad. Leigh was so broken up over Andrew's death that she didn't want to live in the States without him, which was why she returned to Jamaica. She passed away two years ago."

Flipper's commanding officer then took up the tale. "Leigh sent for us before she died of stomach cancer, asking us to look out for Swan after she was gone. We would have done that anyway, since we always kept in touch with both Leigh and Swan. In fact, Swan rotated summers with us and our families even after Leigh returned to Jamaica. We took our roles as godfathers seriously. We were even there when Swan graduated from high school and college."

"Did Swan have any American grandparents?" Flipper asked.

He saw both men's lips tighten into frowns. "Yes. However, her paternal grandparents didn't approve of their son's marriage to Leigh," said Commanding Officer Shields.

"So they never accepted their granddaughter." It was more of a statement than a question.

"No, they never did," Admiral Martin confirmed. As if it was a topic he'd rather change, the man added, "We've been given some time to find out the truth, but not much. Luckily, Swan's Godpop 3 has a high-level position at naval intelligence. Otherwise, we wouldn't know about the investigation. We have thirty days to prove Swan is not a traitor and identify the person who is. That's where we need your help. Instead of releasing you to go home as we're doing for the other members of your team, we are assigning you to a special mission, Lieutenant Holloway. You are being sent to Key West."

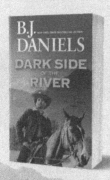

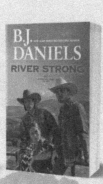